The Unionist

A Novel of the Civil War

W. Steven Harrell

SUMMERHILL
Senior Living Community
500 Stanley St
Perry, GA 31069-3145

PublishAmerica
Baltimore

© 2002 by W. Steven Harrell.
All rights reserved. No part of this book may be reproduced in any form without written permission from the publishers, except by a reviewer who may quote brief passages in a review to be printed in a newspaper or magazine.

First printing

ISBN: 1-59129-584-x
PUBLISHED BY PUBLISH AMERICA BOOK PUBLISHERS
www.publishamerica.com
Baltimore

Printed in the United States of America

July 30, 2002

Chapter One

Two wagons rolled northwest along a dusty Baldwin County road. It was August, and it was hot and dry. A young David Snelling drove the lead wagon full of dried field corn, pulled by two pretty grey mules. His uncle's slave, Zack Dawson, drove the second wagon. Two red mules, a jack and a mare, teamed up to pull the second wagon, which was also filled to capacity with dry field corn. David spent most of the morning on this road, first waiting for Zack's wagon to catch up and then driving toward his uncle's gristmill in Putnam County. The mules were in no great hurry to get there, and the deer flies buzzed and assaulted them fiercely along the way.

David's uncle, William Floyd, had his hands load both wagons early that morning. While the wagons were being loaded by ten of the slaves, William had instructed David about the quantities of corn meal and grits that he wanted ground from each load. William was the type of man that paid attention to details, and overlooked nothing when a task was to be done. Two thirds of each load of corn would be ground for corn meal. The other third of each load would be ground for grits. The wagons were headed toward a gristmill in Putnam County owned by another of David's uncles, Uriah Snelling. David had been sent to Boston five years before to purchase much of the machinery for the construction of the gristmill. It had been built as a joint venture between Uriah Snelling and William Floyd's cotton plantation, and it now supplied most of the corn meal and grits for the area.

David was a graduate of Franklin College in Athens. He had attended college there with his cousin, Joseph Floyd, William's son. David had excelled in his studies there, which included mathematics and engineering. Joseph was brown haired, slightly shorter than six feet, and handsome. He was not the same sort of student as David, and careful tutoring was needed to pull him through his course of study, natural philosophy. Joseph was very popular, both with the Athens girls and the other students. He was elected a drill sergeant in the local militia in Clarke County. He now commanded a militia company in Baldwin County. David's thoughts that hot morning could not concentrate on the task at hand. He instead was engrossed in thoughts of winning over the affections of Angela Collins. He liked his cousin Joseph a great deal, but he believed that Joseph could have any girl he wanted in Middle Georgia. His father owned two thousand acres of prime land and over seventy–five slaves.

Joseph was handsome and popular. Why did he want the same girl that David did?

David then began to attempt to rationalize the situation between him and Angela. His mind was always quick to deal with pending problems. He was an orphan at only ten years of age. His parents had died from yellow fever at their farm in Laurens County. The farm did not sell at a price sufficient to pay off his father's debts. David had no fortune to speak of. He could only succeed by using his mind. His talent for engineering and mechanics had earned him a reputation in the area.

His Uncle William was also well impressed with his ability. He had not only entrusted him with acquiring the gristmill machinery, but he had recently sent David to Pennsylvania to buy a steam engine and other equipment needed to construct a steam powered saw mill.

David had prepared the designs of the sawmill himself, and had the saw blades ground and cut to the specifications of his original design. The mill had been operating for two months now, and it was successful. David's uncle saw a bright future for his nephew. His thoughts at the moment centered on how to convince Angela to marry him instead of his cousin Joseph. They rounded a bend in the road, which approached a small, swampy creek. A large canebrake also appeared to the left on the downhill side. David saw an object stretched out across the road. His eyes gleamed with instant recognition. Even though the object was now forty yards away, David drew back on the reins and halted his team of mules. He then put up his hand and signaled Zack to stop his rig. He turned around to speak to Zack.

"What yo stopping heah for Mista David?"

"Zack, there's a big rattlesnake out in the road up there. He'll spook the mules for sure. I don't want to lose our wagons or our loads. I want you to stay here and keep the mules quiet."

"What you gonna do?"

"I came prepared for this situation."

David stepped down from his rig and drew a short muzzle loader shotgun from behind the seat. He checked to make sure the percussion cap was in place over the nipple, and he half–cocked the piece as he walked toward the snake. He gave Lucifer, his lead mule, a friendly pat on his rump as he passed him, and began to focus on the problem that was crawling across the road. As he got closer, he began to appreciate the reasons that made him stop the wagons as quickly as he did.

The rattlesnake was a Canebrake rattler, with a dull tan color from his tail to the front of its head. Circling the body of the snake, and spaced several inches apart were black rings that were bordered in smaller white outlines, which resembled chevrons. As David approached, the snake stopped his forward progress in the roadway. He was at least five feet long.

A snake that large had few natural enemies. David stepped between the edge of the road and the front of the snake to cut him off. The rattler halted, flicked out its tongue a few times, and picked up its head and tail. His string of rattles was over five inches long, and the snake began to sing them loudly at this new enemy blocking his path.

David became a little nervous when he heard the rattles, and he knew the mules would soon hear the noise also. He did not want the mules to spook and stampede with their loads of corn in the wagons. He drew the hammer of the shotgun to full cock, aimed, and fired at the head of the rattlesnake. His lead mule snorted and flinched a bit, but the other mules had heard gunfire before, and did not move. David looked down after the smoke had cleared, and noticed that the bird shot from the shotgun had blown the snake's head off. The snake's body began to coil up, even though its head was now missing. The snake's body was as thick as David's thighs. He walked back to Zack's wagon, reloading the shotgun on the walk.

"Can I go down and get that snake, Mista David? Eula May's cooked 'em for me for years."

"You mean you cook and eat rattlesnakes?" David found that kind of hard to believe, since most Negroes he had known were afraid of rattlers.

"Yes sah, we eats' em. Eula May cuts 'em up and fries 'em up like chicken. Dey taste good. Dat's good white meat on that snake, Mr. David."

"Go ahead and get him then, I guess. Put him in this croaker sack here. I don't want the mules to see or smell him. They may bolt anyway if they smell that big snake. I hope Eula May will appreciate the size of that snake."

"Yes sah, Mr. David." Zack took the cloth sack from David and retrieved the snake. David noticed that Zack carefully handled the snake as he placed it into the bag. They then continued on their way to Uriah Snelling's gristmill. The road soon ran into a series of small red hills, covered with hardwood trees. They soon rounded a bend in the road and climbed a small hill. They saw Uriah's gristmill in the valley down below. The gristmill was built in 1859 along the banks of Murder Creek. The creek current there was swift enough to turn the large water wheel located on the side of the building. Uriah's mill was built on a joint partnership between Uriah and David's uncle, William Floyd. It ran most of the year, and served several surrounding counties. Uriah had erected several large storage buildings, and sold corn meal and grits, which he had obtained from farmers or plantation owners that paid for his services in ground corn.

A large white frame house had been built several yards from the mill. Uriah lived there with his wife, Faith. Faith was a Quaker, or a member of the Society of Friends. Uriah met and married Faith when he was called to Washington as a special advisor to Secretary of War Jefferson Davis in the 1850's. Uriah was a former soldier. He had served with distinction in the U.S. mounted dragoons during the Mexican War. He was later promoted from captain to the rank of major. He greatly assisted Jefferson Davis in the organizing of the 1st and 2nd U.S. Cavalry Regiments during the 1850's. He retired from the U.S. Army after being passed over for promotion in 1858.

Local residents simply called him "the major". David and Zack pulled their wagons near the side door of the gristmill. A black man that David knew only as Nate, helped them unload their dry corn onto the bottom floor of the gristmill. David then went upstairs to the grinding room to look for his Uncle Uriah.

The upstairs portion of the gristmill had several storage rooms for ground meal, flour, and grits. David saw a thin black man working the bagged corn around the millstones, pouring on dry corn on the stones, while a stout white man in a white shirt scooped up the ground corn meal and shoveled the meal into a nearby oak barrel. David immediately recognized the bulky form of his Uncle Uriah. He watched them grind up three large bags of shelled corn before making his presence known to his uncle. He then walked over to the millstone and tapped his uncle on the back. The miller turned around and greeted his nephew.

"David, it is so good to see you. I haven't seen you in several weeks. How's things over at Greenbrier Plantation? How is your Uncle William and your cousin Joseph?"

"They are both doing fine, thank you. I brought Zack Dawson and two wagons of shelled corn over for you to grind for us, Uncle Uriah."

Uriah pulled a rag from his trouser back pocket, and began to wipe the sweat from his brow.

"It sure has been hot this week, we could use some more rain."

He then pulled a small book from his left rear pocket, and began to calculate the amount of grits and corn meal he had ground for Greenbrier Plantation the previous year.

"I did about forty three bushels of corn for y'all last year, David. How much did you bring in today?"

"We have about fifty–nine bushels of corn in the wagons out there. Uncle William told me to tell you he wanted thirty percent of the corn ground for grits, and the rest would be ground for corn meal."

"I figured that he would want it done that way. Does he have any cash to pay me this year, or does he want to pay me in meal and grits?"

"He asked me to get a receipt from you, along with your charges per bushel of corn, and he will write you a check when I return to Greenbrier."

"William's check is good enough for me. It's as good as gold up at the Merchant's and Farmer's Bank over at Milledgeville. Let's walk down to the creek. We can let Nate and Zack unload the wagons and water your mules. I need to talk to you about some things."

David had wondered what was bothering his Uncle Uriah. He could not imagine the importance that he had attached to their conversation. His uncle usually did not quit work before sundown in the afternoon, unless he had a good reason. Uriah directed Nate to see after the mules, and went off with David.

They took a trail that led down by a patch of willow trees. David looked out in the middle of the creek and spied a couple of river turtles sunning themselves on the sunny side of a Blackgum log. The late summer heat caused both of them to sweat profusely, and they soon stopped to rest in the shade of two giant Water Oaks.

"David, have you been keeping up with political matters this year?"

"Yes sir. I have followed the presidential campaign in the newspapers. I'm for Mr. Douglas, but the Southern people probably will not support him."

"You are correct. They have abandoned him when they bolted the Democratic convention over in Charleston. You studied mathematics up at college, didn't you?"

"Yes, sir, I sure did."

"Well, you should appreciate the situation that now presents itself with the presidential campaign."

"I don't really understand what you are getting at, Uncle."

"You should. Lincoln is running as a Republican. He will get a lot of support from New England, New York, Illinois, and the rest of the northern states. Douglas will be strong in Kentucky and Missouri and the Upper Middle West. He is, after all, the Democratic nominee. But the Democrats are splitting their votes. John Bell is running from Tennessee under a party called the Constitutional Union Party. I'm supporting him. He'll draw off votes in Virginia and Tennessee. A good many Democrats there will support him. Mr. Breckenridge is running as the Southern

Democratic Party candidate. He will carry all of the Deep South votes. He'll also be real strong in Kentucky, his home state."

"So who do you think will win this election, then?"

"I hate to tell you this, but the numbers here just do not lie. Popular vote doesn't determine the outcomes of presidential elections. You have to look at the electoral vote. The candidate that wins a particular state gets all of that state's votes in the Electoral College. The candidate with the most electoral votes is declared the winner of the election. You have to look at the mathematics here."

"What are you telling me?" David at this point was really puzzled.

"If it were Lincoln against Douglas or Lincoln against Breckenridge, I do not believe that the Republicans would have a chance at all to win this election. That has not happened. Instead, the Democratic votes are going to be split between Breckenridge and Bell and Douglas. Lincoln will win most of the northern states. Any close races in any of the northern states will go his way because Breckenridge and Bell and Douglas will take votes away from each other. There are more people in the northern states. Each state has more electoral votes than the Southern states. Breckenridge could win all of the Southern states, and still lose this election. If Lincoln wins most of the northern states, he will have enough electoral votes to win the election."

"So you are telling me all Lincoln has to do is finish his campaign, and he will be elected the next president?"

"You are correct. He can't lose this race, barring some unforeseen disaster. He will be the next President of the United States."

"It means that the politicians around here know that Lincoln's election is a certainty and they are making plans as we speak."

"What plans?"

"Howell Cobb has been going in to see the governor at least twice a week for the past month. I have seen Alec Stephens and other politicians come to the capitol this summer for conferences with the governor and members of the General Assembly.

"But Mr. Stephens is a U.S. Congressman, and the Assembly should not even be in session during the summer."

"That's right. That means that something really big is cooking up over in town.

I have been reading the *Macon Daily Telegraph*, and the paper says that the politicians in South Carolina have been talking about seceding from the union should Lincoln get elected president in November."

"Isn't that what John Calhoun threatened over the tariff way back when?" David remembered his school lessons on recent history.

Uriah stopped, scratched his chin. "Yeah. I was just a young pup back then. Old Andy Jackson was president. He didn't put up with any of that talk. He told Calhoun and the governor of South Carolina that he would blockade Charleston with the Navy and send in federal troops if they were to carry out their threat. He was a strong president. He made 'em back down."

David began to remember things he had heard from his Uncle William back home.

"I have heard Uncle William say that the states have the right to secede if the federal government should somehow refuse to acknowledge the planter's rights to property. He said that the Southern states did have the right to leave the Union if the Federal Government becomes belligerent in its attitude toward the Southern states."

"So I guess his argument presupposes that each state legislature will meet and vote to leave the Union if Lincoln is elected president?"

"That's correct. And the governor has been entertaining visiting planters and dignitaries all this summer at the executive mansion just for that purpose. We had several large orders to fill over in town for meal and grits on account of all the governor's entertaining. He wants Georgia to go with all the other cotton states. He will tell you that the abolitionists are going to take over the Federal Executive branch of government, and the states must do something about it. I have spoken to the governor many times this summer, and he says that the Federal Government sooner or later will vote to abolish slavery in the Southern states, at the expense of each of the Southern states. He says it would wreck our economy, destroy our social structure, and punish all the white people from the rich planter to the poor day laborer."

"What is your opinion about this issue, Uncle Uriah?" David wanted to know where his uncle stood in the face of this great debate.

"This great country of ours is about to fall apart. Your grandfather served as a lieutenant aboard the *U.S.S. Constitution*. He told me years ago that the United States was the greatest experiment in democracy ever made on this earth. Your father fought with me in Mexico in '46. You know, he was a sergeant in the 1st U.S. Dragoons. We did not fight to extend slavery. We fought because our country called us to serve. This Union was made by men that fought England to abolish tyranny. They drew a constitution that gave each state sovereignty and rights, and each citizen rights under the law.

Those cotton planters and politicians now anticipate that Lincoln and the 'Black Republicans' will do something on the federal level to harm the institution of slavery. So now, after all those years, when they anticipate that the Democrats may lose a presidential election, they think they can go in and change the rules of the game altogether. It's sort of like wanting to change the rules of a baseball game after the other side scores a run."

David chuckled to himself when he heard that comparison.

"David, Toombs and Brown are idiots. Nothing detrimental to slavery could ever be voted in if the South remains in the Union. Alexander Stephens has assured me of that for years. You know, he came by here not too long ago, and told me that the Northern states need us just as much as we need them, and the Union will not be dissolved for that reason."

"Does he really believe that?" David asked.

"Alex told me that he knew Lincoln very well, that they had both served as Whigs in the U.S. Congress, and that Lincoln would never do anything rash or disruptive to the South should he be elected."

"So why do we have all of these problems then?" "Toombs and the other fire–eaters have for years threatened to pull out of the Union if slavery is tampered with in any way. The problem here is that the politicians have staked out positions that are doomed to clash with one another. Lincoln wants to stop the spread of slavery into the territories. Toombs and the governor fear that if slavery is blocked in the territories, that the free states will soon get a majority in the Congress, and vote to get rid of slavery altogether. So they want to take action now to preempt moves they anticipate Lincoln will make against the South."

"But why do anything now?"

"I have thought about this situation, and can only tell you this. Money is the root of all evil. The Bible says that a man cannot serve two masters, but he love the one, and despise the other. "Ye cannot serve God and 'manna.' The 'manna' here is cotton. Slavery is the cheapest means of planting and harvesting cotton that we know of today. The cotton planters control most of the money, and the politicians are planters mostly in the South. David, you have been up north. You have visited cities up there. Have you talked to any people up there to get their opinions?"

"Yes sir, I have. I have spoken to many a businessman on trains from Boston to Philadelphia, and over in Pittsburgh. The people up North believe that slavery is a backward and worn out institution that should have been outlawed years ago. I even got the chance to talk to some British subjects in my travels. Believe it or not, the English people feel the same way about slavery. They also abhor the institution."

"I understand. What about you, David? How do you feel about the institution of slavery?"

"Uncle Uriah, in all the years I have known you, I have never heard you express an opinion in this area, one way or the other. I am quite surprised."

"I know, boy, but please speak your mind."

"I have been with my Uncle William to many auctions of slaves across this state. I was at Louisville several years ago, and witnessed a whole family, a wife, husband, and two children, sold to separate owners right before my eyes. You should have seen it. The scene would have broke your heart. I never forgot the crying and wailing those people did when they were separated.

I was in Wilkinson County two years ago, and came across an overseer beating the hell out of a young slave with a horsewhip. I saw the look in the overseer's eyes while he was giving this beating. It was pure evil."

"What did you do about it?" Uriah was curious.

"I got down off my wagon and told him the boy had had enough. The idiot then drew back to hit me. I pulled my pistol out of my belt and cold cocked him up 'side his head."

"I remember that now. The sheriff came over and talked about arresting you for that."

"He did, but when I told him I was defending myself, he let me go. No charges were pressed. I never forgot the look in that slave boy's eyes, though. He was very grateful."

"Enough about slavery. The reason I wanted to talk to you was to let you know that you need to be thinking about your future. You may be faced with difficult choices to make in the months ahead. Your cousin Joseph has been drilling a militia company, the Thompson Rifles?"

"Yes sir, he has."

"Well, if war breaks out, the governor will probably call those types of units into state service. Joseph will probably want you to fight with his outfit. How would you feel about serving as a militia officer under your cousin's command?"

"I don't know. We get along with each other, but we also lead separate lives. He has his foxhunts and barbeques. I work for my uncle most of the week, and go hunting or fishing by myself when I have free time. I do not want to serve in any type of military unit under Joseph. At times he can be overbearing and abusive."

"You know that your Uncle William will probably expect you to serve with your cousin's regiment, don't you?"

David had not given any thought to the chances of being called to join a militia unit. He began to show his uncertainty.

"...Well, I expect that they would want me to..."

"David, let me ask you some things. You have been out of college quite some time, have you not?"

"Yes, sir."

"And you have helped your Uncle William purchase this mill equipment and build the sawmill on his place, did you not?"

"Yes, sir, I did."

"And you work daily on the cotton crops and cotton harvesting on his plantation also?" "Yes sir, I do."

"Does William pay you a salary, or has he decided to make you a full partner over at Greenbrier?"

"No sir, not really. He pays me a small monthly stipend, and whenever I need clothes or other necessaries, I go into town and can purchase items on the Greenbrier accounts."

"And what does William's heir, Joseph, do each day, David?"

"Not a whole lot, to tell you the truth, sir. He occasionally reviews the bookkeeper's accounts, he helps some at harvest time, and he socializes and fox hunts a great deal."

"And for all of his efforts, his father will leave Greenbrier to him in his will."

"That's probably true. I haven't really thought about all of that too much, to tell you the truth."

"Just keep this in mind, David. Your Uncle William is the kind of person that takes things personally if he believes his family honor has been slighted in any way. He may turn on you if you refuse to join your cousin's militia regiment."

"There is something I need to tell you, Uncle Uriah. You may hold it against me, but I cannot fight to uphold the institution of slavery."

Uriah could see fear on David's young face. "Fear not, boy. Your secret and your beliefs are safe with me. I will tell you this. Over the past ten years, I have also come to believe that slavery is wrong. It has put a stranglehold on our political system in this country for the past thirty years. We cannot grow as a nation or achieve anything without addressing the issues raised by slavery. Your Aunt Faith worked on me for years, and finally convinced me that slavery is wrong, and must be ended.

"I understand, I knew that you were not per se opposed to slavery years ago."

"People change, David. Even an old dog can learn new tricks. Will you be staying for supper, David?"

"Thank you, no. I really need to drive back over to Greenbrier tonight. I have to get up and ride into Milledgeville in the morning and see if my new saw blades have come in from New Haven."

"Very well. When will you return for your grits and your corn meal?"

"In about four weeks. Our wheat will be ready to cut and thresh then, and we will have the cotton crop in by then."

They walked back up to the mill. David later said goodbye to his Uncle Uriah and Aunt Faith, and started back with Zack over the twelve miles of dirt road that led back to Greenbrier Plantation.

As the sun began to set over the pine trees, David heard the whistle of a train engine over at the station at Nona, some five miles away. The train whistle jolted him out of his day dreaming of Angela.

As he looked back at Zack's wagon, and noticed that Zack's team of mules had picked up their pace and had picked up their ears. Feeding time was now, and they knew the way home. Nearly an hour later, they rounded a bend in the road, and saw the square white columns on the front porch of Greenbrier Plantation.

They pulled their teams around the gravel drive and over to the large carriage house and stables. The stables were made entirely of brick, and two black stable boys there with grey breeches and white shirts relieved them of their teams of mules, and rolled their wagons around to stalls on the side of the building.

Whale oil lights on the porch were already lit, and Savannah, the Floyd's black cook and house servant, greeted David as he walked around to the front steps.

"Mista David, I made you rice soup and baked chicken. I kep' it warm fo' you, come back with me to the kitchen. Mista Joseph and Mista William's done had their supper."

"Thank you, Savannah, I'll be in directly." David looked out over the front porch and admired his uncle's home. Greenbrier was a Greek Revival building with square columns, and a porch that wrapped around the entire two story main house.

The home was constructed of heart pine lumber with hand–hewn beams, some as large as sixteen inches square. All of the lumber was cut on the plantation property, and processed in an earlier version of the plantation sawmill. The brick used to build the carriage house, some of the walkways, the fireplace and foundation piers were made on the plantation brick mill. Clay for the bricks was hauled from the banks of the Oconee River and the Little River.

The house had black window shutters, and was painted white. William Floyd built the house in 1840 with the help of a Jones County contractor, Daniel Pratt. At the time, William's wife Janet was alive and helped to choose the color schemes of the various rooms of the mansion. David thought a moment about his Aunt Janet. She had died four years before from diphtheria during a bitter cold January. She was a raven-haired beauty with blue eyes and an hourglass figure. The thing that David most remembered about her was her beauty and her kindness. She had helped to raise him after the death of his own mother and father.

David finished his supper, strolled out of the kitchen, across the brick dog run, and back into the main house. His cousin Joseph would not have taken a late supper in the kitchen area. He would have made Savannah bring his meal in covered tureens across the dog run and into the main dining room.

David thought of what his Uncle Uriah had told him. He and his cousin really are different. Joseph is treated as an heir apparent to the large plantation. David is treated more like an overseer or paid employee. For the first time in his life, David finally realized his Uncle William did not regard him and Joseph as peers.

He strode into his uncle's large study, which was lined with pine paneling and bookcases around each of the walls. A whale oil lamp was lit, and William Floyd was seated at a corner desk, studying a column of figures in his large account books. He was pulling on a homemade briar pipe, made from the same briar roots that gave the plantation its name. He was short and rotund, and was dressed in a cotton duck suit but wore carpet slippers near his bedtime.

He looked up as David entered the room.

"Well, young David, did you get our corn delivered to Uriah's mill?"

"Yes sir, but we encountered a little problem along the way."

"What was that?"

"A great big Canebrake rattlesnake. I took care of him with my shotgun though, and no harm came to us or the animals."

"What did you do with the snake?" William was curious.

"Zack cleaned him for Eula May. He says she will cut him up and fry him for breakfast in the morning." A look of surprise crossed William's face. "You know, darkies usually don't fool with snakes at all, much less eat them. That is pretty odd. Her mama was a 'Gechee' nigger, though. They have some odd practices. Damn fine cooks, though. That is a fact. Their low country boil is somethin' else. Enough about food. Are you going into town tomorrow?"

"Yes sir. I was going to take a wagon and see if my saw blades had arrived at Ivey's General Store. I also wanted to take in an estimate of our cotton harvest acreage over to Mr. Collins' office, if the figures are ready."

"I have that estimate here. David, this year's harvest is going to be our biggest one yet. 1860 will be a year to remember if these numbers are correct. Mr. Collins will need these estimates in order to arrange for railroad car space to Savannah. You may want to get these over to his office by noon."

He handed David two sheets of folded paper sealed with wax, addressed to George Collins.

"I also want you to tell Buck tomorrow to start cutting skid poles and flat board lumber to size so we will have some way to stack and move our cotton bales to the gin. I will also need you to inspect and oil the gin machinery by the end of the week. If you need any replacement parts for the gin, you will need to order them now. I want to be completely prepared to handle this year's harvest. If it's gonna be a big 'un, I want us to be ready to handle it."

"Yes sir." David got up, picked up the letter to George Collins, and walked toward the end of the room.

"And David." David stopped and turned around.

"Yes sir?"

"Please say hello to Angela for me." David saw the smile across his uncle's face, and saw him wink his eye.

"Yes sir, I sure will. Good night, Uncle William."

"Good night, young man."

David exited the room and went upstairs to bed. As he removed his clothes and turned out his lamp, he heard the call of a Whippoorwill in the Water Locust bushes outside. He was excited and keyed up, anticipating his visit with Angela Collins on the morrow. Just the thought of seeing her generated high excitement and anticipation. He had never felt this way about a woman before. His feelings about her were new and at the same time were hard to control. The only way he could sleep that night was to remind himself that he would get to see Angela the next day. He finally nodded off to sleep after midnight. His dreams were those of her.

Chapter Two

The next morning, David had two strong mules hitched to the buckboard, and drove the ten miles south down the Eatonton Factory Pike into the small town of Milledgeville. Milledgeville in 1860 was the capital of the State of Georgia, but its population only numbered around 2,000 full–time residents. Legislators and other temporary residents bolstered the numbers to 3,500 during the first fifty days of the year when the General Assembly was in session.

Most of the year, Milledgeville played the role of a small farming and mercantile community. On the first forty eight to fifty days of the year, the Georgia General Assembly would meet at the State Capitol during the annual session. The governor, Joe Brown, resided in a large columned Greek revival mansion a little over a mile from the capitol building, located on a hill overlooking most of the downtown area.

David pulled his wagon up to Collins & Bloodworth's Factor House on South Wayne Street, where he spied George Collins through one of the upstairs windows. He made out his tall beaver hat and his side–whiskers, which were his distinguishing features. He tied off his mules' reins near the front post of the building, and entered the front door. A clerk with a blue shirt and an eyeshade greeted him. He stood behind a large wooden counter.

"Hello, young David. What can I do for you today?"

"My Uncle William had prepared a list of estimates of our cotton acreage for Greenbrier for Mr. Collins. He indicated he would need to get those to Mr. Collins in order for him to arrange rail transport with the railroad for our cotton crop."

The clerk took the folded paper from David eagerly.

"Thank you, Master David, we have been expecting these numbers for the past two weeks. I will telegraph the Central of Georgia Railroad today."

David wanted to linger around the Factor House a bit longer in order to get the opportunity to see Angela. He began to engage the clerk in conversation.

"Uncle William believes that we will have our best cotton crop ever this year. He has asked me to come in and pick up saw blades for the gin today. They were ordered out of New Haven."

The clerk knew about the large Griswold–built gin at Greenbrier. "Your gin has eighty saws, doesn't it? It is about the largest gin around here, isn't it?"

"Yes sir. I have to replace around twenty–five of the saws over the next two weeks. I have to get the gin ready for the cotton harvest. The steam engine and belts are in great working order. I just need to oil and grease some of the moving parts, and replace some of the saws." "Good luck, David," the clerk said, nodding his head, "I know you will do a fine job for your Uncle William."

"Thank you. Good day, Mr. Blankenship."

David walked out the front door, and began to mount up on the wagon. Angela Collins walked up behind him, and gently tapped him on his left shoulder. He turned around and looked into her beaming face.

"Hello, Angela. It is really nice to see you today. I was on my way to Ivey's General Store to pick up our saw blades. What have you been up to this summer?"

David was truly smitten by this girl. He started the conversation in order to hide his nervous demeanor.

"Gladys Fielding and I went up to Clarksville and stayed with her aunt and uncle up in the mountains the last part of June for about four weeks. We saw apple orchards and we even got to go to Tallulah Falls. David, that gorge at Tallulah Falls was a spectacular sight. I have never witnessed anything so beautiful."

David looked down at her. He had never witnessed anything as beautiful. She had on a pretty gingham dress with a baby blue checked pattern, and a wide straw hat with a long hatband that matched the pattern of her dress. Her jet–black hair was done up in a bun, with two curls set around her face. Her blue eyes matched the color of her dress, which was a deep ocean blue. David was already weak in the knees. He knew he had to ask her to the Harvest Ball in October, and it was now or never. He bit his upper lip, ignored the weakness in his knees, and began to ask her, "Angela…er…do you have an escort to the Harvest Ball next month? I really would like to escort you if you are willing to go with me."

The girl did not display her emotions as publicly as David did, but he could tell that she was pleased that he had asked her to the ball.

"Well, I had other offers, David, one even from your cousin Joseph, and I had put them all off. But I want to go with you."

She walked up and poked him in the chest with her right hand. She looked him in the eyes, and began to tell him her reasons for declining the other offers.

"I have always been interested in you, David. You are so different from the other boys. You are so serious and business–like. I wish you were more fun, and more socially conscious."

"I don't really understand what you mean, but I'm really happy you want to go to the Harvest Ball with me, Angela."

A look of relief came over his face.

"David, my daddy may have a problem with you coming to escort me to the Ball without coming over on Sundays. You need to come at least once a week and call on me, so that Daddy and Mother may accept you."

David knew when to take advantage of favorable offers.

"Would this Sunday be too soon, Angela? Could we go for a buggy ride then? I can arrange for a proper chaperone, of course."

Angela consented to the buggy ride for the following Sunday. The only thing that David could remember that afternoon was the sight of her as she waved him goodbye with her straw hat. He did remember to go by Avery's Haberdashery & Dry Goods to pick up two suits of clothing his uncle had ordered.

He drove his rig back to Greenbrier, where he spent the remainder of the day changing out saw blades on the cotton gin, and on the steam saw mill. His helper on this and most other jobs was an older slave in his 50's named Joe Buck McGee. Joe Buck was an interesting person as far as slaves went.

He was originally from down near the River Plate in South America, but was sold to a tobacco farmer in Cuba. The Cuban tobacco farmer brought him up to Charleston, South Carolina in 1841. At a high stakes poker game, Joe Buck's former master ran out of ready cash funds, and was allowed to draw house credit against the value of his servant, Joe Buck. William Floyd drew three kings on the last hand, and Joe Buck's former master, Fernando Hernandez, drew a pair of twos. That is how Greenbrier Plantation obtained a skilled carpenter for the price of William Floyd's initial stake in a poker game.

Joe Buck was worldly, because he had been to many parts and places in North America, the Caribbean, and South America. He was wise, and he was intelligent. Although he was black and was a slave, David looked to Joe Buck as a mentor, a confidant, and as his particular friend. David grew up without his parents, and Joe Buck was a father figure to him. Joe Buck had particular skill as a carpenter. He made David a turkey call in the form of a varnished cedar box, and showed him how to use it in the spring to kill a wild turkey gobbler. Joe Buck made most of the slaves' furniture in the form of split–bottom chairs from white oak, and tables from oak and cherry.

When David built and installed the steam powered sawmill, Joe Buck's duties increased at Greenbrier. He became responsible for supplying all lumber, fence rails, and skid poles on the plantation. He supervised wood cutting parties during the winter months. His work parties would go out and cut Georgia Loblolly pines, oaks, and hickory trees, and drag the felled trees back to the sawmill with oxen and mule teams.

The trees were formerly split with sledgehammer and steel wedges, with the work taking hour after backbreaking hour. Once the steam–powered sawmill was built, however, whole logs could be ripped into board lumber of almost any size with relative ease. Rails for fences, lumber for building and construction, skid poles, wagon bodies, and furniture could be cut to size, even to order.

The steam sawmill had also turned into a profitable operation for Greenbrier, as other planters ordered and paid for lumber to be cut by Joe Buck McGee. After the new saw blades were bolted into place, David and Joe Buck began to cut Loblolly Pine wood into skid poles. While they were handling the pine lumber, David sought out his friend's advice concerning matters of the heart.

"Joe Buck, I saw Angela Collins when I went into town yesterday. She said that she would go to the Harvest Ball with me, but she wanted me to call on her on Sundays between now and then, so her parents can get to know me."

Joe Buck leaned back against the trunk of a Water Oak tree, and took out a briar pipe from a front pocket in his denim overalls. He fumbled around for his pouch of tobacco, stuffed the bowl of the pipe full, and lit the pipe with a Lucifer match. He looked over at David, smiled, and began to interrogate him.

"Do you know what they means, boy?"

"Not really, what does it mean?"

"They are gonna size you up as potential 'husband material' for their daughter. They are gonna look at your manners, your bearing, and temperament, and your worldly goods."

"How do you think I will measure up?"

"Are you really serious about pursuing this girl? What makes her so special?"

"I don't really know, I just know that she is the only girl I want to be around and talk to and spend time with. I have never felt that way about anybody like this before. I'm scared to death, really."

"Well son, it looks like you have been bit by the love bug. You are 'gonna need to get some serious help if you want to spark this girl, David.

From what I hear, you got some serious competition out there. You are a good boy, but you are a little rough around the edges. I'll talk with Savannah, and see if she can help you with your table manners. She's from Virginny, and mammies up there are taught everything in that department."

David was puzzled. "What do you mean, I need a lesson in manners? I don't understand." Joe Buck sat up higher against the tree, and took another pull on his pipe.

"David, you work all of the time. You don't go to the fancy dinners, dances, and cotillions that Joseph attends each week. You don't know the difference between your salad fork and your shrimp fork. You don't know about dancing and dance cards. You need some trainin'. But don't give up, you are a bright boy, and you learn quickly."

David trusted the advice of Joe Buck. If Joe Buck said he needed lessons, then he must need them.

"All right. Please talk to Savannah for me, and see if she can give me lessons maybe two or three nights each week after supper."

"I'll talk to her tonight." Over the next few weeks, David took lessons during the evenings after supper from Savannah. She taught him complete and proper table manners, and tutored him on proper etiquette at formal balls and cotillions. He learned the waltz and the Virginia Reel. Joe Buck could play several tunes on the violin, and Savannah taught him the appropriate dance steps, and the proper procedures for use of a dance card.

During the weekends, on Sunday afternoons, David would call on Angela and took her on picnics, to church social functions, and on buggy rides out near the Oconee River.

Each of their outings were chaperoned, of course, and David barely ever had the opportunity to steal a kiss from Angela. He did get to kiss her on a recent buggy ride out to the river, when the chaperone, Julia Bonner, was distracted by a large horsefly.

He pulled Angela behind a Sycamore tree and kissed her, and she kissed him back. Near the end of September, though, David's free time began to dry up. The harvest season for the cotton crop soon consumed all of David's time.

Near the middle of September, David, Joe Buck, Zack, and a small gang of field hands cut and threshed Greenbrier's small crop of summer wheat. David and Zack carried the wheat to Uriah's mill, and then hurriedly joined the other workers at Greenbrier that had begun the harvest of the largest cotton crop in Georgia ever seen, the fabulous cotton harvest of 1860.

Greenbrier had four hundred acres of high quality Sea Island cotton to harvest in the fall of 1860. The summer had brought frequent thunderstorms and ample rains, and the humid weather had produced a high quality crop. The crop was also of a high yield per acre, and the harvesting required several gangs of experienced hands.

Joseph supervised one gang of twenty hands, and was assigned a one hundred–acre tract to harvest. David had supervision over thirty–five other field hands, and was given the task of harvesting an additional two hundred acres across the creek from Joseph's tract.

Joe Buck ran a smaller crew of fifteen field hands and five white paid day laborers, who were mostly schoolboys. They were to harvest the one hundred–acre field near the Little River. The cotton pickers would each have a long cotton sack made of a strong canvas material, which had a sturdy shoulder strap. The sack was six feet in length. Each picker was required to fill his sack, by picking the cotton lint off of each bowl on the plant. The Sea Island cotton was a tall plant, growing over the waist of each cotton picker. The bottom of each cotton bowl contained a rough, fibrous material, and cotton pickers needed tough, strong hands to keep up a day's work of harvesting the cotton. As each picker's sack filled, each crew had a system of runners to exchange empty sacks for filled ones, in order to keep the pickers constantly at their work of pulling cotton off the plants.

The runners ran the filled sacks down to large wagons parked at the edge of the cotton fields. Those wagons were double–teamed, and had high wooden side bodies built by Joe Buck McGee. Once each wagon was filled, it was then sent to the cotton gin house at Greenbrier, where its contents were unloaded at the lint room.

After the harvesting crews were sent out, around the middle of the day, when several loads of cotton were brought to the gin house, David would leave another man in charge of his cotton picking crew, and began his other duties, which required him to run the cotton gin.

The gin house at Greenbrier was one of the largest in Middle Georgia. It was built on a hillside, and was powered by a steam engine David had purchased in Pennsylvania. The gin itself was a device containing saws that separated the cotton fibers from the seeds and trash contained at the bottom of the cotton bowls. The saws, gin brush, and screens were located on the second story level of the gin house.

The wagons from the fields would drive up to the rear door of the gin house, and there the cotton was unloaded by hand into large baskets. If the cotton was still wet with morning dew, it was piled onto a large platform near the rear of the gin house to dry.

Under the gin house, the steam engine turned a crankshaft, which drove a large wooden running gear, which drove the gin. The small steam engine that powered the gin was located at the side of the gin house at the end of a long crankshaft. David perfected the placement of the steam engine in this manner, in order to minimize the fire hazard for the cotton lint.

Cotton was fed into the gin box after the engine gears were engaged. Several boys would fill up cotton baskets with raw dry cotton, and the raw cotton was fed into the gin. The saws of the gin, turning constantly, ripped the cotton fiber apart, separating the fiber from the seeds and trash. The gin box was located on the upper story of the gin house.

The doffing brush would then blow the lint cotton down a chute to the lint room on ground level. Next to the lint room, the lint cotton was then packed into a screw box, where it was packed into bales.

Also near the lint room was a seed room where seeds that were separated from the cotton lint were blown. Some of the seeds were retained in seed pens for use to re-seed the next year's cotton crop. Most of the seeds were shoveled into piles where they deteriorated, and were later used as fertilizer on vegetable crops. Other portions of the seeds were mixed with cracked corn, and used to feed livestock on the plantation.

The lint room was built large enough to handle three days' worth of cotton ginning. Once it was filled, hands were called in from the fields to assist in pressing out the cotton bales. The lint cotton was packed out into bales by a huge wooden screw. The screw was supported on a huge wooden frame. The frame was supported by a cross-sill at the bottom. At the bottom of the frame was a cotton box, which had doors at both ends and sides on its lower part.

A follow block was built above the lower box, and located to one side. While the box below was being filled with cotton, two hands would get into the follow box and tramp down the loose cotton as it was put in. Steps were built up to this box from the ground, where the cotton was carried up in large white oak baskets.

When the box was tramped full, the follow block was turned into it, a large piece of burlap bagging was placed under the cotton, and the screw was started down. At the top of a screw-pin was a large cross beam, which was connected to a set of large levers which dropped down from the second story level to near the ground. The larger of the two levers contained leather harnesses to which two strong mules were hitched.

Those mules turned in a counterclockwise circle, thus turning the screw pin. This produced a large and tight bale of cotton at the bottom of the cotton box. The doors of the cotton box were then opened, and the bagging was pulled up the sides and ends of the bale. The bagging was sewed up with twine, and ropes were pulled around the bale with a lever and a windlass, and were drawn up tight and tied in knots. Five or six ropes were used to tie up the bale.

    Sam Griswold originally built the gin house and bale screw in 1840. He was an expert builder of the bale press, selecting the timber himself, and drying the timber to his specifications. David had added the steam engine power to the gin in 1858. David added another innovation to the operation of the cotton gin. On a trip to Philadelphia in 1858, David met a naval officer that had described in some detail the life aboard a naval ship. When he described the ship's lanterns, and the way that they provided light with a minimum of a hazard for causing fires, David immediately saw a use for ship's lanterns at Greenbrier.

    David purchased two dozen ships' lanterns in Philadelphia, and hung them in the gin house when he returned to Greenbrier from his northern trip in 1858. The metal plates at the rear of the lanterns kept the device spark–free, and yet provided illumination needed to work in the gin house after dark.

    As a result of the installation of the ship lanterns, the gin house could operate into the night. David trained Zack Dawson in the operating of the gin house machinery, and Joe Buck McGee was also trained to run the cotton gin. This allowed the men the opportunity to relieve each other during the harvest process, and to increase their output to fifteen bales of cotton per day. After the cotton was baled, it was hauled down to the railroad station in Milledgeville by large wagons drawn by teams of six strong mules.

    Once the cotton got to the station at Milledgeville, it was loaded on railroad cars for transport to the depot at Gordon, Georgia, on the Central of Georgia Railroad. Mr. Collins had then arranged rail transport of the Greenbrier cotton to Millen, Georgia, and then on to the Savannah Cotton Exchange via the Georgia Central Railroad. After shipment of the cotton crop at Greenbrier, David ran the cotton gin for other plantation owners, ginning their cotton and baling their cotton in exchange for a fee charged for each bale ginned. The gin proved to be a substantial success that fall, both in speed of operation, and in the quality of refined cotton it produced.

    While cotton was being harvested and ginned at Greenbrier and all over the South, political speakers were stumping all over the United States, seeking votes for the 1860 presidential election. Word came in from the various cotton factors around the state of the huge cotton crop, and of the nice prices that foreign buyers were paying to import the southern cotton to England and France. The excellent cotton crop brought huge profits for the planters and extreme overconfidence in their single commodity. This overconfidence brought arrogance on the political leaders of the South, and this arrogance brought the North and South to the brink of war.

The planters were overjoyed by their good fortune, and soon to be realized profits. The Harvest Ball in Milledgeville, an annual affair, was relocated to the State Capitol because its planners wanted a larger, more formal cotillion than originally planned. The Farmers and Merchants Bank in Milledgeville, together with a consortium of local planters, planned two full days of festivities for Friday and Saturday on October 20th and 21st. A caterer named Alice Horn was hired to provide the food for the Harvest Ball and for a reception, which would precede a band concert on the Friday night.

Mrs. Horn came to the governor's mansion on Monday, and began baking on Monday, in order to have her baked goods ready for the coming festivities on Friday. On early Friday afternoon, the State Capitol building was decorated with dyed paper banners, cut flowers, and a banquet table was prepared. At the ends of a pair of crossed tables sat hams, a turkey, a roast pig with an apple in his mouth, and a leg of lamb. Piled onto the table were plates of fried chicken, pickles, salads, and sliced fruits.

In the next room sat a large punch bowl, on the sideboard were gin, brandy, rum, and Kentucky Bourbon whiskey. At the center of another table cakes, pies, mounds of whipped cream and nuts, and "cotton" bales made of spun sugar candy. The afternoon before the Friday band concert, William Floyd sent Savannah to summon David to his study for a conference. David met his Uncle William at the study, where he was reviewing a telegram from Collins & Bloodworth's offices at the Savannah Cotton Exchange. He looked up from the telegram when David walked in. The old man was dressed in a bottle green coat, and a gold watch fob hung from his green waistcoat. The look on his face was one of elation. As soon as he laid eyes on David, he began to speak.

"David, this year was the best cotton crop yet! We have surpassed anything I could have ever hoped for in terms of yield. Collins says that our Sea Island cotton got to market before any other Middle Georgia cotton. We beat others to market, and the demand was high when our crop sold. David, we made over three hundred bales this year!"

"What did that do for us in terms of prices?" David did not have a great deal of experience in the workings of commodity prices.

"David, our prices were sky high! At the time our cotton got to market, no one else had delivered large quantities of good Sea Island cotton. Demand from foreign buyers was high, and our cotton was one of the first large crops to hit the Cotton Exchange. Collins' telegram said that we had the best quality in a big crop that they had seen so far this season. We got an excellent price for the crop, David. And Mr. Stone says that the per bale fees from the gin paid to us by the other planters will be quite substantial indeed."

David knew that Dan Stone's figures were generally accurate. Mr. Stone was hired by William Floyd as an overseer at Greenbrier, but he had never performed any services out in the field. David had considered the man only a first rate clerk, but his numerical estimates were always accurate.

David was glad that he had been able to contribute to the success of Greenbrier's operation that year. He was genuinely grateful to his Uncle William for taking him in as a boy, and for allowing him to complete his education.

"Uncle William, I am really glad that Greenbrier was successful financially this year. Everything I have ever done for you was done to help make this plantation a success."

"I know that young man, and that is why I sent for you. I know that you will be escorting Miss Angela Collins to the festivities this weekend, and I want you to do so in style."

He peered around David, and called for Savannah, who came through the doorway with a long, flat object wrapped in brown paper. She handed the object to William, who began to unwrap it, explaining as he went.

"You see...boy...a few months ago, I had you go by Avery's Haberdashery and have them take your measurements for some work clothes?"

"Yes sir. But I got those in last month."

"I know, son. But I also had them make you a formal tailed coat and trousers that would be fine enough to wear to a black tie affair such as the Harvest Ball."

He unwrapped the package, and showed David a formal suit of clothes made of black broadcloth, with the coat being pleated and tailed in the rear. The tailor had also made David a beautiful starched white shirt with long sleeves, and a large black bow tie and waistcoat out of the same broadcloth material as his coat.

David had planned on borrowing a formal suit from his cousin Joseph, but this generous gift took care of that problem.

"Thank you kindly, Uncle William, I have never owned a suit as nice as this. I really appreciate what you have done for me."

"No David. It is me who appreciates what you have done for me. You were instrumental to our success this year. This suit of clothes is merely a small token of my appreciation for the work you have done for Greenbrier."

David graciously accepted the suit of clothes from his Uncle William. As he was about to leave the room, William gave him another wink from his left eye, and a nod.

"David, please have a good time escorting Miss Angela this weekend. Please enjoy yourselves. You are only young once, you know."

"I know sir. Thank you again."

David went up to his room and tried on the shirt, coat, and trousers. They fit perfectly. He was escorting Angela Collins to the Harvest Ball and to the band concert in impressive style!

Chapter Three

The next morning after breakfast, David ran into Joseph, who was just returning from a morning ride on Hercules, Uncle William's fabulous black stallion. David had a great admiration for the horse. William Floyd had bought Hercules to race in half–mile derby–style races. His former owner lived near Columbus, and Uriah Snelling spotted the horse while returning on a trip from Montgomery. Uriah's prior services in the U.S. Cavalry made him a keen judge of horseflesh, and he purchased the horse on the spot.

He then had him transported by rail from Talbotton to Macon. He then saddled the horse at the livery stables in Gordon, and rode him all the way up to Milledgeville and out to Greenbrier. William bought Hercules on sight.

The horse had a fiery eye, a spirited disposition, and loved to run. He had a white star in the middle of his forehead, and the rest of his coloring was jet black. Joseph trotted up with him at the stables, and dismounted under the shade of a nearby Sweetgum tree. He was dressed in whipcord riding pants, tall knee boots, and a blue denim shirt. He had worked Hercules up to a good lather, and he was winded from his morning ride.

He strode up to David, and began a discussion about the Harvest Ball festivities.

"David, Pa told me about getting you the new suit to wear at the Harvest Ball. He also told me that he wanted me to loan one of my old suits to Joe Buck so he can drive us into town together in the cabriolet coach."

"Who are you escorting to the ball, Joseph?"

"Barbara Wood. She told me that she was going to be staying with Angela Collins, so we will be able to drive by and pick them both up in town together."

"This is going to be a rather grand affair, Joseph. Have you seen the spread they are putting together for this?"

"Yeah, I have. I also heard that the governor and Congressman Stephens and Robert Toombs and Howell Cobb are coming on Friday and Saturday nights."

"Well, you can't have that many people of influence get together in any one place, and not have politicians there, too. Barbara is from down in Wilkinson County, is that right?"

"Yeah, her father has around 2500 acres of cotton down off Commissioner's Creek. Barbara's a charming girl, blonde hair and green eyes. You may have met her, already, but if not, I can introduce you on Friday night. If it's okay with you, I'll tell Joe Buck to leave here around four o'clock."

"That's fine, Joseph. I'll be ready then."

David wondered to himself if Barbara Wood even had a brother, or if the man that tried to prosecute him those years ago was related to her. He saddled his horse, and rode into Milledgeville to buy a pair of decent shoes to wear on Friday night. When he got into town, he noticed a number of politicians giving stump speeches over near the Capitol Building. He tied his horse on Wayne Street, and walked over toward Avery's Haberdashery. He saw fishmongers across the street selling bass and catfish from the Oconee River. As he passed a corner grocery store, he spied his Uncle Uriah crossing the street ahead of him, wearing a dark gray suit and a stovepipe hat. He walked up behind him and tapped him on the shoulder.

"What brings you into Milledgeville today, Uncle Uriah?"

"Urgent business, boy. I am just returning from completing it. Come over and have a beer with me at Sean's Tavern, and I will tell you about it."

"You lead the way."

They walked over to a brick tavern off of South Wayne Street, and entered through the front door. The tavern had a bar, tended by a jovial rotund man in his early 40's named Sean Roberts, whom it was said had many friends but no enemies in Baldwin County. He saw Uriah as he entered the building and greeted him at once.

"Major! How good to see you. You, too, young David! Your Uncle William has been bragging about your ability these past few weeks. Come in and have a drink."

"Sean, we would like a table in the back over there, where it's quiet. We have some business to discuss in private."

"I understand, sure. What may I get for you?"

"Two mugs and a pitcher of beer."

"Coming up, fresh off the tap." Sean left to pour them some beer, and they walked to the back of the bar and sat at a small table.

Uriah began to speak, and spoke in soft, low tones but in a way that noted a sense of urgency. "David, what I tell you now must remain a total secret. You must promise me not to repeat a word of what I tell you now to anyone."

"Sure, you can trust me, Uncle Uriah."

"Good! I thought so. I have spent most of the afternoon at the governor's mansion at a reception with Robert Toombs and Howell Cobb. One of Cobb's aides at the Treasury Department served in my regiment in Mexico. He sent me a note last night, and asked me to attend the reception today. David, I have uncovered an insidious plot to break up the Union."

"What are you talking about?"

"Howell Cobb is Secretary of the Treasury. He was speaker of the House of Representatives. He has huge political ambitions. Robert Toombs is one of our U.S. Senators. He has similar ambitions to Howell Cobb's. Cobb has told my friend that President Buchanan has taken the position that secession by the states is illegal, but the Federal Government can do nothing to stop it once it has begun. Robert Toombs has learned that Abraham Lincoln will be declared the winner of the presidential election in the Electoral College."

"...But Uncle Uriah...you predicted that..."

"I know. But Robert Toombs cannot hold his liquor. Just one mint julep, or two beers, and he falls under the influence of alcohol and says anything that comes to his mind."

The beer was delivered to their table, and David paid Sean fifty cents for the pitcher and the two mugs.

Uriah smiled at Sean and resumed his intense conversation.

"Yesterday, Toombs drinks a couple of juleps, and starts talking about a meeting he had with Robert Rhet and some others from South Carolina concerning a 'contingency plan' they had cooked up in the event of Lincoln's election. Their 'plan', as I was told includes some legal opinion they obtained which affirms Buchanan's views concerning Federal intervention."

"Uncle, this explanation is a little too complex for me, please simplify your explanation, if you can."

"Very well. If Lincoln is elected president, he cannot be inaugurated until March 6, 1861. The Electoral College results will be published on November 6th."

"That's in roughly two weeks."

"Exactly. Their 'contingency plan', in the event Lincoln is elected president, is to call conventions in each of the cotton states, and to vote on articles of secession for each state. Then, the goal is to call for a congress of the delegates of the seceded states, for the express purpose of forming a Southern Confederacy. This is to be done with a great deal of speed, say before March 6, 1861."

"Why is that?" David was really curious now.

"Well, Buchanan has already taken the legal position that the Federal Government has no power to prevent a state or states from leaving the Union. If they do this thing as quickly as they say they can, Lincoln will be presented with a fait accompli. He will have a Southern Confederacy staring him down the second he is sworn into office."

"So what did I miss? Why are they going to do this?"

"The reason why they want to arrange for secession and the creation of a Confederacy before March 6th is to avoid bloodshed. In their logic, the United States will not send troops to force states back into a union that they left voluntarily. These people are convinced that there will be no blood shed if they accomplish secession before March 6th."

"So what are you going to do about this, now that you know their plans?"

"David, I have served in the General Assembly. If a convention is called for Georgia on the article of secession, I know that I will be sent as a delegate. I have had some influence in this state. There are many men of some influence in different parts of the state that served under me in Mexico. I am going to send telegrams to those men, and I am going to tell them what I told you just now, and I am going to do everything I can to prevent Georgia from leaving the Union. I have got to do all in my power to stop the formation of a Southern Confederacy. I can't be of service in the other states, but I can sure make a difference here in Georgia! I will influence as many votes as I can."

"When will you leave?"

"I have got to get over to the telegraph office and send telegrams to some of my friends. I will then need to buy some train tickets and write up an itinerary, and pack my bags. I will be gone at least a month, David, so please look in on your Aunt Faith for me."

"I sure will, sir. Uncle, good luck and God speed."

"Thank you, David."

They gulped down their beers and headed out of the tavern, and into the bright, sunny afternoon. Uriah headed up to the telegraph office, and David went down the street in a different direction to buy a pair of shoes.

"What a different set of errands we have set out on," he thought. Uriah was going out to save the State of Georgia from secession, while he was going out to win the love of a lovely young lady. Would there ever come a day when he would be more like his Uncle Uriah? When would he ever put his beliefs to the test as his Uncle Uriah was doing? Those questions would be answered on another day.

The afternoon of the band concert was crisp and cool, but sunny. Joe Buck had put on an old suit of Joseph's, and had two pretty white horses hitched to the cabriolet coach. David put on his new suit, and walked around to the coach house to meet Joseph and Joe Buck. Joseph was dressed in a similar black suit with tails and waistcoat, and sported a new black Panama Hat as well. They both walked up at the same time, and Joe Buck reviewed their attire favorably.

"You boys both look like southern gentlemen. I am proud to drive you both in to town this afternoon."

David spoke first. "Thank you Joe Buck. You know that you are to take us to Miss Collins' residence in town, and then on to the Capitol Gate?"

"Yes sir. We need to leave now, Mr. David. Y'all please get in, if you will."

David and Joseph climbed into the coach, and Joe Buck flipped the reins. The powerful team of horses pulled off, and began their trot toward the Milledgeville Pike.

On the way down the pike, David began to discuss the results of the cotton crop with Joseph.

"You know Joseph, there are several planters in this county and down in Wilkinson County that rely on steamers and flatboats to get their cotton to market. The Greenbrier cotton has been shipped down to Savannah and sold before their cotton even reached port."

Joseph did not normally discuss the business affairs of Greenbrier, but he was involved in the harvesting and ginning of the cotton crop.

"I was over in Gordon the other day, and was told that the more recent prices in Savannah and Charleston were not all that good. The bumper crop this year has, so they say, caused recent prices per bale to drop."

"Well, they attribute that to the law of supply and demand. Because we relied on rail transportation, our crop got to market faster, and brought an excellent price at the Cotton Exchange."

"David, I just don't have a head for business like you have. I know that Pa wants me to take a more active role at Greenbrier, but I just can't seem to concentrate on these things."

"Why not?"

"Well, I have devoted a lot of time to drilling with my militia company. I do a lot of socializing, hunting, and visiting, and it takes up most of my time. Business interests bore me, David. I can't really explain it. I don't want to disappoint Pa, but I know that I will never be involved in running the plantation like you have been."

"Joseph, if there is ever anything you may want to learn about or get interested in at Greenbrier, you know that I would be glad to help you."

"Thank you kindly, David. I appreciate the offer."

The cabriolet coach wheeled into Milledgeville, and Joe Buck turned the rig down Wilkinson Street, and up to the front gate of the Collins' home. George and Nancy Collins and their children lived in a two–story townhouse several blocks from the Governor's Mansion. The white clapboard house was handsome, and was framed by a high set of boxwoods that grew on either side of a broad brick walkway. A white picket fence separated the end of the walkway from Wilkinson Street. Joe Buck halted the team of horses near the fence, pulled the brake on the carriage, and opened the door for David and Joseph. Joseph strode up the brick walkway, up to a small flight of steps, where he handed a small calling card to the house servant at the door.

"Mister Joseph Floyd and Mister David Snelling calling for Miss Barbara Wood and Miss Angela Collins."

The tall house servant was dressed in a black suit, and had on a pair of starched linen gloves.

"Yes suh. I will pass word on to Mista Collins. You and Mista Snelling please come into the foyer, Mista Floyd."

"Thank you."

Joseph led the way into the large hallway, which had a granite tile floor, and was lined with wooden chairs. A portrait of Mrs. Nancy Collins graced the end of the foyer, near where it joined the rest of the house.

George Collins appeared several minutes later. He was also dressed for the band concert, with a gray suit and a large white bow tie. He was tall and thin, and gray hair decorated the sides of his scalp just above his ears. His blue eyes always twinkled, and David had always considered him a thoughtful man and a dedicated father.

He came right up to both David and Joseph, and pretended to look them over.

"My, my, you boys sure look dressed up to me." How can you stand to look so good? I have never seen you sporting such elegant suits of clothes. Angela and Barbara may have trouble recognizing you."

A minute or two later, Angela Collins and Barbara Wood came downstairs in their gowns. Angela wore a blue and white taffeta gown decorated with blue bows on the skirt and the bodice. Her hair was pulled back and pinned from the rear with a studded sapphire pin.

Miss Barbara Wood was dressed in a crinoline gown, which was white lace around the bottom of the skirt, with yellow trim around the outside of the bodice, and the top of her hoop skirt. She had blue eyes of the same shade as Angela's, and she had blonde curly hair.

Mr. Collins spoke first.

"My, my, if you aren't a couple of beautiful girls tonight. While any young man in the South would be honored and privileged to escort you young belles to the band concert tonight."

David and Joseph bowed politely to their ladies, and escorted them out to the waiting coach and Joe Buck. Mr. Collins called out to Angela: "I've got to wait for your mother. You all go on ahead. We will be along directly." Joe Buck flicked his wrist, and the pretty white team of horses pulled off toward the Georgia State Capitol.

The carriage later pulled up to the Capitol Gate, where large black stewards in white coats, white waistcoats, and white knit gloves opened the carriage doors, and assisted the ladies in dismounting from the carriage.

Another black steward stepped up and pointed the way to the Capitol Building.

"Please come through the right arch of the gate, Mr. Joseph, as the Senate Chambers shall be the banquet hall tonight."

Joseph recognized the large black man with flashy white teeth as Robert Jackson, one of Howell Cobb's trusted servants.

"Thank you kindly, Robert."

The Capitol Gate was constructed entirely of marble, and contained three separate arches. The top of the Capitol Gate closely resembled the top of the Capitol Building itself, as large ramparts were constructed from stone, thus allowing a soldier to fire down at an attacking enemy. David viewed the construction, and recalled that the Georgia State Capitol was constructed over forty years before, when nearby Creek Indians posed a threat to the young Georgia State Government House. They walked through the Capitol Gate, and up the walk to the Senate Chamber. As they entered the chamber, they noticed the large tables of food that had been prepared by the hired caterer. They also noticed that the chamber had been divided again into smaller tables, which were reserved for the various families.

David did not know where they were supposed to sit. He saw numerous men and women in their party finery milling about, and talking with each other. He began to ask Joseph where they were supposed to sit, and then he spied a table that was decorated with bouquets of cut flowers, and a placard stating "Floyd–Collins Families."

He steered their party up to their table. Angela began to recognize some of the dignitaries in attendance.

"Look Barbara, there's the Governor, and there's Howell Cobb and Alexander Stephens."

Joseph saw them and remarked wryly: "Alexander Stephens is a man after your own heart, David. He is opposed to secession absolutely."

David maintained his silence. He had previously promised Angela that the subject of politics would not be mentioned at the festivities. They took their seats, and were later joined by Mr. and Mrs. Collins, and William Floyd. A black servant soon brought them a large silver tray containing many plates of food, which were portions of all of the food prepared by the caterer. Another servant in a white linen jacket fixed plates for each of the guests, and then served each of the persons seated, with the ladies being served first. Another servant passed glasses of beer, wine, and water for each guest, as indicated by their preference.

When all of the glasses were filled, William Floyd stood up, and addressed the guests at his table. "Here's to a successful and bountiful harvest, and a wonderful cotton crop for 1860. May the coming years be bountiful for us all."

George Collins raised his glass in a show of affirmation. "Here, here. Well said."

They then commenced eating, and feasted on a wonderful assortment of food. David felt that he was in a dream. Angela never looked prettier. She was at the festivities with him, and she was the prettiest girl there!

Near the end of the meal, William Floyd arose, and stepped down to a platform near the well of the Senate Chamber, and he began to address all of the guests.

"Ladies and gentlemen. Thank you for attending the festivities of the Harvest Ball this November weekend. The Lord has been good to us this year, and this is our way of showing our appreciation for the people of this community, and for the many shops and businesses that support the planters here. I would at this time like to present to you, the distinguished Governor of the great State of Georgia, his Excellency, Governor Joseph Brown."

The gallery erupted in applause, and Governor Brown walked up to the Senate well to address the guests. He was a grizzled old man from North Georgia, with a long gray beard that reached almost to his waist

He was dressed in a black suit, and wore a white shirt and black bow tie. He had a fiery demeanor. He removed his stovepipe hat, and began to speak.

"Friends, ladies, and gentlemen. Fellow citizens of the great State of Georgia. Each year, the Farmers and Merchants Bank, and a committee of local planters form a consortium for the purpose of celebrating the years' harvest. For the past fifteen years, we have celebrated the years' harvest by underwriting festivities known to you as the Harvest Ball. This year, we decided to offer the facilities of the State Capitol Building and grounds, for your pleasure and enjoyment.

This year, we also decided to underwrite a five hundred dollar award, and to award a deserving individual who, on account of his efforts, has done the most this year to further the cotton trade, and the planting and production of the cotton crop for this area of the State. We shall call this award the "Steward of the Year" Award. The winner of the award shall receive this engraved gold cup, containing ten fifty–dollar gold pieces. I will announce the name of winner directly, but would first describe his achievements to you:

He pioneered the use of steam power to local cotton ginning facilities. He enabled his steam–powered cotton gin to operate at night, thus doubling the ginning capacity. He has pioneered the technique of pre–purchasing rail transportation for an entire cotton harvest, enabling rapid delivery of the harvested crop to the Cotton Exchange in Savannah. His production and harvesting techniques allowed his plantation to enjoy the advantage of favorable cotton pricing from foreign purchasers at the Savannah Cotton Exchange. His efficient production techniques also enabled his friends and neighbors to gin and ship their cotton crop to the Savannah Exchange while prices continued to be favorable.

I want you to all applaud and stand, and give a warm ovation for this years' 'Steward of the Year', Mr. David R. Snelling."

The applause erupted from the seats around David's table. He could not believe his ears. Did the governor just call out his name? Joseph slapped him on the back, and encouraged him to rise and greet Governor Joseph Brown.

"Get up and accept your award old man. You sure earned it. Go ahead." David quickly rose and strode down to the podium. He remembered Angela reaching up and kissing him on the cheek, and he started down to accept the award with a frog in his throat. He was totally surprised.

He walked up to the podium amid the applause, and shook Governor Brown's hand. Governor Brown shook his hand, and greeted him warmly.

"Mister Snelling, the State of Georgia needs bold and energetic young men like you. Georgia will soon need all of her sons for the rough times that may lie ahead. Please accept this cash award with the thanks of your fellow planters."

Governor Brown handed David the gold plated cup with the cash award.

"Please say a few words to your friends and neighbors. Say what is on your mind." David turned toward the podium, cleared his throat, and began to speak.

"I was taught...by my dearly departed mother...to serve the Lord and to love my neighbor as myself. For the past few years, I have served my Uncle William as best I could. I did what I did on Greenbrier not for reward or recognition, but because I loved my uncle. My Uncle William gave me a home and a roof over my head, and I always appreciated what he did for me. I am completely surprised about this award, and I am really grateful. Thank you all."

David turned and bowed to the governor, and asked his Excellency if he could take his leave. The governor bowed back politely, and David walked back to his table amid another round of applause. He glanced down at Angela, and noticed that she was beaming.

The next evening went by in David's mind like a dream. He and Joseph escorted Angela and Barbara down to the ballroom of the Milledgeville Hotel for the Planters' Ball.

David was one of the most popular men in the room the entire evening. His dance card remained full, and he danced with many lovely Southern belles that evening. However, he only had eyes for beautiful Angela Collins, who wore a crinoline dress that night that was the envy of all the girls at the Ball.

It consisted of overlapping concentric layers of blue crinoline fabric, with white trim on each layer. She wore her hair back in a bun, with ringlets of curls around her face, which framed her blue eyes perfectly.

David danced with her, and whispered into her ear that he loved her and wanted to ask her a question later that evening. She knew the question that he would ask before he was even ready to ask it, for her feelings were the same as his.

They later walked out on to the hotel verandah, and gazed up at a golden harvest moon. David knew the time was right to ask Angela the big question. He took her by the hand, and looked deeply into her eyes. "Will you marry me, Angela? I love you, and I want to spend the rest of my life with you."

Angela did not hesitate.

"Oh David, yes. Of course I will. But you will need to speak to Papa first."

"I'll ride over and speak to him this Sunday, if you don't mind."

"Oh David, we'll be so happy together. Let us plan a June wedding. I always dreamed of getting married in June at the Level Grove Church."

The Level Grove Baptist Church was a small but pretty church around four miles above town on the Eatonton Factory Pike. David and Angela had often ridden by the church in the spring buggy on Sunday afternoon. David attended church with Angela on most Sundays, and also had visions of being married in the same building.

"David, we'll announce our plans the Monday after you speak to Pa."

"I wouldn't have it any other way, darling."

He pulled her close to him, and kissed his bride–to–be tenderly.

Chapter Four

The following Sunday, David rode down to Milledgeville and spoke to George Collins about his desire to marry Angela. George gave his consent to the marriage, but asked that the wedding be postponed to July to give Angela's cousin Martha Jane and her Uncle Frank Collins extra time to attend the ceremony, since they resided in Richmond.

David thought that such a request was rather odd, since they could easily arrive by train from Richmond inside of ten days. However, the request seemed reasonable, and he was in an agreeable frame of mind.

The following Tuesday was the general election, and of course the Presidential election. David and Joseph and William drove to the balloting precinct, where they cast their secret ballots. David voted for Stephen Douglas for President. Joseph and William cast their ballots for John C. Breckenridge.

The ballots were tallied around the country, and the results from the various states were quickly transmitted to the Electoral College members via telegraph. The mathematical outcome of the election was an Abraham Lincoln victory. Abraham Lincoln had defeated Stephen Douglas, John C. Breckenridge, and John Bell for the Presidency of the United States.

Immediately after the Presidential Election results were made known, a number of cotton state governors called their legislatures into special session to consider the question of calling for a secession convention. Governor Joe Brown of Georgia called the General Assembly into session on November 13, 1860.

David was in Milledgeville on November 12th, when a courier from the telegraph office delivered a written message to him.

"Are you Mr. David Snelling?"

"Yes sir, I am."

"I have a telegram for you. Please sign this receipt first." David signed the receipt, and handed it back to the courier. "Thank you, Have a good day sir."

"You too."

David tore open the sealed envelope, and read the contents of the telegram.

TO: David R. Snelling, Esq.
FROM: Uriah Snelling

> MESSAGE: I WILL BE ARRIVING MILLEDGEVILLE ON GEORGIA CENTRAL TRAIN AT 8:30 AM ON 11/13/60 STOP NEED YOU TO MEET ME AT DEPOT ON SAID DATE AND TIME STOP NEED YOUR ASSISTANCE THAT DAY AT STATE CAPITOL STOP CONGRATULATIONS ON YOUR AWARD STOP
> URIAH

David reread the telegram, and then rode over to Avery's Haberdashery to conclude his business in town. He then rode back up to Greenbrier that afternoon, after calling on his fiancé and her family. When he arrived at Greenbrier, Savannah informed him that William was in the study, and had been asking for him. David walked into the study, where William and Joseph were engaged in a serious discussion.

"But Pa, I am telling you that we will be asked to drill the company more, 'cause the governor will call us into service soon. I will need to spend more time in town."

Joseph looked up and saw David walk into the room. He then continued his conversation.

"The Yankees will not allow us to secede from the Union without a fight. The governor is not going to leave the State of Georgia without a defense..."

"I hear what you are saying, son, but I believe the Yankees will allow us to secede from the Union without a fight. Even that Black Republican Lincoln will decline a fight if a Southern Confederacy is in place when he is inaugurated. I do not believe any blood will be shed. Hello, David, I have been looking for you. Have you set a wedding date yet with Angela?"

David was relieved that the conversation was switching away from politics.

"Yes, sir. We have set a date for July 15th. The announcement will be made publicly some time next week."

"Splendid. I have always wanted another woman around the house. David, I also wanted to talk to you about the Special Legislative Session tomorrow. I think both of you boys should come and hear the debates. Robert Toombs and Alex Stephens are both scheduled to speak. You might receive an education in the real world of politics if you attend. Joseph, are you also attending?"

"Yes sir, Pa. I am supposed to meet with Colonel George Doles tomorrow also."

"Very good, then we can ride down together. What about you David?"

"I received a telegram from Uncle Uriah. He is coming into Milledgeville on the 8:30 a.m. express. He wants me to drive him from the train depot to the Capitol."

"Very well then. Take the spring buggy. And please ask him about his lumber order. He said he was going to buy some lumber for an addition to his house."

"Yes sir."

The next morning was clear, crisp, and cool. David pulled his linen duster over his jacket, and drove the spring buggy down to Milledgeville just before breakfast. Savannah had packed him a basket with several ham biscuits, and a small stone jug of hot coffee. David ate his breakfast while riding down on the Eatonton Factory Pike. He saved a couple of biscuits and a little coffee for his Uncle Uriah, as he knew Uriah had been riding the train for hours. He drove down near the train depot as the train was pulling out of the station.

He pulled the buggy around across the road from the station, and allowed the grey horse to drink deeply at the water trough. He saw a number of smartly dressed men and women leaving the station. The local residents had servants meet them at the front of the depot. The travelers from out of town hired coaches to take them to the Milledgeville Hotel or the livery stables.

David walked down to the depot, and began to search for his Uncle Uriah.

He soon found him on a wooden bench in the middle of the station, wearing a navy blue suit, and a black slouch hat. He was pulling on a Greenbrier pipe when David walked up to greet him.

"Hello Uncle Uriah. I got your telegram. May I help you with your baggage?"

"This is all of my baggage, boy."

David looked down at his feet, and spied a small, rather weather–beaten leather trunk. He lifted the trunk with ease.

"Where shall I take you, straight to the Capitol, or would you want a room at the Milledgeville Hotel?

"We will go to the telegraph office first, and then on to the Capitol Building. I have some banking business to conclude, and then I have some political business to see about. I will arise early in the morning and ride down here to the State Capitol Building, so I will not spend the night here in town, but you will need to drive me back home tonight."

They loaded Uriah's trunk into the back of the buggy, and David turned the buggy out onto the Garrison Road toward town. It was a cloudy, breezy day, with some threat of rain. David's curiosity regarding the telegraph office caused him to question his uncle.

"Uncle Uriah, what banking business would you have at the telegraph office?"

"Don't tell this to anyone, David, but I have withdrawn funds from the Farmers & Merchants Bank here, and have opened accounts in banks in New York and Baltimore. Some of my former Army associates have assisted me with this."

"Why would that be necessary, Uncle Uriah?"

"Well David, during times of political unrest, there can also be financial panic. Now that Lincoln has been elected President of the United States, there is going to be an attempt by the Cotton States to secede from the Union. If this attempt takes place, and if a war breaks out, financial resources down South may be exhausted."

David found his uncle's statements difficult to comprehend.

"Uncle Uriah, the South has just recorded a record cotton harvest. Even if a secession movement is successful, how does that translate into financial ruin? David found driving and heavy conversation to be quite difficult to do at the same time.

"Look at the situation involving currency and value, as we know it. An ounce of gold in the United States is now worth around $125.00. In London, that same ounce would be worth around fifty pounds. A denomination of currency minted by a nation is only as good as the credit of the issuing nation. If there is no strong central government in the South, currency down here can only become devalued. Don't tell others what I am doing, David. This business must be done discretely."

"Yes sir. Uncle Uriah?"

"What is it, David?"

"Some time in the next few weeks, could you please open a bank account up North for me?"

"Surely, boy. You normally don't concern yourself with financial matters, why the sudden sense of urgency?"

"Because I have asked Angela Collins to marry me, and we have set a date for July 15th of next year."

"Where are you going to live after you are married?" Uriah had no idea how far their romance had progressed, until just then.

"Uncle William has told me that we can live at Greenbrier. He also told me that I would be taken in as a full partner this next season."

"I suppose congratulations are in order, David, but the way the political winds are blowing, your world and my world will be changing very shortly."

They arrived at the telegraph office, and David dropped his Uncle Uriah off, and then headed over to the livery stables. He gave the stable boy a couple of dollars to feed and water the horse, and to put him up in the livery for the day. He also received permission to store Uriah's trunk near the front of the stables, where it could be watched more closely. He then walked up Greene Street, and over to the State Capitol Building, where Uriah soon met him at the Capitol Gate. They were greeted by several local legislators that had known Uriah for years. Uriah spoke to the two men briefly, and then began to walk to the House Chamber.

David did not understand why he was there. He felt dumb and stupid, and very out of place at the Capitol. He finally got up the nerve to speak, and asked his Uncle Uriah the obvious question.

"Uncle Uriah, what may I do to assist you here?"

"I'm sorry that I failed to tell you, David. My train ride was long from Atlanta, and I was half asleep and groggy this morning."

He stopped on the sidewalk, and turned to face his nephew. He then began to speak, more slowly, and more clearly." Governor Brown has called a joint session of the General Assembly to consider the calling of a convention in January to consider secession from the Union. Over the last three and a half weeks, I have been to almost every county of any size in the northern third of Georgia. I have talked with legislators in each of these districts, and I have spoken with some men up in North Georgia that served with me in the Army.

Today, Robert Toombs is going to address the General Assembly, and request a secession vote for a secession convention. Governor Brown will also request a secession convention. Alec Stephens will speak tomorrow, and will speak out against a secession convention. There are a number of legislators from South Georgia here that favor secession. My friends and compatriots in North Georgia have identified some legislators from South Georgia who are not yet committed to secession, that might be amenable to some persuasion."

"What may I do to assist you?"

"While Mr. Toombs and the Governor are speaking, I will arrange meetings out in the halls and anteroom with legislators that I can possibly persuade or influence on the secession question. I will give you handwritten notes addressed to two or three individuals, and you will lead them over to me. I will meet with them, say my piece, and you will get me three more legislators, until I speak to every legislator on my list. Now do you understand?"

"Yes sir, but if this process must last longer than say five o'clock this afternoon, could we get a room over at the hotel? And Uncle, I will also need to find Uncle William, and let him know that I may not be home this evening."

"Very well. David, you will need to do that now. Mr. Toombs is scheduled to speak at 1:00 p.m., and I will need to line up an anteroom for our meetings. Please meet me back here in one hour."

"Yes sir."

David then went into the House Chamber, and began to search the gallery for his Uncle William. He filed his way past men with tall stove pipe hats, and gold watch fobs, and spied a crowd of men around Robert Toombs. One of the men near the back of the crowd was his Uncle William. He walked up to his uncle, and gave him an affectionate pat on his back." Uncle William, Uncle Uriah wants me to assist him here at the State House today. We will be riding back fairly late this evening. I have the horses and buggy over at the livery off Greene Street."

"What sort of duties are you performing, young man?" William was already raising his eyebrows at David's planned day of activities.

"I will be passing written messages to legislators, scheduling meetings, caucuses and such."

"Well then, young David, maybe you will learn something useful about politics. I have been wanting you to take more of an interest in national affairs for some time. Now that the action is closer to home, maybe this will now spark your interest, eh?"

William patted David on the back, gave a nod and a wink, and stepped over toward a vendor selling small bowls of parched peanuts. David stepped out of the House Chambers, and walked back to the small caucus room where Uriah Snelling was lining up couriers.

"Oh there you are, David. I need you to take these notes to Alec Stephens and William Vann. When you get back, I will have some other people for you to contact over at the Senate Chamber."

"Yes sir."

David spent the rest of the day passing written messages to pro–Union legislators.

Robert Toombs and Governor Joseph Brown both addressed the Georgia General Assembly that day. While they were speaking, David passed messages and scheduled meetings between the pro–Union legislators. David went over to the Milledgeville Hotel at seven o'clock that evening, and rented a small room for himself and his Uncle Uriah.

The next day, Alexander Stephens gave a lengthy speech before the Georgia General Assembly which denounced secession, and demonstrated continued loyalty and support to the Union. At the end of Stephens' speech, a motion was made to schedule an election of delegates for a secession convention. The motion passed, 160 to 130, and the legislature was to reconvene on January 2, 1861, to elect convention delegates to the secession convention. Uriah and his compatriots had done their work well, but the secession proponents from South Georgia were too influential.

David drove Uriah back home from Milledgeville on a dark and blustery afternoon. Uriah was somewhat dejected, but was encouraged that the vote to schedule the delegate election was closer than others had been lead to believe.

"David, we gave them a run for their money. The only problem I see for us now is the length of time between now and January 2nd. A lot can happen in seven weeks. According to what I have been reading in the *Macon Daily Telegraph*, South Carolina will vote on its ordinance of secession and leave the Union sometime next week."

"How does that affect us?"

"Well, there will probably be some type of civil war if the Southern states secede the way I think the process will pan out. There are Federal military installations and arsenals that will be attacked or occupied by each state that secedes. No seceding state will allow the Federal government to maintain arsenals or forts on its soil."

"So you feel that conflict between the Federal Government and the South is inevitable?"

"Yes, David, I believe the die has been cast."

They drove down to Uriah's mill, where a large black worker helped unload Uriah's trunk and travel bag. David said his good byes to his uncle, and his Aunt Faith, and turned the buggy down the road toward Greenbrier. It had been a long two days, and David needed his rest, for the following Monday, he had planned a trip to Savannah. The next Monday, Joe Buck drove David down to the train depot in Milledgeville. He had a train to catch at 9:05, which would carry him to Gordon, and then on to Millen and Savannah.

The previous day, David went to the Collins' residence for Sunday diner. David took Nancy Collins aside and asked her two questions concerning Angela. What was her ring size? And what gemstone would she prefer in an engagement ring?

Mrs. Collins assured David that Angela wore a size six ring, and that she loved blue sapphire. David told Mrs. Collins to keep their discussion about the ring confidential. He had been advanced some funds against his stipend by his Uncle William, for the purpose of purchasing an engagement ring for Angela. He had decided to journey out of town to purchase Angela's ring, so the fact of its purchase could remain a secret.

He caught the Gordon train at the proper time, and made the trip down to Savannah by midnight of the same day. He booked a room in a hotel off of Bay Street, down near the Cotton Exchange. He washed up in his room, and put on a clean shirt and coat. The day was brisk and windy, and he could see steam boats pulling up the Savannah River to their berths on River Street.

He checked the money in his wallet, placed his wallet in a pocket in his coat, and headed downstairs. The street was full of cotton wagons, blacks, fish and crab mongers, and farmers with two wheel carts selling fresh vegetables, such as cabbage.

He crossed a busy Bay Street, and spied a slave auction in progress down below the Cotton Exchange. He strolled down to River Street to a shop in a two story brick building that sported a red painted sign with white letters. The sign read "A. Rayfield Marx, Fine Jewelry and Watch Repair." Joseph had told David about Mr. Marx and his reputation as a jeweler. David only wanted the best quality engagement ring for his bride to be.

He walked confidently into the jewelry store, and greeted a short, balding man with a visor who was wearing a black apron, and had black sleeve guards across his elbows. He had a thick lens in his hand, and was eyeballing a diamond when David walked in.

"Hello there, young man, what may I help you with today?"

"I need to purchase an engagement ring with a blue sapphire stone."

"I have several sapphire rings in stock, and I have a selection of stones I can set for you if one of the rings fails to suit you." He walked over to a large chest of drawers, and pulled out a black box lined with felt. Many sapphire rings were sealed in a folded area at the bottom of the box. Loose sapphire stones were in the other compartment of the box.

"What ring size is the lady in question, your bride–to–be?"

"Uh, size six."

"I have three rings on the top row there that are a size six. Here, have a look at them."

He handed the two rings to David, who took them into his right hand, and held them up toward the light coming through the shop window. One of the rings was a pale blue, the other was beautifully cut, and had a deep blue shade. The deep blue stone just matched Angela's eyes.

"Sir, I believe I will take this one. What is the price for this ring?"

"That one I will sell you for $200.00. But you need to pay me in cash."

"That is no problem, sir. I have that right here."

David pulled out his wallet, and counted out two hundred dollars in bank notes, and gave them to Mr. Marx.

"I would like a bill of sale and a receipt, sir, if it is not too much trouble. And sir, could you please wrap the ring in a box for me?"

"Certainly. I will be back with your ring and your receipt in five minutes."

The jeweler stepped into the back of the shop to wrap David's ring and write him a receipt.

David began to stare out the shop window, and noticed a gathering of people on the public square between Bay Street and River Street. He noticed a number of hoop skirted ladies, and saw three companies of militia drilling out of the grass on the public square. The militias were dressed in grey wool uniforms.

Mr. Marx appeared a few minutes later with the bill of sale and the wrapped ring. David had to ask Mr. Marx about the gathering of people on the square.

"That is Major Lawton's regiment of militia. They have been out there for over two weeks. I have been told that these men will take over Fort Jackson and Fort Pulaski when Georgia secedes from the Union. I have also been told that they only take orders from Joe Brown himself. Once the war starts, they will be one of the first units to go in for Georgia."

"Do you really think there will be a war?"

David was interested in Mr. Marx's opinion of the political situation.

"Yes, I do. The Yankees hate and despise us. They are a different people than us. We cannot live peaceably in the same Union with one another. I don't know who will pull the trigger first and start the war, but I know that right now, you have two sides spoiling for a fight. And that fight is coming soon. You in the militia yet, son?"

"No sir, not yet."

"Well, if you ever join up, do be careful. And be careful going back to your hotel. There are thugs and footpads all about River Street. Especially at night."

"Thank you, Mr. Marx. Good day to you, sir."

David walked back to his hotel room in a depressed frame of mind. The country is about to go to war within itself, and he did not know which side he should take. The truth was that he must choose one side or the other. He could not sit the war out. It was coming, and it would directly affect his future. He soon developed a headache and went up to his hotel room to lay down.

Later that evening, he walked down to the Savannah River House, and ordered a large meal of fresh seafood. He sat after dinner drinking a beer down near the river front, watching the steamboats full of cotton load up at the Exchange, and steam down the Savannah River to the ocean.

He watched women and girls in hoop skirts walk arm in arm with their husbands and sweethearts in the grey uniforms of the Georgia Militia. He began to think to himself 'How can Angela love me and live with me if I refuse to join a militia unit? How can she possibly love me if I refuse to fight for the South in this war? How can I fight to preserve and protect the wicked institution of slavery? What will I do when my beliefs are put to the test?'

He walked back to the hotel just before dark, washed his face, and tried to sleep. He could not close his eyes until 3:00 a.m. the next morning.

Chapter Five

David returned to Milledgeville two days later by the Georgia Central Railroad. He had deep concerns over his role in the coming war, but decided to address his concerns on another day. He soon lost himself in the daily chores around Greenbrier. During the first part of December, he helped Joe Buck cut down and haul trees from wooded areas with two mule teams.

They ran the steam sawmill and cut lumber for orders Uriah had made for the new addition to his house. On Sundays, he attended church services at the Episcopal Church in Milledgeville with Angela Collins and her family. He then stayed for Sunday dinner, and would earn his dinner by splitting firewood for Mrs. Collins. The following Saturday, Savannah had asked David to go down to the Little River with his shotgun, and shoot some ducks for their Sunday dinner.

David arose before daylight, saddled his horse, and pulled on his oilskin jacket. The morning was cold, windy, and rainy, a perfect day for water fowling. He had hidden a wooden john boat under some willow bushes on the riverbank, near a pronounced bend in the Little River. He tied his horse to a tree, and got into the boat. He knew where a large wooded creek emptied into the river, and had scouted the area earlier that week. Across from the mouth of the creek was a large sandbar. He got into the punt, rowed across the river, and pulled the boat onto the sandbar. He then took his knife and cut several reeds, bamboo stalks and bushes, and built himself a blind around the boat.

He then sat down in the boat, loaded his shotgun, and waited for the ducks. He waited until he could see the red sun rays breaking over the eastern sky. It was then light enough to allow him to see more than a hundred yards ahead of his position.

He soon heard the squeal of several Wood Duck drakes, and saw four ducks rapidly winging toward him. He waited until the oncoming ducks were over the river, then raised his shotgun and fired. Two of the Wood Ducks pitched over and fell forward, striking the edge of the sandbar in front of him. He got out of the punt and picked up the two birds, and placed them into a canvas bag. He then realized that the ducks were using the creek as a corridor and a landmark, in order to guide their flight down the river. He set up again in the same spot, and reloaded his gun. Soon another flight of six ducks appeared, and he fired at the last minute, and dropped one drake Wood Duck.

It soon began to sleet, and the wind began to blow, as the heavy clouds moved in over the river. David killed several more ducks, including some Mallards, but the storm began to increase in its intensity. He loaded his ducks and shotgun into the john boat, and pulled his oilskin coat more closely about his neck.

His hat had already become soaked with rain, and he had water blown directly into his face. He paddled the punt across the river, and pulled the boat and his day's kill out over the bank. The sleet and rain were soaking his jean cloth breeches, in spite of the protection of his oilskin coat.

He pulled the boat into its riverbank hiding place, and walked over to where his horse was tied. The horse was an old hand at hunting, and had turned his hindquarters toward the wind, while leaving his face against the tree trunk for extra protection from the wind. David threw his haversack with the birds over the pommel, and holstered his shotgun in a sling beside the saddle.

He rode back to Greenbrier in the driving rain and sleet. The grey sky continued to bring more storm clouds from over the horizon. David noticed the beautiful colors of the fall foliage on the trees as he rode by the forest. He compared the deep purple of the Sweetgums and Dogwood leaves with the yellow and gold leaves of the Beech and Hickory trees. He was chilled to the bone, and began to cough.

At the time he rode into Greenbrier, he could barely stay in the saddle. He saw Joe Buck in the coach house, and asked him to clean the ducks for Savannah's Sunday dinner. He pulled off his wet clothing, and went down and hung them before the fireplace in the kitchen to dry. Joe Buck helped him into some dry blankets, and hustled him over to bed in the main house. The following morning was dry, but was cloudy, cold, and windy. William had asked David to go out with Joe Buck and a wood cutting crew of Negroes to cut some hardwood timber over near the Little River. David drove one wagon of hands, while Joe Buck drove another wagon filled with saws, axes, and several sets of trace chains. Two strong draft mules followed along behind Joe Buck's wagon.

The wood cutting party spent the day felling several large oak trees, and splitting the tree trunks into four or six large slabs.

They then cut the slabs to proper size, and loaded the slabs on small log carts. The log carts were then pulled by the mule teams out to the main road, which was the Eatonton Factory Pike. William then sent a work party of twenty hands with Joseph and Zack Dawson, driving two long bodied wagons, pulled with four mule teams. The hands loaded the large slabs of oak logs onto the wagons, and hauled them back to the sawmill at Greenbrier.

Joe Buck would later cut the boards up to the ordered sizes with the steam powered saw, and stack the lumber in a large shed to cure.

David developed a pronounced cough by mid morning, and soon became too weak to work out in the cold weather. At dinnertime, Joe Buck drove him home, and put him to bed. His illness worsened, and he developed a fever. Savannah attended David, and placed a boiled mustard poultice on his chest, and spooned him chicken soup. She also dosed him on rose hips and herb tea.

His fever got worse over the next few days, and he developed cold sweats. Savannah sent Joe Buck down to the river to strip off some willow bark, and she boiled the bark in a small pot. She later gave David small doses of this concoction from a stone jar. Angela came down to his bedside and helped to wait on him some during the next week.

David was supposed to escort her to a Christmas reception at the Governor's Mansion on December 15th. However, on December 12th, David was still too weak to move out of the house.

He called for Joseph, and asked him to escort Miss Angela to Governor Brown's Christmas reception. Joseph gladly accepted. The Governor's Christmas reception was by invitation only, and was one of the highlighted events of the social season in Milledgeville. David knew that Angela wanted to attend, and he knew she would be disappointed if she did not go on account of his illness.

He had planned on giving the engagement ring to Angela the night of the Christmas reception, but decided to wrap it up and give it to her on Christmas Eve instead. The Collins held a large dinner on Christmas Eve, and invited their family members and close friends for dinner, and they exchanged gifts afterwards.

Joe Buck drove David down in the cabriolet coach, and had David wrapped in blankets to keep out the winter chill. The house servants brought David into the Collins' foyer, and bore much of his weight themselves. Mr. Collins soon came out and spoke to David, noticing at once that he was not well.

"David, you continue to try and overdo. You are too ill to be out in the cold weather today."

"I know, sir, but I wanted Angela to have this Christmas present. Will you give it to her for me?"

He handed George Collins the small wrapped box that contained Angela's sapphire engagement ring. Mr. Collins took the ring, and gave David a wink and a nod of the head.

"I sure will, son. I hope when Angela sees fit to show her appreciation for your gift that you will be well again. Please try to go home and get some rest now."

"Yes sir."

"Oh, by the way, did you hear that South Carolina seceded from the Union?"

"When was that, sir?"

"December 20th. Our legislature will revisit this issue on January 2nd, and I hope you will be well enough to come up to the Capitol then."

"I hope so too."

David coughed, and had some trouble regaining his breath.

"You go rest now, young David. Please take care of yourself. I'll have Angela look in on you over the next few days."

"Thank you, Mr. Collins. I appreciate you."

David returned to Greenbrier, and his illness became worse. On Christmas Day, his fever broke, and he later could sit up in bed and take a small amount of broth. He began to improve on December 30th, but was too ill to attend the special session of the Georgia General Assembly on January 2, 1861.The legislature on that date selected the delegates to represent the many districts and counties of Georgia at the secession convention scheduled for January 18th. William Floyd was elected as a delegate for Baldwin County. Uriah Snelling was elected as a delegate for Putnam County.

David steadily began to improve after January 3rd, and sat up and began to eat solid food again. His cough had also subsided. By the beginning of the next week, was able to walk about without difficulty. On January 16th, David obtained permission from his Uncle William to ride down to the State Capitol in Milledgeville, and attend the convention and the vote on the proposed ordinance of secession.

Joe Buck drove David down to Milledgeville for the debate on secession, and dropped him off at Statehouse Square the morning of January 18th. David had on his wool gloves and great coat for maximum protection that cold morning, and slowly climbed up the hill to the Capitol building.

The Capitol of the State of Georgia was situated on the highest hill in the small town, and it commanded the town with its imposing presence. It was a large stucco structure, with brick columns across the top of each wall, that were staggered to create battlements. The doorway into the Hall of Representatives was graced with a Gothic styled arch, and the windows on the top story of the building were formed in a similar graceful arch, which lit the Hall of Representatives with natural light from the sun.

David saw delegates walking up the hill to the State House from Newell's Hall across Greene Street, and he began to enter the building himself, to avoid the rush. He wandered the smoke filled halls, looking for his Uncle Uriah. He spied him at the end of the hall, huddled with delegates in dark suits, and wearing stove pipe hats. Uriah was deeply engaged in conversation with Alexander Stephens, a demure, clean shaven man, who seemed like a boy in a grey suit. After their meeting concluded, most of the men, including Alec Stephens, headed into the Hall of Representatives. Uriah spied David sitting at the end of the hall, and walked up to speak to him.

"David, you are sight for sore eyes, boy! How good it is to see you up and about. Do you know what is taking place here?"

"Not really, Uncle Uriah. I was told that a vote on the secession question would come today. I came to view the proceedings."

"Let me brief you on the present situation. Last night, Robert Toombs gave a long speech that advocated secession. He had a great deal of support. Alec Stephens and my people have spent most of last night, and all of this morning lining up votes against secession. I expect the delegates will vote on the question right after Congressman Stephens gives his speech. Would you like to hear him, David?"

"Yes sir, I would."

"Very well, we will find a seat in the Hall of Representatives."

David and Uriah heard Alec Stephens give a passionate speech that asked for coolness and level headed dealings between the South and the North. Alec spoke his stand against secession. "This step, secession, once taken, can never be recalled," he warned. Stephens had no illusions regarding the result of a secession vote. Secession meant war.

"We and our posterity shall see our lovely South desolated by the demon of war." Later in his speech, he reminded the audience of Robert Toombs' declaration that he would take the sword and fight the North, Toombs himself shouted out "I will!" The gallery erupted with vigorous and enthusiastic cheers. David saw the depression on Alec Stephens' face, and his speech concluded soon thereafter.

The vote was then taken on the proposed ordinance of secession. All of Uriah's past work of the last three months was put to the test. When all of the votes were counted, secession won by 166 votes to 130 votes. Immediately after the vote was taken, one Eugenius A. Nisbet proposed that all of the delegates present sign the ordinance of secession, on the grounds that all of the delegates should show their support for the State of Georgia. Uriah Snelling refused to sign the ordinance. Augustus R. Kenan, also a Unionist, signed the secession ordinance, and then threw away his pen in disgust. William Floyd voted for the ordinance of secession, and expressed his disgust at Uriah for working fervently against the passage of the ordinance.

David later left the State House with Uriah, and they watched Old Glory being hauled down the flagpole, and be replaced with the Georgia State flag. David spoke to Uriah on their way out to the Capitol Gate.

"Uncle Uriah, now that Georgia has seceded, what will you do now?"

Uriah turned and answered his nephew quickly.

"I will work with the Governor for a while, to try and keep the State of Georgia out of chaos while this secession business can be sorted out. You know Alabama, Mississippi, and Florida seceded from the Union last week, David."

"Yes sir, I read that in the *Macon Daily Telegraph*."

"Louisiana and Texas will go out next, and Georgia and other states will send representatives to a convention in Montgomery in February to draw a constitution, and to implement a Southern Confederacy. What will you do, David?"

"Go back home, cut more wood, and help my Uncle William plant a crop."

"What if we have a war, and you are called on to fight for Georgia, what will you do?"

"I don't really know, to tell you the truth. I can honestly say that I do not want to volunteer into the militia or the army."

"David, just remember this, if you decline to serve in the militia, and if you are treated harshly because of that, you will always be able to come and live with me and your Aunt Faith. You know that don't you?"

"Yes sir, I do."

"When are you going to deliver the rest of my lumber?"

"Next week, I promise. We will have it all loaded and delivered by then."

As they walked down the hill and over to the livery stable, they had to weave their way through mobs of yelling, ecstatic men. Some groups of men ran down to the Methodist Church and the Baptist Church, and began to ring their church bells.

Uriah stopped, and then began to show signs of anger." The fools! God forgive them all, for they know not what they do. They think they have accomplished something. All they are doing is plunging their country into civil war. Lincoln and the Congress will not permit this nation to dissolve into small dictatorships."

David had done some recent soul searching on his trip to Savannah. He decided that in spite of Uriah's anger, he should ask him pertinent questions regarding the military readiness of the state, and the South in general.

"Uncle Uriah, you have been in the United States Army for years. Surely during your time in Washington, some form of planning was done in the event of war with the South. It has been threatened by Robert Toombs and other politicians for years."

Uriah's anger began to cool a bit, and he and David stopped walking, amid a crowd of people that were constantly running, shouting, and proclaiming their huzzahs over Georgia's secession from the Union.

"David, please remember that the conversations we have are made in the strictest confidence."

"Yes, Uncle Uriah, I understand. Please go on."

"The United States is the largest manufacturer of firearms in the world. There are only two rolling mills in the South that are capable of producing railroad iron. There is only one mill in the South capable of manufacturing railroad locomotives. The North has many more people than the South. The numbers of available men for conscription in the North far exceed the available numbers in the South. The South has few miles of railroad track compared to the North. The South has no navy to speak of. With few industries, the South will have a great deal of difficulty in producing manufactured goods to equip standing armies in the field."

"I understand. What should I do, Uncle Uriah, considering the situation I am in?"

"Son, you eventually will have a choice to make. You will either fight for your state, or for your country and against your state. Or you can, if you are able, sit the war out entirely. Whatever you do, you should follow the dictates of your conscience, and not be led by the whims and desires of others. Do you understand me, David?"

"Yes sir, I do. I really appreciate your advice, Uncle Uriah. And I appreciate you and Aunt Faith, very much."

"We love you, too, boy. Now let us get out of here, and go home and get some rest. We all have work to do tomorrow."

They walked on to the livery stable, where Uriah got his horse, and where Joe Buck was waiting with the carriage. The first Wednesday morning in February, 1861, was clear, frosty, and cold. David arose that morning, and felt strong enough to ride over with Joe Buck and deliver the lumber Uriah had ordered from Greenbrier's lumber mill. The shipment was large, and required four mules and two large wagons to deliver both loads.

Zack Dawson drove one wagon, and David and Joe Buck rode in the other wagon.

William had agreed to loan out Zack and Joe Buck to Uriah to lend their carpentry skills to Uriah, while Uriah was working for Governor Brown. David helped Joe Buck lay the corner supports of the room from granite blocks. He then helped build the sill and supporting joists for the new addition to Uriah's home.

David's Aunt Faith fed them a dinner of fried chicken and buckwheat biscuits with honey, which they washed down with hot coffee.

Zack and Joe Buck then began to nail down the White Oak floor to the supporting timbers, and Joe Buck took exacting measurements, and worked methodically. At the end of the day, the floor was laid, and the bottom boards for the outside of the room were nailed up. They carefully propped up the exterior boards, and began to load up for the return trip to Greenbrier.

They took their leave of Aunt Faith, and promised to return the next morning. On their way down the road toward the main pike, they met Uriah, who was riding a large bay stallion. He dismounted, and let his horse rest from his efforts of the past hour. David spoke first." Uncle Uriah, what are you doing for Governor Brown? How goes your work in Milledgeville?"

"It has not gone that smoothly. I have had to convince the governor that even though banks may issue paper currency, that the newly formed Confederacy may also issue its own paper money."

"What will that do to prices?"

"It will create an inflation effect on prices. The currency will naturally devalue. That is why I am convincing the governor to base our system of taxation on a percentage of agricultural products grown by each plantation or farm. The tax commissioners in each county will levy a ten percent tax on each agricultural product as it is harvested. The tax authorities will store the grain or produce that can be stored, and later sell the produce and grain on the open market to raise revenues."

"What about the planters that want to grow only cotton?'

"We have discussed that problem in detail. Governor Brown is going to issue an advisory that would inform planters that they should only plant a maximum of fifteen percent of their available acreage in cotton."

"Why is that?"

"The governments of the states and the Southern Confederacy will need food to feed the soldiers and the civilian population. Importing of agricultural items is not practical by sea, and the exporting of cotton products by sea will also be impractical."

"So your plans count on a Union blockade of Southern ports."

"Yes, it does. David, it is getting late. You men need to get home and get some rest. I will stop in and see you tomorrow afternoon. My business in Milledgeville should wind up early then. You boys go home and get some rest."

"Yes, sir. See you tomorrow."

David asked Joe Buck to ease on, and the wagons rolled on toward Greenbrier.

The following morning, David, Zack Dawson, and Joe Buck once again delivered too more loads of lumber to Uriah's place. They began the task of framing the walls for Uriah's new room. David and Joe Buck took the measurements for the layout of the wall studs, and Zack and Archie West, Uriah's black hand, sawed the boards to the proper length.

David and Joe Buck then nailed the stud boards together, and the room was fully framed out by mid–afternoon. David's Aunt Faith brought them lunch at 1:30, consisting of a roast chicken and boiled red potatoes, with cornbread.

Faith was a Quaker woman from Frederick, Maryland, that fell in love with Uriah when he was an officer in the U.S. Army. He met the black haired, blue–eyed woman while he worked for the War Department in Washington. She gave up her Quaker faith to marry him, as he worshiped at the Episcopal Church.

Uriah was twelve years older than Faith, but the love that they showed was strong. David loved Faith, and looked up to her as he would his own mother.

They began to cut the long pine boards for the roof and rafters, and they put together a crude scaffold to assist them in putting up the rafters of the roof. They had nailed together the main supports for the roof by five o'clock, when Uriah came riding up. He was dressed in a grey wool suit, and wore his old U.S. Army cloak. He dismounted from his horse and took notice of Joe Buck's fine carpentry work.

"Nice job, Joe Buck. You have learned carpentry well."

"Thank you, Major." Joe Buck bowed to Uriah.

David was curious for news from Montgomery.

"Uncle Uriah. What have you heard about the convention down in Montgomery?"

"Come down to the barn with me, and help me hang up this saddle."

David climbed down from the scaffold, and led Uriah's horse down to the barn. He untied the saddle from the back of the black mare, and put it in its place in the tack room. He removed her bridle while Uriah unbuttoned and hung up his cloak.

"David, there are four major candidates for President of the Confederacy; Howell Cobb, Robert Toombs, Jefferson Davis, and Alexander Stephens. The Georgia delegates will split their support among their three candidates, and I have been told that Jefferson Davis will be elected President by the delegates."

"What else is to be done in Montgomery?"

"Stephens and Cobb and others will probably draft a provisional constitution, similar to the United States Constitution, but one that guarantees slavery."

"What then?"

"They will begin to organize a government, create governmental departments, and print money."

"You told me some things about money and taxation yesterday, is that what you are working on with Governor Brown?"

"Yes, David. I have convinced the governor to set up a system of taxation based on returns of agricultural produce rather than hard currency. You know, Senator Wigfall from Texas always said that the South did not need any industries. He was just dead wrong."

"Why did the senator say that?"

"It was his position that cotton equaled instant wealth. If you could grow enough cotton and sell it overseas, you can buy enough manufactured goods, and never be in need. Unfortunately, you can't get any hard currency for your cotton crop if you do not control the seas, and your seaports are under a blockade."

"So you have told the governor that the South is not really prepared for war?"

"I have already told him everything I know concerning the lack of military readiness. I have been working with the governor on some ideas to prop up the currency situation. We have been assembling a catalog of 1860 U.S. currency prices on all available dry goods and produce sold here."

"Won't banks print money and issue notes also?"

"Sure they will. But if we base our system of taxation on agricultural commodities, the tax collectors will get paid in produce and grain, and the government can feed troops and retain solvency. And the paper money that is issued will retain more of its face value."

"You are making those assumptions with the understanding that U.S. currency will be hoarded, or go out of circulation?"

"Yes, for now, we are."

"As we discussed yesterday, what about the planters that want to do business as usual, and plant a full cotton crop?"

"The legislature is about to enact the advisory into law, and will not allow more than fifteen percent of all acreage to be planted in cotton."

"So what does this mean on the average plantation?"

"It means that both farmers and planters must plant more corn, sorghum, sweet potatoes, and Irish potatoes, for example. The county tax commissioners will go out during growing season to estimate the amount of yields and time of harvest. At harvest times, a return will be made, and ten percent of all crops will go to the State."

"This is really going to be unpopular with the people."

"I know it is. But it is the only real wealth that the South possesses. All crops returned to the State will be stored locally, and shipped for sale or barter by revenue commissioners.

This way, soldiers may be fed, city people will have enough food to allow them to work in factories and hospitals, and the government can impose a barter system to prop up the currency."

"When will your work be completed?"

"In four or five weeks. Then I will come home and help you finish this room."

Several weeks later, Uriah's new room was completely finished, and he drove Faith down to Milledgeville in their buggy to go shopping on a Saturday afternoon. The day was windy and cold, and Uriah tied the horses at the livery stable, and went up Greene Street searching for a cup of hot coffee.

He was about to enter a tavern when he saw David walking hunched over up the street, bundled in a wool pea jacket. His eyes lit up when he saw his Uncle Uriah.

"Hey Uncle Uriah, what a surprise! I was out here hunting something hot to drink. How about you?"

"Lets go in to the McComb House and get a cup of coffee."

They walked up Greene Street to Wayne Street, and entered McComb House, near the Statehouse Square. It was a popular hostelry with the state legislature, and did a brisk business when the General Assembly was in session.

A pretty young black woman in a navy dress and a long white apron greeted them at the door of the café, and directed them to a table in the corner of the room. The room had several tables in the center, and was surrounded by solid pine paneling. The floor was made of brick, and gas lights burned on the walls. Several gentlemen in dark suits were seated in the café, some eating, others were smoking cigars and drinking coffee.

They placed their orders and began to discuss the matter of national politics.

"David, now that Jefferson Davis and Alexander Stephens have been elected and have formed a government, everything has began to build up toward a war."

"I don't really follow you, sir."

"Well, first, Stephens gave a speech in Savannah recently, where he emphatically states that the 'cornerstone' of the Southern Confederacy was the 'great truth' that the black man is inferior to the white man, and that slavery is his natural condition. In short, the speech denies the principles of Jefferson that says 'all men are created equal."

"I read excerpts of that 'cornerstone' speech in the *Macon Daily Telegraph*. In a way, the speech disgusted me. For one thing, it appears that Mr. Stephens has completely changed his principles once he lost the secession vote in January. Like some kind of a new tiger, he has completely changed his stripes."

Uriah chuckled at David's metaphor.

"New tiger, change of stripes, David, you are so right. That speech really embarrassed Jeff Davis, though. There are a number of planters and politicians that never even call a slave a slave. They never refer to them by that name. Instead, they speak publicly about their 'right to property' being guaranteed under the Constitution."

"Does that not disgust you, Uncle Uriah? They have destroyed the Union over slavery and yet many of the same people that accomplished that are unable to publicly state the reasons behind what they are doing. I'll have to hand it to Mr. Stephens, at least he is honest in declaring what he stands for."

"That is the truth. David, I read in a Baltimore newspaper that Abraham Lincoln had to sneak into Washington City in order to avoid assassination at the hands of southern sympathizers. Federal forts in several states have been seized by state militias. Georgia took over Fort Pulaski back in January.

Florida, Alabama, and Louisiana have also seized Federal forts and arsenals. But there is one or two forts that have not surrendered, and will not give up without blood being shed."

"I know that Fort Pickens in Florida near Pensacola had not surrendered, but I did not hear much about the situation in South Carolina."

"A Federal major by the name of Robert Anderson had a small garrison at Fort Moultrie, near Charleston Harbor. He moved his garrison out to a brick fort named Fort Sumter around Christmas time."

He refuses to surrender, and has asked President Lincoln for food and provisions. His cabinet has debated the issue of resupplying Anderson at Fort Sumter. Lincoln is in a tough position here. If he attempts to resupply Sumter, that can be interpreted as a hostile act of war. If he fails to resupply Sumter, and allows Anderson and his garrison to starve to death, that would be taken as a sign of weakness by the Confederate leaders."

"What will the Confederate troops do if an attempt is made to resupply Fort Sumter by sea?"

"Well, young David, there is where Lincoln holds the upper hand, in my opinion. If Confederate troops fire on the fort or on supply ships first, he can say that the south fired the first shots of the war. In the eyes of the world, whatever actions he takes in response to aggression would be justified."

"If what you say is correct, Uncle Uriah, Fort Sumter will be the spark that ignites the whole powder keg."

"In a manner of speaking, boy, yes, I believe so."

"Uncle, I am going to change the subject on you. Did you ever work out terms of payment with Uncle William on the lumber for your room?"

"Yes, I finally came to an agreement with him. I paid him half in U.S. currency, and the other half of what I owed him in corn meal and grits, based on December 1860 U.S. prices."

"Have you prepared to plant this years' crops at Greenbrier yet?"

"Not quite. We have purchased some seed, and some plows, and some of the hands have begun breaking land. According to the legislature's advisory, we are planting mostly corn, potatoes, sweet potatoes, beans, and field peas. Only about twenty percent of our acreage will be in cotton, but that may be even less."

"It will be less, once war breaks out."

Their coffee was brought out, along with some oatmeal cookies, and Uriah paid the waitress with State of Georgia bank notes.

"Speaking of the topic of money, David, if you don't mind me asking, on top of your $500.00 cash award you won last fall, did William compensate you for your efforts in getting his cotton crop to market?"

"Yes sir, he did. He paid me a five percent commission on all the ginning fees, and all cotton sold at the Savannah Cotton Exchange from this years' crop."

"Have you been paid yet?"

"Yes sir. The funds are on deposit at the State Bank here in town."

"After you repaid William for the cost of Angela's engagement ring, how much money do you have left?"

"Around thirty one hundred dollars. And that does not count the two hundred and fifty dollars I have on deposit at the Merchants and Farmers Bank."

"You asked me to open an account for you up in Baltimore. Here is your deposit book. I opened an account with the Maritime Bank in Baltimore with a twenty five dollar initial deposit."

Uriah handed David the bankbook. David accepted it, and gratefully acknowledged his uncle's efforts.

"Thank you for opening the account for me, Uncle Uriah. I will write a large check drawn on the State Bank account, and make a two thousand dollar deposit into the Maritime Bank at once."

"That would be a wise move, David. I have been in contact with several people that work for Robert Toombs. You know he was named Secretary of State for the Confederacy."

"Yes sir."

"Well, the new government in Montgomery has concocted all kinds of schemes involving cotton to raise money. The latest version calls for a large bond issue, backed by an export duty of $5.00 per bale of cotton. Other schemes call for a pledge or consignment of cotton from planters to the government of a portion of their cotton crops, in exchange for Confederate bonds. None of those things will work."

"Why do you say so?"

"Because the Confederacy has no merchant marine, and cannot ensure delivery of cotton to market in the event of a U.S. Naval blockade. A bond is a promise to pay in the future. It involves giving away something of value in the present. Take my advice David; do not invest in any Confederate bonds. Only trust gold, or a commodity that has ready value. Do you understand what I am telling you?"

"Yes sir. I will have most of my funds transferred and converted to U.S. currency in Baltimore while I still can do it."

"A wise decision."

Faith Snelling walked into the room at that moment carrying a large shopping basket filled with cloth. Both men arose as she entered the room. Uriah spoke first.

"Hello, Dear. Did you find the cloth you were looking for?"

"Yes I did. There was plenty of this type in stock at Avery's Store."

She held out a bolt of dark blue grey kersey wool cloth, imported from England. She also had several bolts of black colored cotton jean cloth, and a small bolt of a shiny gold–colored silk fabric.

Faith appeared to be ready to return home, but wanted to inquire about David's upcoming marriage plans and some of the parties scheduled in the spring for him and Angela.

"David, we received an invitation to a barbeque for you and Angela over in Tenille. Who is giving that for you?"

"That is on April 20th. Mary Westmoreland, a close friend of Angela, and her parents are having the barbeque at their home over there. I have been by there before. They have a nice plantation there. The plantation is about a mile or two out on the Sandersville Road. It is a large white Greek Revival mansion. You can't miss it. Are you and Uncle Uriah going?"

"Yes we are, young man. We would not miss your party for anything in the world. Are you ready, darling?" Faith gave a loving glance to Uriah, who arose and took her by the hand.

"Yes, dear. The buggy is tied up at the livery just up the street. You might want to tie up your cloak, dear. It is really windy and cold out today. See you later, David, we need to get back."

"Take care, Uncle Uriah. Aunt Faith, I will see you at the barbeque."

"Yes, David, please stay and finish your coffee."

David watched them leave the McComb House, walking and holding hands. He finished his coffee, and wondered if his life with Angela would be similar to his Uncle's marriage to Faith. He sure hoped so.

Chapter Six

President Jefferson Davis sent commissioners to Washington at the end of March, 1861, to negotiate the surrender of Fort Sumter. President Lincoln's Secretary of State, William H. Seward, who had presidential ambitions of his own, made representations to the Southern emissaries that Lincoln would not resupply or reinforce Fort Sumter.

On April 6th, Lincoln informed his cabinet that he had decided to reinforce and resupply Fort Sumter. Seward informed Commissioner John A. Campbell that Lincoln intended to resupply Fort Sumter only. Campbell telegraphed President Davis in Montgomery concerning Lincoln's decision, and Jefferson Davis called a cabinet meeting.

Mr. Davis informed his cabinet in Montgomery concerning Lincoln's decision to resupply Fort Sumter. He decided that the Fort should be bombarded by Confederate forces in and around Charleston Harbor.

Robert Toombs, the Confederate Secretary of State, a fire eater about the war in public, paced the room, and strongly argued against firing the first shots of the war.

"The firing on that fort will inaugurate a civil war greater than any the world has yet seen. Mr. President, at this time it is suicide, murder, and you will lose us every friend at the North. You will wantonly strike a hornets' nest, which extends from mountains to oceans. Legions now quiet will swarm out and sting us to death. It is unnecessary. It puts us in the wrong. It is fatal."

Jefferson Davis made the opposite decision, and telegraphed the Confederate general commanding at Charleston, General P.G.T. Beauregard.

General Beauregard was instructed to contact Major Anderson under a flag of truce, and demand the immediate Federal evacuation of Fort Sumter. Anderson, who was Beauregard's artillery instructor at West Point, refused to surrender.

Around four a.m. on April 12, 1861, Beauregard's batteries opened fired on Fort Sumter. His batteries soon threw over 4000 rounds into Fort Sumter. On Friday, April 13th, almost two days after the commencement of the bombardment, Major Anderson surrendered Fort Sumter.

On Sunday, the news of the surrender of Fort Sumter to Confederate troops was telegraphed all over the North. The firing of artillery at Old Glory electrified the North as nothing had before.

Hundreds of callers came by the White House, and assured President Lincoln of their support and loyalty. Senators and members of Congress pledged the resources of their states to the Union.

On Sunday, April 15th, Lincoln assembled his cabinet, and formed a proclamation calling on the states to send 75,000 militia to serve for 90 days to serve against "combinations too powerful to be suppressed by the ordinary course of judicial proceedings."

He then called a special session of Congress to meet on July 4th.

The militia draft was telegraphed to the states on April 15th, to all except the seven that had seceded, and gave quotas to be sent by each state.

The reply to the call for troops was also electric and momentous. Many northern states quickly oversubscribed their quotas of troops. However, President Lincoln's call for troops to fight the seven seceded states quickly galvanized opinions among the border states in the South. The governors of Virginia, Arkansas, Tennessee, and North Carolina wrote President Lincoln, and informed him that they would furnish no troops to suppress their sister states. Virginia seceded from the Union two days later, then Arkansas, Tennessee, and North Carolina. The area of the Confederacy was greatly increased, from seven states to eleven states. Her chances for achieving victory in the war also dramatically increased when Virginia seceded, but for another reason.

On April 20th, Angela's friend, Mary Westmoreland, gave an afternoon barbeque to honor Angela and David. All of Angela's friends and near relations were invited, and David's friends and close relatives also attended.

The large white Greek Revival mansion was located on a hill between Sandersville and Tenille. James Westmoreland, a fiery secessionist, owned the thousand–acre plantation, and lived there with his 20–year–old daughter Mary, and his lovely wife, Paula.

After dinner, the girls went upstairs for a nap, while the men gathered in the study to smoke cigars and discuss politics. Shortly after the Saturday afternoon conversations commenced, Joseph walked into the room, wearing the grey uniform of a Captain of the

Thompson Rifles. He walked to the center of the room and sought out the tall figure of James Westmoreland, and asked him a short question.

Westmoreland nodded his head, and waved his arms to get the attention of the men standing in the study.

"Men, Joseph Floyd has asked me to allow him to make an announcement to you. I do not mean to steal his thunder in any way, but I will tell you that today, Governor Brown has ordered his militia unit down to Eden, Georgia by the middle of next week. Joseph, I will let you tell the men the rest, if you please."

"Thank you, Mr. Westmoreland. His Excellency Governor Brown has ordered the Thompson rifles to board rail cars on Monday at Milledgeville, and to ride near Savannah, Georgia, to report to General Alexander Lawton at Eden, Georgia. This regiment, along with other regiments, has been called into active service by the Governor to defend against a Yankee invasion from the sea.

However, at this time, our regiment is short some 14 men from full strength. I am here today to recruit at least a dozen of you here into the service of the State, if I can. The Governor needs you. Your state needs you. Will you respond to the call?"

Mr. Westmoreland, an attorney for some fourteen years, was an experienced orator, and saw that young Joseph Floyd had some trouble in speaking before bodies of men. He quickly sized up the situation, and decided to offer his assistance.

"Men, Captain Floyd is here to ask those men who are not enrolled in the militia to show some patriotism and join his regiment. I will get the enlistment papers from him, and will proceed to enroll as many of you as he needs to complete his company quota. I will also tell you right now that there are several lovely ladies upstairs who I promise will hear of your noble decision to fight for this land, and you may be rewarded with their attention and their gratitude, should you decide to enlist."

The room was filled with mostly young men in their twenties and thirties, around thirty men all total. Some of the men were eager and ready to join up and fight Yankees. Others were not interested, and were hanging around the edge of the study.

Joseph came back with his saddlebags, and a small table was set up for Mr. Westmoreland to commence enrolling the militia recruits. A dozen young men soon lined up to enlist.

Joseph strode over to David, and made a motion with his hands that indicated that he wanted to talk to him outside of the study.

They walked out of the room, and into the hallway, where they stepped under the alcove created by the large spiral staircase.

Joseph spoke first.

"I'm sorry to spoil your party, David, but we were telegraphed our orders this morning, and we were over a dozen men short of a full company. This was the only gathering of men I could find on such short notice. Please forgive me."

The Unionist

"You don't have to apologize, Joseph, I know you have a job to do, and this is the best way for you to accomplish it. I wish you nothing but success."

"Thank you. While we are on the topic, Colonel Doles advised me that I can appoint one more officer as a lieutenant to complete the roster of the regiment. The only person I could think of to offer the commission to was you. Will you enlist and come down to the coast with us, David?"

David knew that this moment was coming. He knew for months that he would be asked to join his cousin's regiment. He would not, for any reason, hurt his cousin's feelings by refusing him publicly, or use any unkind words in refusing the commission privately. He had given considerable effort to how he would refuse service in his cousin's regiment, and the only reason that was acceptable was related to Greenbrier.

"Joseph, I really appreciate your offer of a commission in your company. I am deeply honored, believe me. But I am needed at Greenbrier, especially since you will be gone. I will need to see that the crops are planted and harvested. It will be up to us on the plantation to see that everyone is supplied with food. Please remember that I deeply appreciate your offer, but at this time, I cannot join the army."

Joseph did not appear to be angered or disappointed.

"Sure, David, I understand. I will just need to step into the study, and inform Mr. Westmoreland that we will need another volunteer added onto the roster. I'll let the company vote and elect another officer once we get to Savannah."

Joseph stepped into the room to inform Mr. Westmoreland that another recruit could be enlisted. David heard voices raised in the next room, and saw his Uncle William rush out toward him, his face flushed with rage. The old man was dressed in a grey light wool suit, and had an unlit cigar clinched in his fist. He walked right up to David, and lit into him at once.

"What's this I hear that you are refusing service in Joseph's regiment? How could you do something so disloyal? Didn't we take you in and raise you when you were an orphan? Why on earth did you refuse him when he asked you to join up?"

David remained calm in the face of his Uncle's anger.

"Uncle William, I meant you and Joseph no disrespect, none whatsoever. I simply told him that spring planting was in progress, and that I would be needed at Greenbrier. I will especially be needed there if Joseph is gone off to war."

"That is not true. I have Dan Stone to help me run the plantation. You could enlist if you really wanted to."

"With all due respect, Uncle William, Mr. Stone is a first rate clerk, but he has never given you any service out in the field. You need someone at Greenbrier who can see that the crops are properly planted, tilled, and harvested. That involves field work, and to my knowledge, Mr. Stone has never done that for you."

William glanced around the room and saw that a small crowd had begun to gather. His anger had already begun to wane, and he knew that David was correct to assume that his services were badly needed at Greenbrier. However, he had publicly stated a position, and he could not back down now.

"Son, I understand what you are trying to tell me, but I am publicly questioning your loyalty, to this state, and to this land. I believe that you are disloyal."

Uriah had heard the commotion in the hall from the front porch of the house, where he had been standing, smoking a cigar. He walked into the room at the same moment that William had questioned David's loyalty. He knew that David's reputation required some immediate aid. He came to David's assistance at once.

"Now see here, William. It takes all kinds of contributions to supply an army, and to win a war. Just because a man is not in uniform, and is not in action on a battlefield, that doesn't mean he cannot be of service elsewhere. It takes a great deal of foodstuffs to feed an army. Food does not grow and harvest itself. David says he has a contribution to make at home, and I believe that he is sincere in his efforts for you. He meant no disrespect in not joining Joseph's regiment. There was no harm done here. There will be other opportunities."

Uriah's words seemed to calm William down, and he put his arm around his shoulder, and asked him if he had any more Cuban cigars left to smoke.

A moment later, Mr. Westmoreland came out into the hall to speak to David.

"Well, it looks like you won't be the goat after all, David. A real Yankee hater from Wilkinson County, a boy by the name of James Wood, signed up to fill out the company roster. You have nothing to feel guilty about young man, unless it is the knowledge that you were less than enthusiastic when your Governor called you into his service."

He left the room, and David soon noticed George Collins standing in the doorway, staring at him. The look on his face was one of total disgust.

Before David could speak to him, Mr. Collins turned away and headed upstairs.

An hour later, Mr. Westmoreland had a large wagon hitched to a team of strong horses, and most of the new recruits were seated in the wagon, ready to go over to Milledgeville.

Most of the ladies at the party had walked down from upstairs, and had walked out to say their goodbyes to the departing troops. There were hugs and kisses, and promises to write each other every week.

David noticed that Angela had walked down to say goodbye to Joseph. From a distance, he saw her hug his neck, and kiss him goodbye. He then saw Joseph pull on his forage cap, mount his horse, and head out ahead of the wagon.

The following Sunday, David drove the spring buggy down to Milledgeville, in order to escort Angela to the morning church services. She had a house servant instruct him to tie up the buggy, and for him to meet her around back at her mother's rose garden.

David tied the horses to the hitching post on the corner, and was escorted back around the side of the house past a large privet hedge, and into the rose garden.

Mrs. Collins' garden had four or five rose varieties, with varying colors, from crimson to yellow to white. The roses were in beautiful condition, and a series of wooden benches had been built in the garden for seating. Several white trellises provided privacy and climbing opportunities for the rose bushes.

Five minutes later, Angela appeared, wearing a white and blue dress, and a white large brimmed hat, with a blue ribbon around its crown. She was lovely, as usual. She was hanging her head, and walked through the garden slowly toward the spot where David was standing.

David spoke first, concerned about Angela's demeanor.

"Why are you so forlorn and sad, my dear? This is a lovely day, and you look so beautiful."

She raised her head, and David noticed that tears were streaming down her cheeks.

"Oh David, I can't marry you. Daddy has asked me to return your engagement ring. He says that you are disloyal, or you are a coward, and he does not want me to marry you."

David was stunned. Angela's words were like daggers running through his heart.

His heart began to beat wildly, and he struggled to think clearly.

"He's just wrong, darling. He's just badly mistaken...maybe I could talk to him and reason with him. He doesn't know me very well at all...."

"No David. His mind is made up. There is no way you could convince him otherwise. I have seen him get like this before."

"But Angela, you are a grown woman. If you really loved me, you can marry me without his blessing or approval. It is your life, honey. I love you dearly. I want to spend my life with you."

Angela then began to cry. She pulled out a small handkerchief, and wiped the tears from her face.

"I love you too, David. But I will never go against my father's wishes. He would make things miserable for you if I married you despite his wishes. I could not do that to him or to you."

She pulled David's ring off her finger, and carefully handed it over to him. She also walked up, and kissed him full on both lips.

"I will always love you, David Snelling, no matter what. You will always hold a special place in my heart. Daddy has told me that he does not want you to call on me again. If you return here David, he will ask the sheriff to come and arrest you."

David was stunned. He could not think of a way to deal with the situation. He put the ring in his pocket, and the words he spoke to her came from his heart, not from his head.

"I love you too, Angela Collins. You are the one great love of my life. I am not a coward, and I will fight one day. And I hope the day comes when you will be able to see me again."

He turned and walked away, and drove the spring buggy five miles down to a grove of White Oak trees. He tied up the horse, walked into the grove, sat against a tree, and wept. He wept for the life he could have had with Angela. He wept because he had been branded a coward. He wept because he knew he could never fit in with the other men, and fight for the Confederacy. He began to pray. He prayed for wisdom and understanding. He prayed for courage and strength. And lastly, he prayed that the Lord would remove Angela Collins from his heart.

Chapter Seven

In June of 1861, Joseph's regiment was ordered north from the Savannah area to Richmond, Virginia. Richmond had become the new Capital of the Confederacy, and the risk of invasion from the north was greatest there.

Jefferson Davis subsequently ordered many of the newly organized regiments to protect Virginia and the Confederate Capital from Union attack.

David corresponded with Joseph regularly, and informed Joseph that Angela had broken off their engagement. The Confederate Congress was scheduled to meet in Richmond on July 20, 1861. Many politicians and leaders in the Union wanted the Federal army to invade Virginia and capture Richmond before the Confederate Congress could meet on July 20th. General Irvin McDowell had a small army of 35,000 men positioned near Washington, D.C.

Opposing the Federal forces near Centreville, Virginia, were forces commanded by General Joe Johnston, and General Beauregard, the hero of Fort Sumter, who commanded around 34,000 men.

On July 21, 1861, General McDowell's forces attacked the Confederate forces near Manassas, Virginia. The Federal troops had some initial success early on in the battle, but gave way when Confederate brigades counterattacked after being reinforced later in the day.

Joseph's regiment was attached to Bernard Bee's brigade, and saw little fighting until the middle of the day. They withstood an attack by a New Jersey regiment, and then counterattacked along with Thomas J. Jackson's brigade. They swept the New Jersey troops off the field.

The green Union troops failed to take the Henry House Hill, and gave way rapidly to Confederate counterattacks.

The orderly retreat became a rout, and regiments and companies of troops ran pell–mell across the Stone Bridge over Bull Run, and toward Centreville, and the safety of the Washington defenses.

Congressmen and other civilians had brought their buggies and picnic lunches down from Washington to view the battle. They also became caught up in the mad rush toward Washington, to escape capture from the Confederate Army. Bull Run was a major defeat for the Union, and a major victory for the Confederacy. Only a few brigades at Bull Run fought fiercely, and these units became the rear guard that protected the retreat of the Union Army back to Washington. One of these brigades at Bull Run that fought well, and held together as the rear guard, allowed the rest of the Union Army to escape destruction. That brigade was commanded by an Ohio volunteer colonel named William T. Sherman.

Several weeks later, David and Joe Buck were sent into town to sell some sweet corn and vegetables they had grown out at Greenbrier. They pulled their wagon over near the State House Square, and spent most of the day selling sweet corn and other vegetables to the townspeople, in exchange for Confederate paper money and Georgia bank notes.

They ate a meager lunch of sliced ham sandwiches and sliced tomatoes, while watching a slave auction, and a recruitment officer sign up volunteers for a new Baldwin County regiment.

An hour later, David saw William Floyd walking down Greene Street toward the livery stable. He noticed that William had been by the Post Office, as he noticed several letters in his hands.

He got up and walked toward his uncle, and waved his hand to get his attention. He noticed that his Uncle William was in his shirt sleeves, and was having a difficult time walking in the summer heat.

"Uncle William. I did not expect to see you in town today."

"I was told I had some letters in from Joseph up in Virginia." He began to fumble around in his pockets, but could not find what he was searching for.

"Oh David, could you read these letters to me? I seem to have left my spectacles at home."

"Certainly, Uncle William. Just allow me to break the seal of the envelope. With your permission, I will read the older letter first."

"Certainly. Go ahead."

David broke the seal on the envelope, and read the contents verbatim:

Near Centreville, Virginia, July 23, 1861

Dear Papa:

We have won a great victory here over the Yankee Army. We pushed them back after a real sharp fight at Henry House Hill.

The Yankees retreated over Bull Run, and all the way back to Washington City. They ran away like a mob. They threw down their guns and knapsacks, and ran back to the Potomac as fast as they ever could run. Some of the officers are saying that we have won the war. Others say that they will be more fights and bigger fights to come with the Yankee Army.

I was very proud of our men, and the way they handled themselves. Colonel Bee was killed, though. Please send my regards to Angela, Joe Buck, and even to David. Please tell him I have no hard feelings about him not joining up with us. We may have won the war without him.

Love, your son

Joseph

William took out his handkerchief, and began to wipe away tears that had run down his cheeks. When he was done, he motioned for David to open the second letter.

David broke the seal, and noted that the letter was written on an officer's letterhead, and not on the plain foolscap that Joseph's letter had been written on.

Mr. William Floyd
Greenbrier Plantation
C/o General Delivery
Milledgeville, Georgia

Headquarters near Centreville, Virginia
August 12, 1861
Dear Mr. Floyd:

I regret to inform you that your son, Captain Joseph Floyd, has fallen ill with typhoid fever. We have transported him by rail to the Confederate Army Hospital in Richmond.

The nurses there will take good care of him. Your son distinguished himself in battle at Manassas on July 21st. He and his men were a credit to my brigade, and to this army. You may contact your son in Richmond, or through my brigade headquarters.

Your faithful servant,
Brig. General Nathan Evans, C.S.A.

William appeared to grow faint, and nearly collapsed. David grabbed his arm, and slowly helped William regain his feet. William's face had grown ashen in color, and he displayed visible signs of grief. He began to speak, but slowly.

"I must think…of what to do. David, I need to tell you first that Joseph has been corresponding with Angela since he went off to the army."

"I know that, Uncle William, and I understand."

"Then you must know that since they have been corresponding with one another, that I have a duty here to disclose the contents of these letters to her."

David did not want to deal with his continued feelings for Angela at the moment, but knew that she should be contacted at once.

"Uncle William, would you like me to go to the livery and get your buggy, and drive you over to Angela's house?"

"Yes boy, please do that for me. But first, go ahead and tell Joe Buck to pack up his produce and head back to Greenbrier. Have him turn all his cash receipts over to you."

After telling Joe Buck where they were going, and collecting his cash receipts, David picked up the spring buggy at the livery, and drove William over to Angela's house off Wilkinson Street.

David gave William's card to the house servant, and requested an immediate audience with Miss Angela. Angela came down a few minutes later to the back door, wearing a green calico dress and a matching hat, looking as lovely as ever. She had a look of surprise on her face.

"David, what are you doing here?"

"Angela…Uncle William has received some letters from Joseph up in Virginia…"

"From Joseph! Oh, David, is he well, please, please tell me he is well…"

"That is why we are here, Angela. He survived the battle at Manassas, but his general sent a letter that says he has typhoid fever. Please come out to the buggy, and we will let you read them."

She ran out the back door, and down to the waiting spring buggy, where William was waiting. She briefly asked his permission to read the letters, and William handed them to her. Angela read through the first letter, and then the second. After reading the second letter, her demeanor changed from excitement to one of grief. She began to cry, and then covered her mouth and ran up to meet David.

"Oh David, I must buy a train ticket to Richmond. I can go and stay with my cousin, Martha Jane up there. I can then go and see about Joseph at the hospital."

She ran upstairs to pack her bags, and prepare for her trip to Virginia.

David turned and began to walk out the back door of the Collins' house, and down the brick walk to his uncle's buggy.

He got about halfway down the walk, when he heard an angry George Collins calling out from the upstairs portion of the house. He began walking back to the buggy, when he heard footsteps behind him, and felt a hand on his right shoulder.

"You stop right there, young man. I told you not to ever come calling here again. You have come back over here to stir up trouble, and I aim to stop you."

David was outraged.

"Now see here, Mr. Collins. I did not come here to cause trouble. I came here at the request of my Uncle William, to give Angela news about Joseph. That had nothing to do with you."

Collins was highly agitated, and David could see he was not himself. "You coward! If you had joined the army with Joseph, Angela would not be leaving us now. After staying home and letting Joseph do the fighting, you have the nerve to come here and violate my wishes. I am going to beat the hell out of you, and teach you a lesson!"

He swung at David with his brass tipped cane, causing David to deftly duck out the way. The blow struck near the front seat of the buggy. David reached into the rear of the buggy, and pulled out a Hickory ax handle from a bundle that was purchased earlier that day at the general store. Collins swung again, and David used the ax handle to parry the blow from the cane.

David became angry, and decided then and there to teach Collins a lesson.

He stepped to the side, and swung the ax handle at an angle, and struck George Collins hard on his collarbone. Collins went to one knee, and screamed out in pain.

David ran to the man, and seized him by the throat. He looked into his eyes, and spoke his words to Collins slowly.

"I...am no coward. If you ever call me a coward in public again you lily livered bastard, I will kill you."

William had observed the bizarre fight in silence, but soon came to his senses.

"David, let go of Mr. Collins. Go to the house and ask the houseboy to run and get a doctor. He has a broken bone that needs to be set."

William climbed down from the buggy, and propped George Collins up off the sidewalk.

"George, I cannot begin to tell you how sorry I am for the trouble we have caused you this afternoon. I can only beg yours and your family's forgiveness."

Collins was too stunned to speak. William asked David to immediately drive him back to Greenbrier, as he knew that neighbors and town folk would come and make inquiries concerning David's mean handling of George Collins.

He did not want to be embarrassed in any way on account of his nephew.

David drove William back home in silence. He was angry at the situation he had been put into, and he was angry at the blatant stupidity that George Collins had displayed in town.

William also did not speak, as he knew a real situation had occurred that must be handled. His problem was that he did not know how exactly the situation should be handled. He rode back to Greenbrier in silence, although he did come to a decision about David by the time they pulled around to Greenbrier's coach house.

When they pulled up to the coach house, William's head cleared, and he was able to speak his mind.

"David, please have Zack unhitch the horses, and feed and put them up for the night. After you wash up and eat your supper, I want you to meet me in my study."

"Yes sir."

David had the horses fed, watered, and rubbed down. He then washed up and ate a quick supper of beef stew down in the kitchen. One half-hour later, he reported to his Uncle William in the study.

His uncle was seated behind his desk, with a glass of Kentucky Bourbon in his hand when David walked in.

"Close the door, David."

David reached behind him, and pulled the white oak door shut.

"David, have you read *Uncle Tom's Cabin*?"

"Yes sir, I have. That was when I was in college."

"And do you believe all of the stuff in that book?"

"That's a tough question, to be honest with you. There were some exaggerations and distortions with the characters."

"But you agree in principal with the idea set forth in the book?"

"Let's put it this way. Slavery has been outlawed and abolished in England, France, and almost all of Europe. It is considered a backward and barbaric institution up North, and around the world."

"Let me ask you this. Do you believe a nigger is equal to a white man or a white woman?"

"I can't come out and say that, no. But I will tell you that I believe there is a place at God's table for all races, white, black, or yellow. Let me ask you, Uncle William, do you believe that blacks go to heaven when they die?"

"Not the same way you or I would get to heaven, no. They may have their heaven, but it is gonna be separate and apart from ours, you better believe it"

"And you can look Joe Buck in the eye and tell him that, as devout a Christian as he is?"

"I have before, and I probably will again."

"Why all of the questions tonight?"

"Well, I was told by others that you were a coward, and you were afraid to fight in the army. The way you handled George Collins today simply proves that to be a lie.

If you ain't no coward like they said you were, then that means you chose not to fight for the South because you are a damn Black Republican or an abolitionist."

"That's not true. I voted for Stephen Douglas, and you know it."

William had a fiery look in his eyes, and his face began to grow red. He drew a Colt Navy revolver from his desk drawer, and pointed it at David.

David was stunned. He did not move or do anything to anger his uncle, but did raise his hands above his head.

William continued with his tirade. David could tell that he was drunk, as his speech was slightly slurred.

"A vote for Douglas was the same as a vote for Lincoln in the last election. I saw you working with Uriah at the Capitol last November, and never put two and two together until now. You are a damn Yankee lover, and a Black Republican, and you have beat and hurt my close friend, and disgraced me."

"He attacked me. I defended myself."

"You are through here. Get out. Get out of my house. You don't deserve to live here when you refused to fight for this land; this home."

"Very well. I will pack my bag and leave."

William brought the Colt Navy revolver to full cock and pointed it at David.

"You will leave here with the clothing on your back. Now!"

He meant business. David backed away slowly, and eased himself out the door. He then went downstairs, and walked down through the kitchen.

Savannah was down there, cleaning pots and pans. She looked up from her work, and noticed the terrified look on David's face.

"Mista David, where you goin' this time o night?"

"Savannah, I have been ordered out of the house by Uncle William. I have to leave now. Goodbye."

He hugged her neck, and walked out the back door, and down the driveway. He remembered that his Uncle Uriah had offered him a place to live, and hoped his offer was still open to him.

He was told to leave the house "as he was", with nothing but the clothing on his back. He reached into his left pocket, and noticed that he had around $75.50 in Confederate and State notes in his pocket that was turned over to him by Joe Buck that afternoon. 'Oh, well,' he thought, 'he told me to get out with what I had on my back, and that includes what was in my pockets as well.'

He continued to walk for two more miles, when Joe Buck McGee drove up beside him in the spring buggy. David stopped, and noticed that Joe Buck had packed up some of his personal belongings.

"What are you doing, Joe Buck? Does Uncle William know you're here?"

Joe Buck climbed down off the wagon, and walked around to David's side.

"He has passed out, David. He drunk himself into a stupor. If you come back in the mornin', I think he will have forgot all about what he said tonight."

"No, Joe Buck, I can't go back. He pointed a gun at me, and asked me to leave, and I believe he meant what he said. I'll go and stay with Uncle Uriah and Aunt Faith. He told me that he would let me come live with them. What do you have there?"

Joe Buck handed him a canvas bag that was stuffed with David's clothing, both summer and winter clothing. It had his pea jacket, his oil skin coat, and his black felt hat.

Joe Buck brought David's canvas shaving kit, which contained his razor, shaving soap, toothbrush, and needles and thread for mending his clothing.

Joe Buck also brought David's compass and pocketknife. David looked at his shaving kit, and also noticed that Joe Buck had brought his bank deposit books. David looked over and expressed his appreciation.

"Thank you, old friend. You always know how to help. I promise you that the next time I return to Greenbrier, that I will be wearing a blue uniform. The next time I go there Joe Buck, you will be a free man."

Joe Buck was puzzled.

"What are you talking about?"

"Just drive me over to my Uncle Uriah's place, Joe Buck. We will talk about that some other time. You will need to get back before Uncle William awakes."

David climbed into the buggy, and Joe Buck flapped the reins across the backside of the horse. The buggy lurched forward, with the horse pacing off a fast walk.

They pulled into Uriah's place around nine thirty, about an hour after dark. Joe Buck unloaded David's bag on Uriah's porch, and said goodbye to his old friend. He watered the horse at the trough, and then began the return trip to Greenbrier. David saw lights in the windows upstairs, and knocked on the front door of Uriah's house.

Uriah soon came down and unbolted the front door, wearing his nightshirt, and bearing an oil lamp in his hand.

"David, your Aunt and I were about to go to bed. What brings you out this late?"

"My Uncle William. He threw me out today, Uncle Uriah, even at gunpoint. He tossed me out without even a blanket. If Joe Buck hadn't done me a favor, I would have been thrown out with only the clothes on my back."

"What happened? Why did William do that?"

David told Uriah about the entire events of the afternoon, from Joseph's letters through George Collins' physical attack on his person. When he finished recounting the day's events, David was interrupted by his Aunt Faith, who came downstairs in her dressing gown, with her hair unpinned.

"Uriah, what is going on? Who is here?"

"David is here, darling. He is going to stay with us from now on. Please go ahead and prepare the guest room for him. Go ahead and turn his bed down, too. I know he has had a long day."

Faith gave David a peck on the cheek, and carried her oil lamp back to the new room, which was now a guest room. Uriah stepped over and placed his hand on David's shoulder.

"You see...David, I have foreseen this. I knew you would be required to leave Greenbrier once William became offended by you. That is not knocking you, boy, but you see, William Floyd is a man that cares deeply about his reputation and standing in the community. When you refused to join Joseph's regiment, he was publicly disgraced.

When you got into it with George Collins, that was the last straw. Your Uncle does not hate or despise you, he feels that you have embarrassed him, and he can regain his social standing around here by claiming he has disowned you. Do you understand me, David?"

"Yes sir, I understand you. But I will tell you this. I am damn tired of being called a coward. I am not a coward. I want to fight. I can't sit out the war and be called a coward. But I will not fight for the South. Can you help me?"

"Yes, boy, I can. I will train you, but you must earn your keep while you are here. I will train you three hours per day and on Saturdays, but you will need to help me at the grist mill."

"Certainly. You know I am no stranger to work."

"Very well. Come on over to the guest room with me, and I'll get you squared away. Say goodnight to your Aunt Faith."

David walked over and kissed his Aunt Faith on her forehead, and followed his Uncle Uriah down to the hall to the guest room.

The next morning, David was awakened by the smell of coffee and frying bacon. He threw the handmade quilt off himself, and scrambled into his clothing. He joined Uriah in the kitchen, who was using a small tin pot of water on the cast iron stove as a shaving basin.

David had grown accustomed to the daily routines at Greenbrier. House servants drew and heated his shaving water every morning. Uriah noticed David's awkward appearance in the kitchen, and spoke to him immediately.

"Go get your shaving kit and join me, young David, while the water is still hot."

David complied, and he strapped his razor, lathered his face with his shaving brush and soap, and shaved quickly.

Faith had fried eggs and boiled grits, and began to serve breakfast on the Red Oak table. She pulled a pan of biscuits out of the stove, and gave Uriah a nudge on his back.

"You need to call Archie down to breakfast."

"Okay. Come on David, let us go down to the barn and let Archie know that breakfast is ready."

They walked outside, where the sun was just breaking over the horizon. The mist continued to hug the ground, and David saw Archie at the barn, returning with a pail of fresh milk.

"Well, it looks like Archie's done some of our work already this morning. Hey Archie, Faith has breakfast ready for us."

"Yes, suh. I will be right on."

Archie brought the milk over to the spring house, where he strained it through cheese cloth, and then poured it into stone churns. He saved some of the milk in the tin pail for breakfast, and brought it up to the house with two fresh eggs he had found in the corner of the barn.

Faith had the men sit down to eat, and Uriah said grace. They bowed their heads.

"Lord, make us thankful for all of our many blessings. Bless this food and the one who prepared it, and we ask in Jesus' name, Amen."

David began to eat his aunt's breakfast, and noticed that her cooking was every bit as wonderful as Savannah's. He then began a conversation with Archie.

"How long have you been working here, Archie? I don't remember seeing you here much."

Archie's eyes darted back and forth a few times, and he began to speak slowly.

"I have been here since December, Mista David. I came up from Savannah."

"I understand."

David made the assumption that Archie was a slave that Uriah had purchased in Savannah, and his curiosity was then satisfied.

"What do you want me to do for you this morning, Uncle Uriah?"

"You and Archie go and stack bags of grits and flour in the warehouse of the mill. I will come and get you around three o'clock, when I return from Milledgeville. I have some business with Governor Brown this morning."

David and Archie moved and stacked several fifty pound bags of flour, corn meal, and grits in the warehouse behind the grist mill. At around two thirty, Uriah stuck his head around the door and called for him.

"David, go and saddle the black mare behind the barn, and meet me here in twenty minutes."

"Yes, sir."

David caught and saddled the large but gentle mare, and rode her up to the end of the warehouse. Uriah walked up and asked him to tie her up near the back of the building. He motioned him around to a store room at the rear of the building that was padlocked from the outside.

Uriah produced a key from his pocket, opened the lock, and moved the iron hasp to one side.

"You see...boy...I promised your Aunt Faith that I would keep this room under lock and key after we moved down here. But things have changed greatly, and the War has come upon us. I told her the other day that I could not keep my promise, and she understood me."

They let the sunlight fill the dusty storeroom, and David saw that it was filled with boxes of firearms, several barrels of gunpowder, and lead shot. Uriah walked over to one of the dusty wooden crates, and pried it open with a small pry bar.

He pulled back several scraps of canvas, and pulled a .36 caliber Colt Navy Revolver from the crate. He then reached deeper into the crate, and pulled out a U.S. Model 1841 "Mississippi" Rifle, along with a cartridge box.

"I must have left some cartridge papers down here somewhere. David, step away from the door for a moment, you are blocking my light."

"Yes, sir."

David moved away, and Uriah fumbled around and found his cartridge papers. He soon found the pewter powder flask, and several more Minie' balls. He deftly began to roll the balls into the paper cartridges, and poured powder behind them. He twisted the ends of the paper cartridges, and stuffed them into the cartridge box nearby.

"David, will you hand me that can of percussion caps, please?"

"Do you have any round balls for the pistol?"

"Yeah, they are in the box on that pistol belt. Go out and tell Archie to saddle my grey gelding. I'll go ahead and load the pistol."

David and Archie then saddled the big bay gelding that was grazing behind the barn, and they set off with the Colt Navy Revolver and the 1841 Mississippi Rifle toward the other side of Murder Creek. The afternoon was hot and hazy, and horseflies attacked the rear of the horses as they walked.

David was inquisitive. "Where did you go this morning, Uncle Uriah?"

"I went into Milledgeville to make some inquiries concerning your legal status. It seems that Mr. Collins attempted to have a warrant issued for your arrest on assault charges, but Sheriff Douglas converted that warrant into a peace bond."

"Why did he do that?"

"I went into his office and asked him directly. Mr. Collins attacked you without sufficient provocation with his cane, and you simply defended yourself with an ax handle."

"The Sheriff was not a witness to that, though. Who told him what really happened?"

"Apparently, Angela did. She went by and gave him a sworn affidavit before she boarded her train for Richmond."

"After breaking off our engagement on account of her father's wishes, it seems a little hard to believe she would testify against him."

"David, I know that you are upset about Angela breaking your engagement, but you must remember she is a fine woman. It is one thing to not marry because of your father's wishes. It is another to bear false witness on his account."

"I understand. What is a peace bond?"

"It is simply a conditional warrant that authorizes your arrest if you go into the town limits of Milledgeville, or within one hundred yards of George Collins. Do you have any problem in understanding that you cannot enter the town limits of Milledgeville?"

"No, sir. I will avoid violating the conditions of the bond as long as I live with you. I really appreciate what you have done for me, Uncle Uriah."

"You know that I could not let you go without a home, as long as I live, boy. We will ride over this hill to James Vann's property. He has given me special permission to train you on his property. There will be no militia or sheriff's deputies around to respond to our gunfire there."

Uriah thus began David's instruction: "The cavalry is the eyes and ears of an army. A good commander of a regiment of cavalry can screen the approach of a large body of infantry, and will constantly update his commanding general of any movements of the enemy army.

I have served in the cavalry most of my life. I have trained cadets in cavalry tactics at West Point. If you can somehow leave here and join a Union regiment, your best chance of serving will be in the cavalry."

"Why is that?"

"Because Confederate cavalry will guard the areas you will need to go through in order to reach Union held territory. You cannot outrun these patrols on foot, but I can train you to outride them. I anticipate that the Confederate authorities will be forced to resort to conscription in order to bring their armies up to full strength. When that happens, you will need to leave this area and seek out Union held territory. That will necessarily require you to travel long distances, and that is best done on horseback."

"I understand."

They approached a high red clay hill, which was surrounded by a heavily wooded area.

Uriah reined his horse to a halt, and motioned for David to stop his mount as well.

"You see this hill, David. You could not pick a better place to hold off an approaching enemy force. If you commanded a company of cavalry, along with two or three batteries of artillery, how would you hold this position against an approaching body of infantry?"

David looked down at the road, which traced the long draw for over a mile, and offered an excellent field of fire from their position at the top. He then looked to either side of the hill, and noticed a grove of Sweet Gum trees on the right, and a large stand of oak trees on the left of the roadway.

"I would place two batteries in a hidden position in the grove of Sweet Gum trees there, and one battery over there in those oak trees. I would aim the guns downhill, but converge their fire toward the center of the road near the lower part of the hill."

"Very good, David. Very well done. Now how would you position your cavalry company?"

"How many men in a company, sir?"

"Usually about a hundred. But casualties may bring you down to 75 or 80 men, normally."

"I would dismount three men from each squad of four troopers, and have them spread out on both sides of the road with their carbines. The fourth trooper in each squad would proceed back to the rear of the hill, say seventy yards, and hold the horses away from the battle line."

"Excellent. You have been reading some tactics manuals. But would you deploy all of your men this way?"

"No, sir. I would require one squad to remain mounted, to shuttle messages between me and the artillery batteries. I would also require one squad to remain mounted to shuttle messages back to the commanding field officer in the area."

"Where did you find cavalry tactics manuals to study, David?"

"About two months ago, when Uncle William got on me for not joining the Thompson Rifles, I went to Aunt Faith and begged her to allow me to read your tactics manuals from West Point."

"I see. When would you give the order to fire on the approaching body of infantry?"

"I would have the artillery batteries open fire at around 3/4 of a mile, and the dismounted troopers would be ordered to open fire at one hundred yards."

Excellent, David. And when would you withdraw your force from this position?"

"That depends. Either after I am ordered to withdraw by the commanding officer in the field, or until I see it is too difficult to maintain the position. I could be ordered to hold the position 'at all hazards', or something like that, I guess."

"You are correct. Now here is a tougher question. Assume you were ordered to vacate this position by your commanding officer. Also assume you must do so while you are under attack. How would you do so?'

"That would depend on the situation presented, of course, but I would withdraw the two batteries in the Sweet Gum trees first, as those guns would be the most valuable assets on the field."

"Certainly. Go on."

"Then I would withdraw the last gun from the other side of the road, after ordering the gunners to increase their rate of fire, to compensate for the lack of fire from the other withdrawn guns. I would then order half of all the troopers to remount, and to provide covering fire for the remaining troopers to withdraw on foot.

The retreating troopers would maintain their carbine fire until they join the mounted troopers, who would use their pistols to hold off the attacking force."

"When would you vacate the field?"

"After all troopers are mounted. This assumes that all troopers can get back to their horses, remount, and retreat under fire off the hill."

"That was excellent, David. The retreat you described is one of the most difficult orders an officer can execute."

He reached into his back pocket, and pulled out a torn bag that once held flour.

"David, I am going to ride down near the foot of this hill, and tie off this rag for a target."

Uriah then spurred the bay gelding into a trot, and he kicked off down the hill toward a Dogwood tree. He dismounted, and tied four corners of the rag to opposing branches on the small tree, until a square target was presented. He then spurred the gelding back up the hill. When he got back to the top, he pulled the 1841 Mississippi Rifle out of its case he had tied to his saddle.

He then commenced loading the weapon, putting in powder, a Minie´ ball, and a percussion cap on the nipple below the hammer. He set the rifle to half cock, and then asked David to dismount.

"David, take the rifle and go over to that Sycamore tree over there, and fire at the target from a kneeling position."

David took the rifle from Uriah, along with his haversack containing the powder flask, caps, and Minie´ balls.

"What about the horses? Will the firing bother them?"

"Don't worry about the horses, David. They are used to gunfire."

David walked over to the Sycamore tree, readied the rifle, aimed, and fired. The smoke from the discharge of the rifle stung his eyes, but a moment later, he saw a hole in the flour bag below.

"Good shot, David. Load and fire two or three more rounds."

David then grabbed another cartridge from the box. He bit the end of the paper cartridge off, poured the powder down the gun barrel, and took the ramrod and started the Minie´ ball down the barrel. He rammed the Minie´ ball down with the ramrod, replaced the percussion cap, and half cocked the rifle. He brought the rifle to full cock, took aim, and fired. The second round also cut through the target. He reloaded quickly, fired another round, and broke the target again.

"Very good, David. Bring the rifle back to me, now."

David walked back to Uriah and handed him the 1841 Mississippi Rifle.

"Let's see how you can shoot a pistol. Take this Colt Navy Revolver and ride to within thirty yards of the target. Fire six rounds, and then return."

"Yes, sir."

David took the Colt Navy Revolver, and checked each cylinder to see if all of the percussion caps were properly seated. He climbed up on the big bay gelding, and briefly rode to within thirty yards of the target. He reined in the gelding, and drew the revolver. He took aim and fired all six rounds.

Hitting the target was more difficult than he had first thought, because his horse flinched after each discharge of the pistol. He let the smoke clear a bit, and then rode back to Uriah's position. Uriah was all smiles when he returned up the hill.

"Well done, young man. You hit the target every time. In a couple of days, we will come back out and test your skill with real cavalry carbines."

They began their ride back to Uriah's mill, and David's curiosity about firearms got the better of him. He began to question Uriah about firearms.

"Why did you have Colt Navy Revolvers when you served in the U.S. Army?"

"Young David, I was one of the few Army officers that advocated the use of Colt Navy Revolvers in the cavalry. The army revolver is .44 caliber, and is less handy. It is better for shooting at Indians on the plains, but it has its disadvantages also. Its ammunition is heavier, and that would require extra weight in a regiment's supply wagons."

"Some one told me a couple of months ago that Samuel Griswold was going to turn his cotton gin factory into a pistol factory. Is that true, Uncle Uriah?"

Uriah reined in his horse momentarily, and killed a large horsefly that had lit on the horse's neck.

"Yes, David, he is going to manufacture a replica of the .36 caliber Colt Navy Revolver. They are going to melt down leaf springs from wagons for the pistol barrels. They are going to cast the frames and trigger guards out of brass."

"Can a gun with that much brass in its frame function properly?"

"It may not hold up over time after say, a thousand rounds are fired, but time will tell. I will say this: If anyone can make a quality firearm in Jones County, Georgia, Samuel Griswold can do it."

"I would assume that similar arms contracts are being let out all over the South?"

"Yes, but in the North, there are hundreds and hundreds of contracts being let out to competent and capable firms. U.S. agents have also gone to Europe to buy arms up over there."

"What does all this mean?"

"It means that one day, a great number of soldiers on both sides will bear these arms and fire them at one another. You will see great casualties and great bloodshed. This war will decide the fate of our nation. The stakes just cannot be higher."

They went back to the mill, and put away their firearms in the store room. David washed up and helped his Aunt Faith prepare their dinner. It had been a long day, and tomorrow would bring chance for him to learn the art of war.

Chapter Eight

The following day brought clouds and rain, and Uriah set David and Archie to work at the mill grinding corn into cornmeal. David was assigned the task of shoveling the meal into bags, and sewing up the ends of the bags with strong cord. Faith brought them a lunch of cold ham, biscuits, and fresh milk.

At three in the afternoon, Uriah walked over and asked David to come with him. They walked over to a grove of willow trees near Murder Creek, where Uriah had set up two folding wooden chairs.

"I need to give up some classroom instruction, David. Welcome to my classroom. When John Brown led his insurrection up in Virginia in '59, many of the Southern states ordered extra small arms from Federal arsenals. One of these types of weapons was this weapon, a 1859 Sharps Carbine."

Uriah picked up the carbine for David, and opened up its breach block by pulling its lever forward.

"This carbine is shorter than a muzzle loading rifle. It is handier for use on horseback."

"Explain how the carbine works, please."

"When you pull down on the lever here, the breach block is exposed, and you insert a linen or paper cartridge into the rear of the firing chamber. The bullet is cone shaped, like a Minie ball. You then insert a percussion cap over the nipple, and return the lever to the trigger guard position. The carbine is then cocked and ready to fire. After firing, you repeat the process to reload."

"This is a single shot carbine?"

"Yes, that is correct. But it can be reloaded more rapidly than the standard Springfield Carbine, and it is just as accurate."

"I have been told that several repeating carbines are under contract for development up north. Is that correct?"

"Yes, you are correct.

"What does that do to cavalry operations?"

"It may do many things. A brigade of cavalry armed with these types of weapons would have the fire power of a division of infantry. The tactics manuals should have been revised years ago, anyway. These types of weapons make the old tactics manuals obsolete."

"How so?"

"Napoleon did not like rifles. In his day, they took extra time to load. Infantry tactics involved firing in massed volleys. Marksmanship was not important with smoothbore muskets. Cavalry regiments were outfitted with sabers and lances. Infantry units had to form squares and repel cavalry with rows of bayonets, because they could not fire accurately at long distances."

"What has changed since the time of Napoleon? Aren't most of the tactics manuals based on Napoleon's experiences?"

"Yes, but two things have occurred since Napoleon to change warfare. A few years ago, a French officer named Minie invented a conical bullet that was hollow on the end. It is loose enough to slide down a rifle barrel, and the hollow end expands when the rifle is fired. The expansion allows the bullet to take the grooves of the rifle, and creates an accurate shot out over one hundred yards."

"What impact will that have in this war?"

"It will cause casualties to increase dramatically. It will require many more men to assail a position than to defend a position. It will give advantage to a defending force rather than an attacking force. Remember what happened in 1815, at the Battle of New Orleans?"

"Andrew Jackson's men with squirrel rifles defeated a British invasion force."

"Right. And not just any invasion force. Those British troops were some of Wellington's best soldiers. And they were utterly defeated. The dead in their ranks counted over thirty five hundred. The dead in Jackson's army totaled around one hundred and fifty men. The rifle caused that mismatch."

"Will that impact this war the same way?"

"Yes, it will. Many more men will go into battle in 1862 than at New Orleans in 1815.

These modern rifles will fire better in damp weather, and will be more accurate. Carnage at battlefields will be commonplace."

"What was the other factor?"

"The other factor is the six shot revolver. With a fully armed company holding revolvers, a dismounted unit can hold off a larger infantry unit for some time. This weapon can be used also while a trooper is on horseback, and even on the charge. Properly equipped with carbines and revolvers, a cavalry unit can be highly mobile, and can have the military impact of a much larger body of infantry."

"What other things do I need to learn about the cavalry service?"

"You must remember to take care of mount at all times. If you override your horse, dismount from the animal, and lead him on foot until he gets his wind. You will need to pack a curry comb, a tool for plucking debris from his horseshoes, and a feed bag for the animal's muzzle. I need to teach you about service in a cavalry regiment. Do you have any questions about that branch of the service?"

"Yes, sir. When is the best time to use a saber, or a carbine, as opposed to a revolver, and vice versa?"

"That is a fair question. With rifles on the battlefield, the old style lancers and even the saber charge may become a thing of the past. The best time to use the saber is in a fast charge, preferably when you are in a column. This is especially true if you are trying to cut your way out of a fixed position, say, behind enemy lines."

"And the best time to use a pistol?"

"When you are at close quarters with other enemy cavalry or infantry units, when you are fighting mounted or dismounted. If you are fighting dismounted, use your carbines first, until your ammunition runs low, or until the enemy is close upon you. Then you use your pistols. That will conclude our sit–down instruction for today. Now, would you like to go out behind the barn and test fire this carbine?"

"I sure would."

"There is a cedar shingle over there we can use for a target. I will bring it out to that oak tree, and you can practice your marksmanship with this carbine."

David and Uriah spent the rest of the afternoon firing the carbine at the fixed target. Uriah trained David to shoot from horseback and from standing and sitting positions that afternoon.

* * * * * *

After several weeks of training, David was asked by Uriah to saddle a horse and ride north across Murder Creek toward Eatonton Factory. He mounted the big bay gelding, and headed up the pike toward Eatonton. When he got two miles up the pike, he heard the crack of a gunshot, saw a puff of smoke, and heard a round whistle over his head. He stopped the bay by pulling back on the reins.

He then heard another report, saw another puff of smoke, and heard a pistol ball whiz by several feet over his head. He cupped his hands and hollered "Hey!" and was about to yell again, when Uriah began riding down a nearby hill on his mare.

When Uriah got close, David began to question him.

"Why did you shoot at me like that?"

"To test you under fire. You did quite well, David. Much of being a soldier deals with encountering the unexpected. You did alright."

"Was that anything like being fired upon in battle?"

"Heavens, no. In a real battle, you will have muskets and carbines and all kinds of artillery fired your way. You will see men and horses and mules get hit by shells, and see arms and limbs and entrails thrown all over the battlefield. There is nothing like it, and you never quite get used to it, even as a hardened veteran."

"What else do I need to do to complete my training?"

"I have several weeks of field and 'classroom' instruction for you, David. Then I will take on the weighty task of finding a way to get you into the Union Army."

"I did have one more question, Uncle Uriah."

"What was your question?"

"What is the best time and the best way to use a saber?"

"That is another good question. Draw and use your saber only when you run out of ammunition. Use the point of the saber if you can, as opposed to whacking with its edge like you are using an ax."

"When will I learn the proper way to handle the saber?"

"Tomorrow, young man. Tonight, we will go and rub down the horses and eat some supper."

They rode back over the hot and hazy countryside, while the Katydids sang their familiar tune in the trees beside the road.

* * * * * *

Near the end of December, 1861, David and Archie were hard at work stacking bags of corn meal in the warehouse. It was cold enough to require both men to don their heavy wool jackets.

A few moments later, Uriah came into the warehouse, holding what appeared to be a letter. He called out to David, who saw the steam of his breath in the damp light of the warehouse.

"Oh there you are, David. I have a letter here for you. It was addressed to David R. Snelling c/o Uriah Snelling, General Delivery, Milledgeville, Georgia. It is from Angela. Take a break outside and go read over it."

He handed David the letter, and he accepted it reluctantly. He pulled off his gloves and handled the envelope. It was postmarked in Richmond, Augusta, and by the Milledgeville post office.

He went outside, and sat on part of an oak log they had sawed up into small stools. He broke the seal on the envelope and began to read the letter, which was dated November 15th.

Mr. David R. Snelling
c/o Mr. Uriah Snelling
General Delivery
Milledgeville, Georgia

Dearest David:

I wanted to write you and give you our latest news by my own hand, as I did not want you to find this out from anyone else. Joseph obtained a furlough of one week from his regiment in Warrenton ten days ago, and we were married in Richmond three days ago. The church was near the Chickahominy River, and it was just beautiful, David. Joseph made a handsome groom in his captain's uniform, with all the braid on the sleeves of his tunic.

He was really sick this past Fall, David. It took weeks to nurse him back to health. We are very happy together, and I know that the Lord meant for us to be together.

I now know that Father attacked you wrongfully, and without provocation. What I want you to know is that I am happy with my life and my work in the hospital, and you also deserve a chance at happiness.

I have written Governor Brown in Milledgeville, and asked him to give you a pardon. You were born and raised around Milledgeville, and deserve the ability to journey into town and conduct business. Please try to forgive my father for breaking us up. I know you have forgiveness in your heart. I will always love and admire you, David, and wish you nothing but a lifetime of happiness.

Love,

Angela

David wiped the tears from his eyes, and began to realize the news that had been handed to him. Another man had married the woman he loved, in a small church that was probably similar to the church he had picked for their ceremony.

His loss of Angela was Joseph's gain. Yet he could not feel jealous of Joseph. Joseph was like a brother to him. He could not wish him any ill will. He opposed his involvement on the Confederate side, but he wished Joseph nothing but success.

He bowed his head and prayed for Joseph and for his safety. He also prayed for Angela and her happiness. What had happened to them was God's will. He must accept God's will, and dedicate his life toward becoming a soldier.

A few moments later, Uriah interrupted David's train of thought by asking him the obvious question.

"News from Angela, David? From the look on your face, it appears to be bad news for you."

"Well, yes sir, it is. Angela and Joseph were married in Richmond last month, while Joseph was on furlough."

"I see. Well, after Angela decided to stay up in Richmond, I figured that she had made a decision concerning Joseph. Does this anger you, David?"

"No, sir. It only disappoints me. I have to be a man about this. Don't worry about me, Uncle Uriah. I will get over Angela."

"Well, the news today is not all bad. I heard in Milledgeville today that Captain Du Pont and the Union Navy has captured Port Royal in South Carolina.

"From the look on your face, it appears that you also have some other news."

"Yes, David, I do. Two months ago, I filed an application for a pardon for you with the governor's office. I met with the governor's general counsel back then, and he told me that I needed a second person to propose the pardon before Governor Brown would consider it."

"It is funny that you should mention that. Angela said in her letter that she had asked the governor to pardon me."

"Well son, that was the second person! Angela's letter to the governor has persuaded him to pardon you. You can expect a full pardon to be issued in due course next month."

"What does that do for me?"

"It will relieve you of your legal disabilities. The peace bond with the sheriff will be recalled, and you will be allowed to return to Milledgeville freely, and without any restrictions."

"That is good news. I can now make deliveries for you in town."

"It means even more than that, David. I have a contact up in Tennessee that I am waiting to hear from. Once he contacts me, I believe I can figure out a way to get you out of the state, and into the Union Army."

"That is really good news, Uncle Uriah."

"Yes, it is, boy. Let's get back to work. I would like to finish our warehouse work before supper time."

"Yes, sir."

They walked back into the warehouse, and began to finish the job they had started that morning. The work went quicker, and seemed lighter to David, as his spirits had been lifted by Uriah's news.

Chapter Nine

In mid January of 1862, Uriah returned home one afternoon with a pardon for David R. Snelling, which was signed by Governor Joseph Brown. This pardon relieved David of all his legal disabilities, and enabled him to travel into Milledgeville without fear of arrest or prosecution. David would train with Uriah in army and cavalry tactics on Saturdays, and worked in Uriah's mill and made deliveries from Monday through mid afternoon on Fridays.

David developed a Friday afternoon routine. Every Friday afternoon, he would saddle a horse and ride into town, and buy a newspaper. He generally read the *Milledgeville Southern Recorder*, but on occasion would purchase a *Macon Daily Telegraph*.

He would purchase a newspaper, ride over to the State Capitol, and sit on a bench and read the news about the war.

The news of the war excited David, but also greatly frustrated him, because he was stuck in Milledgeville, away from all of the action. In early February, David read about General Grant's capture of Fort Henry on the Tennessee River.

Around the twentieth of February, David read of General Grant's capture of Fort Donelson on the Cumberland River. He also read of General Burnside's capture of Roanoke Island in North Carolina.

During the second week of March, 1862, he read about Union General Lyons' victory at the Battle of Pea Ridge, in Arkansas. He also read about a Confederate General named "Stonewall" Jackson, who had commenced a campaign against Union forces in the Shenandoah Valley, up in Virginia.

He also read of the embarkment of Union troops under General McClellan for the York River in Virginia, during the second week of April.

That same week, news of a titanic battle near Shiloh Church, Tennessee, began to filter in around the South. Confederate General Albert Sidney Johnston was wounded and killed, and General Grant's army had defeated the Confederate forces after two days of battle.

Yet Shiloh presented an opportunity for David that Uriah believed he could not pass up. A large Union Army group had penetrated deep into Tennessee, just over the Alabama and Mississippi state lines.

Near the end of April, 1862, David came home one Friday afternoon to find Uriah meeting with a funny looking stranger, one James C.

McBurney. Uriah promptly introduced him to David, and explained his presence there.

"Mr. McBurney owns a commission house on Cherry Street in Macon. He is also a sutler, and sells hats and canteens and other items to both Union and Confederate forces. What we tell you now is in the strictest confidence, David."

"Yes, sir, go ahead."

"Mr. McBurney is an intelligence agent for the Union Army. He put me in contact with Parson Brownlow, a prominent Union man in East Tennessee. They put me in contact with the War Department through Mr. McBurney's travels, and I have some news for you."

"What is the news?"

"Several Union cavalry regiments are being raised in Tennessee. Senator Andrew Johnston of Tennessee has remained loyal to the Union, and has helped the War Department recruit Union men from his home state."

"So how does this apply to me?"

"Let me get there, son. Mr. McBurney, tell us, sir, about out joint venture, if you will."

The rotund and short man stood up, cleared his throat, and began to speak. He was dark haired, with long side whiskers. He wore a frumpy grey wool suit, and a stovepipe hat.

"Certainly. Master David, Major Snelling and myself have executed a contract with the State of Georgia to supply pikes to the State Arsenal in Milledgeville. We will have them manufactured in Rome, Georgia, and we will ship them by rail to Gordon, and up to Milledgeville. These pikes are highly thought of by Governor Brown. Uriah knows, however, that they are only good for sticking pigs in hog killin' weather, ha, ha, ha."

Uriah and McBurney both laughed heartily, but David was not amused.

"What has all of this got to do with me?"

Uriah began to explain.

"This gives Mr. McBurney a reason to be in North Georgia in a month or so. I will then have him make contact with you, probably in the vicinity of Chattanooga. He will then put you in contact with a Union man in North Alabama, a William Looney. Looney has been in contact with me, and he has agreed to guide you to the Union lines over there. A large Union force has invaded that part of Alabama, and southern Tennessee. We think it can be done. But there is a catch."

"What is that?"

"In order to get you to the vicinity of Chattanooga, you must join a Confederate regiment, and then desert."

"What! That is crazy, Uncle Uriah. Why would I want to do the very thing that I have refused to do before? Why would I want to do that, when all I really want is to fight on the other side?"

Uriah's face hardened, and he looked into David's eyes, and began to speak slowly.

"This is not some high handed principal that I am trying to uphold, boy. This is war. The situation we are presented with is this: A conscription law has been enacted by the Confederate Congress last week, and was signed by Jefferson Davis. If you do not join a Confederate unit, or the state militia, you will be conscripted into a coastal defense unit, a Virginia bound unit, or thrown into prison. I have gone to some degree of trouble to determine the planned movement of Georgia regiments into Tennessee."

"I'm sorry, Uncle Uriah, please continue."

"I'm not angry boy, but this is what you need to do. I have determined that the 57th Georgia Regiment is being raised and organized and will be ordered to reinforce Chattanooga, Tennessee. I have contacted your cousin, Julia Bonner."

"What for?"

"Her husband, John, will be captain of Company H of the 57th Georgia Infantry. They will form up and sign the muster books in Fortville and Milledgeville, and then move out by rail the following week. I told Julia that you had a change of heart, and wanted to serve as a private in her husband's regiment."

"What did Julia say?"

"She said that John would be glad to have you. You need to listen to this next part, David, 'cause this is very important. You are to muster in the first week of May, and they will load you on rail cars and ship you up to Atlanta, and to Camp McDonald, just above Kennesaw Mountain. You will drill there for three weeks, and then you will be transferred to Chattanooga. It is there that Mr. McBurney will make contact with you."

"How will he do that?"

"He will come into your camp as a sutler. He will be selling haversacks, canteens, mess kits, and other such items. You will have only one good chance to desert and leave your regiment, and that is when you draw picket duty."

"What should I do when I draw picket duty?"

"We have worked out a system of signals that can tip Mr. McBurney as to your picket duty assignment. If you are going to draw picket duty that

The Unionist

day, go to Mr. McBurney's tent and purchase a light colored haversack. If you are going to draw picket duty at night, go over to his tent and purchase a dark colored oilskin cover for your kepi."

"How will I escape?"

"Whenever you draw picket duty, get down to the Tennessee River. Mr. McBurney will hide a john boat on the riverbank for you. Take your oilskin, your haversack and your canteen with you. Once you get into the boat, there will be no going back. You will paddle the boat across to the other side of the river from your post, where Mr. McBurney will meet you.

He will then get you a horse, and you will ride toward Lewis Mountain in Alabama, where Mr. Looney will rendezvous with you."

David was stunned, but also elated. He could not believe that this was actually about to happen. But he deplored the idea of enlisting in a Confederate regiment just to desert.

"I don't really like your plan all that much Uncle Uriah..."

Uriah changed his tone of voice, and began to use his power of persuasion.

"David, I have been into town, and have seen you reading about the war in the newspapers. I saw you just fuming because you have seen no action in this war. This is your best chance to enroll in a Union cavalry regiment. If I didn't think you could do this, I would never have set this up."

David was then convinced. If Uriah thought it was the thing to do, he would do it.

"All right, sir. I'll do it. Can I go ahead and purchase my gear now?"

"Sure, son. Mr. McBurney's wagon is parked out back. Come on out and we'll get you a mess kit, a canteen, a bedroll, and even a kepi. Come on outside."

He put his arm around David, and led him out back to purchase equipment from Mr. McBurney.

David bought a bedroll, a solid black kepi with a leather bill, a fine tin canteen with a leather strap; a mess kit, and a folding fork and spoon set that could fit into his pocket.

After they had packed away his gear, David then thought of an obvious question that he should have asked before.

"What about a uniform?"

"Come around to the guest room, and I'll let your Aunt Faith show you her handiwork."

They walked around into the house, and to the guest room, where Faith was laying out a military uniform on his bed.

David looked at the uniform, and could not believe his eyes. It was beautiful.

"Aunt Faith, I can't believe that you did this or me. Your handiwork is flawless! You even put brass buttons with eagles on the coat!"

"It was a real pleasure to make it for you, David. I would not want you to go off to war naked, now would I? Please try it on for me."

David slipped on the uniform coat. The outside portion of the coat was made of blue–grey Kersey wool. David noticed that the inside of the coat was navy blue. Uriah immediately offered an explanation.

"That is not just any uniform coat, David. Please reach in and pull the sleeves on the coat inside out."

David did as he was told. Much to his astonishment, there were pockets and brass buttons on the navy blue side of the coat as well.

"When you leave the Confederate lines, all you have to do is turn your coat inside out, and you will be wearing Union blue."

"Let's take a look at the trousers."

The trousers were made of black jean cloth, and were double seated. Faith's seems sewn into the garment were double stitched, and were flawlessly done. He then remembered that she had purchased all of the cloth for this uniform back in March of 1861. It had taken her an entire year to secretly sew this uniform for him. Uriah added another explanation.

"Those are not just any uniform pants, David. They are double seated, so they will last you a while in cavalry service. The uniform coat is a little shorter than the infantry coat. That will help you sit a horse easier than with a longer coat."

"I don't know how I can ever repay you for what you both have done for me. I love both of you."

David gave his aunt Faith a big hug.

"Just return home safely, son. We both want you to survive this terrible war. Enough with the war, let us start supper."

David obeyed his aunt, and put his uniform down long enough to peel a bowl of potatoes.

After supper, Archie went back to his room in the loft over the warehouse, and David reviewed his plans with Uriah and Mr. McBurney.

"David, do you know the call of the barred owl? Have you heard a barred owl call out in the forest?"

"Yes, sir."

"It is a distinctive call that sounds like who–cooks–for–you–who–cooks–for–your–all."

"I have heard it many times, believe me."

"Okay. When you draw picket duty on the night or the morning that you are to desert, Mr. McBurney will approach your post and make the front part of the barred owl's call, like I just did for you."

"And?"

"And then, you respond and answer him with just the same call as another barred owl would make in reply, which is: 'Who–who–who–who–who–who–whowaaw' Do you remember that? Can you remember to do that?"

"Yes sir, I believe that I can."

"If you are near the Tennessee River at all, look for a small canoe or boat near the shoreline. You will paddle over to the other side, and Mr. McBurney will arrange to get you to a rendezvous with Bill Looney. It will be Looney's job to get you over Lewis Mountain, and through to Union lines. Mr. McBurney will have papers for you that will identify you as a private in the Middle Tennessee Union Cavalry. You should not forget to turn your coat inside out. I will also have some revolvers and some other equipment for you when you meet with Mr. McBurney.

David, for your protection, you will need to change your personal appearance after you leave the 57th Georgia Regiment. I suggest growing some facial hair. Maybe a mustache, if you can grow one. Do you have any questions?"

"Yes, sir. I have two questions?"

"Go ahead."

"Have you taught me everything you know?"

"Yes, I have, except for one thing. When I was a soldier in the Mexican War, we were a cohesive professional body of ten thousand, and we conquered all of Mexico. Most of us were consummate professionals, and many of us were trained at West Point. Both armies in this war are now mostly volunteers. Many of the officers are appointed because of their politics, and not because of their ability or military skill.

David, don't ever let some greenhorn officer get you killed on account of his stupidity. Take care of yourself at all times, do you understand?"

"Yes sir, I do."

"Well, now that I have taught you all that I know, I have prepared a letter of introduction for Mr. McBurney to forward to the Federal officer commanding the forces in North Alabama and Middle Tennessee. I am requesting an appointment for you as a first lieutenant of a calvary regiment."

David was stunned, but was also elated. He could not believe that his Uncle Uriah had that much confidence in him.

"Thank you, Uncle Uriah, thank you for everything."

"Well David, there is also something else that I want you to do for me and your Aunt Faith."

"What is that?"

"You will not be in a position to send mail and letters back to us once you leave your Confederate regiment. So what I would like you to do is to take this journal, and write us letters twice per week in there, as if you were going to post the letters out to us."

"What will I do with the journal?"

"Keep it up, and record your experiences, and then give it to us when you return home to us."

"That could be after the end of the war."

"I know that, but please humor us. We want to know what happens to you after you join the Union Army."

"When do I join the 57th Georgia and ship out?"

"You will muster in on Monday morning, and board the train for Gordon and Atlanta the following Monday at noon."

"Will you be there to see me off?"

"You bet we will. We will drive you down to the depot. David, there is one other question I need to ask you. How do you feel about the blacks bearing arms and fighting in this war?"

"They have as big a stake in this fight as any of the rest of us. Some people say that they have even more at stake, because their eventual freedom will be decided. Freedom is worth fighting and dying for. If they want to help us do some of the work, then I am all for it. Does that answer your question?"

"Yeah, it really does, boy. Let us get ready for bed."

David let Mr. McBurney have his bed, while he made himself a pallet on the floor. He was so excited about his chance for action that he had difficulty getting to sleep that night. Monday morning could not arrive soon enough for him.

He would finally have a part to play in this war, and he wanted to make his aunt and uncle proud of him. He wanted to do his part, and now his opportunity had presented itself. It was not to be wasted!

Chapter Ten

Monday morning came sooner than David expected, and Uriah drove him down to Milledgeville in his spring buggy to enlist in the 57th Georgia Regiment, Co. H, and to sign the muster book.

They left the mill at seven o'clock in the morning, and they enjoyed the dawn in all of its scarlet splendor while they rode down the pike.

Uriah had hitched a red and sleek mule named Sophie to the buggy, and she loved to trot down the turnpike. Uriah let her eat up as much road as she wanted. Uriah made David dress in his uniform and kepi, in order to show Captain Bonner that he was serious about his enlistment in the 57th Georgia.

Their conversation focused on items that David should take with him in his haversack and knapsack.

"You will have some baking soda that Faith will give you in a small tin flask to take with you. You need to brush your teeth with that."

"Yes, sir."

"Faith has also boiled and prepared a powerful salve with sage in it. You need to put that on you in case you get ticks or red bugs on you."

"Yes, sir, I understand."

"I will also give you some hand fishing lines in a small canvass bag. You may need to use them later, to catch fish for your supper in those Alabama mountains."

"Yes, sir."

"David, your regiment may depart quickly after you muster in. You may pull out early in the morning. I will help you pack up all of your gear this afternoon, and Faith and I can see you down here to the depot early in the morning, if that is necessary."

Sophie continued her torrid pace on the turnpike, and finally pulled the buggy over toward the depot. Several tents were set up on the grounds adjacent to the depot. Each tent was filled with lines of young men, checking in with enrolling officers, and signing muster books.

The grounds around the depot were crowded, and the atmosphere on that hot and hazy morning resembled that of a traveling circus.

David saw the Confederate Battle Flag flying on a makeshift pole near the tents, along with the regimental colors of the 57th Georgia. The Confederate Battle Flag flying at the depot was the first one David had ever seen.

There were lovely young ladies wearing homespun dresses and palmetto woven hats, there to greet the enlisting soldiers. Young boys ran around the grounds, running and playing with wooden toy muskets.

A regimental band was assembled, with a banjo player, a fiddler, a guitar player, and a vocalist. David recognized the tune that was being played, a minstrel tune named "Dixie", but he had never heard the lyrics sung the way the band's vocalist was singing. A tall man in a gray tunic, with a wonderful baritone voice, sang the unfamiliar lyrics to the tune of "Dixie":

> Southerns here your country call ye...
> Up, lest worse than death befall ye...
> To arms! To arms! To arms! In Dixie...
> The walls are peaked, the fires are lighted...
> Let our hearts be now united...
> To arms! To arms! To arms! In Dixie...
>
> Advance the flag of Dixie, Hurrah! Hurrah!
> For Dixie's land, we take our stand,
> To live or die for Dixie...
> To arms! To arms!
> And conquer peace for Dixie!
> To arms! To arms! And conquer peace for Dixie!
>
> Hear no danger, shun no labor!
> Lift up rifle, pike, and saber...
> To arms! To arms! To arms! In Dixie...
> Shoulders breast and post to shoulder...
> Let the odds make each heart bolder...
> To arms! To arms! To arms! In Dixie!
> Advance the flag of Dixie! Hurrah! Hurrah!
> In Dixie's land, I'll take my stand...
> To live or die for Dixie!
> Away, away, away down south in Dixie...

David and Uriah tied the buggy up the street, and walked through the masses of people gathered in front of the depot. They got into line a few yards off the street, where locals greeted Uriah and his nephew.

A young man ahead of Uriah recognized him, and immediately spoke.

"Hello, Major Snelling, do you remember me? I'm George Thompson, Claude Thompson's son. We've bought meal and flour from you for years."

Uriah then recognized the sandy–haired, freckle faced lad.

"Your family has a farm down on the Little River, not far off the Eatonton Factory pike. I remember your place. You have some pretty pastures on rolling hills."

"Yes, sir. I came down to enroll in this new regiment. You remember my brother, Howard?"

"I sure do. He was older than you, had reddish hair."

"That's him. Well, he joined up with Captain Floyd's regiment last year. We got a letter from him last week. Says he is on the Chickahominy River. Where would that be?"

"Just outside of Richmond, Virginia."

"Pa said he could spare me off the farm, 'cause he just hired a guy up the road from us, John Morgan, to help him with the chores while I am gone off to the war."

"Your father is a resourceful man. I'm sure he can find a way to manage while you are gone."

"Are you joining up with the regiment, David?"

"I sure am. You see I'm here in uniform."

"I know. I just didn't know you were gonna sign up with our outfit. We sure are glad to have you."

David managed to smile.

"Same here."

The time passed quickly, as George Thompson was a pleasant young man who loved to talk. He told them about his Blue Tick coon dog, and his sweet heart over in Clinton, Alison Childs.

Uriah also reminded David of some items that his Aunt Faith had packed for him.

"Your Aunt Faith has packed you a tin drinking cup and a small sewing kit into your haversack. You need to remember that you will be sewing and cooking for yourself from now on after you enter the service."

"That's not a pleasant thought, but I will probably be reminded of that at mealtimes, Uncle Uriah."

The lines had moved along, and David soon found himself before the enrolling officer for Company H of the 57th Georgia Infantry, a Lieutenant Mathew Kline.

"I will need your name and rank, and place of birth and your current age, soldier. State your first name, middle initial, and last name, if you will."

David looked at the impeccably dressed lieutenant in the light gray tunic and embroidered kepi, and recited the necessary information.

"David R. Snelling, private. Milledgeville, Georgia. 25 years of age."

"Very good. You will need to sign the muster book on this line here, and place your initials on this roster sheet here. I do need to tell you that the train departure has been scheduled for Friday morning at nine a.m. That was the first available time for the number of cars needed for our transport train."

"So I am to report back here on Friday morning?"

"Yes, but be here by eight a.m. It will take at least an hour for all of the company and officers to board the train and load their baggage."

"I will be here on Friday morning, bright and early and ready to go, sir."

David waited for George Thompson to sign his enlistment papers and muster book, and then told him where he would meet him on Friday morning.

"My Uncle Uriah and Aunt Faith will be with me on Friday, but I would like to ride up to camp in the same car with you, if you don't mind."

"Sure, I would like that. My sweet heart may be in town to see me on Friday. I'm headed to the telegraph office to send her a wire. I will see you on Friday, David, take care."

They walked back to the spring buggy, untied Sophie, and let her trot down the road back to the mill.

On the way back, David could not help but recall the similar chaotic scene that they witnessed on the Capitol Square the year before.

"That place was like a circus, today Uncle Uriah. It reminded me of all the people running around and shouting their huzzahs after Georgia voted to secede from the Union."

"You know, I had those same thoughts when I saw all the crowds and the running around of the children, and heard all of the noise at the depot."

"Uncle Uriah, I now feel guilty about enlisting in a regiment that I know I could never serve in."

"I don't want you to even think about all of the rights and wrongs of your situation now, boy. I only want you to concentrate on the task at hand. If you let your feelings of guilt get to you, you might end up shot dead, or swinging at the end of a hangman's rope, do you understand me?"

"Yes sir, I do."

"Your Aunt Faith is packing your haversack and your kit as we speak. She is going to pack you two extra pair of drawers, three extra pairs of socks, two extra shirts, and three handkerchiefs. She will give you a bar of soap to take with you. Use it to wash your body and your clothes."

Sophie ate up the road on the way home faster than she did when she was heading into town. When she got within three miles of the mill, her ears pricked up, and her gait became quicker.

David took his mind off the war, and enjoyed the ride home. He had fought too hard against too many causes of late. He decided to let his Uncle Uriah do all of the planning of his military career. His part was execution of the master plan.

He would enjoy his last few days at home with his aunt and uncle, and worry about the war when his train departs on Friday.

* * * * *

Friday morning came bright and early, and David rose at four a.m., donned his uniform, and helped his Aunt Faith fix a small breakfast. At five thirty, Archie had two strong horses hitched to the wagon, and they were soon off to Milledgeville. David's haversack was fully packed, and Uriah had lashed his bedroll and oilskin to his knapsack. His mess kit, canteen, and shaving kit were all neatly packed and stowed away.

Lieutenant Kline had advised David that rifles and cartridge boxes would not be issued to the company until they had arrived at Camp McDonald. That would save room in the cars for the men and their gear to be stowed on the trip through Atlanta.

The horses trotted quickly down the macadamized pike, and quickly pulled the wagon across the Fishing Creek bridge and into Milledgeville in less than ninety minutes.

There were lines of soldiers, and their wives and sweet hearts waiting at the depot, as the sun began to rise. It appeared as a red ball in the eastern sky, as the morning was already developing into a hot and hazy day.

They tied up the wagon across the street from the depot, and David began to look for young George Thompson. He did not have to look long before he spied him in his gray uniform and black slouch hat, walking arm in arm with a beautiful girl of nineteen years. David had never seen Alison Childs before, but the sight of her was enough to stop his heart.

She was in a gingham dress with a full hoop underneath, with a crocheted wrap around her shoulders. She wore a matching powder blue hat to match her dress. Her lovely bosom accentuated her hourglass figure. She had auburn hair that fell to shoulder length, and bewitching royal blue eyes.

No wonder George Thompson was smitten with her! She was enough to break any man's heart, and place other men in the same condition as young George Thompson.

The feelings David experienced when he saw Alison reminded him of his old feelings he had for Angela. It was a brief reminder of his lost love. He hoped that George Thompson would never experience the pain of losing the love of his life.

He stepped up to George and Alison and boldly introduced himself.

"I'm David Snelling. And you must be Alison Childs."

He bowed, and took her hand and kissed it. The fragrance of her perfume was wonderful. As he rose to look at her, he saw her eyes light up as she looked at him.

"George, I have never met this charming man before. Do you ever get to Clinton, Mr. Snelling?"

"Every once in a while, to make deliveries for my Uncle Uriah. Let me properly introduce you to my Uncle Uriah and Aunt Faith."

David brought his Aunt Faith and Uncle Uriah forward to meet the lovely Alison Childs. Uriah and Faith were both impressed with Miss Childs, and even offered to drive her down to the McComb House later that morning. Alison was to catch a 3:15 train back to Griswoldville that afternoon.

George remained in a jovial mood, and all of them enjoyed conversing with each other prior to the train's arrival at the station. The wives, children, sweet hearts, and parents of the regiment's soldiers filled the yard all around the depot.

The train soon arrived at the station, blowing its whistle, and blowing smoke and steam from its engine as it pulled through the depot. The train was to be loaded from last car up through the first car, in that order. David and George were part of a group that would load into the first two cars behind the engine.

They made the most of the time that they had left, as the train was being loaded. David kissed his Aunt Faith, and shook his Uncle Uriah's hand. Uriah spoke to him first.

"Stay alive, boy. Return home from the war. Remember what we taught you, and make us proud of you."

David saw tears in Uriah's eyes as he spoke the words to him. All he could hope to tell him at that moment was a weak "I will, I love you both". He began to get emotional himself.

He saw George kiss Alison full on the lips, and tell her that he would be back after his regiment licks the Yankees.

David stepped forward with his gear, and could not resist approaching Alison boldly once more.

"Don't I get a kiss too, since I am also going off to whip the dirty Yankees?"

Alison rolled her pretty eyes, and gave him her answer right off.

"You are mighty forward, sir, but I guess this is war, and you are risking your life for us, too. You may kiss me also."

David stepped forward, took off his kepi, put his arms around her, and kissed her full on the lips. Oh, what soft lips!

David thanked the beautiful Alison for the kiss, and she just rolled her blue eyes at him. He then begged apologies to George, whom he did not want to insult.

"George, I'm sorry to be so forward with your sweet heart, it's just that where we're going, we may not see any pretty girls for years."

"I understand, David. Let's board the train now."

They said their last good byes, and climbed into the cars with their packed gear. They were fortunate that the front portion of the make-shift troop train consisted of real passenger cars. The cars at the rear of the train were simply wooden freight cars that had make-shift seats nailed into them.

David looked out across the yard of the depot as the train pulled out, and waved to his Uncle Uriah and Aunt Faith until they were out of sight. His old life was over, and his life in the army was just beginning.

* * * * *

The troop train took them through Macon and Atlanta on the Western & Atlantic Railroad, and their train stopped at Allatoona Station. Allatoona Station was above Big Shanty and Kennesaw Mountain, and just above Red Top Mountain.

The soldiers of Company H were ordered to march, with their baggage, around seventeen miles to Camp McDonald, near Canton, Georgia, in Cherokee County. The march took all of the night, and a portion of the next morning.

Other companies soon joined theirs. Company A was called the "Dixie Boys", from Thomas County. Companies B through K were from different counties in Middle Georgia.

In theory, each company should have contained at least one hundred men, giving the regiment a total of one thousand men. In practice, each company contained anywhere from 75 to 150 men each. There were roughly 1,000 men in the 57th Georgia Regiment of Infantry.

The camp known as Camp McDonald was located in the mountains, and consisted of a series of crude buildings for the officers, and rows of small "dog–tents" for the enlisted men. The enlisted men slept in the "dog tents" two at a time, as there was only room for two men to sleep in each small tent.

The 57th Georgia Regiment was soon joined by other Confederate regiments, the 34th Georgia Infantry, and the 36th Georgia Infantry.

The camp was soon filled with men dressed in all types and colors of uniforms. There were blue–gray colored tunics with sky blue, black, or gray breeches. Some wore slouch hats; others wore kepis and forage caps of various colors, from gray to blue and even red. Some troops wore high shakos, similar to those worn during the War of 1812. Others were dressed more modestly, in homespun pants of wool or jean cloth, and woven uniform coats dyed gray or a butternut color, from homemade dyes.

A few days after arriving in camp, the quartermaster began to distribute firearms to each of the companies. Company H of the 57th Georgia received their firearms near the first part of the week. David was issued a .577 caliber British Enfield rifle, a cartridge box, a powder flask, cartridge papers, and a bullet mold. He was also issued a tool for servicing the rifle, and a bayonet. His rifle had a leather sling which allowed him to sling the weapon on his shoulder while he was on the march.

During the next three weeks, David drilled with the regiment. The companies drilled by companies, and later began drilling with entire regiments, or with all of the companies in the regiment.

In the mornings, typically, there would be a roll call around 6:30 a.m. Then companies stood down and drew their morning rations for mess. There would be an inspection by the captain or the major or colonel next, and then officers would drill the troops until one o'clock. The troops would then draw rations, and prepare a mid–day meal.

After the mid–day meal, the officers would drill the troops again, and on some days, schedule a dress parade for the colonel commanding the regiment.

On June 24th, Captain Bonner assembled the men of Company H, and informed them of their next movement. They were to March by companies to Allatoona Station, and take a train north to the vicinity of Chattanooga. They were to march out on the 26th of June, at 6:00 a.m. They would march out with Company I to Allatoona Station on the 26th.

The morning of the 26th, the men of Companies H and I strapped on their knapsacks, shouldered their rifles and haversacks, and marched over to Allatoona Station.

The bugles sounded, and they fell into line and marched over the mountain to Allatoona Station. The head of the column arrived at Allatoona by four o'clock in the afternoon. A special train from the Western & Atlantic Railroad, pulled by the engine *Texas*, was waiting for them at Allatoona Station.

David noticed the height of the small mountains around the station, and took note of the area where the railroad tracks were laid. Allatoona Pass was just beyond the train station, and was a narrow gap through the mountain where the railroad tracks were laid up from Big Shanty, toward Kingston and Resacca.

The mountain rose up on either side of the pass at a height over eight hundred feet above the rail line, and the pass itself created a gorge around one mile in length. David surmised that the engineers constructing this part of the railroad were required to blast out larger gaps in the pass for the railroad trains to run.

They took three hours to board their train, and the *Texas* pulled them up through north Georgia, through Tunnel Hill and around Missionary Ridge, and into Chattanooga.

The regiment exited the train at the depot in Chattanooga, and marched out to a make shift camp around four miles from the center of the town.

Chattanooga was situated at the base of towering Lookout Mountain, on a famous bend in the Tennessee River known as Moccasin Bend. From the top of Lookout Mountain, a person viewing Moccasin Bend would see a bend in the Tennessee River exactly in the shape of the shoe of an Indian, hence its name, Moccasin Bend.

David and George Thompson shared another dog tent at their camp, and all of the men were exhausted from their long march and train ride from Camp McDonald. David kept pretty much to himself, and only socialized and conversed regularly with George Thompson. He was not interested in conversing with the other men in the regiment, as he would overhear others bragging about the Yankees they would shoot or 'whip' in battle.

He heard the officers in other companies pontificating on the nature of 'States' Rights', and their 'rights of property', which ultimately meant slavery. He was dying to get away from there, and wondered when James McBurney would arrive at their camp.

* * * * *

Two weeks later, Mr. McBurney did arrive in their camp as a sutler. He set up a tent, and did a brisk business with soldiers in the different companies. David walked by his tent and made eye contact with Mr. McBurney a few times, but he could not approach him as of yet. He had not yet been assigned picket duty, and they had agreed on a prearranged set of signals to be given when the time was right.

The second week of July, the 57th Georgia was ordered to march into town, and the troops were ordered to board rail cars, and were sent over to Long Island, Alabama. They marched from the train station there to the Memphis & Western Railroad bridge over the Tennessee River near Bridgeport, Alabama.

David was apprehensive during the march from the railhead, as he worried that James McBurney might have been unable to follow their advance into Alabama. His fears were somewhat quelled by the fact that the 57th Georgia Regiment had just moved him ever closer to the Union lines.

The 57th Georgia Regiment was ordered by General Henry Heth to guard the Memphis & Western Railroad bridge over the Tennessee River, and to be on the lookout for the advancing Union forces of Major General Don Carlos Buell. If the bridge could not be held, the officers had orders to set fire or blow up the bridge, and to retreat to Moore Crossing, Tennessee.

Some two days after they had arrived at Long Island, Mr. McBurney's wagon and wares arrived at their camp. The fourth day after Mr. McBurney arrived, George Thompson returned after drawing the mid day rations, and informed David that they and twelve others had been detailed for picket duty on the Tennessee River at 9:00 p.m. that evening.

David immediately cooked his rations, ate his meal of hardtack and bacon, and set out for Mr. McBurney's tent. He tried to make himself walk slowly, and remembered to control his excitement as he approached the sutler's tent.

Mr. McBurney was dressed in gray pants, a checkered blue shirt, and a stovepipe hat that was half covered in road dust. He had a short stump of a cigar in his mouth, and he was unshaven. Nevertheless, he was a wonderful sight to David, because he was his ticket out of there.

David walked straight up and picked up an oilcloth cover for his kepi. Mr. McBurney had just finished selling a tin canteen to an officer when David walked up.

"What may I sell you today, my lad?"

"I would like to buy this oilcloth for my kepi, but I hope it's not too much. We haven't got paid yet, and I only have nine U.S. dollars."

That was the signal for the time that he would be on picket duty, and McBurney acknowledged it by giving David a wink.

"Well, you are in luck my good man, I will let you have that cover for three dollars, and here is six dollars U.S. back for your change."

David put the oilskin cover on his kepi, and walked back to his tent and began to pack his gear. He packed his oilskin, ground cloth, and blanket into his knapsack, and put his mess kit and other items into his haversack.

The troops detailed for picket duty that evening were to report to the corporal of the guard at 8:00 p.m. that evening.

At eight o'clock, David and George Thompson reported with their rifles and gear to the corporal of the guard, who was posted around one mile above the Memphis & Western Railroad bridge.

David and George were instructed to post a picket station about one mile north of the others in their party. This would enable them to watch for and listen out for any activity near the Tennessee state line, and upstream on the Tennessee River. They were detailed to walk picket duty until they were relieved at four a.m.

The river bottom was heavily wooded, with broadleaf trees such as White Oak, Hickory, Sweet Gum, Tulip Poplar, and Maple. The foliage was fully filled out, and the vegetation was thick enough to conceal friend or foe.

The Tennessee River at that point was split by a long wooded island known as Long Island, which was around one half mile wide. Long Island was around eight miles long, and lay in between the 57th Georgia Regiment and the town of Bridgeport, Alabama.

In order to protect the camp from surprise attack from the island, Captain Bonner ordered that two pickets be placed on Long Island with field glasses, in order to warn the others of invasion from the west.

David and George Thompson drew this assignment. They were given field glasses, and were rowed over to the island in two john boats. The river was fifty years wide on the east side of Long Island, and one hundred yards wide on the west side of the island. The river flowed generally from north to south, and the river current ran eight knots.

The corporal of the guard and two other men rowed David and George over to Long Island in separate john boats, leaving one boat on the east shore of the island for them to use on their return trip.

David could not believe the opportunity that now presented itself for his escape. He could not have planned it out any better than it was playing out at the moment. They were on an island, with a broad river at their front, in a lush river valley, surrounded by mountains that offered numerous places to hide.

The larger slope of Lookout Mountain behind the regiment would serve to screen out Confederate units that may come after him from Georgia. David told George that he would walk the picket post at the north end of Long Island. George had a post on the river around six hundred yards further south.

The quarter moon was beginning to rise over the eastern horizon when David started his guard duty. He pulled out his pocket watch and noted the time by the moonlight, which was nine fifteen. After an hour, it became completely dark, as all vestiges of the remaining sunlight from the dusk had gone. He saw Venus and Jupiter in the sky, and noted the Big Dipper above him.

A half hour later, he heard the distinctive call of the barred owl coming from across the Bridgeport side of the river.

"Who–cooks–for–you–who–cooks–for–you awl".

David knew that had to be James McBurney. He cupped his hands and gave the call that he was to make in reply:

"Who–who–who–who–who–who–who Awaw".

He then walked over to the western shore of the island, and began to look for a small boat. It was dark, but the moonlight from the quarter moon was sufficient enough to allow him to see several feet ahead on the riverbank.

He was apprehensive about walking up a riverbank at night, as he could step right on a Cottonmouth Water Moccasin and not realize it until he was bitten. He had walked fifty yards along the bank, when he saw a small john boat and boat paddle hidden under a willow tree.

He pulled the boat off the bank, and into the edge of the river, onto a sandbar. He was in the process of putting his knapsack into the boat when George Thompson walked up.

"David, what are you doing? What was that noise? Where are you going?"

David had to think fast, and utter a believable answer.

"There is a wounded Confederate soldier on the opposite bank of the river, and I am going to pick him up and bring him over here. You will need to row the other boat back to the other side of the river, and report to the corporal of the guard. Tell him what I am doing."

"Sure, no problem, I will report this to the corporal of the guard and request his instructions."

"I will be back shortly, George," David lied completely.

When George left, he put his rifle and gear in, lowered the boat into the current, grabbed the boat paddle, and shoved off. He began making strong paddle strokes in the eight knot river current, aiming the bow of the boat in a southwesterly direction, toward the Bridgeport side of the river.

The Tennessee River at that point was over two hundred yards wide. David found the boat drifting hard downstream in spite of all he could do with the paddle. Even his best effort with the paddle could not stop the river from pulling him downstream. David took the end of the boat paddle and made longer, deeper strokes into the water. He quickly determined that he had to paddle the john boat much differently in the river current than he would in the placid waters of a pond.

He made two strokes on the left side of the boat for every stroke made on the right. He fought the current, and slowly began to push the boat toward the west side of the Tennessee River. A few minutes later, the john boat was near the opposite shore. He searched for a level bank, and then landed and beached the boat. He withdrew his gun, knapsack and haversack, and piled them on the bank near a large Hickory tree.

He then pulled the boat a ways off the river bank, and hid it carefully behind a large Wax Myrtle bush. The heavy vegetation of the bush obscured the boat from any potential trackers that might come searching for him. He remembered to turn his uniform coat, and quickly turned the Union blue sleeves inside out. He donned the uniform jacket, reclaimed his rifle and gear, and began to walk toward the northwest. He figured that the powerful current had pushed him several hundred yards south of the position where he had heard Mr. McBurney from Long Island.

He walked through typical riverbank vegetation of that area, which consisted of Willow trees, Tulip Poplars, Water Oaks, Eastern White Pines, Maples, and Hickories. He went another hundred yards, and stopped to make the second prearranged signal to James McBurney.

They had agreed on a bird call, and on a call that they had all known. This was the call of a bird known as a Towhee, or in Georgia, as a Joe Reed. The bird had a brown back, a black head and neck, and red and white breast, and made a distinctive call that could be reproduced in the field. The bird was sometimes active at night, and after dark calling was not at all unusual.

David pursed his lips, and made the whistle of the Towhee. "Zreet, Zreet."

He listened intently, and presently heard a reply around fifty yards away. He paced steadily toward the area of the Towhee call, and heard horses snorting at twenty yards. He eased forward, and saw a bay gelding in the moonlight that looked familiar. He then saw James McBurney astride a chestnut colored mare, and holding the reins of the bay gelding. He stepped forward and immediately spoke, in a low tone of voice.

"I'm sure glad to see you."

McBurney took his hand, and also spoke softly.

"Glad you could join me. We need to make tracks before troops come over here to look for you. We need to get to the back side of Summerhouse Mountain. Mount up."

David took the reins from McBurney, and heaved himself up over the back of the saddle. He had trouble getting his right foot into the stirrup, because of his protruding haversack. His slung rifle and knapsack also impaired his ability to mount and ride efficiently.

They eased their animals into a trot, and moved north by west, and away from the riverbank. They went through a cane brake, and over and through two small creeks, getting their breeches wet up to their knees. They followed an old Indian path along a swift little creek that McBurney called Jones Creek. The creek soon became rocky and began to narrow, and McBurney soon led them to a small ford.

"We will need to dismount here and lead the horses across, Master David. The rocks are covered in moss, and can be slippery."

They dismounted, and carefully picked and waded through the ford by moonlight, leading their horses across. They let the horses take a drink, and then mounted up. They headed up toward the north and western edge of a small mountain McBurney identified as Summerhouse Mountain.

The terrain was higher than at the river, and the vegetation consisted mostly of hardwood trees, Cedars, and Eastern White Pines. White Oaks and Hickories and Ash were everywhere on the slopes of this mountain, offering numerous hiding places for friends and foes.

They crossed a small valley that McBurney called Dorian Cove, and crossed another small creek. They then began to follow another Indian trail that climbed the slope of an ever larger mountain which McBurney said was Montague Mountain.

They rode over three fourths of the way up to the summit of the mountain, when David noticed a camp fire glittering in between some large boulders on the mountainside. They proceeded a short distance closer, when they were hailed by a sandy haired boy of around twenty years of age.

"Halt, who goes there?"

"A friend of the Union. And of the Black Fox."

"Advance and be recognized."

They dismounted from their horses, and led them into the camp. There were ten men in the camp; some were dressed in Union blue uniforms, others in civilian clothes. Some of the men were eating, others were cleaning their weapons.

The tall, sandy-haired sentry quietly spoke.

"Mr. Looney, these men gave me the correct password. They are the men you have been looking for, I believe."

A short but wiry man seated near the fire stood up, and walked over to greet them. He was dressed in black jean cloth, and wore a black pigskin slouch hat. He answered the sandy haired boy, and went over to greet the newcomers.

"Thankee, James Day. Go ahead and stand your watch. I'll send Anderson over to spell you in three hours. Mister McBurney, we have been looking for you for two days. Where you been?"

McBurney walked over and took Looney's hand, and gave it a shake.

"I had to cross the river at the ferry at Stevenson, and leave my wagon at the livery stable there. I got Uriah's horse and a horse from the livery, and picked up young David here at the river. This is the boy that Uriah wrote you about. His Uncle Uriah gave me some equipment for him, and a letter of introduction for him. He told me to tell you to give the letter to the Federal enrolling officer at Huntsville or Decatur."

"I'll take care of that if you will get me the letter. So you're David Snelling? Your Uncle Uriah says you should be made an officer in the new cavalry regiment."

David walked forward and addressed William Looney directly.

"Yes, sir. He trained me himself. I would like the opportunity to serve my country."

"Well, serving your country is fine and good. Would you agree that the job of an officer is to see to the welfare of his men?"

"Yes sir, I do."

"And would you also agree that solving problems is part of an officer's job?"

"Sure, I do."

"Then tell me something, young David. We rode through a swamp today that was dried up on account of the drought, and the Deer Flies and Black Flies got on us and the horses, and damn near bit us to death. How would you solve that problem?"

David was caught off guard with that question.

"Well, for the bites themselves, Witch Hazel is good, and if we ever get to town, a poultice or salve made from the leaves of a Camphor Tree are good. My aunt made me up a salve from boiled sage and lard which may do you some good for the bites, too."

"Yeah, but what about the flies?"

"My Uncle Uriah told me that they were real bad down in Mexico. His dragoons took bacon grease left over from cooking, and mixed it with gunpowder, and daubed it on their faces and hands. He said the nitre in the gunpowder would keep the flies off of you."

"I knew Uriah would know how to deal with a problem like that. John Wilhite, wash out that empty bean can over there, and let's mix up some bacon grease and gunpowder."

David had been told about William Looney, and could not resist the opportunity to question him about the situation in Alabama.

"My Uncle Uriah told me that you have a price of $500.00 put on your head by the governor of Alabama, and a $700.00 bounty put on you by Jeff Davis himself, why is that?"

Bill Looney walked forward, picked up a Hickory stick, and began whittling it with his knife.

"It's a long story, boy, but it happened this way:

Back in '61, on July 4th, we called a meeting at a tavern I own in Winston County, just above the county seat of Houston. We had sent representatives to the secession convention in Montgomery that voted against secession, just like your Uncle Uriah. They got badly outvoted, and a lot of men in the North Alabama counties wanted to do somethin' about it.

We called a meeting, which we called the convention of Free Winston, and we declared all of Winston County to be the Free State of Winston. We had over 2600 men show up for this meeting. Word of our meeting got out to the governor, and he put a price on my head. They arrested me in Decatur and tried to hang me, but I escaped. If I ever see any one of those bastards that tried to string me up, I'll kill 'em on sight. Jeff Davis put a bounty on me after I escaped hanging in Decatur."

"How did you start recruiting men for the Union Army?"

"Your friend McBurney here was sent to me by the War Department. After Shiloh, they thought I could get some men out of the hills up here, and sign 'em up for the Union Army. All of these boys here came with me to join the new Union regiment of cavalry.

You know the Reb Congress passed the Conscription Act back in April. Ever since May, the Alabama Home Guards have been rounding up and arresting all men that refuse to fight with the Rebel Army. We sent out riders to all the counties in North Alabama. All able–bodied men who did not want to fight for the Rebels were told to hide in the mountains. That is why I came here to this county. I will be riding all over these mountains to recruit mountain men for the Union Army.

We have been asked to bring 'em all to Huntsville, where they can enlist in the new Federal cavalry regiment. Let me ask you a question."

"Yes, sir. Go ahead."

"You were born and raised on a plantation in Central Georgia. You saw the slave system first hand. You know the kind of money that can be made by planters on cotton plantations. Why fight on the other side?"

David considered the question, and proceeded to answer it carefully.

"That's a fair question. I love my country more than any system of agriculture, no matter how wealthy it could make me. I could never fight against the greatest government ever conceived in the history of man. I could not pledge my loyalty to a government that ignores the sanctity of a human soul.

I know you have corresponded with my Uncle Uriah, but that is what I believe. That is why I am here."

William Looney walked over and took his hand.

"Son, you are well spoken. You don't have to convince any of us as to why you are here. I just wanted these boys to hear some of the reasons for the hardships that they will endure. You men come up here and introduce yourselves, and tell young David where you're from, and what you do for a living."

The men lined up, and greeted him one by one; taking his hand, and pumping it hard, one time for each introduction:

After they were done, Bill Looney walked over, and resumed speaking.

"Boys, this young Snelling wants to serve with you. He wants a commission as an officer. Would you serve under him?"

Looney received many "yeas" to the question right off the bat.

"I thought so. I hope they appoint you, son. Right now, we got other problems to deal with. There is a regiment of Home Guards down in Gaylesville, riding north. We are gonna avoid them by riding over the mountains, even over the roughest trails, to get into the Union lines near Huntsville."

We need to get some rest. Mr. McBurney, do you have something to give me?"

"Yes, sir, Mr. Looney."

McBurney reached into his coat pocket, and handed Bill Looney David's letter of introduction.

"I will give this letter to the Federal enrolling officer at Huntsville. Mr. McBurney, you also have some more business with David?"

"Yes, sir. I have more equipment for him."

He walked over toward the campfire, and began to pull objects from a haversack.

"You can swap your brogans for these boots, and you can start packing this Colt now."

He handed David a pair of calf–high cavalry boots, and a Colt .36 caliber Navy revolver, with its gun belt and cartridge boxes.

"You might want to read the inscription on this gun, David."

To Major Uriah Snelling, for valuable services rendered to the United States. Jefferson Davis, Secy. Of War.

David read the inscription aloud.

"This was his prize possession. I can't believe he would part with this pistol."

William Looney walked up.

"Did you hear him read that, boys? Good 'ol Uriah wants Jeff Davis to eat his words now. It's up to us and David to make him eat those words!"

"How did you know my Uncle Uriah, Mr. Looney?"

"He saved my cousin's life at Buena Vista in Mexico. Cousin Ed always told us that Uriah Snelling was a wizard in the saddle. I hope that some of his knowledge has been rubbed off onto you."

"I think so."

"Then I feel a whole lot better about our boys' chances in this war. Let's all get some rest, we'll leave at first light. Go ahead and feed up and water your stock."

When he returned from the animals, the men were banking up the campfire. He began to unroll his bedroll and stretch out. David carried his Colt Navy pistol to his haversack, and placed the gun belt beside his bedroll. He swapped the boots for his brogans, and placed the brogans in his haversack.

His new life as a Union soldier was about to begin. They only had to get to Huntsville.

Chapter Eleven

The next morning, they rose at dawn, and began to eat a breakfast of hard tack, beef jerky, and cold water. They saddled their horses, and began a single file descent down Montague Mountain. David now realized that the bay gelding he was riding belonged to Uriah Snelling. He eased behind Mr. McBurney's mount, and began to question him about the horse.

"Why did Uriah send this horse out here with you?"

"He wanted to make sure that you were well mounted, Master David. In case the animal is bought into the army, he gave me a bill of sale to give you. I'll give it to you when we get down to the valley."

The small party of troopers had smeared their hands and faces with a mixture of gunpowder and bacon grease to ward off the flies and mosquitoes.

They went down the mountain to a creek near Jeffries Cove, where they filled their canteens, and watered their animals. Mr. McBurney gave David the bill of sale for Uriah's horse when they halted.

They then took a series of trails that led over another mountain, which the horses climbed at a slow walk. When they reached the summit of the small mountain, William Looney passed the word for David to ride over to him.

"Get out your field glasses, David, and see if there is any Home Guards or Reb cavalry down in that valley. I fear that some scouts may have made it over to Stevenson."

David looked down into the valley, but saw no militia or Confederate troopers. They resumed their trek over the mountain, and arrived at Collins Spring late that afternoon. They made camp at Collins Spring, and arose the next morning and rode southwest, toward Dudley Pond Mountain.

When they got to Crow Creek, Mr. McBurney parted ways with them.

"I must get back to Stevenson and get my wagon at the livery stables. I have a shipment of pikes to get out of the depot at Rome."

David thanked him for his assistance, and Mr. McBurney rode down the valley toward Stevenson.

They continued over the mountains, crossing Big Coon Creek, and taking a narrow path up the rocky face of Crow Mountain. They rode over the ridge of the mountain, and began to descend into the valley the following afternoon. The trail led out into a large field at the base of Crow Mountain, near Mud Creek.

They rode past a large barn built of split lumber, and faded by the weather. Around the barn and adjoining field of corn was a fence made of split rails, stacked up to chest height. The rails were in staggered rows, contouring to the slope of the field. Each rail in the fence was at least eight feet in length.

A large cabin stood around forty yards from the barn. Smoke was rising from its chimney. A small sandy–haired boy, and a thirteen year old boy were playing with a yellow dog on the front porch.

As they rode up to the cabin, the dog began to bark, and a man came out the door with a flintlock rifle in his hands. When William Looney came into sight, the man smiled, and put up his right hand.

"I know you, Bill Looney, long time no see. What brings you up to these parts?"

"I know you, too, Joe McClusky. I am bringing men with me to Huntsville to enlist in the Union Army. We are just passing through here, but we are looking for all able–bodied men we can find. Are you interested in joining up?"

"Let's eat supper first, and then talk about it. Gail has made some beef stew, and she can make another pan of biscuits for y'all. Y'all tie your horses over on the rail fence, and go wash up at the well. I'll get you a towel and some lye soap."

They were eager for a hot meal, and just could not pass up the welcome invitation. Joseph's boys, Allen and Michael, helped them feed and water their animals. They then washed up at the well, and stepped up to the porch to get their supper of beef stew and biscuits.

Gail had made a fresh pot of Sassafras tea, and began pouring it into cups to serve all of the men. David helped her serve the men their meal of beef stew and biscuits on carved wooden plates. Gail was a dark–haired beauty of twenty five years, with brown eyes, and high cheekbones.

She was dressed in a green calico dress, and wore a woven straw hat tied down with a green ribbon. David could picture her, as lovely as she was, walking arm in arm with a rich planter on the streets of Savannah, Georgia, wearing a beautiful imported dress. Instead, she was the hard working wife of a mountain man.

Joe McClusky was also dark haired, but had blue eyes. He was six feet tall, and had huge shoulders and biceps. His huge shoulders and biceps were the product of his hard work on his lovely farm. He was just the kind of man David wanted in the new regiment.

David walked over to Bill Looney, and made his case for recruiting Joe McClusky.

"He might not want to leave here to fight the Rebels."

"Sooner or later he'll have to fight, or the Confederate provost guards will arrest him. I'd much rather have him ride and fight with us, rather than against us."

"I understand, you're right. I'll talk to him about joining us."

About that time, Anderson Looney came up with young Allen McClusky, a dark haired boy of thirteen, who was wearing a homespun shirt and jean pants.

"Bill, young Allen here wants to know why they call you the Black Fox."

Bill Looney broke out in a grin, and motioned for the others to come in and listen.

"Y'all gather 'round. You're gonna want to hear this story."

Bill Looney took a sip of Sassafras tea, then stood up and cleared his throat.

"Well, there was this Cherokee chief from the mountains over near Guntersville that they used to call the Black Fox, that went by the name Chief John Looney. He went to Oklahoma Territory during the Trail of Tears, when the soldiers ran the Cherokees out of this state. When I was growing up, people that knew about Chief John Looney started calling me the Black Fox, 'cause I could track and shoot as good as any Indian.

Back in July of '61, after we had declared the Free State of Winston, the governor put a $500.00 bounty on my head. I got arrested by a company of Reb cavalry over near Decatur. Two Reb officers took me down to a hotel in Decatur, and they were gonna hang me the next day. They tied me to a bed in the hotel room.

Whilst they were a tying me up, I begged them officers to please send my grandpappy's whiskey home to my brother, 'cause it was his dying wish that us boys have some of his last batch of homemade liquor.

You see...I had a batch of homemade liquor in my haversack. Well, they took the bait real well, 'cause five minutes later, they started pouring my bottle of liquor into their tin cups and drinking it hard. They drank the whole bottle of liquor and passed out.

I worked the knots in my ropes loose; tied my bedclothes together, and climbed out the second story window. When I got to the ground, I picked up a piece of charcoal, and wrote on the wall of the building: 'The Old Black Fox is gone again!'"

The men began to laugh, and some laughed so much that they were doubled over.

Bill Looney then went over to Joe McClusky, put his hand on his shoulder, and began to speak to him in a softer tone of voice.

"Joe, I have known you for many years, and we have had some fun and some good times, but now I need to speak to you about something more serious..."

"If its about the Sassafras tea, well I was down at the store last month, and the price of coffee was absolutely outrageous, and..."

"Its not about the tea, Joe. It's about why we are all here. I am bringing these boys to Huntsville to enlist in the Union Army. In the Gospel of Matthew, Jesus told Simon Peter 'Follow me, and I will make you fishers of men.' Do you see that dark-haired young man in the blue uniform over there?

His name is David, and he has come all the way from Milledgeville, Georgia to enlist in the Union Army. Down the road from you, the Rebs are putting your friends and neighbors into prison because they love their country, and refuse to buy into secession.

You have a lovely wife, wonderful children, and a beautiful place. But right now your very freedom is in question. We want you to ride with us, and join the regiment with these boys in Huntsville. You have two horses. Bring one of them with you and come with us to Huntsville.

If you stay here, the Rebs will only come up and arrest you and put you into prison. Think about it tonight, and come go with us in the morning."

"Bill, I respect and appreciate you. I need to go inside and talk this over with Gail."

"I understand. David and Anderson and the boys can draw some water and wash these dishes. Go ahead and speak to her now."

They washed the dishes, unrolled their bedrolls, and slept out near Joe's rail fence, under the stars. Just before David eased off to sleep, he heard the call of a Barred Owl off toward the side of Crow Mountain.

* * * * *

They arose the next morning and fed and watered their horses. David and Anderson Looney helped Gail McClusky prepare a breakfast of sliced bacon, biscuits, and grits for all of the soldiers. She served them hot biscuits with Wild Plum jelly, grits with butter, and smoked bacon for their breakfast.

They washed their breakfast down with fresh milk from the McClusky's Jersey cow. After they had cleaned the bowls and dishes, David asked Gail if Joe McClusky had made his decision.

"Yes, he has. He is going to enlist with you. Be careful and watch out for him. I want him to return home to his family."

"I would think that you would have persuaded him to stay with you, ma'am."

"No, as long as he is here, the Rebels and provost guards would never let him stay in peace. We don't care about secession. We didn't want any part in their war. If they had left us alone, it would have been fine. The only way my Joe will ever have any peace is if them Rebels are whipped for good."

David thanked Mrs. McClusky for her hospitality, and he and the other men began to saddle their horses. Joe McClusky saddled his horse while Gail packed his haversack. He led his horse around the barn and over toward the cabin. He then called for his sons, and asked them to join him. He bent down and hugged his sons, and told them he had to go off to the Union Army, but that he would be back in a year or two.

He told his oldest son, Allen, to be the man of the house while he was gone, and to plow and gather the crops, and mind his Ma. He hugged and kissed his sons, and stood up and slung the flintlock rifle and haversack that Gail handed him over his left shoulder. She gave him his cartridge box, slouch hat, and canteen, and a bundle of food to take with him on the trip. He grabbed her, kissed her deeply, and whispered sweet promises into her ears.

She cried when he mounted his black mare, and began to ride off with the others. David cried some tears for her and her boys, too. If such good men wanted to ride and fight with him, he owed their families a debt he could never repay.

* * * * *

They rode down the side of the mountain into a broad river valley that Bill Looney called Paint Rock Valley. Looney warned of an increased risk of running into provost guards or Reb cavalry here, because the valley was like a funnel which narrowed as it approached Huntsville. As they passed Jacobs Mountain, they encountered some clouds and rain. David and the other men broke out their oilskins and black rubber raincoats.

They rode another twelve miles or so past Jacobs Mountain, on the south side of the Paint Rock River. Near Bingham Mountain, across from the little town of Trenton, they encountered three mounted Home Guards dressed in gray uniforms, with gray kepis.

Bill Looney was riding out at the head of the column, and Anderson Looney was riding behind him. In the blink of an eye, before the Home

Guards could draw rein or draw weapons, Bill Looney grabbed his Adams revolver from his belt, and fired two rounds. They hit the first two riders in the chest. Anderson Looney threw up his carbine and shot the third Home Guard in the chest.

Anderson Looney rode over to the first dead militiaman, who was an officer. Bill Looney just rode his horse past the man's body, as if it were not there. The dead officer was wearing braid on his sleeve that indicated he was a major or a captain.

"Who was that officer, Bill? You just rode by him like he was nothing."

"Look here, Anderson. That is Major Philip Walker, one of those men that tried to hang me down in Decatur. I told you the next time I saw him that I'd kill him.

David, they were headed up the trail toward that cave up yonder. Take two men and see if they were after any of our Union boys."

"Yes, sir."

David and the Jett brothers rode halfway up the mountain to a large cave that had a wide and tall entrance. He dismounted, and walked into the mouth of the cave.

The only way he could make contact with anyone hidden there was to call out for them.

"Hello—Bill Looney is here. Y'all come on out. It's safe now. The Home Guards are gone."

A few moments later, two young men walked out of the cave, carrying little more than haversacks and pistols. David wasted no time introducing himself and the Jett brothers to the men.

A black haired, skinny young man spoke first.

"I'm Eli Hughes, from Madison County. This here's Thomas Wiley. We both farm the same patch of bottomland in Madison County."

Thomas Wiley was red haired and freckle faced, and was also nineteen years old. He spoke next.

"Both of our Pas gave us permission to enlist in the new regiment and fight the Rebs. We were on our way to Huntsville to join up when we seen them Home Guards a tracking us. Y'all got here just in time."

"You can ride double with the Jett boys. We got some mounts for you when we get down to the river."

They rode back down the mountain, and joined the rest of the party below in the Paint Rock valley. The men had caught the horses the guardsmen were riding, and had them tied off to small trees. Bill Looney had the new men mounted on the militiamen's horses. David led the other horse, as they rode past Gurley Mountain, and avoided the small town of Gurley, for fear of Confederate cavalry patrols.

It began to rain again, and they once again broke out their oilskins and rain slickers. Anderson Looney rode up to David, and handed him a pistol and some cartridges.

"We got this pistol and shells off one of the dead Rebels back there. Bill told me to give 'em to you. He says an Adams double–action pistol is good to have in a pinch. Especially when it's raining. These pistols use metal cased shells, see? He says it could mean the difference between living and dying."

David thanked Anderson and his brother for the Adams revolver, and shoved the pistol into his belt. He put the box of cartridges into his coat pocket. They continued riding down the old Gurley Road, within eye shot of the Memphis & Western Railroad tracks.

A few miles down the road, near Chapman Mountain, they were hailed by Federal sentries, manning a picket post with five men. Bill Looney gave the correct password, and they rode down the old Gurley Road into the corporate limits of the town of Huntsville.

They rode past the courthouse, and over to the Huntsville Depot, a sandy colored three story brick building with dark shutters. Bill Looney directed them to the Federal Army headquarters there.

As they dismounted, David looked up to the flag pole, and saw Old Glory flying at its top. He had not seen that flag since January of 1861. Tears streamed down his cheeks as he dismounted from the bay gelding. He stood at attention and saluted Old Glory. The other men in their party dismounted, and did the same.

Chapter Twelve

(David makes his first journal entry, in the form of a serial letter to his Uncle Uriah and Aunt Faith:)

August 13, 1862
Huntsville, Alabama

Dear Uncle Uriah and Aunt Faith:

I finally made it to the U.S. Army Headquarters at Huntsville. Mr. Bill Looney gave your letter of introduction to the enrolling officer, a Captain William Bankhead of the Fifth U.S. Infantry. I am sorry to say that he later told me that the current quota of lieutenants had been filled, and he could not authorize a commission for me as of yet. He did promise me a commission, though, once an opening becomes available.

If more regiments are recruited, for instance, that would create a need for another officer or officers to command companies. One of the officers on General Buell's staff knew you, and said that your recommendation of me was as good as gold to the Army.

We rode into town with thirteen men (including myself) who joined the new regiment. Bill Looney immediately went back into the mountains to recruit more soldiers for the new regiment. His brother, Anderson Looney, was made first sergeant of our new company. The other men that rode over with us have also enrolled in our outfit. We are now Company "D", in the First Middle Tennessee Cavalry.

They issued me a sky blue pair of double–seated uniform pants, with a yellow stripe down the outside of the pants leg. I also got a gold cavalry insignia of crossed sabers, and a gold numeral "1", which I proudly sewed onto the top of my kepi with Aunt Faith's sewing kit. I also got a pair of braces for my new pants.

Captain Thomas Jones is in command of the company. We also have a first lieutenant, William Beasley. I have been enrolled as a private, and that is all right for now. We drill as a company in the mornings, draw rations at mid–day, and have inspections in the evening hours. I have been on two scouting expeditions (or "scouts", as we call them), since I arrived the last week of July. Over two hundred men have enlisted in the new regiment over the last month, and more are coming into the depot building every day.

I will write you two installments per week, so you will have some idea about my times in the service.

Until next time, I am

Sincerely yours,
David

* * * * *

The rest of the month of August, 1862, was business as usual, until the 29th, when Anderson Looney came over to David's dog tent that they shared, and informed him of new orders.
"Well, William just got back, and told the general officers that General Bragg has crossed the Tennessee River with twenty five regiments, and artillery. This was at Chattanooga. We got orders to pack up and march toward Stevenson, and take the cars north through Decherd to Murfreesboro and Nashville."
"Didn't the infantry capture Stevenson several weeks ago?"
"Yeah. They turned it into a big supply depot from the supply line up in Louisville. John Morgan and Bedford Forrest cut the rail roads twice, and now Bragg's whole army's marching north, and we gotta go after him."
"Have you talked to Lieutenant Beasley since you heard about the orders?"
"Not yet. He's been down at the latrines most of the morning. That man has had dyspepsia and stomach problems ever since he enlisted. I don't think he has the stomach for the army."
"Well, he is thirty five years old. I wonder if he'll have even less of a stomach for combat."

"You said it David, I didn't. You better go ahead and pack up your haversack and knapsack, brother. We'll pull out at first light on the first."

"Yes, Sergeant Looney."

David looked at the four stripes on Anderson Looney's sleeve as he turned to walk away from the dog tent. James Day had been elected fourth sergeant by the men, as there were five sergeants and eight corporals in the company. He just had to wait his turn for promotion.

Late that afternoon, David learned that the other company, Company E, was also ordered to Nashville. After drawing his afternoon ration, David took his bay gelding from the corral, and led him over to the company farrier, James Johnson. James was a strapping man of six feet two inches and twenty five years that could handle horses well. He was also adept at trimming the horses' hooves, and kept all of the horses in both companies well shod.

David brought the bay gelding over, and asked James to check his shoes, and to trim out the horse's hooves. David wasted no time in getting this done, since he knew that Johnson's services would soon be in demand by others in Companies D and E. When James Johnson was done with the bay gelding, David gave him a U.S. greenback dollar, and genuinely thanked him for his efforts.

The companies were later told to draw three days rations, and an additional three days of rations were packed away in the wagon trains that were to follow the troopers to Nashville. They moved out two mornings later.

The men were ordered to stand for roll call, and then drew and cooked their morning rations, and fed and watered their horses. The buglers then sounded "Boots and Saddles" and then "Assembly". The officers inspected the troopers as they stood at attention with their mounts. Another order was given to "mount". Captain David Smith then gave the order to "move by the left flank, column of twos", and "forward march". This caused the two companies of troopers to march up the road in a column, with two riders moving abreast of the other.

They followed the rear guard of the infantry, which was an Indiana regiment, out the Gurley Road, along the Memphis & Charleston Railroad tracks. They followed the railroad bed generally, easing out by Splitrock Mountain. They rode on flanks of the blue–coated infantry until their horses became winded.

Captain David Smith was in command of the two companies. He was 37 years of age, and was an imposing six feet tall. He had long side whiskers, and wore a Hardee style black felt hat. He was born in Henry

County, Georgia, and transferred from the 21st Ohio Volunteers to take command of Company E.

He gave the orders to the column to dismount and walk the horses. Anderson Looney gave the order for David's squadron to dismount, and walk the animals. They began walking beside an Indiana regiment of infantry. David noticed how the road dust settled on the men's blue uniforms. They marched with a determined pace. All of the men were determined to reach Nashville before General Bragg's Rebel army.

Anderson Looney soon noticed a tall red haired sergeant major leading a company of infantry down the Gurley Road. The sergeant major had four yellow stripes at the top of the chevron on his sleeve, and three yellow stripes on the bottom. He was large and muscular, and wore a tall forage cap with the infantry horn insignia on the front. Each of the infantrymen had fully packed knapsacks and haversacks, and were all armed with Springfield rifles.

Anderson could not pass up the opportunity to speak to the sergeant major. He walked beside him, and engaged him in conversation.

"Sure is hot dusty weather for marching, ain't it?"

The sergeant major looked up.

"You got a southern accent. Is this the outfit they call the First Middle Tennessee Cavalry?"

"Yes, sir. That would be us."

"And most of you are from North Alabama?"

Anderson spat out a mouthful of dust onto the ground.

"That's right. Most of us, anyway."

"If you don't mind my asking, why fight on our side? Since you are from the South?"

"That's a fair question. We don't want the country to break up into a bunch of little kingdoms. And we are against secession. Why do you fight, if you don't mind my asking. To free the slaves?"

The sergeant major's face turned red.

"Hell no! We don't give a damn about the Niggers. We don't want New Orleans to be a foreign port. We want the Mississippi River opened up permanently. We also want the Union restored, but we are fighting mainly over the river. We want a free river for our commerce and traffic."

"I understand. I'm glad we are on the same side. We'll be chewing on the same piece of dirt before long. You take care, soldier."

"You too, cavalry. Nice talking to ya."

The order soon came for the column to mount up, and they rode ahead past Pikeville, and set up a bivouac for the night. They ate their rations cold that evening, and a picket was detailed from Company E. The men unsaddled their horses and slept under the stars.

* * * * *

The bugler sounded reveille the next morning at four a.m. The troopers arose and fed the horses from the forage in the supply wagons. They watered the animals from the nearby creek. They then drew their own rations and cooked a breakfast of boiled coffee, bacon, and hardtack fried in bacon grease. The men washed up their fry pans and mess kits, and readied themselves for the day's march.

David and some of the other cavalrymen saved some hot water from breakfast for shaving each morning. David had remembered Uriah's advice, and had begun to grow a mustache. Some of the men went into the nearby mountain stream to wash themselves.

An hour later, the bugler sounded "Boots and Saddles". Each trooper caught his mount, folded a blue saddle blanket on his horse's back, and saddled the animal with a McClellan saddle. They then slipped the horse's bridle into place, and placed the bit into the horse's mouth. Each trooper then took the reins and mounted up.

When Captain Smith sounded the order to advance at the walk, David noticed that they had once again slipped behind the rear guard infantry of Buell's army. The day was cloudy, and was also hazy, as the troops and troopers marched past McCoy Mountain and Cotton Mountain, and marched toward the looming Poorhouse Mountain.

At four o'clock in the afternoon, they marched past Walker Mountain, and were approaching the town of Stevenson. A mile further in toward town, Captain Smith was hailed by a major on horseback. Major Daniel Grayson, who was an assistant adjutant general on General Buell's staff, discussed their marching orders with Captain Smith. Major Grayson instructed Captain Smith to bivouac the companies of cavalry in the forest just south of Stevenson.

The cavalry companies were to report to the train depot the next morning a nine a.m., and board the cars for a ride on the Nashville & Chattanooga Railroad line into Nashville. They went into bivouac in the woods just south of town, and a picket line was detailed from Company D. Around nine o'clock that night, David unrolled his bedroll and stretched out. He was serenaded by the snoring of Anderson Looney. He counted stars until he got drowsy, and then he fell asleep.

* * * * *

The next morning was hazy and warm. After rations were drawn and cooked, Captain Smith, Anderson Looney, and the other officers conducted roll call for each of the men of Companies D and E. "Boots and Saddles", sounded at seven a.m. At eight a.m., the companies mounted their horses and moved out, marching in a column of twos into Stevenson.

David and Anderson had already said their goodbyes to Bill Looney, who had cooked his ration and headed west after daylight. They soon arrived at the train station, where an engine with a wide cowcatcher and balloon shaped smokestack was waiting. The train had a long line of boxcars, cattle cars, and flatcars, and passenger cars for the men. The rear guard regiment of Indiana infantry had marched in an hour beforehand, and had loaded into several of the cars near the front of the train.

The troopers were instructed to unsaddle their horses, and to stack their saddles and blankets in two boxcars. The bits and bridles were to be rolled up and tucked under each saddle.

The horses were loaded into separate cars with stalls, and then the troopers loaded into passenger cars with their weapons and gear. A Lieutenant Hoskins of the U.S. Military Railroads assisted them with loading their horses and saddles on the train. There was even an adequate supply of flat cars to allow them to load their supply wagons and ammunition wagons on the train.

The mules were put into separate cattle cars for transport into Nashville. All of the animals were fed and watered immediately prior to loading, and would be fed and watered at various intervals along the way.

The wagons and animals were not loaded and secured until twelve thirty. The train did not pull away from the Stevenson station until one p.m.

It was twelve miles to the Tennessee state line via the railroad, and then another seventy five miles to Murfreesboro via Decherd, Tullahoma and Wartrace. The men ate cold hardtack and drank water from their canteens for their dinner. The troop train began its slow pull up through the mountain gaps toward Decherd.

On the way, David and Anderson Looney made conversation with Sergeant James Day, who shared their seat on the passenger car.

"Some of those Indiana infantrymen said that General Buell had to get out of Alabama 'cause Bedford Forrest and John Morgan's cavalry wrecked the railroad lines at Murfreesboro and at Gallatin."

"Well, Jim, that's what I heard, too. They said Forrest wrecked some bridges at Murfreesboro, but Buell had them rebuilt and the line repaired in one week."

David had been told even more about General Buell's troubles.

"I was told that Morgan and his men set fire to a bunch of boxcars at Gallatin, and pushed 'em into a tunnel, and it burned up the timbers in the tunnel, and made it cave in. That put the L&N Railroad out of business, I was told."

Anderson was amused.

"What fiendish business, destroying railroads in the name of war. Morgan is a devilishly clever man."

"A man after your own heart, Anderson?"

"I don't believe that I could be so clever."

"We may have to be one day, my friend."

David did not know how true his words would be until later on in the war.

* * * * *

Their train was overloaded, and did not pull into Murfreesboro until around six p.m. The train had to take on fuel and water at Murfreesboro, and Lt. Hoskins went into each of the cars and told the men that they were to stop for two hours, in order to let the transport trains in Nashville clear the station up there.

The slim Lieutenant Hoskins suggested that the men walk into the nearby woods and cook their rations. They were issued a ration of canned beans, coffee, and bacon that could be cooked immediately. Hoskins told the men that he would see that they had plenty of time to eat their rations before the train would leave the station.

Captain Smith passed the word for the officers and sergeants to meet at the station platform. James Day and Anderson Looney slipped out of their seats in the passenger car, and left for the officers' meeting.

David went out into the woods with the others, gathered some firewood, and proceeded to cook his ration of coffee, beans, and bacon. After he had finished his meal, Anderson and James Day walked up.

"We had to water and feed the stock before we could join you for grub. We got another problem, David."

"What is that?"

"We got to find Lieutenant Beasley. The semimonthly reports and company returns are overdue. If headquarters don't have those returns when we report, they will stop all of our pay. Do you know where he is?"

"He's down in one of the train cars, puking up into a slop bucket. I guess riding on a steam train does not agree with him."

"Don't tell me that, man. I gotta get those reports done or it's my ass."

"Relax, Anderson. I have a degree from Franklin College. I think I can handle your reports without too much difficulty. Where are your muster rolls and your report forms?"

"In my haversack here."

Anderson pulled out the muster roll books, and the printed semimonthly return forms and handed them to David.

"Do you have a pencil, Anderson?"

"Yeah, let me dig around in this haversack."

After a few minutes of fumbling around in his haversack, Anderson handed David two small pencils.

"I'll go up to the depot where it's well lit, and sharpen these pencils with my penknife, and get these returns and reports filled out for you. Do you want to sign them? Or do you want me to sign Lieutenant Beasley's name to them?"

"Let me sign 'em. We'll put Beasley's name on the next set of semimonthly reports we'll do."

"Good enough. Y'all get some grub down you. We will be pulling out in a couple of hours."

David walked up to the train depot, where he could sit and complete the company returns and reports. Anderson and James Day began cooking their ration of coffee, canned beans, and raw bacon.

"You know Jim, David really ought to be in command of this company. If I ever get a chance, I'm gonna find a general officer and put in a good word for him."

"Do you really mean that, or are you just happy that you got your reports done?"

"I really mean it. If you ever get the chance, talk him up to Captain Smith. A little wire pulling goes far in this army sometimes."

"I understand. You got those beans hot yet?"

The men ate their rations, and stowed their mess kits after washing them out with water from their canteens. They boarded the train with plenty of time to spare before it left the station for Nashville.

* * * * *

The train pulled into the depot in Nashville just after midnight. They unloaded their saddles, blankets, and bridles, and saddled and bridled their horses by the moonlight. They then rode their horses and the supply wagons followed the two companies down the Nolensville Pike. They marched almost two miles to Camp Campbell, a large camp of dog tents and cabins on Brown's Creek.

Each pair of troopers claimed a dog tent, and they unsaddled and picketed their horses by tying them off to a series of pre tied lines behind the camp. The men cached their equipment in their dog tents, stacked arms in the common areas, and got some much needed rest.

The following morning after roll call, Sergeant Anderson Looney was ordered to report to the regimental headquarters building, a crudely built wooden structure near the front of the camp. He was led into the office of the colonel. Colonel William B. Stokes, the commanding officer of the First Middle Tennessee Cavalry, had summoned Sergeant Looney for the purpose of reviewing the muster rolls and semimonthly reports of Company "D".

Looney handed the reports and muster rolls to Colonel Stokes, a six foot tall officer with dark hair and a short dark beard. The colonel had an unlit cigar in his mouth, and reviewed the muster rolls and semimonthly reports carefully while Sergeant Looney stood at attention, with his slouch hat under his arm.

"Sergeant, these reports and muster rolls were not only well done, they were clearly written and legible. I know you had some help with them. Who helped you prepare these? Keep in mind when you answer this question that I know Captain Jones went to the hospital today with typhoid fever. Lieutenant Beasley also went over there. He has the worst case of the trots I have ever seen."

"A private in our company named David Snelling wrote those reports, sir. He is college educated. He even brought over a letter of introduction from his uncle, Uriah Snelling, who was a major in the U.S. Army during the last war."

"One of my officers graduated from West Point when Uriah Snelling was the cavalry instructor there. Who has that letter, Sergeant Looney?"

"Captain Bankhead gave all of those types of letters and documents to Captain Smith of Company E, sir. It was to be sent up with the headquarters papers."

"You see, sergeant, Washington is putting a great deal of pressure on the army to attack the Rebels and close out the war. We need all the capable officers we can get, and we need them now. Would David Snelling make a good officer in your company?"

"Oh, yes sir, I believe he would."

"Well, you need to know what is going to happen. Captain Jones and Lieutenant Beasley are going to be discharged out of the service on account of health reasons. It takes over one year to properly train a cavalryman. It takes more than one year to train a good cavalry officer. I don't have a year. I need a man that I can rely on right now.

We are mustering in four other companies of the First Middle Tennessee Cavalry. We will be ordered to engage the enemy immediately. I need to review that letter of introduction from Uriah Snelling now.

Sergeant Major Withers!"

"Yes, sir."

A burly man with long red side whiskers and red hair entered the room, and saluted Colonel Stokes.

"Go to Captain David Smith, and ask him to please forward the headquarters packet to me at once."

"Yes, sir."

"That will be all for now, Sergeant Looney. You are dismissed."

"Thank you, sir."

Looney saluted and spun around, and headed out toward the Company D area. He had done his share of wire pulling for David. He walked back to his dog tent, whistling a merry tune. He was hopeful that his wire pulling had paid off for his friend.

* * * * *

The remainder of the month of September was one of activity and preparation for the First Middle Tennessee Cavalry regiment. They spent most of that month preparing the fortifications around Nashville, and scouting the roads and pikes around Nashville for enemy cavalry patrols.

Chapter Thirteen

Camp Campbell, Tennessee
October 10, 1862

Dear Uncle Uriah and Aunt Faith:

An opportunity has arisen that creates an opening for an officer in my company.
Captain Thomas Jones was taken ill with typhoid fever, and is so sick that the post physician has discharged him from the service. Lieutenant William Beasley was also examined by the same physician, and was discharged from the army on account of dyspepsia.

Sergeant Looney claims that he has done some "wire pulling", for me with Colonel William Stokes, who commands the First Middle Tennessee Cavalry regiment. I have discussed my appointment as first lieutenant with the colonel, who says that he will recommend me for a commission to General Buell when the army returns from Kentucky.

We have drawn a number of strange duties since we have been posted here. We have guarded supply wagons and gunboats, and have assisted the provost guard in policing the streets of Nashville. We even saw the new governor of Tennessee the other day. Mr. Andrew Johnson is a tall, dark haired man, who maintained a serious countenance the entire time we were near the State Capitol building. We were ordered near the Capitol to assist in the construction of breastworks and lunettes for the artillery pieces.

Governor Johnson was appointed by President Lincoln after Nashville was captured last Spring. He has authorized the raising of many regiments of Union cavalry and infantry from Tennessee. Our own Colonel Stokes was commissioned by Governor Johnson. I have had a chance to read several New York newspapers, and issues of *Harper's Weekly* since we have been posted here. It seems that in Virginia, the war has not gone well for the Union. General McClellan drove General Lee's army out of Maryland after a huge battle at Antietam Creek. The War Department is claiming this was a victory, but the casualty figures make this by far the bloodiest day of the war. You were right about General Robert Lee. He is by far the best soldier in America.

The colonel has a substantial library in his quarters, and he allows some of the men in the regiment to borrow and read his books. Last week after duty hours, I read *Bleak House*. Next week, I will read *A Tale of Two Cities*. We have been ordered to construct wooden sides for our dog tents in contemplation of the winter season. I have been helping the regimental carpenters with this work.

A number of the men have become ill with the measles, typhoid fever, and even smallpox. Most of the men in the regiment are small farmers, and have never been in large towns before, or even around large groups of people. Some of the latrines are not well placed. The lack of decent sanitation in some of the camps, and susceptibility of some of the troops to disease has caused widespread illness in the regiment.

We have lost more good men to illness and disease than to enemy action. I need to finish this letter now. I have volunteered to go out and round up some beef cattle from the countryside in the morning.

Until next time, I am

Sincerely yours,

David

* * * * *

On November 7, 1862, after roll call and morning mess, David was summoned to Colonel Stokes' quarters. He knew that he was being considered for promotion, but he had not yet been notified by his commanding officer. He brushed out his uniform coat, shined his boots and saber, and marched up to Colonel Stokes' quarters. He received a smile from the sentry, and was greeted by Captain David Smith, who was serving as regimental adjutant that week.

"Snelling. We've been expecting you. Go on in. Colonel Stokes has something for you."

He gave David a wink and a nod, as he opened the door and entered the makeshift office of Colonel William Stokes. The colonel's quarters consisted of a small three room frame building, which had a porch built across its front. He saluted the colonel, and stood at attention.

"At ease, Snelling. The headquarters staff of General Rosecrans has approved and issued your commission as a first lieutenant in the First Middle Tennessee Cavalry. Congratulations, son. You will be eating with the officers now. I have four cloth patches with your first lieutenant's bars here for you to sew onto your uniform jackets. In the meantime, I'm going to ask Captain David Smith for some assistance, and we're gonna pin you on a set of lieutenant's bars right now."

He stepped to the door and called for Captain Smith. Captain Smith came in with a smaller cloth patch for each of David's shoulders that contained the bars of a first lieutenant.

They quickly pinned the patches on David's uniform jacket. David saluted Colonel Stokes.

"Thank you for giving me this opportunity, sir."

"Snelling, the reports that you and Sergeant Looney have forwarded us are the best done in the regiment. But we need much more from you than the services of a first rate clerk. We are expecting big things from you, son. Since you will be in command of your company, you will be entitled to draw the pay of a company commander, starting today."

"Thank you, sir."

"There's another thing. Here is your written commission, by the way."

He handed David the coveted commission, which was on rolled up parchment paper.

"Since you will not have a captain over you, the U.S. Army regulations require that a second lieutenant be appointed to serve under you. It is my understanding that the men of your company took a straw poll to select a second lieutenant. Who did they select?"

"James B. Day, sir. He's a bright young man. He will do his best for us, sir."

"I'm sure he will. Captain Smith, write out a commission for Second Lieutenant James B. Day, and then pass the word for him to come here. We have another officer to appoint for Company D."

"Yes, sir. With pleasure, sir."

* * * * *

On November 4, 1862, the First Middle Tennessee Regiment of cavalry was ordered on a reconnaissance down the Franklin Pike below the Harpeth River. The weather had begun to turn colder, and the officers and enlisted men had been issued overcoats, which were paid for by deductions from their military pay.

The air was crisp and chilly as "Boots and Saddles" was sounded that morning, and the steam billowed from the horses' nostrils as they trotted down the Franklin Pike. Single scouts or vedettes had reported that Confederate Brigadier General Nathan Bedford Forrest was in the area with at least three regiments of cavalry, and two pieces of horse-drawn artillery.

The Unionists were in motion with seven companies of cavalry, ("A" through "G"), to find and attack the most able and feared of all Confederate cavalry commanders, Nathan Bedford Forrest.

Forrest was perhaps the most unusual military genius of the age. He would soon earn the nickname "Wizard of the Saddle". His motto was "Get there first with the most men."

On November 5, 1862, he had the most men, even though some of his troopers were out recruiting, and he was down to three regiments of cavalry. However, Colonel Stokes had only one regiment of cavalry, and he had to make the most of the men that he had at his disposal.

Colonel Stokes' cavalrymen crossed the Harpeth River below Nashville, and began to march south on the macadamized Franklin Pike. The air was crisp and still, and the leaves on the trees signaled that Autumn had arrived.

Just above the little town of Franklin, near Spencer's Creek, they ran head on into General Forrest's troopers, who had been ordered over from Smyrna on a reconnaissance in force.

Forrest's troopers were mostly veterans, whereas the First Middle Tennessee Cavalry Regiment consisted of mostly untried troopers. The lead companies of Union troops collided with General Forrest's lead companies on the Franklin Pike. General Forrest ordered an attack with his usual vigor, and Confederate cavalrymen began a charge up the pike with their sabers and pistols drawn.

Colonel Stokes' men began to fire on the troopers riding up the Franklin Pike, and emptied several saddles. More Confederate troopers charged up the pike, and Stokes' Union troopers were driven back gradually.

David's Company "D", and Captain Smith's "E" Company were ordered to guard the flanks of the regiment on the east side of the Franklin Pike. They were situated in a heavily wooded area, which was thick with small Sweet Gum trees, Water Oaks, and Hickory trees. A large cane brake was nearby, and led down toward Spencer's Creek. It was an excellent position, as they had a hill behind them, and a heavily wooded position that they could defend while dismounted.

David heard the gunfire on the pike, and saw the advantages of fighting on the wooded hill known as Roper's Knob. He had Sergeant Looney suggest to Captain Smith that they defend the ridge line while dismounted. Captain Smith rode over to confer with David, and began to scan the hill with his field glasses.

"You're right, David. We need to occupy that hill. It will give us an edge if we're attacked."

"I was just thinking, sir, that with the standard Springfield and Enfield rifles, the men would be better off fighting dismounted up there at the top of that ridge."

"I agree. Order every fourth man to stay back behind that ridge and to hold all four horses from each squad. Order the dismounted men to occupy the top of that wooded hill. My men will follow you."

"Yes, sir. Sergeant Looney, make it so."

The fourth man in each squad was ordered to hold all four horses, and three men from each squad grabbed their rifles and gear, and began to climb Roper's Knob. They each formed a skirmish line near the top of the ridge, loaded their rifles, and waited for the enemy.

A half hour later, small groups of gray backed cavalrymen began to advance in rushes toward Roper's Knob. David sent Private Jesse Davis out to look for Sergeant Anderson Looney. Anderson reported in several minutes later.

"Sergeant, I see Reb cavalry coming up on foot, in small groups. Pass the word down the line to each squad to open fire on my order when the Rebs get to seventy five yards of our position. Can you do that now?"

"Yes, sir."

"Go ahead and pass the word, then."

Looney passed the word to the troopers to open fire when the Rebs had closed to seventy five yards. The gray backed cavalrymen began to ascend Roper's Knob, and began firing at the blue coated troopers.

David had the men build a hastily constructed barricade out of fallen trees and rocks, and made the men lie down near the top of the hill. He cocked his Enfield rifle, and crouched down on one knee to await the

Confederate cavalry charge being made from below by dismounted troopers.

He saw a line of gray uniformed men advancing up the wooded slope of the hill. He waited several seconds until he thought they were seventy five yards away. He then gave the order to fire, and he pulled the trigger of his own rifle. The effect on the attackers was electric. Each of the rounds knocked cavalrymen down to the ground, leaving only a handful of men standing. They soon sought cover in the trees down the hill, and remained content to fire at them with shotguns and pistols. The Confederate troopers thought they were attacking an infantry column, because they were receiving fire from rifles, as opposed to shotguns and pistols.

General Forrest had succeeded in driving Colonel Stokes' mounted troopers back up the Franklin Pike, but received a written dispatch that his men were having trouble advancing up Roper's Knob. He ordered a staff officer to find the commander of the regiment that was advancing up the hill, and to have him order more men into the attack. He wanted to increase the pressure on the Union cavalrymen at the top of the ridge, and wanted his troopers to "put the skeer on 'em".

One hour later, David noticed even more troopers attacking them from the base of the hill. He ordered his men to fire at will, and to shoot any enemy troops in sight. The attack this time drew the Rebel cavalrymen closer in, where they were more effective with their pistols and shotguns. David's men began to get hit by shotgun pellets and pistol fire.

David's immediate position was again attacked, and he tossed his Enfield rifle down to the ground, and drew his Adams revolver. Two Confederate troopers began to charge his way, armed with sawed off shotguns. David aimed his Adams pistol at a gray haired trooper, and shot him in the chest. He shot the second trooper through his neck, and shot a third trooper in the chest a moment later.

Captain Smith's position was also attacked, and his company also drove General Forrest's cavalrymen off the ridge. The enemy troopers took their colors and withdrew down the ridge shortly after the smoke had cleared from their last assault. It soon began to grow dark, and David received a written order from Captain Smith.

The captain ordered him to withdraw his company down the back side of Roper's Knob two hours after sunset. David sent for Sergeant Looney, who walked down from near the summit of Roper's Knob.

"Report our status, First Sergeant Looney."

"No one dead, sir. No one missing. Five wounded, though. One is pretty serious."

"Who is that?"

"Corporal Al Bain, sir. He's shot in the gut."

"Rig a litter for him and the other wounded out of blankets and some of these little Sweetgum trees. Go ahead and carry the wounded down the hill behind our position. We have orders to pull out ourselves and get to the turnpike in two hours."

"Yes sir."

They got the wounded men down off the ridge, and soon began a complete withdrawal from Roper's Knob. After one o'clock, all of the troopers of Companies "D" and "E" were in the saddle, and were riding north on the Franklin Turnpike.

* * * * *

At four a.m. the following morning, General Nathan Bedford Forrest roused his Confederate troopers, and began to assemble his men for the march north on the Franklin Pike. He had been informed by his scouts that only two companies of Yankee troopers had held the crest of Roper's Knob. They had fought well, but now they were marching away from their covered positions, and were vulnerable to an attack from the rear.

His blood was up, and he was ready to move against the enemy with vigor that morning. If his men moved quickly, he could put the 'skeer' on them, and infect all of the Yankees with panic. If he played his cards right, he and his men would bag half of the Yankee troopers, and open up the Franklin Pike toward Nashville.

His brother, Captain William Forrest, a twenty two year old man with a light gray tunic and short beard, walked over to his campfire and handed him a dispatch.

"It's from General Bragg, sir. A courier just brought it in this morning. I thought you would like to see it right away."

He looked up at his handsome younger brother, and took the dispatch and opened the seal, and began to read:

Murfreesboro, Tennessee
November 5, 1862.

Brig. Gen. Nathan B. Forrest
Commanding Div. Cavalry Army of Tennessee
General:

You are ordered to throw your command rapidly over the Tennessee River, and precipitate it upon the enemy's lines, break up railroads, burn bridges, destroy depots, capture hospitals and guards, and harass him generally.

Two regiments of cavalry are ordered to rendezvous with you at Columbia, and you are to have a four gun battery of artillery. You are to cross the Tennessee River at Clifton, march thence to Lexington and Jackson, and on to Union City. Withdraw your command by way of Paris or Parker's Cross Roads.

Your obedient servant,

Braxton Bragg, General
Commanding Army of Tennessee

Forrest read the dispatch and fumed. Damn! And the Yankees on the pike were as good as in the bag! He controlled his conflicting and explosive emotions, and remembered his duty as a brigadier general.
"Will, get me two buglers. Have them sound recall now. Issue orders for the men to head south down the pike toward Columbia. We have to rendezvous there with two other regiments. General Bragg has given us business to tend to in West Tennessee."
"Yes, sir. Right away."
William Forrest saluted his brother, and carried out his commander's orders. Bedford Forrest mounted his horse, and turned his head south toward Columbia. "Oh, it's just as well", He thought to himself. He would fight these Yankee troopers another day. He knew it in his bones. The regiments soon formed a column of fours, and began to march south on the pike.
The horses blew steam from their nostrils as they carried their gray clad riders south toward Columbia, and down the turnpike.

Chapter Fourteen

Camp Campbell, Tennessee
December 8, 1862
Dear Uncle Uriah and Aunt Faith:
This is the first opportunity I have had to make a journal entry since we went on our scouting expedition on November 5th. We had a brief fight with two companies of dismounted cavalry commanded by General Nathan B. Forrest. We picked a strong position at the top of Roper's Knob off the Franklin Pike, and we drove off two companies that charged us on foot up the ridge.

We got away from that skirmish in pretty good shape, though we had some men wounded. Corporal Al Bain died of a gunshot wound this morning. Five other men died of cold and sickness after we returned to camp. Some of the men were ill at roll call this morning, and will probably be in the hospital later on. Anyhow, we took on Bedford Forrest, and lived to tell about it.

It has turned very cold up here. I expect it to snow or sleet well before January. The men should actually have gone into winter quarters already, but the War Department will not allow us to remain idle. I have read an edition of *Harper's Weekly* since we returned, and the present situation concerning the war has been made known to the troopers here.

We have lost men to cold weather and to illness. General William Rosecrans of Ohio is our new commanding general of the Army of the Cumberland. The army has built up rapidly around Nashville. There are over 80,000 soldiers here. Gen. Crittenden, Gen. Thomas, and Gen. McCook command the three army corps. We saw General Thomas off the Franklin Pike the other day. He is a large, heavy set man with an iron gray beard with a white streak in it. His soldiers call him "Pap". He sure looks like a Pap to me.

The army has piled up many stores and rations in anticipation of the coming campaign.

There is talk that we will be sent on a scout down to Franklin in search of Forrest's cavalry, and that could happen next week.

I have to go now, Lt. James Day and myself have to kill and issue a beef cow to the men today.

Very truly yours,

David

* * * * *

On December 11th, the First Middle Tennessee Cavalry Regiment was ordered on a reconnaissance south to Franklin. After morning rations were cooked and eaten, and after roll call, "Boots and Saddles" was sounded. The troopers then were ordered forward down the turnpike in a column of fours. The weather had turned colder again, and the troopers were all wearing their overcoats.

They rode at a steady pace toward Franklin, retracing their route they had taken a little more than a month before. They marched past Roper's Knob at the walk, and did not encounter any Rebel troops or skirmishers, as they did before.

They spent the night out in the open just above the town of Franklin. The men kept themselves warm by the cooking fires, while David and Captain Smith set a strong guard of pickets for the night watch.

They rode into Franklin the next morning, but found no sign of General Forrest's cavalry.

General Forrest and his three regiments of cavalry had been ordered to west Tennessee to break up General Grant's communications and supply lines. David and Captain Smith's cavalry companies were detailed to ride below Franklin to search for Forrest's command. Local Union sympathizers advised scouts from the companies that Forrest's command had gone south through town toward Columbia just two days before their arrival.

Captain Smith's troopers rode back above Franklin, and advised Colonel Stokes that General Forrest had moved his troopers south to Columbia. Colonel Stokes ordered the entire regiment back to Nashville, and to Camp Campbell.

When they arrived there, the troopers noticed that the entire army was being placed in a state of readiness for an invasion of Middle Tennessee.

* * * * *

December 24, 1862
Camp Campbell, Tennessee

Dear Uncle Uriah and Aunt Faith:

This has been a most unhappy Christmas season for those that love the Union. General Burnside has led the Army of the Potomac to a disastrous defeat at Fredericksburg.

The New York newspapers and *Harper's Weekly* have been freely distributed among the men here, and Burnside's bloody defeat has been chronicled as the signal disaster of this war. General Longstreet's command held a fortified position with good artillery that should never have been attacked by any sane commander.

The enlisted men in the infantry cannot help but be suspicious of their officers when they act so foolishly in ordering men to their death for nothing. I stare into the stars at night and pray daily for wisdom in the execution of my orders. I also pray that I will never ever throw away a single trooper's life under my command for the sake of personal glory or promotion.

General Burnside's stupid blundering has cost the Army of the Potomac over 12,000 good men in one day. It has cost all of us that seek to end this rebellion without dividing the Union.
To make matters worse, Colonel Stokes has told us at the officer's mess that the War Department has demanded that General Rosecrans attack General Bragg's army immediately.

The British Parliament meets in January, and the latest Confederate victory may assure them recognition by Britain and France. All eyes are now on the Army of the Cumberland. We are to move out with General McCook's corps on the 26th, and the entire army has been ordered to Murfreesboro over different routes.

The weather has been bitterly cold, and several troopers have died from sickness and exposure to the elements. Active campaigning in summer and winter is a grueling existence, and only the most fit of men can endure it.

I have never before seen the large battle groups of troops that are now assembled by our army. Stockpiles of rations and supplies have been built up in the depots in preparation for this campaign, and now the order to march has come. General Thomas commands the middle corps, and General Crittenden the left wing of the army.

We will receive a special Christmas food and beverage ration, and then we will be ordered to cook three day's rations and move out of our encampment. This fight will be large, bloody, and dangerous. Cavalry scouts have reported that Bragg has Hardee's corps and Polk's corps concentrating between Triune and Murfreesboro. That is right where we are headed. There will be a fight to come, and the outcome of that fight may decide the war.

My next entry will appear after the coming battle. I can only pray that God gives us the victory needed for us to carry on the war.

Until next time, I am

Very truly yours,

David

* * * * *

The Army of the Cumberland had orders to march toward Murfreesboro at dawn on December 26, 1862. "Boots and Saddles" was blown early for David's entire regiment, and they were mounted and on the Nolensville Pike by seven thirty a.m. The day was overcast, cold, windy, and bleak. The broadleaf trees around them had all shed their leaves, and the dark and bleak branches stretched out into the gray sky.

The First Middle Tennessee Regiment of cavalry rode with other Federal cavalry regiments on the flank of General McCook's corps. They marched down the turnpike through Nolensville, then veered east on the Rocky Fork Road, toward Gibbs Knob. They then rode on the west side of Gibbs Knob until they reached Burnt Knob Road. They rode east on Burnt Knob Road until they arrived at Overall Creek, a slow and sluggish stream that flowed northeast toward Stones River.

General McCook's engineers had laid a pontoon bridge across Overall Creek, and the long line of infantrymen began to march across the creek to form a line of battle at right angles to Stones River.

That night, General Joe Wheeler, a 1859 graduate of West Point, took a column of 2000 Confederate troopers up to LaVerne, where he captured and burned 300 supply wagons of McCook's corps. Wheeler had gobbled up McCook's entire supply train. The results of the raid caused McCook's infantry and cavalry to run short of ammunition and food during the upcoming battle.

General Bragg ordered General Hardee's corps and General Polk's corps to oppose the Federal advance above Murfreesboro. Bragg had around 37,700 Confederate troops, which was 45% of the number of Federal troops in the advancing army. Bragg made the most of what he had by attacking first, and attacking ferociously.

Bragg's plan was to have his men attack in force on the enemy's right, and to throw the enemy forces northward, and pin them against the banks of Stones River as they were to wheel north, and to the right.

On the morning of December 30th, at dawn, 10,000 Confederate troops under Patrick Cleburne and General McCown charged General McCook's troops as they were cooking breakfast. General Polk's corps joined in the advance upon Thomas' corps of Union troops, which drove the entire Union lines back almost three miles.

The Union line folded back on itself like a jack knife, and Rosecrans lost 300 troops and 28 guns in just over two hours. Union commands and divisions became intermingled in confusion down near the river. It was there that General McCook and General Thomas set up a line of stragglers. They directed the troops of different commands to refill their cartridge boxes from nearby supply wagons, and the units were readied for the next round of Rebel infantry attacks.

David's regiment had been ordered to Williams' Cross Roads on the 29th. They were ordered to take positions near the pontoon trains across Overall Creek, to guard General McCook's right flank. On the morning of December 30th, David's Company D, and Captain Smith's Company E were dismounted and deployed in a line of battle near a wooded area of Oak and Hickory trees.

When General Hardee's men attacked McCook's infantry, the troopers could do nothing more than watch the Federal infantry get swept back three miles toward Stones River. Isolated from the rest of the army, David and Captain Smith decided to fortify their position and wait. Troopers were dismounted, and riders were sent down to the engineer companies down at Overall Creek to borrow axes and picks.

When the troopers returned, details were ordered to cut down trees and pile up dead logs in their front. Breastworks were then constructed which consisted of dirt, dead logs, rocks, live trees, and anything that could stop a bullet.

Near the middle of the day, the crude breastworks was completed, and the dismounted troopers awaited a Rebel attack with their rifles. They did not have to wait long. General Wheeler soon threw his 2000 troopers at them from the southeast, from Stones River. Companies D and E were well entrenched, and Colonel Stokes' other companies were dug in above them toward McCook's original lines. Wheeler's men charged them on horseback with pistols and sawed off shotguns. The Union troopers cooly allowed them to close the range, and then fired into the Rebel troopers' ranks. Horses were thrown into somersaults, riders were hit in the chest and in their extremities, and saddles were emptied.

The Union troopers reloaded their rifles, and a fresh regiment of Wheeler's troopers again assaulted their position. The Rebel troopers were again allowed to approach to seventy five yards before the Federal troopers opened fire. The result was another blood letting. Wheeler's troopers suffered the same check as before, and left their dead and wounded on the field. The Confederate cavalrymen retreated toward General Hardee's lines near the Murfreesboro Pike.

After the smoke had cleared and the Rebel horsemen had withdrawn, the Federal cavalry officers began to take stock of their situation. The various company commanders began to call in their sergeants, and took a head count of their dead and wounded.

David sent for First Sergeant Anderson Looney. He reported with a face blackened from gunpowder, and saluted his First Lieutenant.

"Report our status, First Sergeant."

"Three dead, ten wounded, sir. Lieutenant, there are a lot of wounded Rebs out on the field. I would like permission to help them sir, if we can. They'll freeze to death tonight if nothing is done for them."

"Take ten men and start to bring those wounded in front of our position into our lines. Bring some water with you. Send two men over to

Colonel Stokes, and see if he will order the same for all of our companies. Carry on, sergeant."

"Thank you, sir."

Looney saluted David, and went off toward the other end of the fortified line. The temperature was dropping rapidly as darkness approached, and it was apparent that any wounded soldier could not survive the cold that evening unless help was made available.

Lieutenant Day then reported in. "Sir, all of the men are now out of rations. A staff officer from General McCook told us that all of the supply wagons have been burned by Wheeler's cavalry. We can't sit out here all night and all day without any food, it's just too cold. Man, I tell you sir, I could eat a horse right now."

"A horse!" The idea went through David's mind at once. "Why not!" he thought to himself. His Uncle Uriah had told him of the time when U.S. Dragoons in Mexico ate horse meat when their supplies ran out in the desert. His eyes got large with the realization that the answer to the men's hunger was right before them. He gave the orders quickly.

"Jim, get five troopers. Do you see those caissons over there that the Rebs left behind when they captured those guns?"

"Yes, sir."

"Go out there with axes and chop the spokes out of the carriage wheels. Take four more troopers and have them cut the reins and bridles off those dead horses out there. Then cut the lids off the caisson chests. Then I want you to take four more troopers and have them bring their sabers and report to me."

"If you don't mind my asking, sir, what is all this for?"

"If I am successful, you are going to eat your words tonight!"

They made forks out of the spokes from the caisson wheels, which they tied together with reins cut from the dead horses. They then made spits with the iron axles. David and four other troopers cut large portions of horsemeat with sharpened sabers, and placed the meat onto the spits to cook over their campfires.

Soon the smell of cooking meat wafted down the lines, and Captain Smith's men began cooking horse meat as well. A courier from Colonel Stokes sent word that the Colonel was coming to reprimand them for disobeying orders not to kindle cooking fires. When Colonel Stokes finally arrived, most of the horse meat was done.

As he began to reprimand Captain Smith, David brought the colonel a searing horse steak on his mess kit, together with a hot tin cup full of coffee.

"You men are disobeying orders...wow! This is delicious...this is best piece of steak I have ever had in my life! Who made this?"

David had to come forward, since he had prepared the meat himself. "I did, sir. I took a little molasses and some black pepper, and mixed it with some whiskey, and applied it to the meat while it was cooking..."

"This is first rate. It is a meal fit for a king! To hell with the general's orders. Captain Smith!"

"Sir."

"Send a corporal from Company E down to the other companies, and tell them to cut meat from those dead Reb horses, and cook enough for each trooper to have a fair sized steak."

"Yes, sir."

The rest of the officers from Company E and Company D gathered around the cooking fires, and enjoyed the delicious horse meat David had prepared. Soon, they noticed flaming firebrands moving down the fortified lines of the cavalry. As one fire was kindled, another fire brand would be lit, and move down the line, until the whole line contained a series of cooking fires.

A Major Roland Kendall, a staff officer from General Crittenden's staff, soon rode over, to repeat General Rosecrans' order against cooking fires. As soon as he dismounted and stated the nature of his business, David handed him a steaming mess kit containing a horse steak, and a hot tin cup of coffee.

"Tell General Crittenden where he can get a first–rate *beef* steak, Major Kendall. The major sat down and ate the horse meat with relish. When he arose, he shook David's hand, and accepted a closed mess kit containing a piping hot horse steak. He rode away from their camp with a full belly, and a smile on his face. He would surely win favor with General Crittenden by bringing him a hot meal on this bitterly cold night.

David's regiment loaded their wounded and the Rebel wounded onto ambulances late that night. The men could hear the ambulances from the other units rumbling up the Murfreesboro Pike toward Nashville for the rest of the night. The weather was freezing cold, and that added to the misery of the wounded men.

* * * * *

The following morning, Colonel Stokes rode over to David's company to check on the wounded. As he rode up, David was using his field glasses, and was scanning the far bank of Stones River. He saluted the colonel as he dismounted.

"As you were, lieutenant. You did an excellent job of foraging for food last night. Even though you disobeyed orders, you took care of your men. I admire that in a soldier. Are you ready for a fight today?"

"Yes, sir. I was looking at the officers of the artillery corps across the river, sir. We counted over fifty five guns over there. Who is that officer over there, sir, with the red kepi and red shoulder straps? Here is my field glasses, sir. Pray tell me who that officer is."

Colonel Stokes took the field glasses and looked at a mounted artillery officer across Stones River, arranging a vast array of artillery pieces.

"That David, is Captain John Mendenhall, Chief of Artillery for General Crittenden's corps. With all of the guns he has set up over there, he will make it hot for the Rebs if they charge through the Round Forest today."

"Where is the Round Forest, sir? I heard a staff officer speak of it last night, but did not know where it was."

"It's that area with all those Cedar trees, between here and the river. If the Rebs are to attack the army's lines today, they will have to advance into the Round Forest."

"And that's where Captain Mendenhall has sited his guns, I'll bet."

"You would be correct, lieutenant."

* * * * *

Later that day, David witnessed the fruitless assault on the Round Forest by the Confederate troops of General John C. Breckenridge.. At around four o'clock in the afternoon, General Breckenridge's five brigades of 4500 men assaulted the lines of Union General Van Cleve's division. The Confederate troops formed ranks and descended down the hill, and began to climb the opposite slope of the hill held by Van Cleve's Union troops. They opened fire at the Union troops when they were halfway up the opposite slope of the hill.

Van Cleve's troops began to run for the rear after the first rounds were fired by Breckenridge's soldiers. Captain Mendenhall's Union guns on the opposite side of Stones River then began to fire, with devastating effect. After a few minutes of suffering hideous losses from the shelling of the guns, the Confederate troops turned and broke back the way they had come.

General Breckenridge greeted his men as they returned with tearful eyes, and he later noted that 1700 of his men had fallen in less than ninety minutes.

General Bragg was convinced that a large Federal force was in front of his army, and his corps commanders also urged him to retreat. On January 3rd, Bragg and his army pulled out and marched south to Tullahoma, Tennessee. Even though Bragg's troops had forced the Union troops back over three miles on the first day of the battle, General Rosecrans claimed a victory.

* * * * *

Murfreesboro, Tennessee
January 16, 1863

Dear Uncle Uriah and Aunt Faith:

Our regiment survived the bloody battle of Stones River, which ended on the 2nd day of this month. We were detailed to bury and dispose of some of the casualties of that great battle. I saw carnage and the shedding of blood on a gigantic scale over those three days.

Men in the ranks were decimated by artillery and musket fire. The first day of the battle, the Confederate soldiers threw our infantry back nearly three miles. The second day, we were attacked by Joe Wheeler's cavalry, and we beat off every attack from our breastworks. General Wheeler's cavalry withdrew, and they left their dead and wounded men out on the battlefield. The last day of the battle, General Breckenridge sent at least four brigades against our infantry's lines near Stones River. They were beaten off with the well placed fire of at least fifty five pieces of field artillery. Bragg retreated with his army the next day after Breckenridge's attack failed.

The Confederate soldiers were brave, and they dressed their lines beautifully when they moved forward on the attack. Their gallant charge into the face of hell and death was a spectacle to behold. Two days after the Rebel troops were thrown back, we were detailed the grisly task of burying some of the dead from the battle. All of those fire–eating public speakers that were not afraid of bloodshed before this war should have been at Stones River on the third day. The dead were piled up almost in windrows.

What have they fought and died for? President Lincoln has freed the slaves in the Confederate states as of January 1st, but many Union troops say that emancipation is not the reason for their service in this army. The Confederate troops fight for independence and the right to secede. All I can see is that President Lincoln used his Emancipation Proclamation as a political weapon against the South. After the so called victory at Antietam Creek, and the victory at Stones River, the British and French may stay out of this war.

General Bragg has withdrawn his army south toward Tullahoma, and we will be sent on a scout in that direction shortly. Our regiment only lost around sixteen men. In this cold weather, that is nothing short of a miracle. God spared my life in this large and bloody battle, and I now live to serve Him, and to serve the Union.

May the Lord bless and keep you. Until next time, I am

Sincerely yours,

David

Chapter Fifteen

The First Middle Tennessee Regiment was ordered on a scouting mission to Auburntown, Liberty, and Cainsville, Tennessee from January 20th through January 22nd, 1863. The regiment returned without any major fighting. Company E did skirmish with a company of General Morgan's cavalry near Milton, Tennessee on January 21st.

General John Hunt Morgan's Confederate cavalry was reported near Auburntown, Tennessee, around the end of February, 1863. A large force was assembled to confront Morgan's cavalry, and to drive him out of Middle Tennessee. On March 8, 1863, Colonel Stokes' First Middle Tennessee cavalry was ordered to rendezvous near Auburntown with a 1700 man force of infantry under the command of Colonel A.S. Hall.

They met Colonel Hall's troops on March 14th near Lofton, Tennessee. The combined Federal force of cavalry and infantry now numbered nearly 2000 men. They marched east by north, back through the towns of Milton and toward Auburntown. David's Company D was near the end of the column. The weather was cold and rainy, and most of the troopers were busy trying to keep their bodies and their gunpowder dry.

About a mile west of Milton, David noticed a large hill covered with Eastern Red Cedar trees. The hill reminded him of the Round Forest at the Stones River battlefield near Murfreesboro. When Captain Smith rode over from his position with the Company E troopers, David mentioned the similarities of the terrain to him. The Federal troopers continued to scout in a northeasterly direction, moving into the small town of Prosperity, Tennessee. The column spent two days in Prosperity, taking advantage of an excellent blacksmith shop in the town. Every trooper had his horse reshod during that two day period, and saddlers also took advantage of the break in the march to repair saddles and bridles.

The troops then moved out the next day, and rode up to Auburntown. There in town, Union sympathizers informed Colonel Hall that General John Hunt Morgan was moving north from McMinnville, Tennessee, with a large force of cavalry. Colonel Hall decided to concentrate his forces below Auburntown, and to prepare his men in a defensive position and await General Morgan's certain attack.

On the road into Auburntown, David asked Captain Smith if he could recommend the hill west of Milton as a place to defend against the coming attack of General Morgan. David rode over to the rear of the column, and up the pike, until he found Colonel Hall. Colonel Hall was a small man, only five feet nine inches tall, but he wore a full beard and a tall black slouch hat.

He was seated on a white bay mare, talking to an infantry major when David rode up. He saluted the officers, and was given permission to speak. "Colonel Hall, I am First Lieutenant David Snelling. Captain Smith of Company E of the Middle Tennessee Cavalry has asked me to suggest a fine defensive position about one mile west of Milton, sir. It's a fine large hill with Cedar trees, and reminds us of the Round Forest at Murfreesboro, sir."

"Have you reconnoitered the position yourself, lieutenant?"

"Oh, yes, sir. We rode over here on a scout back in January, sir. It is a fine defensive position. I can go with some of your infantry officers, sir, and lay out a line of breastworks in advance of the whole force this afternoon."

"Take Major Jernigan with you. This man is a damn fine engineer. Go ahead and take your company of cavalry, and get some axes and picks, and prepare some breastworks. When you have laid out the defense lines, report to me immediately, and I will see that the lines are occupied."

"Yes, sir. Right away, sir."

"Carry on, lieutenant. It is nice to see an officer display some initiative."

"Thank you, sir."

They rode back to the cedar tree hill west of Milton, where David's company and Major Jernigan worked on a strong defense line. They rode to the crest of the hill, where Major Jernigan determined the military crest of the ridge. They then began to cut trees, and constructed a breastwork of rocks, dead trees, and dirt. At midnight that evening, they had completed a strong defensive line that ran around the crest of the large hill.

David then sent couriers to Colonel Hall, and to each regiment under his command. Colonel Hall immediately ordered the works occupied. The Union infantry troops marched down the pike through Milton, and began to file into their places on the line as directed by Major Jernigan.

The First Middle Tennessee Cavalry dismounted all their troopers, and had the fourth man in each squad take the horses several hundred yards to the rear of their position. At two o'clock, it began to rain a cold rain. The Federal troops and troopers kept their powder dry, and waited for John Hunt Morgan's troopers to come calling.

General Morgan was a handsome young cavalryman, with a full beard and a red ostrich plume in his gray hat. He cut a dashing figure in his short cavalry jacket. He was at the height of his fame, and his 1200 troopers would ride anywhere under his command.

General Morgan decided to attack Colonel Hall's force at daybreak, and his bugler sounded "Boots and Saddles' at two a.m. They saddled their horses in a cold rain, and moved down the pike toward Auburntown.

At four a.m., the Confederate troopers began to ride through Auburntown. Citizens in the town were partisan supporters of the Confederacy. Men and women alike peered out their windows in their nightshirts and dressing gowns. The women cheered the troopers, and the men of the town waved their white handkerchiefs out their windows.

Halfway between Auburntown and Milton, Colonel Hall had ordered Captain Smith's company east to picket the road as "bait" for Morgan's Confederate troopers. Smith's orders required his troopers to fire one pistol round at Morgan's men, and then to ride hard toward the other side of Milton.

Morgan's lead companies took the "bait" perfectly. They charged Captain Smith's company with drawn sabers. The Union troopers fired one round, and emptied some Rebel saddles. Morgan's men were undeterred, however, and spurred their mounts even harder up the pike.

Captain Smith's men then wheeled about, and spurred their horses the five miles down the pike into Milton. They slowed their pace a little as they rode through town, and then rode into their own lines just outside Milton, with the Confederate troopers close behind.

When Morgan's lead troopers closed to within seventy yards of the fortified line, Colonel Hall gave the order to fire. Over one thousand muskets discharged at once, filling the rainy air with smoke and flames. The lead companies of Morgan's force were decimated. Troopers were dispatched to ride back to General Morgan, who was riding out to meet them when he heard the sound of the guns.

When General Morgan arrived on the field, he thought that his men had only run into one brigade of Union troops. He ordered three of his cavalry companies to dismount, and to make an attempt to outflank the Yankees entrenched on the hill. He ordered three other companies to dismount, and to fight uphill as skirmishers.

The Union troops had chosen a fine defensive position. They were well protected by their hastily constructed breastworks. Morgan did not realize the size of the Union force in front of him. He had not scouted the Union position, and did not understand the advantage of his enemy in fighting near the top of the hill. He blindly directed company after company to dismount and attack the large Union force at the crest of the hill.

David's immediate position came under attack by twenty five dismounted Rebel troopers. Sergeant Looney shot one trooper with his rifle, and Lieutenant Day shot two troopers with his Colt revolver. David heard a bullet whiz past his left ear as he drew his Adams revolver from his belt. He immediately shot three more troopers in the chest. Just as the rest of the dismounted troopers were closing on their position, a line of Union infantrymen appeared behind them. An infantry captain yelled at David, "You men get down now!"

David ordered his men to go down on one knee. He then heard the captain yell, "Fire!" A line of flame and smoke erupted from their rifles, and the Rebel troopers charging uphill were gunned down to a man.

Colonel Grigsby, commanding one of the last remaining regiments of Morgan's command, was ordered to assault the line with his men two hours later. Some two hours after the infantry column appeared behind David's position, some of the troopers in Company D began to run out of ammunition. David passed the word for First Sergeant Looney.

"Sergeant pass the word down the line. As each trooper runs out of ammunition, he is to fall out of the line, and change places with each man holding horses at the rear of our position. Pass the word that as the last trooper holding horses is relieved, he is to notify me at once. That way, I will know when all of the fresh troopers have taken their place at the front of the line. Do you understand me?"

"Yes sir, I'll tell the men at once, sir."

After Sergeant Looney spread the word of David's order down the line, troopers began falling back to the rear as their ammunition became exhausted. Troopers from the rear that had been holding horses then filed into position to take their place at the line.

Colonel Grigsby then ordered more troopers on the attack. Company by company, he fed them into the mill of battle that was raging on the hill. A steady rate of fire was laid on the Confederate troopers, and Major Jernigan had cleared away so much brush in their front, that they had no secure way of approaching the Union defense line.

They attempted to rush the line in small groups, and they were repulsed by rifle fire time and time again. Near the end of the third hour, Grigsby's men had closed to within seventy yards of the Union lines. At that point, the Confederate troopers simply ran out of ammunition.

Colonel Hall noticed that the combined fire from the Rebel troopers had diminished entirely. He summoned his adjutant, Major Gregory Steele, and ordered him to form one regiment of infantry into line for a bayonet charge. The infantrymen were formed into a line at the top of the ridge, and were ordered to fix bayonets. Major Steele then ordered them forward at the walk, and ordered them to present arms.

Once they had walked out beyond the defense line, the Michigan infantryman were ordered to "charge bayonets". They went forward at the double quick, and swept Colonel Grigsby's Rebel troopers down the hill.

David saw the opportunity to pursue with cavalry, and sent Lieutenant Day to Colonel Hall to request permission to pursue General Morgan's troopers. Lieutenant James Day soon returned with orders for Company D and Company E to pursue the Rebel troopers.

They ran to the rear and mounted their horses, and formed a column of fours on the pike.

They pursued General Morgan's troopers hard down the pike, back through Milton, and even through the other side of Auburntown. Captain Smith had the bugler sound the recall. They had won the battle and the field. It was time to return to Murfreesboro.

They returned to the battlefield, where they helped bury the dead, and where they carried the wounded Confederates over into Milton with wagons and ox carts.

The Confederates lost over three hundred killed and wounded in the short battle. David asked Sergeant Looney for a report on Company D's casualties.

"Three wounded in all. Two only slightly grazed, sir."

"Who is seriously wounded, sergeant?"

"Bill Owen, sir. He took a carbine round in the gut."

"Find an ambulance to put him and the others in, and we will take 'em back with us to Nashville."

* * * * *

They rode into Murfreesboro, and then boarded train cars back to Camp Campbell near Nashville. Two days after arriving at Camp Campbell, a courier came over from General Rosecrans' headquarters, and asked David to report there at four o'clock that afternoon. The courier also instructed David to ride over to headquarters with Captain David Smith.

David got Sergeant John Reid to help him brush and press out his best uniform coat and trousers, and Private Allen Self shined David's boots for his meeting with General Rosecrans.

He changed into his best uniform and his shiny boots, and mounted the bay gelding. He rode over to Captain Smith's quarters, and rode with Captain Smith over toward the Granny White Pike.

General Rosecrans' headquarters was established in a Greek Revival mansion owned by a banker that had Unionist views, a John Mixon. David and Captain Smith left their horses with headquarters orderlies, and returned the salutes of the guards as they mounted the steps of the mansion.

They walked down the entrance hall, where an officer seated at a walnut desk was there to greet them. He had the rank of a bird colonel on his shoulder straps, so David and Captain Smith snapped to attention and immediately saluted him.

The bearded colonel was easy going, and spoke at once. "At ease, Captain Smith and Lieutenant Snelling. You are among friends here. You have impressed a lot of people in this army."

Captain Smith was curious. "I don't really understand you, sir."

Colonel Garfield smiled and scratched the back of his head. "You boys have led two companies in pitched battle against Generals Nathan Bedford Forrest, Joe Wheeler, and John Hunt Morgan and won each time! No one else in this entire army can claim that. Colonel Hall was especially impressed with the both of you, and you have been recommended for a new assignment."

He then rose from his desk, and showed them into another room down the hall, where another colonel was seated in an armchair, holding his slouch hat in his left hand. The hat contained the horn insignia of the infantry, and the colonel rose and placed the hat on his head when they entered the room.

David and Captain Smith immediately saluted, and the colonel was quick to acknowledge them. "At ease, gentlemen. You came recommended to me highly. Colonel Garfield, may I make my presentation to them now?"

"Yes sir, Colonel Streight. I'll shut this door and let you brief these officers."

The colonel was tall, and was around forty years old, with dark brown hair and a beard that was beginning to turn gray. He was large framed and muscular, and spoke with a Midwestern accent.

"My name is Colonel Abel D. Streight, of the Fifty First Indiana Volunteers. Last month, I proposed to General Rosecrans the idea of putting together a large mounted column for the purpose of raiding deep behind General Bragg's lines.

Specifically, I proposed a raid through North Alabama over into North Georgia, for the purpose of severing the Western and Atlantic Railroad, and breaking up General Bragg's communications around Rome, Georgia. This plan has been approved here at headquarters.

I am in the process of assembling a provisional brigade which will consist of around 2,000 men. I will take the Fifty First Indiana Regiment;

the Seventy Third Indiana, the Third Ohio, the Eightieth Illinois, and I want to take your two companies with us."

Captain Smith had an immediate question. "Colonel Streight, all of those units you just mentioned except our companies are infantry units. How will you obtain mounts for a cavalry raid?"

"That is an excellent question, captain. I intend on using mules as mounts. We will receive half of our mules for mounts in Nashville, and embark on steamers down the Cumberland and up the Tennessee River to Eastport, Mississippi. We are to rendezvous there with an 8,000 man force under the command of Brigadier General Grenville Dodge.

We are to obtain other mounts from General Dodge, and we have been authorized to seize any animals necessary to mount my command."

Captain Smith chimed in again. "You mean steal them along the way, sir?"

"No captain, appropriate them as needed. A quartermaster's receipt shall be given to each owner which will instruct any regimental quartermaster of the Union Army to pay the bearer of the receipt the sum indicated for the animal in U.S. greenbacks. However, if we are pursued by the enemy or run short of time, we have been instructed to appropriate animals without issuing any receipts.

I understand that your men are mostly from North Alabama, is that correct?"

Captain Smith spoke up again. "Yes sir, they are mostly from North Alabama, but a few of us even hail from Georgia. I was born and raised in Henry County, Georgia, and married an Ohio girl and moved up there. Lieutenant Snelling here is from Milledgeville, Georgia. He was born and raised on a cotton plantation, and has worked horses and mules all of his life. His uncle was a cavalry instructor at West Point, and he has the best eye for ground I have ever seen. You can rely on his expertise, sir."

"I see. Lieutenant Snelling, what do you think about our proposed enterprise? Would you want to volunteer to go with us?"

David cleared his throat, and began to speak. "Well, sir...I have worked with horses and mules all of my life. A mule can be a very stubborn and independent critter, but he's got some good attributes. He will never eat or drink himself to death like a horse can. He will lay down and rest when he is tired and overworked, and won't work himself to death as a horse will.

You may also have some problems with mules on a raid such as this. They can be slower than horses. A lot of mules are just worked in the harness all their life, and are never ridden. You would have to break a mule like that in just like you would a green colt. When you tell me you want to mount most of your infantry brigade on mules, can I assume sir, that you are doing that because of a shortage of horses around these parts?"

"Yes, you may draw those conclusions. Proceed with your opinion, lieutenant."

"Well, sir, if you can get enough healthy mules that will allow themselves to carry riders, I think you can mount a formidable column. But sir, there is one thing I need to tell you."

"Go on, lieutenant."

"We fought General Forrest's cavalry and General Wheeler's and General Morgan's commands from breastworks, because we have been issued only Springfield and Enfield rifles to fight with. Those weapons only allow us the opportunity to fight while we are dismounted. We need weapons such as carbines that would be better suited for the cavalry service, colonel."

"I hear you, Lieutenant Snelling, and I understand you. If you and Captain Smith will prepare a requisition for carbines and get it to Lieutenant Jim Doughty, my quartermaster, we can get you new carbines out of Cairo.

When your carbines arrive, you can swap them out for your standard issue rifles. Any other questions?"

David had not asked the obvious question. "When do we leave out, sir?"

"On April 9th. So get your requisitions filled out and sent in today. You will be the scouts for our brigade. I am expecting a lot out of you, but you have already shown me you can get things done. Don't disappoint me."

Captain Smith answered for them. "We won't let you down, sir. Your confidence in us will be justified."

They saluted Colonel Streight, turned, and left the building. On the way back to Camp Campbell, both David and Captain Smith could not help but question the proposed expedition.

"Horses would be faster than mules, David. The column could reach its objectives faster if all of the men were mounted on horses."

"That's true. The other problem is that the infantry soldiers may not be used to riding. They may have a hard time keeping pace with the column."

They rode to the area designated for use as headquarters for the provisional brigade, where they submitted written requisitions for carbines. David submitted a requisition for arms for the two officers and seventy-eight men of his company. Lieutenant Doughty told them that their requisitions would be filled on the 7th of April, and that both companies should report to his quarters on that date to exchange arms.

The next few days were filed with activity related to fitting out for the expedition. Each man engaged in the expedition was required to have a minimum kit of equipment for the march. Any clothing or item of equipment needed for the march had to be obtained from the quartermaster, and accounted for on the company's books. Every item supplied by the government had to be paid for by an income deduction from the respective trooper's pay. David and Sergeant Looney were required to keep those detailed records on the company books. They then had a great deal of bookkeeping work that was generated by the equipment and clothing transfers to the men of the company.

On the evening of the 7th, Lieutenant Doughty sent word to David that the Burnside carbines had arrived on the steamer *Westmoreland*. David had the buglers blow "Boots and Saddles", and "Assembly". The company then rode over to the provisional headquarters, and was instructed to dismount, and form a single file.

Each trooper was to file past a large wooden rack, and was required to hand his rifle and cartridge box to a quartermaster sergeant, who quickly stacked them in rows. The quartermaster corporal would then hand each trooper a Burnside carbine, a carbine tool, and a new cartridge box. Each trooper would then sign a receipt for the items, mount up, and form a column along the pike.

David directed Sergeant Looney and Lieutenant Day to bring several empty wooden crates, and to ride up to Granny White Pike to a large field. The entire company was ordered down the pike with them.

A farmer had laid his rows and furrows out, and a long row of small Sweet Gum trees had been allowed to sprout up along the edge of the field. David asked the company carpenter to go to each decent sized tree, and nail up one board from each crate on a single tree. Bull's eyes were then drawn on the boards with charcoal, and then David asked Sergeant Looney to lead the company in target practice.

One fourth of the troopers were ordered to take all of the horses two hundred yards to the rear, and to hold them. David then instructed the other remaining troopers in the use of the Burnside carbine. After stepping off seventy five yards, David held up his carbine, and began to instruct his men on its proper use.

"The trigger guard is in itself a lever, which pulls out and away. This then exposes the breechblock. Take a brass cartridge, insert it into the breech, and snap the trigger guard back to its horizontal position. Then you bring the carbine to the half cocked position by pulling back the hammer, and you seat a musket cap over the nipple. Then you pull the hammer back to fully cock the weapon, aim at the target, and open fire."

David dropped down to one knee, aimed at a board on a Sweetgum tree, and fired the Burnside. The little weapon gave him a kick in his shoulder, and reminded him that it was .54 caliber. After the smoke from the discharge had cleared, they saw that a hole had been cut in the board, an inch away to the right of the bull's eye.

"Does anyone have any questions?"

Sergeant Looney was the first. How does the fire get to the powder in the metal cartridge?"

David knew the answer. "There is a small hole in the base of the metal cartridge through which a spark will pass when the musket cap is fired. Sergeant, go ahead and fire some rounds yourself, and then let's have all of the boys line up and fire at least three rounds at one target."

They began their target practice in the early afternoon. At four o'clock, Colonel Streight had heard the firing, and rode over to investigate. He rode up as some of the last rounds were discharged.

"What is going on here, Lieutenant Snelling?"

David saluted, and began to respond at once. "Sir, I am teaching these men how to use a Burnside carbine."

"Some commanders might complain that you are wasting ammunition. How would you respond to that, Lieutenant?"

"Well sir, I would tell him that I would expect a man to be able to use a weapon effectively, especially by the time he takes the field. Before I could expect to order a man to shoot the enemy, I would want to know if the trooper can first hit a board nailed to a tree."

"That is an excellent answer. Carry on, Lieutenant Snelling."

"Thank you, sir."

Colonel Streight and his staff officers rode back down the Granny White Pike toward his provisional headquarters. David looked at the infantrymen as they rode away, all mounted on mules. He could see the long ears of the mules sticking up way up the pike.

'This has got to be the weirdest cavalry assignment of this war', he thought to himself. He then thought about the men's equipment, and he remembered something that he had forgotten that morning.

He walked over to where Sergeant Looney was firing his Burnside carbine, and began to give him an order. "Sergeant, I want you to get a list tonight of every man in the company that does not have a revolver. I want you and each of these men to report to the quartermaster's in the morning, and get a revolver. I don't want any trooper in this company to go out on this mission with a single shot horse pistol. Even boys like Joe McClusky need the edge of six shots in some engagements.

This needs to be done, even if the cost of the weapons are stopped from their pay. Do you understand?"

"Yes, sir. I'll have them down there after they have roll call and morning mess, sir."

"I'll finish up the quarterly and monthly returns first thing in the morning, sergeant. You can bring them over to Colonel Stokes' headquarters tomorrow afternoon."

"Yes, sir."

The company completed its target practice, and returned to camp late that afternoon. The next morning, most of Company D had completed all the necessary preparations for the mission. Ten troopers reported to First Sergeant Looney, who went with them to the quartermaster to obtain Colt revolvers and cartridge boxes.

Later that morning, a courier from Colonel Garfield brought David orders to embark his company on the steamer *Westmoreland*, which was tied up at the Cumberland River docks below the state capitol building.

David had the buglers blow "Boots and Saddles", and "Assembly", and they were soon marching in a column of fours on the Nolensville Pike. The marched down to the town limits of Nashville. They marched through the city streets, and down to the docks, where eight steamers were tied up at landings along the Cumberland River. A river pilot and the captain of the *Westmoreland*, Henry Ward, came out and greeted David when he halted his command at the landing.

Captain Ward was clad in civilian clothes, with a blue and gold navy cap. David surmised that he was not in the Union Navy, but hired his vessel out per day to the Union Army. He was short and squat, and wore black jean cloth trousers, and a red checked shirt.

The river pilot wore a white navy cap, and was lean and tall, with long side whiskers that curved down to the sides of his mouth. He wore a blue pair of trousers, a blue shirt, and a white linen jacket. He greeted David with a nod and a handshake.

"Lieutenant, I was told by Colonel Streight to lead your horses on board in two hours. You are to feed and water them on shore, and load them after your saddles and weapons are stowed in the aft section of the steamer. I have stalls for all of your horses. Colonel Streight also asked you to send five men over to his headquarters to help them drive their mules down to the other steamers."

"Thank you, sir. I'll attend to that at once. Lieutenant Day."

James Day heard their conversation, and came up at once. "Yes, sir."

"Take Sergeant John Reid and four other men, and go to Colonel Streight's headquarters. They will need you to drive some of their mules down to the other steamers to transport them out. After their mules are loaded, report back to me, and unsaddle your mounts and stow them in the aft section of this steamer. Do you understand my orders?"

"Yes, sir. I'll go at once, sir."

"Be careful, Jim. I'll see you on board the *Westmoreland*."

* * * * *

They departed from the Nashville landing around six thirty that evening, after all their equipment and the animals had been loaded aboard the eight steamers.

The steamers pulled out into the river channel of the Cumberland River, and began to steam downstream toward Palmyra.

David and Sergeant Looney stood at the taffrail of the paddle wheeled *Westmoreland*, and watched the city of Nashville slip by them. They then began to steam in single file down the Cumberland, with two armored gunboats leading the way.

David saw that Dogwood trees on the banks of the river had begun to bloom. He was then reminded that the following Sunday was Easter Sunday. He then had a thought, which he shared with Sergeant Looney.

"Anderson, you know that this Sunday is Easter Sunday?"

"Yes, sir, I believe it is."

"It seems strange that during the time that we recognize the death and resurrection of Jesus Christ, we are engaged in a huge civil war, with months of killing and bloodshed."

"Didn't Jesus say in the scriptures that 'Ye shall hear of wars and rumors of wars'? Was that not something he would have anticipated, sir?"

"You are probably right. There are times when I began to feel that this struggle was preordained. I just never quite feel right about it, either."

"I understand, sir. Some of us may not survive this mission. So we need to stay sharp and keep our heads about us, don't we, sir?"

"You are right about that sergeant. We shall face some hazards on this assignment."

They continued to stand on the railing, and they watched the sun sink away in the west. The steamboats ahead of them trailed streaming clouds of smoke off into the orange sky before them.

* * * * *

They arrived at the little town of Palmyra the next day, on the left bank of the Cumberland River. Once all of the steamers were tied up and the landing boards were attached to the steamers, couriers were dispatched summoning the officers to a field just above the river landing.

David and Captain Smith and Lieutenant Day attended the conference, where they met the other regimental officers of the expedition. Colonel Streight introduced them to Colonel Ben Lawson of the Third Ohio Regiment, to Captain D.L. Wright, Fifty First Indiana Volunteers, and to Captain David Driscoll, Third Ohio Infantry, who was acting assistant inspector general.

Colonel Streight laid out their orders at the conference. Colonel Lawson and four companies of the Fifty First Indiana Volunteers were detailed to travel with the eight steamers down the Cumberland River, into the Ohio River, and then up the Tennessee River to Fort Henry. His command was to stop at Smithland, Kentucky, and take on rations and forage for their column, and for General Dodge's command in Mississippi.

David's company and the other regiments were ordered to saddle their horses and mules, and to march from Palmyra, Tennessee, over to Fort Henry, and to seize horses and mules along the way. Each company commander was given eighty pre printed quartermaster forms which acted as receipts for each horse or mule taken or seized.

The infantry soldiers were sent to catch and saddle the mules that were brought over from Nashville. As the men went to work, Colonel Streight noticed that something was very wrong. He sent a courier to summon David over to their temporary corral in the field above the landing.

David rode over with Sergeant Looney, and immediately saw what was wrong. He rode over to Colonel Streight, and gave him his assessment.

"Colonel, about sixty of these mules have the horse distemper. You see how that one is down on his knees there? Those you see like that will be too near dead to travel at all. Some of those mules over there are dying as we speak. Many of the rest of these mules are just green and unbroken. If you get around twenty five troopers over here, they can take turns breaking these mules and puttin' 'em in the saddle before dark."

"What else would you have me do, Lieutenant Snelling?"

David scratched his head. "Well, sir, first, I would detail fifty men to drag the bodies over into that field over there, pile wood on top of 'em, and burn them up. I would then send out fifty troopers and twenty of your soldiers, and try to scare up about a hundred head of horses and mules within the next day."

Colonel Streight pulled on his beard, and then quickly reached a decision. "Captain Wright."

A tall infantry officer walked up and saluted Colonel Streight. "Yes, sir."

"Go get fifty men from the Third Ohio and Fifty First Indiana to drag those sick and dead mules out into that field. Shoot the sick animals in the head, and pile wood on their carcasses, and burn them.

Send a courier to Captain David Smith of the E Company of the First Middle Tennessee Cavalry Regiment. Tell him I need twenty five troopers to break and saddle green mules for the next day. Make it so, captain."

"Yes, sir. Right away, sir." Captain Wright mounted his mule, and rode off to carry out the colonel's orders.

"Lieutenant Snelling, I have orders for you, sir."

"Yes, sir."

"You just named your own poison. Take fifty men from your company, and twenty men from the Eightieth Illinois, and ride out and scare us up about one hundred head of horses and mules. Meet me back here in twenty four hours."

"Yes, sir. Right away, sir."

David rode back to the steamer, and ordered his men to mount and assemble in the field beyond Palmyra landing. He sent out a courier to summon twenty volunteers from the Eightieth Illinois Infantry for their detail.

Once the troopers and the troops were ready, David ordered the column forward. Over the next fifteen hours, they split off into separate columns, taking separate roads into small towns below Palmyra. One column rode into Shiloh; another column went to Slayden, and David and his group rode over to Ellis Mills.

They took mules standing out in fields, and mules and horses in lots and barnyards. They wrote out the U.S. Quartermaster receipts for the animals to the owners, if they saw them. The animal's value was appraised on the spot, and the owner could redeem the receipt at any U.S. Army post that had a quartermaster. A decent mule was worth $75.00, a good horse, at least $100.00.

David had intended the men to rendezvous at twelve noon the next day at Canaan, a small town below Palmyra. When they did meet up, their combined total of horses and mules was tallied by Lieutenant Day. He counted one hundred and fifty five animals.

They then drove the stock up the road and into Palmyra, where the mules and horses were herded into a make shift corral of fence rails. They had fulfilled their mission with three hours to spare. David reported personally to Colonel Streight. The colonel was well pleased with David's efforts.

"You didn't disappoint me, Lieutenant Snelling. You brought in some fine animals. From what I could see, they are in excellent condition."

"What are our orders now, sir?"

"You and your men go turn in and get some sleep. We will pull out in the morning, and commence our march over to Fort Henry. I am going to detail some of Captain Smith's men as scouts to find us some more animals on the way. Good work, lieutenant. See you in the morning."

David saluted Colonel Streight, and rode back to his company's encampment.

* * * * *

Early the next morning, the entire brigade left Palmyra, and began to march in a southwesterly direction toward Fort Henry. Some of the soldiers were not mounted, so several of the mules carried two saddles and no riders. A number of soldiers were required to march on foot at the rear of the column.

They all camped that evening at Yellow Creek, a swampy and sluggish stream that emptied into the Cumberland River. They had only managed to march fifteen miles, because many of the soldiers could not keep up the pace on foot.

Around nine o'clock that evening, Captain David Smith and his detail rode in, with only twenty five mules with them. Farmers and townspeople nearby had heard about Streight's roundup of horses and mules, and hid their stock from the Federal troops.

They resumed their march the next morning, and David and thirty men under his command were ordered to round up more mules and horses. They rode out early in the morning, before the main column got moving. David's idea was to ride over to Brownsville, which was a small town ahead on their line of march. There were several farms and one plantation along the way, and a decent sized livery stable at Brownsville. The troopers found mules in each of these locations, and had forty animals at the end of the day. They camped at Old Sykes Spring, tied off the horses and mules on picket lines, and waited for the main column to catch up.

The rest of Streight's brigade came up around eight o'clock that evening, and encamped above them on Old Sykes Spring. They broke camp the next morning, and began to march to the northwest, up to Fort Henry on the Tennessee River.

They had just crossed Lost Creek when a courier rode up from Colonel Streight. The colonel had ordered David and forty troopers to ride behind the column and bring up any stragglers. He was also ordered to count any dead mules or horses left behind the column. They rode back on the old road toward Brownsville, and picked up several soldiers that were required to abandon dead or sick mules. Half of David's troopers had to dismount, in order to carry the saddles of the newly dismounted soldiers. David and his men arrived at Fort Henry at midnight, where he reported to Colonel Streight personally.

"We picked up twenty five stragglers from the column, sir. We also brought in the saddles and bridles on the animals they were riding. My men counted sixty dead and near-dead mules between here and Brownsville."

Colonel Streight had his jacket off, and popped his suspenders up against his checked shirt. "That means we have lost a hundred animals between here and Palmyra. We still have around twelve hundred horses and mules left, though. Go ahead and turn in, Lieutenant Snelling. We'll see if the gunboats make it here tomorrow."

"Yes, sir."

David rode over to where his company was bivouacked for the night, and sacked out himself.

* * * * *

The gunboats and steamers did not arrive that morning, so David and Sergeant Looney took the delay as an opportunity to survey the sights of Fort Henry.

They spent most of the day around the fort talking to the engineer officers and some of the garrison soldiers, when a courier from Colonel Streight brought David a message. The signal corps wig wag station several miles downstream had spotted the steamers. All troops and troopers were ordered to prepare for embarkation aboard the steamboats once they reached Fort Henry.

They had been ordered to prepare and cook two day's rations that morning, and they led their animals aboard the steamers once they were tied up near Fort Henry. David's Company D and the Eightieth Illiinois were ordered to board the steamer *Westmoreland*.

The *Westmoreland* also had fifty marines from General Ellet's U.S. Marine Brigade. The U.S. Marines had been ordered to proceed with Streight's command as far south as Eastport, Mississippi.

The troops and troopers loaded their animals and gear aboard the transports, and the steamers headed south against the river current. The steamers only went twenty miles upriver down to Johnstonville, where they put into shore and tied up near the Union fortifications there. David was curious as to why the flotilla had stopped. He sent Sergeant John Reid to find the river pilot, and obtain an explanation.

Sergeant Reid returned twenty minutes later with the reason for the halting. "Sir, the pilot says the river bed is extremely low for this time of year. The pilots have all concluded that there are too many snags and log jams in the channel for nighttime navigation. He said that we all can sleep at night, and the flotilla will move out at first light."

"What about our animals? Can we feed and water them now?"

"Yes, sir. That is what he suggested."

"Very well. See to that, Sergeant Reid."

"Yes, sir."

After the animals were fed and watered, and after a miserable supper of lousy bacon, water, and hardtack, David tried to get some sleep.

He awoke at four a.m., sick to his stomach. He pulled on his uniform coat and his kepi, and walked up to the main deck and railing of the *Westmoreland*. He vomited over the side of the steamer, and began to hear two marine sentries engaged in conversation.

"Wyman, why did you join the Corps before the war?"

"I had to get away from my bossy wife down in Maryland. All I ever heard her say to me was 'I don't like you worth a shit, Wyman, yer feet stink.' I got told that one time too many, and I decided it was time to see the world."

David heard both marines begin to laugh, and they rounded the railing carrying their weapons at shoulder arms. He saw their stiff blue uniform coats with red trimmed collars, and noticed that one of them was a sergeant. His three yellow stripes were edged in red. Both men wore caps with the infantry horn insignia with the letter "M" in the middle of the horn.

The snapped at attention once they saw that David was an officer. He wiped his mouth with his sleeve, and acknowledged them.

"As you were, men. I got ahold of some bad bacon. I just need to get some fresh air on the deck. Carry on."

"Aye, Aye, sir."

* * * * *

The pilots gave the steamboat captains the go ahead to untie the steamers and proceed down river after daylight, and the steamers finally reached Eastport, Mississippi on the afternoon of April 19th. Colonel Streight had made every effort to urge the flotilla to steam ahead as quickly as possible, but he and his men were only passengers, and had no authority over the river boat captains in the flotilla. The flotilla tied up at Eastport, which was a small community on the Mississippi / Alabama state line. Colonel Streight sent a courier for David and for Captain Smith, requesting them and twenty men to ride with him some twelve miles up Bear Creek to General Dodge's's headquarters.

Colonel Streight left Colonel Lawson in command at Eastport, and issued orders requiring the mules they had brought with them to be corralled in a nearby field. The troops were building a crude corral of fence rails when David and Captain Smith rode up Bear Creek with Colonel Streight.

General Dodge had his command of 8,000 men encamped twelve miles up Bear Creek. General Dodge had commanded a brigade of troops at Stones River, and was placed in command of the Department of Mississippi and North Alabama right after the battle.

He had several brigades of infantry, and the First Alabama Regiment of cavalry with him at Bear Creek. They rode along the edge of Bear Creek down toward the Natchez Trace, near where General Dodge was encamped. On the way to the camp, Colonel Streight told them about General Dodge, and his prior accomplishments as a designer and builder of railroads. Colonel Streight bragged on General Dodge's engineering ability, and overall ability as a soldier.

They finally arrived at General Dodge's camp at suppertime, when his troops were drawing and cooking their evening rations. The men shared bacon and beans with Colonel Streight and his escort, and then General Dodge briefed them on their line of march for the next two days.

At the end of their briefing, General Dodge introduced himself and his staff officers to Colonel Streight and his men. General Dodge was a short and stocky man, five foot ten inches tall, with graying hair, and a dark mustache. We wore a tall black hat with the infantry horn insignia, and was almost bow–legged in his gait. He shook hands with all of Colonel Streight's men, and hesitated when he saw the cavalry insignia on David's kepi and Captain Smith's Hardee–style hat.

"You two are in a cavalry regiment, which is that?"

David was quick to answer. "Sir, we are detailed to serve with the First Middle Tennessee Cavalry, but our companies were raised in Huntsville this summer."

"So you fought at Stones River near Overalls Creek?"

"Yes, sir, we were in Stokes' Brigade."

"Lieutenant, we need troopers like yours in this Department. You men were raised in Alabama. You belong back here. When this expedition is concluded, I am going to request the War Department to transfer your two companies back to the First Alabama."

"It would be a pleasure to serve under you, General Dodge." David saluted General Dodge, and he and Captain Smith rode back to Eastport with Colonel Streight.

They arrived back at Eastport around midnight, where Sergeant Reid and Colonel Lawson were waiting for them. Colonel Lawson had a worried look on his face.

"What is our situation, Colonel Lawson?"

Lawson removed his hat and began to explain, "Sir, we...built corrals for the mules out of fence rails. Some of the animals were very intelligent. They kicked the top rails off the corral, and then started jumping over the rails. We had 400 animals escape, sir."

Streight threw his hat into the ground.

"Damn! We can't ever get moving on this mission because the damn animals keep messing us up! Captain Smith."

"Yes, sir."

"Take Lieutenant Snelling and both of your companies out, and ride south and west for fifteen miles, and then circle back to Eastport. Round up all of the mules and horses you can find."

"Yes, sir." Captain Smith saluted, and the sound of "Boots and Saddles" was heard among David's and Captain Smith's companies. They were out on the road at two a.m., and they rode south for the next day. They found some mules along the way, and recovered more animals on the return trip to Eastport. Their search was only directed to the south and west of Eastport, since they were surrounded by water on two sides. At ten p.m. on the following day, the troopers rode into Eastport with 200 mules. Other mules brought down from Nashville fell ill with horse distemper, and were left in Eastport.

At twelve o'clock the following afternoon, Colonel Streight led his provisional brigade out of Eastport toward General Dodge's headquarters. They arrived at his headquarters at eight o'clock the next morning. They then marched in the rear of General Dodge's entire force, marching from the Natchez Trace to Tuscumbia, Alabama. They collected several horses and mules along the route to Tuscumbia. However, the brigade was short of animals, and General Dodge gave Colonel Streight two hundred mules and six wagons to haul ammunition and rations.

Colonel Streight also ordered his surgeon, Major William Peck of the Third Ohio, to examine each man, and to send back any man unfit for the mission with General Dodge and his command. Doctor Peck culled out two hundred men from Streight's brigade, leaving him with 1,800 men fit and present for duty.

David was summoned by a courier from Colonel Streight for a conference with General Dodge. He met Captain Smith near General Dodge's headquarters, which he had made in an old barn just outside of Tuscumbia.

They stepped into an area of the barn that was lit by several Wax Myrtle candles, where General Dodge and a small group of officers were seated on wooden boxes. David and Captain Smith saluted General Dodge and Colonel Streight.

General Dodge was to the point. "As you were, men. Now that you all are here, we can begin. Bill Looney and some scouts reported to me yesterday that General Forrest and a sizable force of cavalry has crossed the Tennessee River, and is now located near Town Creek. Captain Spencer, please hand me our maps of the area."

A tall infantry captain with a half beard and dark hair unrolled a large map and handed it to General Dodge. General Dodge unrolled the map on the top of a wooden cracker box, and continued with the briefing.

"Colonel, I know that all of your men are not yet mounted. We will advance in front of you on the Decatur Road to Courtland, and drive Forrest's command in that direction. That should enable your column to slip south and east of us, toward Moulton." General Dodge then began to point out their line of march on the map.

"Now you are going to march to Moulton by marching due south to Russellville from Tuscumbia, and then due east through Mt. Hope to Moulton. You will in effect cover the two short sides of the Isosceles Triangle, but this will keep you out of contact with Forrest's forces. Forrest has a substantial number of troopers, and some brass six pound artillery. My force alone is over twice his number, though.

If Forrest turns his forces due south toward Moulton, I will attack him with all of my cavalry regiments, and will request you to send me your two companies of Alabama cavalry to join us. You will then engage Forrest's cavalry with your force, until my infantry can come up to give him battle. You are still short several mounts, is that correct, Colonel?"

Colonel Streight rubbed his face and responded. "Yes, sir, we are short around 150 animals."

"I expect that you will be able to find a substantial number of mounts before you arrive at Moulton. If there are no questions, gentlemen, the briefing is concluded."

"Thank you for all of your assistance, General Dodge." Colonel Streight and the junior officers saluted General Dodge, and left the barn. David asked the General if he could stay and speak to him.

"What is on your mind lieutenant?"

"Lieutenant David Snelling, sir. Sir, with all due respect to Colonel Streight, nothing has gone right so far on this mission. I have an item that was given to me by my Uncle Uriah Snelling that has some value, and I was wondering if you could keep it for me until I return."

"Show me what you have, lieutenant."

David handed him the Colt Navy Revolver that had been inscribed by Jefferson Davis. General Dodge handled the weapon, and read the inscription.

"This is somewhat irregular, but under the circumstances, I believe you are correct to safeguard a possession of value such as this. However, should you not return alive from your expedition, it would not be appropriate for me to keep this.

I think the proper thing for me to do here is to treat this as a pawn transaction, and I shall give you twenty dollars to pawn this pistol, and I will have Captain Spencer, my chief of staff, write you out a receipt. You can redeem the pawn ticket when you return from your mission, and report to my department."

"Yes sir, thank you very much, sir. I greatly appreciate this."

"Captain Spencer, please write Lieutenant Snelling out a pawn ticket for twenty dollars for one 1851 Colt Navy Revolver, inscribed by Jefferson Davis. Lieutenant, here is twenty dollars in U.S. greenbacks. Good luck to you, young man."

David saluted the general, and took his receipt and the twenty dollars with him.

* * * * *

The provisional brigade began its march from Tuscumbia at 11:00 o'clock in the evening in a heavy spring downpour. The men broke out their oilskins and rubber raincoats, and slogged their way south in the mud and the darkness. One hundred and fifty men in Colonel Streight's command did not have mounts. Another one hundred and fifty men carried only saddles on their own mounts, and had to proceed on foot as well.

The progress of the column was slow, and soon, stragglers on foot began to lag behind the entire column. Colonel Streight sent a courier to General Dodge, indicating that he would halt his advance at Mount Hope, and wait for those on foot to catch up with the rest of his command.

The following night, at Mount Hope, General Dodge sent word to Colonel Streight that he had engaged and driven the enemy cavalry, and that Colonel Streight should push on. David's company, and some of the other companies began to round up some horses and mules, and 110 of the troopers that were walking were now mounted. They arrived at Moulton at dark, with the only contact with the Reb cavalry being small run–ins with pickets posted on the roads.

They made for Day's Gap, a gap in the mountains between Bugaboo Mountain and Burney Mountain. They marched thirty five miles that day, and bivouacked for the night at Day's Gap. Every man in the brigade was now mounted, as some Confederate supply wagons had been captured, and the draft animals had been converted into remounts.

Many of the supply wagons held arms and tents, and were burned by Streight's Union troops. The country had many small mountains, and many stony roads and pathways. The footing was hard on the unshod animals, and the rocky ground would take its toll on the mules.

Some of David's men and Captain Smith's men began to pass by the homes of some of their relations, who greeted the troopers with open arms.

David's company and Captain Smith's company were ordered to command the rear guard of the column. The rest of the brigade moved out at daylight, and began to climb through Day's Gap, and up onto Brindley Mountain.

* * * * *

Bedford Forrest had driven the 1000 troopers under his command hard from Moulton to just outside of Day's Gap. The day before, a Confederate scout had advised him that 2000 Union troopers were heading east from Mount Hope. He was determined to beat Streight's command to Day's Gap and cut him off, but he was a few hours late.

He ordered his brigade to attack the Yankees at day light, and to open fire with his brass six pounders, and all of the muskets that could be brought to bear. He was determined to capture or kill all of the Yankee troopers, and he would prevent them from reaching the Georgia state line.

General Forrest bit down on a piece of hardtack, and heard his brass guns begin to boom a greeting to the enemy. He saw the smoke rise from the batteries, and a smile began to appear on the corners of his mouth. His men were ready, and they began to move out and take their positions. He would charge the enemy troops before their morning rations could be eaten.

* * * * *

David saw the puffs of smoke from Forrest's batteries, and then heard the shells shriek past their position, and explode behind them. He immediately sent for Sergeant Looney.
Sergeant Looney reported and saluted with an unlit cigar stump in his mouth.
"First Sergeant, we are under attack. Order every fourth man in the rear to hold the horses, two hundred yards from this position to the rear. Send Sergeant Reid to Colonel Streight's column to tell him we are under attack, and to request further orders from him. Order the remaining men to form a skirmish line to receive the enemy attack, carbines at the ready"
"Yes, sir! Right away, sir."
They immediately prepared for an attack that came quickly. Dismounted troopers and mounted units began to move up the gap, and up onto Brindley Mountain.
David ordered the men to fire at will, and soon, gray clad troopers began to assault their position. Several squads of Union cavalrymen fired their Burnside carbines, and the first wave of attackers was shot down.
Meanwhile, Sergeant Looney rode up Brindley Mountain near the head of the column to find Colonel Streight. As he rode across the top of the ridge, he noticed that the Indiana and Ohio troops had formed a battle line at the top of the ridge. Skirmishers were deployed on the flanks and at the rear of the ridge to guard against a rearward surprise attack.
Streight had formed his battle line well, as he anchored it on the right beside a deep ravine, and on his left with a marshy creek. The mules were led down the ravine on the right, to shelter them from the enemy gunfire. Sergeant Looney found Colonel Streight near the ravine, and dismounted and gave his report while saluting the colonel.
"Sir, Captain Smith's command is under attack from Reb cavalry, sir. They have driven in our pickets, and are attacking in force."
"I heard their artillery just now, sergeant. We have prepared an ambush here for them. I have written out a message for Captain Smith. He is to hold his position until the enemy assaults him closely. He is then to retreat rapidly, right up through this pass, and over the top of this ridge. You are to draw the enemy in toward us. Do you understand my orders?"
"Yes, sir. I'll take them down now, sir."
"Very well. Good luck, sergeant."

Looney mounted his black mare and rode pell mell down the pass toward David's position. He met the other troopers at the rear of the line holding their horses, and ordered them to move up closer toward the firing line. When he got to David's position, he repeated Colonel Streight's orders, and David ordered Sergeant Reid to ride over to Captain Smith and relay the colonel's orders to his company.

David asked Lieutenant Day to have their horses brought closer, as he had seen the enemy below with his field glasses, and he anticipated a charge was forthcoming.

He passed the word for Sergeant Looney.

"First Sergeant, order the men to sling their carbines, and mount up and draw their pistols. When the enemy charges us, the men are to fire one round, and ride hard for the top of the ridge."

"Yes, sir! Right away, sir." Looney relayed the order among his men quickly, and they were soon ready.

A wave of rebel yells split the forest as the Confederate troopers charged at them up the slope. The Union troopers lowered their pistols and fired one round, and spurred their mounts toward the top of the draw.

Forrest's Rebel cavalrymen followed them closely, firing at them with sawed off shotguns and pistols. The Unionists rode through the gap, and through Colonel Streight's defense line at the top of the ridge. Just as the Confederate troopers closed the range, Streight's artillery opened fire on them, and his whole line of blue coated troops arose and fired on them.

Horses were killed and thrown head over heals, men were thrown; others were blown to bits. Other men were simply shot out of the saddle and killed.

General Forrest's attack had driven in the Federal pickets, and had brought their horse artillery within 300 yards of the Union lines. The Rebel troopers from the bottom of the ridge rode up and supported their attack, and dismounted and attacked up hill in small groups.

Colonel Streight ordered Colonel Hathaway of the Seventy Third Indiana, and Lieutenant Colonel Sheets of the Fifty First Indiana to charge into the advancing cavalrymen. Colonel Lawson of the Third Ohio, and Lieutenant Colonel Rodgers of the Eightieth Illinois were ordered to charge the enemy batteries.

The blue–coated Union troops fired their muskets and charged forward. One of their first volleys struck Captain William H. Forrest in the thigh, knocking him from his horse. The charge overran the Confederate artillery battery of two brass guns and two cannons. Forrest's Confederate cavalry retreated back in confusion, leaving thirty dead on the field, and over one hundred men wounded.

Streight's losses were thirty killed and wounded. After the firing had ceased, David summoned First Sergeant Looney, and requested a report as to the casualties in their company.

"None dead, none wounded, two troopers missing. Private Thomas Forsyth and Private Riley Williams."

Colonel Streight gave the orders to move out, and the entire column swung south toward Crooked Creek. A strong rear guard was detached from the Eightieth Illinois, and Forrest's troopers soon began to engage them severely.

Colonel Streight rode ahead of the column, and selected a ridge known as Hog Mountain to stage a defensive stand with their artillery. The troops and troopers in the column prepared a skirmish line at the top of the ridge. Major Vananda of the Third Ohio placed his four guns to fire down to the bottom of the ridge.

General Forrest had ordered his Confederate troopers to "Keep up the scare", and to "shoot at everything blue", and they pressed on up the ridge toward Streight's lines.

Around one hour before dark, Forrest's troopers attacked the right portion of Streight's line, and then the left. The Union troops and troopers beat off each attack, and Major Vananda's artillery killed and wounded a large number of Confederate troopers.

The Rebel cavalry was driven from the front by ten p.m. A large number of dead and wounded Confederates were left on the field. The ammunition from General Forrest's captured guns had been used up, so it was decided to spike these guns and leave them behind.

The moon had arisen brightly in the eastern sky, and the column resumed its march by the moonlight. The country here consisted of open woods of pine, oak, and Sweet Gum, with thickets of Wax Myrtle and Water Locust bushes.

Colonel Streight ordered Colonel Hathaway and the Seventy Third Indiana to lie down and wait in ambush for the head of Forrest's cavalry. The rest of the column continued its march to the southeast toward Blountsville.

Forrest's lead horsemen passed Hathaway's troops without discovering them, and then Hathaway's entire force rose up and fired upon them. The Rebel troopers were taken by surprise, and raced toward the rear in total confusion.

Streight's rear guard was attacked again later than night, but Captain Smith's company ambuscaded the Confederate troops again successfully. The entire column dragged into the town of Blountsville at ten o'clock the following morning. The ride from Day's Gap to Blountsville covered forty miles, and the animals were tired and hungry.

David's company was sent over to the livery to find sufficient corn to feed all of the horses and mules. Sergeant Reid was sent back for the wagons, and they were loaded with corn from the livery stable. The wagons were then pulled out into the streets, where corn was piled out and fed to the horses and mules of the brigade.

Sergeant Reid brought a message to David when he was at the livery stables.

"A courier just came by from Colonel Streight, sir. We have orders to load all of the ammunition from the wagons onto pack mules, and we are to burn the wagons."

"Go get Sergeant Looney and twenty men, and unload all of the wagons on our end of the street. We'll pull them just out of town and burn them there. I don't want to start a hot fire out here that will carry over to these buildings."

"Yes, sir."

The wagons were unloaded, and the ammunition was loaded on pack mules for their trip east. The wagons were pulled out away from the frame buildings of the town, and were burned.

Sergeant Looney rode over and advised David that Colonel Streight had ordered their company "D" and Captain Smith's Company "E" to act as a rear guard for the brigade. The rest of the brigade was to rest for two hours, and then move east toward Gadsden. David ordered pickets posted at various points along the road leading into town.

David and Sergeant Looney had the bugler blow "Boots and Saddles", and they were soon riding west to their post just outside of town. They rode past Colonel Streight and some of his men, who were standing in front of a dry goods store. They were engaged in distributing ammunition out to the mounted troops. They saluted Colonel Streight and Colonel Lawson.

Two hours later, a courier from Colonel Streight rode up on his mule, and advised them that the column was pulling out of Blountsville. The courier had no sooner delivered his report when David heard gunfire up the road. It was General Forrest.

His advance guard had charged Captain Smith's pickets, and were driving them back toward town. David immediately gave orders to deal with the new situation.

"Sergeant Looney, order the men to draw their pistols, and to fight the enemy through town to slow his advance."

"Yes, sir. Men! Draw pistols and prepare to receive mounted attack!"

They spurred their horses and rode forward. Forrest's troopers charged them in small groups of four and five troopers. David and Sergeant Looney brought their men forward and began to engage them immediately.

They shot over the ears of their horses at the gray-clad troopers, who were pushing into Blountsville with greater numbers every five minutes. David shot two Rebel troopers with his Adams revolver. He was then advised by a courier that Captain Smith had ordered the rear guard to march just east of town, and to set up an ambush on the side of the road.

David sent for Anderson Looney. "Sergeant, we are to set up an ambush for the enemy just east of town. You are to stay here with twenty men and fire three rounds at the enemy troopers. Then you'll ride east, and draw the enemy toward our position. Do you understand my orders?"

"Yes, sir. I'll be with you directly, sir."

David ordered the bugler to sound "Recall", and the rest of his company rode east out of Blountsville. They soon joined troopers from Captain Smith, who had dismounted, and were hiding in bushes on the side of the Gadsden Road.

Captain Smith had ordered the men to hide from the approaching Confederate troopers, and to hold their fire until the head of the column had passed by. They rose up and fired into the Confederate horsemen after the head of the column had passed their position. Their firing caused the Rebels to stampede back toward town.

They crossed Graves Creek, a swift little mountain stream, and rode toward the East Fork of the Black Warrior River. Forrest's cavalry began to press them hard from the rear. Captain Smith sent a courier to Colonel Streight, advising him that Forrest's units were pressing his command closely.

Colonel Streight's men found the East Branch of the Black Warrior swollen from heavy rains, and the ford was too deep to allow passage of the column quickly. Colonel Streight deployed the troops in a skirmish line, and ordered Major Vananda to pull his guns across the river, and to unlimber them on the hills above the east bank.

Colonel Streight sent a mounted courier to Captain Smith, ordering his command to fall back and form a line with his unmounted skirmishers. Company D and Company E complied, and a continual skirmish line advanced and drove Forrest's troopers back from sight of the ford.

Streight then ordered his main command to cross the river, and the troops began to cross rapidly at the ford. The water was swift and was waist deep at the ford. Two hours later, Colonel Streight sent a courier to Captain Smith, ordering him to withdraw his command across the river.

Major Vananda began to shell the west bank of the river, lobbing shells in the direction of the Rebels. David hustled his company to the ford, and ordered each trooper to dismount, and to lead their horses across on foot. The other companies of troops deployed as skirmishes crossed over last, at five o'clock that afternoon, and Major Vananda limbered and withdrew his howitzers. The troopers then resumed their march northeastward toward Gadsden.

They rode on through the night, some troops and troopers so weary that they slept in the saddle on the march. Other troopers fell asleep and fell off their mules, and were captured by Forrest's troopers. They navigated by the light of a full moon which had risen in the sky over their shoulders.

They approached the southern end of Lookout Mountain, which the locals called Big Ridge. As they marched toward the mountain, the clouds and mist around the base of the ridge gave it an even more imposing view, compared with the valley they were traversing.

Small parties of Forrest's cavalry continued to harass the column as they neared the ford of Big Wills Creek. Colonel Streight ordered David's company to deploy as skirmishers along the west bank of Big Wills Creek. They were to guard the ford while the rest of the column crossed over. Rains on Lookout Mountain had caused Big Wills Creek to run more swiftly. David noticed that the creek was a typical mountain stream, except the recent rains had swollen the level of the creek at their rocky ford.

David ordered half of the company to deploy forward in a semicircle with their carbines. They were to lie low in the bushes, and guard the ford against attack. The other half of the company, under Lieutenant James Day, had orders to remain mounted, and to hold the reins of their fellow trooper's horses.

If a quick getaway was called for, Lieutenant Day's orders called for them to ride forward and bring the other cavalrymen off. David selected a rocky ridge above the ford at Big Wills Creek, and ordered the men to hide among the rocks and Rhododendron bushes. They loaded their Burnside carbines and waited. Colonel Streight then began crossing his command across the ford at Big Wills Creek. The ford consisted of a rock ledge along a wide stretch of the creek that was normally shallow. Recent rains, however, caused the water to run deeper. Several of their pack mules stepped off the ledge into holes, causing much of the infantrymen's ammunition to become wet.

After most of the command had crossed Big Wills Creek, David heard the hoof beats of several squads of cavalry riding toward them. He began to make out the gray backed riders, as they rode toward them in the mist. He passed the word for Sergeant Looney.

"Anderson, order the men to fire at will at the troopers once they are close to one hundred yards. Shoot their horses in the lead first. Then shoot at the troopers."

"Yes, sir. I will pass the word, sir."

Anderson left, and David cocked his hammer on his carbine. He heard the cavalrymen as they approached a curve in the road just west of the ridge line. As they came into view, he saw at least a dozen troopers with their color bearer in the road. He took aim at the color bearer's horse and fired. A dozen other carbines fired, and their .54 caliber bullets found their marks. Horses were shot down, and their riders were thrown. Some troopers were shot dead, but others were merely stunned after being thrown forward. Another hail of lead was fired their way, and the dismounted Rebel troopers scurried for the cover of big rocks and trees off the road.

Other troopers turned and raced for the rear. A small fire fight soon developed. The rebel troopers fired at David's company with pistols from their concealed positions. David's troopers fired back at the Rebels with their more accurate carbines.

Colonel Streight meanwhile had crossed all of his command at the creek, and Lieutenant Day rode up to advise David to withdraw to the ford.

"Order all the men except Sergeant Looney and four others to mount up and cross at the ford. Have Sergeant Looney to bring my horse and meet me at the ford with his squad."

"Yes, sir." Day saluted and carried out his orders. David maintained fire on the Rebel troopers, pinning them down until his men could safely cross Big Wills Creek. He climbed back past some rocks after several minutes had passed, confident that Sergeant Looney had had sufficient time to bring his horse to the ford. He eased out and down the slope, walking out quickly, and down toward the creek. Sergeant Looney and his men were there, waiting with their pistols drawn.

David returned Looney's salute and mounted his house after inserting his carbine into its saddle holster. "Let's get out of here, First Sergeant."

"Yes, sir. After you, sir."

They rode carefully across the ford, and on toward Black Creek, which was just outside of Gadsden.

Colonel Streight was already crossing his command over Black Creek when they arrived there. A wooden bridge spanned the creek, and it was the only bridge over Black Creek for many miles above and below Gadsden. The bridge spanned several hundred feet, and was constructed of stone piles and a hand sawn wooden frame of pine and oak timbers.

David was ordered to burn the bridge once the last of his command had crossed over onto the eastern side of Black Creek. A rear guard composed of troops from the Eightieth Illinois Regiment was posted upstream.

Sergeant Looney procured some dry timber and some pine straw, and the bridge across Black Creek was soon burning. The pine timber ignited fully, and the oak timbers also caught fire. The flaming wreckage of the bridge soon broke loose, and splashed into the rushing waters of Black Creek.

David's company soon rode into the town of Gadsden, a small hamlet on the Coosa River. The town was composed of wooden frame houses, a post office, and a few government buildings. Colonel Streight ordered some of the men to seize and destroy some rifles and pistols found in the government building in town. All usable ammunition was carried away, and fodder for the animals was procured from the community stores located in the government building.

After destroying all of the Confederate commissary items that they could not use, Streight's command headed northeast again, toward Turkeytown.

* * * * *

General Forrest and his command had problems of their own. Their horses were giving out, and unlike the Yankees, they could not seize replacement animals from the local landowners. General Forrest instead ordered his men to pursue Streight's Yankees in shifts. This gave his men and his horses a chance to rest, while maintaining his pursuit of the Yankee raiders. He had been told that his brother William had been severely wounded at Day's Gap. He sent a wagon and the regimental surgeon back to Day's Gap to assist in treating his brother William.

He ordered his troopers to maintain the pressure on the blue coats, and to give them no rest. His men were beginning to capture small groups of Yankees, whose animals had either given out, or were too weary to stay in the saddle.

A scout had reported that Streight's men had burned the only bridge across Black Creek. The creek ran from the top of Lookout Mountain, and was now swollen from recent rains. Surely there must be a ford across the creek somewhere upstream. He sent some men north upstream to find it.

Sixteen year old Emma Sanson was out rounding up her milk cow in her father's pasture, when she was hailed by two gray coated riders. They wanted to know if there was a ford across Black Creek. Sure there was a ford, her father's cows used it almost every day to get to a green pasture on the other side. Would she show them where it was? Sure she would, she would help them, since it was only her duty. Her brothers both were enlisted in Law's Brigade of Hood's Division of the Army of Northern Virginia. She climbed on back of one of the trooper's horses, and told them where the ford was located. They rode a half mile upstream to the end of the pasture. They followed the narrow trail created by dairy cows, and saw a series of flat rocks that formed the ford across Black Creek. Several puffs of smoke were visible on the opposite bank of the creek, and Emma heard the cracks of rifle fire directed at them. The trooper made her dismount from his horse, and he and his other fellows charged the pickets on the other side of the creek. After several minutes of firing, the Yankee troops were driven off.

One of the troopers summoned General Forrest, who soon ordered his entire command to cross Black Creek at the ford.

General Forrest took a moment to write a note of thanks to the sixteen year old farm girl who showed his men the ford while she was under fire. Her courage was recognized as follows:

Head Quarters in Sadle
May 2, 1863

My highest regards to Miss Ema Sanson for her Gallant conduct while my posse was skirmishing with the Federals across Black Creek near Gadesden Allabama.
N.B. Forrest
Brig. Genl Comding N. Ala.—

* * * * *

The Union troops and troopers pushed on and reached Blount's Plantation, which was located fifteen miles northeast of Gadsden. The plantation was situated near two horseshoe shaped bends in the Coosa River, and was equidistant from both bends of the river.

The plantation house consisted of salt box shaped main dwelling house, with large chimneys on each end. The house was sided with white painted clapboards, and black painted shutters adorned each of the eight windows at the front and rear of the main house.

Blount had constructed many servant cabins on the grounds, and an ice house and a large barn had been built off toward the main road, away from the main house.

Colonel Streight decided that he would rest his command at Blount's Plantation, and procure fodder there for the animals. Captain Smith was detailed to find either Mr. Emory Blount, the owner, or his overseer, and to purchase food for the horses and mules with quartermaster receipts.

Mr. Blount had a great deal of corn and oats in his barn, and Captain Smith's company hauled the forage out in wagons, and began to distribute the forage, including some hay, to the animals. As the animals were being fed and watered, Colonel Streight sent for Captain Milton Russell of the Fifty First Indiana.

Captain Russell was ordered to take 200 of the best mounted men in the infantry units, and proceed to Rome, Georgia. He was to seize the bridge over the Coosa River, and was to hold the bridge until the rest of Streight's command could join them.

David's Company D, and Captain Smith's Company E were then ordered south of the plantation, to act as a rear guard for the brigade. David took his men south of the plantation, and dismounted two thirds of his command, and posted them on either side of the Turkeytown Road.

An hour after they were posted, Forrest's Confederate troopers began to attack them in increasing numbers. David and his company engaged them during the next hour with their Burnside carbines. It soon became apparent that four of five companies of Rebel cavalry were now attacking their position. David decided to send a courier to Captain Smith, in order to inform him about the developing situation. As the firing in their front increased, a courier arrived back from Captain Smith a few minutes later. David was to withdraw his command back on the Turkeytown Road toward Blount's Plantation. Most of Streight's troops were now deployed in a battle line on a ridge just south of the plantation. David and Captain Smith were to mount their companies, and retreat toward the main body of troops.

David sent for a bugler, and asked him to sound "Recall". The "Recall" was blown, and the men mounted up under fire and galloped back up the Turkeytown Road. Forrest's troopers also mounted up, and began to pursue the two companies closely.

Just as the two Alabama companies reached Streight's main line of battle, David saw Major Vananda order his batteries to fire. David heard shot and shells shriek over their heads, and heard the explosions behind him.

The cavalrymen passed through the main line, and David ordered three fourths of the company to dismount and take up stations along the line. The fourth man of each squad held their horses in the rear of the hillside.

Forrest's troopers charged the center of the infantry lines, but were repulsed by troops of the Fifty First and Seventy Third Indiana Regiments.

They then charged the right side of Streight's lines, but were beaten back by troops of the Eightieth Illinois and Third Ohio Regiments. David's company and Captain Smith's company put their carbines to good use at this portion of the line, and assisted the Illinois and Ohio units in holding the line against General Forrest's attacks.

Forrest withdrew his troopers to a ridge back a half mile away, and began to mass his troops for a better and more coordinated attack. It was growing dark, and Colonel Streight decided to withdraw his command back down the road, and to conceal the troop in a large thicket of cane, and to ambush Forrest's troops on their approach.

Colonel Hathaway of the Seventy Third Indiana had received a mortal chest wound in the battle at the plantation, and soon died. Colonel Streight also began to receive reports from his men that most of the ammunition procured from the pack mules was worthless. The cartridges had gotten wet, and the paper had either worn out, or the gunpowder had sifted away.

The men were withdrawn up to Turkeytown Road to a large canebrake, where they were ordered to lie down. An ambush was prepared for Forrest's troopers. Unfortunately, Forrest's troopers began a flanking movement around the area of the proposed ambush. Streight ordered David's company and Captain Smith's company around to block the Confederate flanking movement. He then ordered the balance of his command to slip away in the darkness toward Rome, Georgia.

The troopers and their horses and mules had gone three consecutive nights without adequate sleep. They consequently had to lead their animals because of their fatigue. As a result, their movement and progress was slow, allowing Forrest's troopers the ability to rest, and then catch up to them.

They marched beside the eastern side of Lookout Mountain, which the locals in that area called Shinbone Ridge. They marched along the west bank of the Coosa River, between the river valley and the slopes of Shinbone Ridge. The mules had become tender–footed, because they had marched over rocky ground while being unshod.

They marched in the darkness another ten miles, near the small town of Centre, Alabama, at a point across the Coosa River from a high hill called Billy Goat Hill. David and Captain Smith had orders to lead the advance guard, and as they marched around a bend in the road, they saw a force of gray–clad men posted in ambush ahead.

David mounted his horse and reported this to Colonel Streight. Colonel Streight ordered two companies of troops from the Eightieth Illinois, and Captain Smith's company to engage the Rebels as skirmishers. They were to advance on the Rebels until they were fired upon, and then were to engage the Rebels until Streight's main force had time to pass around them.

The plan worked well. The main column made a detour to the right, and David's company soon led the entire column back onto the main road three miles in the rear of the ambush point. The skirmishers withdrew and fell back to the rear of Streight's column.

The column was now on the west bank of the Chatooga River, a small river that ran from the northeast, and emptied into the Coosa River near Centre, Alabama. Captain Russell and his Indiana troops ferried his command across the Chatooga one hour before Streight's main body could join them. However, Captain Russell failed to post a guard at the ferry.

Local militia, alarmed at discovering Yankees using the ferry, seized the ferry boat, cut it loose from its moorings, and carried it downstream toward Centre.

When the main column reached the ferry, they reported to Colonel Streight that the ferry boat had been carried off, presumably downstream. David was summoned to report to Colonel Streight to deal with this new emergency. Colonel Streight looked terrible. He had bags under his eyes, and David could tell that the strain was becoming too much for him.

"Lieutenant Snelling. What county is this?"

David was almost too tired to think clearly.

"I believe this is Cherokee County, sir."

"Who in your company hails from Cherokee County?"

"I believe William Guthrie, sir. I also believe James Ingram farmed some land between here and Rome, sir, before the war."

"Very good. Go summon them and tell them that they will be our new guides. They need to find another bridge over the Chatooga River."

"Yes, sir." David saluted Colonel Streight, and rode up to find Sergeant Looney. He found him down near the ferry landing, hitching up his breeches.

"Bad news, sir. Corporal Richard Day is missing."

David liked Dick Day, and regretted his loss to the company. "I hate that, Sergeant Looney, but we have other problems. Tell William Guthrie and James Ingram to report to Colonel Streight with me immediately. They are to be our new guides."

"Yes, sir." Looney saluted, and mounted his horse, and rode off toward the company. He soon returned with Guthrie and Ingram, who advised David that there was another bridge above the Chatooga River some seven miles upstream, near Gaylesville, Alabama.

They pushed on as hard as they could in order to reach the bridge over the Chatooga at Gaylesville. One of Streight's worst nightmares then occurred. The road ran into an area where all of the trees on the surrounding hills had been chopped down and cut out to make charcoal for a nearby pig iron furnace.

The main road itself turned into several wagon roads covering a section that spanned more than seven miles.

The guides from David's company became confused. They knew the area and the roads as they existed before the war. However, the war production of pig iron in the area caused the locals to denude the countryside of trees that had served as familiar landmarks. The guides advised Streight's men to take several roads, in order for them to ascertain the main road that led down to the Chatooga River bridge.

Many troops and troopers began to fall asleep, and David and the other officers were constantly having to wake men who had fallen asleep in the saddle. David's company found a trail that led to the Round Mountain Furnace, and David noted that Captain Russell and his men had destroyed the furnace with sledgehammers and powder charges carried from Gadsden for that purpose.

The column had scattered out so much, that it was daylight before all of Streight's men could cross the Chatooga River. The bridge was burned, and the column proceeded on to Cedar Bluff, and then onto the road toward Rome, Georgia, just after daylight. The horses and mules of the command then began to give out, and their progress slowed until 9:00 a.m., when Colonel Streight called a halt to rest and feed the animals.

Some of the troops and troopers began to feed their animals, while other men began to fall asleep in various positions. A courier from Captain Smith rode up a short time later to advise Colonel Streight that a heavy force of the enemy was moving in from the left, and was marching toward them on a parallel route. Streight studied his map, and came to the conclusion that the enemy force was actually closer to Rome than his troops were.

Captain Smith's pickets were then driven in, and Streight ordered all of his command into line of battle. The picture presented was almost comical. Blue coated soldiers in line of battle were falling asleep, while Rebel skirmishers were taking shots at them. A courier from Captain Russell then rode up, and advised Colonel Streight that Captain Russell had been unable to seize the bridge over the Coosa River at Rome. Several pickets were driven in, and several of Colonel Streight's senior officers began to plead with him to surrender their troops to General Forrest. At that point, a sergeant in a gray coat with yellow stripes came riding through the lines, holding a white flag of truce on a wooden staff in his hands, which were covered in gray leather gauntlets.

* * * * *

General Forrest had allowed his men to rest in shifts, which kept his command fresh, even though the Yankees that they were pursuing outnumbered them two to one. He took his command across the Chatooga River at sunup. He had his color sergeant cut a long hickory pole with his saber, and he tested the river bottom at the site of the ferry.

He judged the river bottom to be firm and sandy. He then had two of his brass six pound horse guns dragged across the sandy river bottom with long ropes. The rest of his troopers swam their horses across the Chatooga, and began to march on the Rome Road. That placed his command nearer to Rome than the Yankees, who had to double back south from Gaylesville.

They soon encountered Streight's men, and began to drive in his pickets. General Forrest sensed that something was just not quite right about the Yankee troopers, and began to scan their lines with his field glasses. At last, he began to realize their problem: they were all falling out from lack of sleep.

He summoned one of his artillery lieutenants, a James Carter, and asked him to get some horses, and drive the guns back and forth over the same stretch of road that could be seen at a distance.

He then sat down and composed a note to Colonel Streight, and sent it over with a color sergeant. The note demanded Streight's immediate surrender to stop "the further and useless effusion of blood."

* * * * *

In the meantime, Streight's regimental commanders had called a council of war, and had unanimously agreed to ask Streight to address General Forrest for the terms of their surrender. Colonel Streight sent for

David and for Captain Smith to seek their opinions, since their troopers were only represented by two companies.

David was opposed to surrender entirely.

"Colonel, we have more troops than they have. Our carbines have metal bullets. We have ten rounds left a piece. We could give some of your other troopers our pistols and sabers, and we could cut our way out of here.

If some of us surrender, sir, we could have our necks stretched. Myself included."

"I understand you, Lieutenant Snelling. I promise you that I will ask General Forrest to assure us that all of my command will be treated and respected as prisoners of war. If he cannot assure me that, I will return, and give you the opportunity to take some of your men and get out. Does that satisfy you?"

David was satisfied. He was just a lieutenant, and a full colonel had promised to look after his interests. That was all he could hope to ask for in that situation.

"Yes, sir. I appreciate what you are doing for us, Colonel Streight."

"Thank you. Gentlemen, I am going with the sergeant here to see General Forrest. I will return shortly."

Streight met General Forrest near his lines, and advised the general that he wanted some assurances of certain things before he could surrender his command. First, he wanted assurances that all soldiers surrendered would be treated as prisoners of war. Secondly, he wanted some proof that he was surrendering his command to a superior force.

General Forrest removed his slouch hat and scratched the back of his head, and began to address each issue. All white soldiers would be treated as prisoners of war. No exceptions.

He then raised his hand, and directed Colonel Streight to look at a hill top down a stretch of roadway toward the west. The artillery officer then had the two brass guns pulled across the same section of hill over and over again. This had the appearance of a large number of guns being moved into position.

"Good God! How many guns have you got? I've counted fifteen already."

General Forrest was cool and collected. " I reckon that's all that has kept up with us."

Streight was convinced. He went back and informed his officers that he had decided to surrender. He then returned and announced his decision to General Forrest, and handed him his sword. General Forrest advised him where his men could stack their arms. They were then instructed to march down a hollow and into the road toward Rome.

Streight's remaining command consisted of 1466 men, which were then marched under guard into Rome, Georgia. Captain Russell's detail also surrendered when the column met them on the road into Rome.

They crossed the Coosa River and rode into town, marching the blue coated captives ahead of their column. The mayor of the City of Rome presented General Forrest with a wreath of flowers and a fine horse.

The people of Rome had been busy preparing for a Yankee attack. They then got busy preparing food to feed several hundred dog–tired and half starved Yankees. Forrest's men were also tired and hungry, but not as hungry or as tired as Streight's troops. Streight's men ate like horses when they were served barbequed hams and shoulders and Brunswick stew by the townspeople. They then fell out on the streets, and slept like dead men.

That evening, the provost guard from the local militia separated Streight's men, and David was placed into a group composed of lieutenants, sergeants, and corporals. They were then marched down to the train depot, and loaded into cars for a trip down to Atlanta.

David noticed the locomotive, the *Texas*, which was billowing steam from its balloon – shaped smoke stack. The engine was beautiful, as it was painted red, and the large cow catcher in its front was painted gold. This beautiful engine could be leading him to his death.

If the Confederate authorities ever found his prior enlistment papers from the 57th Georgia Regiment, he would have to face execution. If you are sentenced to be shot for deserting in the face of the enemy, what would they do to you if you deserted to become the enemy? David's thoughts were morbid, but he believed that he would be drawn and quartered if the Confederate authorities knew his actual situation.

They had taken his uncle's horse, and his Adams revolver and his cartridge box. They left him his haversack, his inkwell, and his ink pen. David had sewn a pocket on the inside of his jacket, under his left armpit. It was there that he placed his journal, and the twenty five dollars that General Dodge had given him for pawning his Uncle's Colt Navy revolver.

They were loaded into crude wooden rail cars, which had seats made from planks that were nailed together, and then to the floor. In the corner of the car was a bucket, which was to serve to contain their excrement made during the trip.

The train pulled out after dark, and soon was switched onto the Western & Atlantic Railroad toward Atlanta. They took on water at Big Shanty, and a group of Baptist women handed them pieces of cold corn bread and ham through the two windows of their railroad car. The train did not stop in Atlanta, but continued east onto the Georgia Railroad toward Augusta.

David breathed a sigh of relief when the train switched onto the line of the Georgia Railroad, because he believed that locals from Milledgeville might see him and recognize him if they had made a stop in Macon. David and Sergeant Looney soon drifted off to sleep. Two hours later, the engine pulled into Augusta.

Two provost guards opened the door to their car, while another held an oil–burning lantern. Their slop bucket was emptied, and biscuits, water, and cheese were passed out to the men. The train refueled and took on water, and the *Texas* pulled them off again, this time over into South Carolina.

They went in a similar way through South Carolina, and onto the Wilmington & Manchester Railroad, and then to Florence. They switched trains up into North Carolina. They then ran onto the South side Railroad, and rode into Petersburg, Virginia, and then up into Richmond. They were marched off the train, and down the city streets by a provost guard to Libby Prison, where they were locked into cells of various sizes.

It was May 11, 1863. David saw an opportunity to contact Angela Floyd, and wasted no time. He called one of the guards over, and told him he would pay him five dollars in U.S. greenbacks if he would send a boy over to 105 Broad Street, and take a message to a Mrs. Angela Floyd. He gave the money and a note to the guard, and the guard told him he would honor his request.

David then looked at his ink well, and determined that he had just enough ink to pen a final entry into his journal:

May 11 1863
Libby Prison, Virginia

Dear Uncle Uriah and Aunt Faith:

I have been taken prisoner, along with my entire company, by General Nathan Bedford Forrest, near Rome, Georgia. We were on a raid with a brigade being led by Colonel Abel Streight, and we were chased across North Alabama by Forrest's troopers. We only lost four or five men from our company. Colonel Streight let General Forrest bluff him into surrendering his command at Lawrence Plantation, as Forrest convinced him that he had a larger force than he actually possessed.

I am running out of ink, so I will make this short. Your horse has been captured, and is now in the possession of Rucker's Rebel troopers. They got my Adams revolver, but your Colt Navy revolver was placed in the possession of General Dodge before I left Alabama, for safe keeping.

I am going to contact Angela, and hopefully persuade her to mail this journal to you. I don't know if we are to be exchanged in accordance with the conventions of the cartel or not.

May the Lord bless you and keep you until I return.

Love,

David

    Angela Floyd did receive David's note, and had a house servant drive her over to Libby Prison the next morning. David was led by the guards over to a single cell that had benches set up for visiting.
    Angela was dressed in a plain cotton dress, which was colored a dark gray, and she wore simple lace up shoes. She was as beautiful as ever, but she also appeared somewhat reserved. She lifted her eyes in recognition when she saw him, but David knew deep down inside that she was repulsed somewhat at the sight of him in the blue uniform of the Union Army.
    She sat down, and after the guard stepped outside, she began to speak.
    "Oh David, I did not know you had gone over to fight for the Yankees. I thought you had just decided to leave Milledgeville and Georgia. It is good to see you, though, even if I have to see you like this."
    David reached through the bars of the cell, and took Angela's hand. He had so wanted this woman to be his bride. Now she was the wife of his cousin. He had to cleanse his mind from all emotions, and take care of the business at hand. He began to speak, slowly at first…"Angela,…. I have a journal that I have been keeping that contains a serial letter to Uncle Uriah and Aunt Faith. Please post it to them for me, and let them know that I am all right. I believe that we will be exchanged and sent north on a steamer in the next few days. Will you do that for me?"

He pulled the journal from his hidden pocket, and passed it through the bars to Angela. Angela looked both ways, then slipped the journal into her leather purse.

David then began to discuss her personal life in Richmond. "How is your cousin's place? Do you enjoy living there?"

"Yes, I do. She has a large brick home in town, and we get to see soldiers and government figures all of the time. We see President Davis quite a bit, and General Lee is in town this week to visit his wife, Mary, who lives here in Richmond."

"How is Joseph doing, Angela?"

"He has been promoted to the rank of Major. David, he was slightly wounded at Sharpsburg. You know, he has asked me about you several times in his letters, and when he had leave, but I never knew what to tell him, until now."

David squeezed Angela's hands, and his emotions got the better of him. He had held and restrained them for the duration of the war, until this moment. Tears began to roll down his cheeks, and he then looked her in the eye, and began to speak..."Angela, please don't hate me because I chose to wear this uniform. I have seen hundreds and hundreds of men die on battlefields because of their beliefs. I loved you with all of my heart, and your father came to hate me because I loved my country.

I have done many things in this war. I've killed men, I have ordered men to risk their lives

The last thing I could possibly bear is to hear that you hate me for my beliefs, too. My only desire in life was to love you and to make you happy. This damn war came along and destroyed us and our future. I have no malice toward anyone, and I even wish Joseph well, please believe me."

Angela's reserved demeanor then melted away at David's powerful show of emotion. "Oh David, please don't think I ever hated you. I don't hate you now. It's just that life got too complicated for us. Joseph was more like me in his beliefs. He got leave after Bull Run, David. After we were married, he got another furlough. You have a new cousin. I'll be right back."

She rose from the bench where she was seated, and returned a few moments later with an infant dressed in a small homemade gray shirt and breeches. He even had on a pair of woolen socks that were colored gray, also. The fabric was dyed with a homemade dye that was called butternut, which was just as brown as it was gray. The child was not more than seventeen months old.

He had blue eyes and dark hair like his mother, and had a beautiful smile. Angela sat him up on the bench, and David put his finger out to let the boy squeeze it in his big hand.

"He's a handsome little rascal. What is his name?"

"We decided to name him Matthew, after Joseph's grandfather. He's really a sweet little boy, David. It's a joy to raise him."

David looked out at the little boy, and realized that could be his son looking at him. If only he had been given the opportunity to marry his lovely mother. He reached into his hidden pocket and pulled out fifteen U.S. greenback dollars, and handed the money out to Angela.

"Angela, I want you to take this money. I know with the Union blockade, it's hard to buy food, and the foodstuffs here are really pricey. This child deserves it, here, take it, please."

"I don't know, David. I don't want to take your money."

"You're not taking my money. Angela, just pretend it came from somewhere else. This money came from Jesus. Here, take it."

Angela took the fifteen dollars.

"Thank you, David. You know that I'll put this to good use for Matthew."

"Angela, please promise me that when Matthew grows up, he won't hate me for fighting for the Union."

"Don't worry David, as long as I live, he'll never hate you. You can count on that."

The guard came in, and cut their visit short.

"I'll try and come down and see you tomorrow, David, God bless you."

David blew Angela and Matthew a kiss, and waved goodbye to them, as the guard led them out the door of the prison. He hoped that Angela would mail his journal to Uriah and Faith Snelling, and he hoped that the $15.00 he had given them would be put to good use. He also hoped to see them again tomorrow.

Chapter Sixteen

The Union Army and the Confederate Army accepted a cartel for the exchange of prisoners on July 22, 1862. The cartel was adopted by the U.S. Army, under General Order No. 142, Series 1862. The cartel was agreed upon by Major General John A. Dix of the U.S. Army, and Major General Daniel Harvey Hill of the C.S. Army (who), "in behalf of their respective governments, and by virtue of which all prisoners, of whatever branch of service, are to be exchanged or paroled in ten days from the time of their capture if it be practicable, etc."

The cartel exchanged prisoners using a weighted exchange formula whereby a non–commissioned officer was equal to two privates, a lieutenant to four privates, and on up to a brigadier general being worth 40 privates, and a general of an army being worth sixty privates. Officers of equal rank could of course be swapped on a man – for – man exchange.

Men not exchanged through the cartel could be paroled by either side when captured. This involved a captured prisoner promising not to take up arms again until properly exchanged.

In May of 1863, the exchange of prisoners required the Union prisoners to be loaded into railroad cars in Richmond, where they were taken down to Petersburg, Virginia, on the Richmond & Petersburg Railroad. The prisoners then were transported to cars on the City Point Railroad, and were carried a few miles to the town of City Point, a deep water port on the James River.

A steamer from Point Lookout, Maryland or Fortress Monroe would then tie up at City Point, after embarking Confederate prisoners from those locations. At City Point, the prisoners' names would be read off by the cartel officers, and then the exchanges would actually take place.

David and his group of prisoners were notified early that morning of May 13th that they were to be exchanged. The cartel had been kicked into high gear by the Confederacy's immediate need for more troops.

David's exchange came as part of a large group of privates and NCO's and junior officers that were agreed upon in a larger exchange of troops. However, the senior officers, including Colonel Streight, Colonel Lawson, and Captain Smith were not exchanged. The Union army had simply not captured that many privates, as the war in the east had not gone very well for the Union up to that point in Virginia.

When the guards came for David's group, they were lined up in a single file near the senior officers' cell. David saw Captain Smith, and walked over to accept a letter from him.

"David, would you please post this to my wife in Cincinnati when you return to Washington? I have put the address on the outside for you."

"Certainly. I sure hope they exchange you soon, Captain Smith. I kind of feel guilty about leaving you all behind."

Colonel Streight answered David promptly. "Don't you dare feel guilty about being exchanged, Lieutenant. You go back and win the war. We will be all right here. We will be exchanged shortly. You take care of yourself."

David continued to feel guilty, but instead reached through the bars of the cell and shook hands with Captain Smith and Colonel Streight. The guards began to move the line of prisoners down the hall, and David looked back at the group of Union officers for the last time.

He then marched down the hall, and out the door of Libby Prison, and down the streets of Richmond, to the railroad depot. They were boarded on cars on the Richmond & Petersburg Railroad, and their train left the station and headed south into Petersburg. They were then switched onto the City Point Railroad for a short ride over to City Point.

They were marched away from the train station at City Point, and down to the waterfront at the James River docks. City Point was located at the end of a peninsula that jutted out into the tide water of the James River. Just below City Point, the James River ballooned out over a mile in width, and was a deep, swift, river. City Point was thus an excellent port for deep drafted steamers from the Atlantic Ocean.

David looked out over the wide expanse of the James River, and marveled at the width of the waterway. He spied sea gulls flying low and skimming the surface of the water, and wondered at their speed and grace.

The column of Union prisoners was halted, to allow Confederate cartel officers to call out the name and rank of each prisoner in their group. David had three hundred men in his group from Libby Prison, and all of the men in the group were prisoners from Streight's Brigade.

They rounded a bend in the road near the waterfront, and David saw a large paddle–wheeled transport tied up at the landing. It was a long ship, over nine hundred tons, with high paddle wheels that were fully encased in semicircular wheelhouses. The ship was painted entirely white, except for its smokestacks and iron railing, which were painted black. She flew the U.S. Blue Ensign at her stern, and she was off loading three hundred Confederate prisoners of war from Point Lookout, Maryland.

Union cartel officers were hard at work reading off the name and rank of each Confederate soldier as he stepped down off the gangway. Confederate cartel officers in gray coats were also writing out their enrollment sheets as each Confederate soldier exited the ship.

David and his group were required to give their full name and rank to Confederate cartel officers, who then prepared lists to give their Union cartel counterparts. Soon, the 300 Confederate prisoners were marched down toward the trains at City Point, and the men of David's group were led down the gangway.

As they walked up the gangway, Union cartel officers read off the name and rank of each Union prisoner on their list, and then each man whose name was called was ordered to board the steamer.

David and Anderson Looney boarded the steamer quickly, and said hello to a white coated flag officer who wore a flat topped cap, and white cotton duck breeches. They walked to the stern of the steamer, and stood down near the taffrail.

The sun was beginning to set, and David and Anderson patiently waited while the rest of their group boarded the steamer. There were sailors on the deck attending to their duties, and one of David's men, Bill Blankenship, began to question the sailors about the steamer, and their probable destination. He reported his findings to David a few minutes later.

"They said we are aboard the Steamship *Dove*, sir, and we're headed for Baltimore. The rest of Colonel Streight's exchanged men will be brought to Baltimore on the *Star of the West*. They said she will dock here in the morning."

David began to figure the number of men that had been exchanged out of Streight's command.

"That means it should take around three days to get all of us up to Baltimore, if they only have those two steamers to move troops with. Why are we headed to Baltimore? Did they tell you that, Mr. Blankenship?"

"Yes, sir. The cartel rules require each side to return exchanged prisoners to the area of operations where they were captured. In our case, sir, we have been ordered back to Nashville."

"Did he tell you how we are to get to Tennessee from here?"

"No sir, but he did say that our immediate destination is Baltimore harbor."

"Thank you Mr. Blankenship. I'll find a cartel officer and ask him more details about our orders for movement, once we get underway."

They walked down to the wheel house, where the huge paddle wheel on the port side was located. David noticed that the paddle wheel itself was made entirely of metal, and the paddles and all surfaces that met the salt water were covered with tin.

The smokestacks were located side by side in between the paddle wheels of the steamer, and were mounted just behind the crankshaft. All of the big cranes and lifting equipment for cargo had been removed and cleared away, because of the specialized work the vessel was undertaking. The only cargo that the *Dove* was under government contract to haul was human cargo. A large galley was set up near the stern of the vessel, and the men were soon ordered to line up for mess. They received a tin cup of coffee, one piece of soft bread, and a tin plate of beef stew for their evening meal. Not long after mess, the officers of the *Dove* ordered the moorings cast off, and the large steam engines began to power up.

David noticed that the smoke from the stacks had become darker and more voluminous, and the large paddle wheels began to rotate backward from the gang way and docks. The *Dove* then slowly made its way out into the current of the James River.

When they were more than twenty rods away from the quay, the captain blew the steamer's large whistle, and some of the prisoners on board began to cheer. The engines of the steamer shifted forward, and the large paddle wheels began to turn in a forward direction with greater and greater rapidity. The steamer's wake soon grew steady, as her forward speed increased. They were soon moving downstream on the James River, making twelve knots. They were making over six knots themselves, and were aided by a six knot river current and the beginning of the pull of the ebb tide.

They soon steamed past Jordan's Point on the south side of the James, and Wilcox's Landing and Harrison's Landing on the north side of the river. The sun began to set in the west, and David noticed the striking beauty of its orange reflection on the water of the James, compared to the green pine–tree covered banks of the river.

The James River made a sharp bend to the south, then another bend to the north again, and they began to steam into more open water.

David looked at Jamestown, as the steamer rounded another bend in the river. If Jamestown was this close, then Yorktown was just across the Peninsula, the area between York and James Rivers.

They steamed into Hampton Roads, where the C.S.S. *Virginia* and the U.S.S. *Monitor* had dueled in April of 1862, and past the large port of Norfolk. It was getting dark, and they began to steam past Fortress Monroe, an impregnable fortress that the Union had managed to hold on to at the tip of the Peninsula. He soon spied the outline of a long steamship, and soon recognized her familiar outlines. She was the *Star of the West*, a sister ship to the *Dove*, and she was inbound from Fortress Monroe to City Point.

The captains of each vessel blasted their steam whistles at each other as they steamed by. David could just make out the dark shapes of the Confederate prisoners on the decks of the *Star of the West* as the vessel slipped by on their port side, around forty rods away.

The stars and a quarter moon were soon out, and the steamer veered into Chesapeake Bay, and turned due north. David was about to enquire about their sleeping berths, when he ran into Anderson Looney near the wheelhouse on the starboard side.

"Lieutenant, the sailors are directing us to sleep in shifts, since they only have pallets set up down below for only a hundred and fifty men. I did find a cartel officer, a Major John Kendall, and this is what he told me."

"Go on."

"He said that all of Streight's men except the officers from Captain Smith on up were exchanged, and we are to go to Baltimore. They are to put us on a B&O Railroad train and take us over to Wheeling, and then to Camp Chase, Ohio. From there we are to go to Cincinnati or Indianapolis, and then on the L&N to Louisville and Nashville."

"How long are we to stay in Baltimore?"

"He said at least three days. The U.S. Military Railroad train must be full before it pulls out. They only have three cartel ships a day running up from City Point."

"What is the name of the other steamer?"

"I believe he said it was the *Princeton*, sir."

"I think I have had enough excitement for one day. Pass the word to the men that half will need to stay up with you for a while, and half of the men can sack out below with me. Have the men count off. Every one that says "two" can go below and sack out. All the "ones" will stay up with you. Send a man below to wake me in three hours. We'll sleep in three hour shifts."

"Yes, sir. I'll get to it, sir."

"And tell the men that are up with you that we are to stay together when we get to Baltimore. I don't want to go and dig men out of bawdy–houses when we get there after the first day. We can't miss our train. We need to show the rest of the Union Army we can really do something right. Do you know what I mean, Anderson?"

"Yes, sir, I sure do. Good night, sir."

* * * * *

They slept in three hour shifts, and late the next day, Sergeant Looney came below to wake David from his nap.

"You will want to come topside and see this, sir. We're passing Fort McHenry now."

The *Dove* had just rounded Sparrows Point, and was ascending the tidewater of the Patapsco River. On a point just outside of the river was a large star–shaped brick fort, which rose above the harbor entrance of Baltimore. Anderson was almost giddy with joy.

"It's Fort McHenry, sir. I never believed that I would ever see it. Look at the size of that flag, sir. It's the largest Stars and Stripes I've ever seen!"

"Sergeant, go down below, and tell the rest of the men to come up on deck and line the rail. They need to see this glorious symbol of what we have been fighting for."

"Yes, sir." Anderson went below, and David gazed at the huge and magnificent Stars and Stripes waving above Fort McHenry. All of the Union soldiers came out to the railing and stared at the spectacle. Soon the men began to cheer, and David cheered with them.

* * * * *

Maj. And Mrs. Uriah Snelling
c/o General Delivery
Milledgeville, Georgia C.S.A.

Richmond, Virginia
May 15, 1863

Dear Uncle Uriah and Aunt Faith:

David was here in Richmond yesterday, after being captured in Alabama with Colonel Streight's Brigade. I went to Libby Prison and met with him, after he sent a guard over with a note at my cousin's house.

He is doing fine, but looks quite different from the young man you last saw in Milledgeville. He is riding in the Yankee Cavalry, and has grown a mustache. His features seem more determined and hardened. I brought baby Matthew down to see him, and it lifted his spirits a little.

He gave me some U.S. greenbacks to use to buy Matthew some food, and for that we are truly grateful. He also gave me his journal which I brought out of Libby Prison, which I am forwarding on to you. David has fought in a number of engagements, and though I disagree with him supporting the Yankees, I can only admit that he is a fine officer who has done his duty thus far.

David and the rest of his brigade were exchanged, and were taken down on the cars to City Point yesterday morning. The guards at Libby Prison told me that a prisoner exchange cartel will allow them safe passage on a steamer from City Point to Baltimore.

I just wanted to write and tell you that David is safe, and I am posting his journal to you as per his wishes. We are doing fine up here. Young Matthew is growing like a weed. Please stay in touch. I know David would stay in touch with all of us if he could.

Love Always,

Angela Floyd

* * * * *

The *Dove* soon steamed across Baltimore harbor, and was berthed on a pier in the inner harbor. An officer from the cartel, and several representatives of the United States Sanitary Commission met the steamer at the docks. The Union prisoners were then called out on deck by the captain and his crew, and they were then addressed by the cartel officer, a Major Skyler Carroll. Major Carroll was slim and tall, and had short brown hair, and an elegant mustache. He was with the Fifth U.S. Infantry Regiment, but had not seen combat in several years. Major Carroll dressed in non–regulation but gaudy uniforms, wearing broad gold epaulets, and a red sash about his waist.

He was accompanied by a Miss Marlena Michaels, who was a regional officer on the U.S. Sanitary Commission, and by a local director on the Sanitary Commission, Archibald Ryan.

Miss Michaels was nearly forty, but was an attractive but prudish woman who maintained a fastidious appearance, and wore a plain black dress.

Mr. Ryan wore a black suit and a stovepipe hat, and had a gold watch fob dangling from his waistcoat. Ryan was loyal to the Union cause, but did not think of serving as a combat soldier. He instead devoted his energy to the Sanitary Commission. He established an aid station for the Union prisoners at an old cotton warehouse off of Pratt Street.

At the old warehouse, Union prisoners were provide pallets and free meals, and bathing facilities were also set up for their comfort.

Major Carroll began to address the men, and advised them that they would be sent west on a B&O Railroad train within the next two or three days, depending on the cartel ships' delivery of additional Union prisoners. The War Department had ordered the prisoners west to Camp Chase in Columbus, Ohio, and then the prisoners would be transferred by rail to Louisville, and thence to Nashville.

Major Carroll then read the ground rules to the men. They were to stay at the old warehouse until they were sent for by War Department Officers for their march to the B&O Railroad Station. They would be fed and billeted, and the ladies working for the Sanitary Commission would provide writing materials, and will post letters home for any man who wanted to write to his family.

The ladies of the Commission were there as volunteers, and were not to be touched or trifled with in any way, since they were only there for the comfort of the men. Bathing facilities would also be provided. He demanded that the men must be on their best behavior. No trips to saloons or bawdy houses would be permitted. All of those places were off limits to all soldiers.

If any misconduct occurred, the offending soldier would be arrested and brought to Camp Carroll, where he would be court martialed and punished by Union Army officers.

The men were then marched off the *Dove*, and then marched up Albemarle Street to Pratt Street, to the old cotton warehouse that was now used by the Sanitary Commission.

David and Sergeant Looney noticed the odd collection of buildings off the waterfront. Old federal style clapboard houses with slate or cedar shingle roofs were interspersed with two and three story brick commercial buildings.

Children played and ran through cobblestone streets, while drays pulled by horses and mules brought grain and farm produce from western Maryland down to the markets and the waterfront.

They soon marched their way up Pratt Street, where David spied a barber shop, and saw a branch of the Maritime Bank. He then decided that when the men were settled into their temporary quarters at the warehouse, that he would get down to the bank and make a cash withdrawal.

After the men were settled in and given a tour of the facilities by Miss Michaels and Mr. Ryan, David asked Sergeant Looney to come with him.

"Tell Sergeant Reid to take over for you for a little while, as we have to tend to some business for an hour or two."

David went into the nearby branch of the Maritime Bank, and spent several minutes convincing a vice president there that he was actually David R. Snelling of Milledgeville, Georgia. He procured a copy of his commission as a First Lieutenant in the U.S. Volunteer Cavalry before the bewildered bank officer allowed him to make a $250.00 cash withdrawal from his savings account.

He then brought First Sergeant Looney up Pratt Street to a firearms dealer, where he purchased a Massachuset made Adams revolver, together with a box of one hundred rounds of brass encased cartridges.

He then asked Sergeant Looney if he would accompany him up the street to a barber shop, where he had planned to pay for a shave and a bath for them both. They walked up to a two story brick structure that had a barber pole displayed on its storefront, where they walked inside.

Several men were seated in the back of the shop, playing checkers, and eating crackers and hoop cheese. Two cavalry officers were seated in barber chairs in front of a large mirror, having their faces shaved.

Two men wearing white coats and black jean – cloth trousers were busy shaving the cavalry officers, who wore blue trousers with yellow stripes that ran down the side of their legs.

The barber was a gray haired man of fifty years, and his apprentice was a tall red–haired boy who was no more than seventeen.

The old barber spoke first. "What can I do for you soldiers today? Would you want a shave? Or how about a bath? My man Jesse back there can heat up some water on my stove in the back, and have you a bath ready for just forty cents. What will it be?"

Anderson had never set foot in a barber shop before, and David quickly realized it. He decided to treat his friend and his first sergeant to a bath and a shave.

"We'll have both, and we thank you. Here is two dollars in greenbacks. We'll bathe first, if you don't mind, and then we would like a shave."

The barber took David's greenbacks, and placed them in his cash drawer. He then called for his Negro servant. "Jesse! Get me up some hot water, and prepare two baths for these soldiers."

David then saw a Negro man in his forties appear from the back of the room, wearing a white waistcoat, a blue shirt, and canvas breeches. He responded with a simple "Yes Sah," and asked David and Anderson to step into the rear room of the establishment. In the corner of the room was a pot bellied wood burning stove, with a black stovepipe that ran up and out the rear wall of the shop. Two wooden stalls were over in the corner of the room, containing one iron bathtub in each set of stalls. A set of wooden swinging doors were mounted on each stall, allowing the bather some degree of privacy.

A small window was cut into the side of each stall, which allowed the Negro to pour hot or cold water into each bathtub.

Jesse directed them to the dressing area, where David and Anderson removed their clothing. While they undressed, Jesse poured heated water into both bathtubs, and pumped in cold water from well pumps mounted on the wall into both bathtubs.

David and Anderson got into their respective bathtubs, where they were handed soap and scrubbing brushes and wash rags by Jesse. They soaked their aching bodies in the warm bath, and then rinsed with the cold water. They then dried off on towels hung in each of their stalls. They changed into a clean set of drawers they had brought in their haversacks, and dressed back into their uniforms.

They then went back to the front of the shop, and each sat in the barber's chairs, since the other cavalry officers had completed their shaves, and had paid the barber and left the building.

David once again did the talking for them. "Shave everything off my sergeant, Mister, and you can have your boy shave off my beard. Please have him leave my mustache, though."

"Sure, lieutenant. I never seen you boys before. You come in today on the *Princeton*?"

"No sir, we came in yesterday on the *Dove*."

The barber and his apprentice then went through the steps needed to generate shaving lather. They each poured some soapy hot water into a pewter mug, and began to whisk the contents of the mug with a long brush.

"What outfit are you with? Where did you serve?" The boy then began to lather David's beard with the soapy brush.

"We are with the First Middle Tennessee Cavalry. We were captured with Colonel Streight by General Forrest the first part of May near Rome, Georgia."

"I read about that in the newspaper. We also read about it in *Harper's Weekly*. We are at least glad you were exchanged quickly. You could have been stuck in prison for a while."

"Yes, sir, we feel we have been fortunate in that respect. Colonel Streight and most of his officers were detained at Libby Prison."

The two men playing checkers then began to take part in their conversation. One old man in a checkered shirt and a long white beard began to speak.

"...Those troopers that just left are with the First Maryland Cavalry. They tell us that Jeb Stuart rode around them down on the Chickahominy River. They say that the Reb cavalry can outride and out shoot 'em. Is that true out in Tennessee?"

David took the liberty of speaking, in between the shaving strokes of the barber's razor. It was difficult to speak clearly with his head thrown back in the chair, but David spoke clearly.

"We are better equipped and better mounted than the Rebel troopers. They have better and bolder officers than us. General Forrest engineered our capture with half as many men as we had."

The old man then spoke up again. "We are losing this war in the east. Nobody can match wits with General Bobby Lee in Virginia. That damn fool Joe Hooker will never win this war here. What do you think of General Rosecrans?"

David once again managed to answer the old man in between razor strokes.

"...He has been steady, and has shown a willingness to fight General Bragg's army. He had his whole line knocked back three miles at Stones River. Can he win the war? I don't know. But I will tell you this, we will never win this war unless the War Department cashiers the fools and incompetent generals in this army, and promotes those generals that show ability and aptitude for prosecuting the war."

The men in the barber shop began to mutter and nodded their heads in agreement, and the chorus of "Well said", and "Well spoken" echoed through the barber shop.

* * * * *

They finished their shaves, and David took Anderson down to a tobacco and cigar shop on Pratt Street, where he bought Anderson a small box of imported West Indies cigars. Anderson was curious.

"If you will forgive me for asking this sir, but why are you doing all these things for me?"

David stopped in the edge of the cobblestone street, and put his hand on Anderson's shoulder.

"Sergeant, you are an excellent first sergeant and NCO. Without your ability, I could never have survived this last mission in Alabama. You have taken care of me, and from now until the end of this war, I will take care of you. We had better get back to the old warehouse, or that powder puff Major Carroll might send a provost guard to arrest us."

* * * * *

They arrived at the old cotton warehouse a half hour later, and were immediately greeted by an infantry corporal and two provost guards. The corporal introduced himself as Joseph Ford, and began to question David.

"Where have you been? The major sent us out to arrest you? Why did you leave the warehouse without permission?"

David's face became flushed with anger, and he reached into his holster and swiftly drew his Adams revolver, and aimed it at Corporal Ford's chest.

"See here, corporal. The next time you address me, you will address me as sir, do you understand me? Disarm these men, Sergeant Looney, right now." David pointed the pistol at Corporal Ford's forehead, and Sergeant Looney relieved the provost guards of their Springfield rifles.

"You will be able to collect these rifles tomorrow morning, corporal. For your information, you are addressing a real combat soldier. We didn't spend the war in a big fine city, sleeping every night in a soft, warm bed. We have spent the past ten months in combat, killing Rebels, and getting shot at in the field. When you address me and my men, you will do so with respect. You came to tell me something I believe, Corporal Ford, what was it?"

Ford was absolutely terrified at this unusual behavior. "...Well, sir, first, I was telling you that you were under arrest..."

"I'm not going to let you arrest me today, so go on and tell me something else."

"Well, sir, Major Carroll sent me to also tell you that the rest of Colonel Streight's exchanged men came in this afternoon on the *Princeton*, sir. I am to have you up at six a.m., and after morning mess, you are to form up all of the former prisoners and march them up Pratt Street to the B&O Railroad Station."

"You go back and tell your powder puff major that we will be up at five a.m., will mess at six a.m., and will be marching up Pratt Street at seven a.m. We want to leave here just as bad as you want us out of here. That will be all, corporal."

"Yes, sir."

"Oh, by the way, I had to attend to some important personal business up the street. That is why Sergeant Looney and I were not present when you arrived. Here are your rifles, corporal." David handed Corporal Ford the Springfield rifles of the provost guards, and Corporal Ford nodded a polite "thank you", and left the warehouse with his men.

David asked Sergeant Looney to pass the word among all of the prisoners that they were to arise at five a.m., attend morning mess, and march out to the B&O Station by seven a.m.

David then summoned Sergeant Reid. "Sergeant, what have the men been doing since we left?"

Sgt. Reid's hair was still damp. "Well, sir, most of us bathed, and some have written letters to their kin up north. Those that wrote letters were Colonel Streight's men, though. We had mess thirty minutes ago, sir."

David could smell the hot cornbread and pea soup at the end of the room, along with the aroma of smoked bacon.

"Some of the men asked the women working for the Sanitary Commission about Miss Michaels. They told us that she wanted Major Carroll to court and spark her, but the girls said he would have no truck with that, since he was sparking a pretty young thing down in Annapolis. We were told that girl's family had plenty of money down in Annapolis. What do you think of that, sir?"

"I think we all have been here way too long, 'cause you have been here long enough to repeat all of the ladies' gossip."

Sergeant Looney laughed out loud, and David suggested that all of them get to sleep, since they were to get an early start the following morning.

* * * * *

At seven a.m., after morning mess, Corporal Ford and five provost guards were sent to David, and asked him to order the men to march up Pratt Street in a column of two men abreast.

They marched a mile and a half down Pratt Street, passing two story brick town houses, mercantile establishments, and various shops and even bawdy houses. They then marched down to a wooden train depot, which was situated near Camp Carroll.

Camp Carroll was a large cavalry base and remounting station that had been built on B&O Railroad property in 1862. The 13th Pennsylvania Cavalry, the 1st Connecticut Cavalry, and The 1st Maryland Cavalry were quartered there. David saw the cavalrymen with their horses near wooden corrals across the quadrangle from the station.

A long train of Pullman cars was parked at the depot, and David noticed the familiar features of the American Standard 4-4-0 engine parked above the depot platform. The engine was the *Tom Thumb II*.

The guards directed all of the men to board the train, and a lieutenant from Major Carroll's staff checked the muster roll of the prisoners as each man boarded. David was then handed several baskets of cheese, bread, and hardtack which the Sanitary Commission had prepared for the men's consumption on their journey to Ohio.

The *Tom Thumb II* soon put on a head of steam, and the troop train pulled away from the B&O station. Unlike the austere train that took them from Georgia to the Carolinas, this train had Pullman sleeping cars, and even had water closets in the passenger cars.

David had always loved railroad trains, and had ridden on the B&O Railroad several times on his way to Philadelphia and Washington. David looked out at the countryside rolling by, and remembered that they were riding over the same track that was once served with horse – drawn cars back in the 1820's. He was deep in thought when Sergeant Looney came over to his car, requesting a word with him.

He had eaten his afternoon ration of cheese and hardtack, and brought David his evening ration and his canteen. David asked him what was on his mind, and Anderson began to question David about his past.

"If you don't mind me asking, sir, who was that pretty woman we saw you with at Libby Prison? I didn't know anything about you having a sweetheart or a bank account in a Baltimore Bank, for that matter.

The way you handled that provost guard yesterday was somewhat curious. Is there anything on your mind that you might want to tell me, sir? I am here to help you, if I can."

David thought that Sergeant Looney was being a bit nosy, but he believed that the sergeant was there to help him, and did deserve some kind of explanation.

He began to tell him everything.

"You know when we were down in Alabama, being pursued by General Forrest's troopers?"

"Yes, sir, I remember that well."

"Then you should also remember that there were times when we had to burn bridges behind us to keep the enemy cavalry off of us."

"Yes, sir, I do."

"Well, I have burned plenty of bridges behind me with my personal life. That pretty young woman that some of you saw me with was my fiancé back in '60.

Back then, I was working on my uncle's plantation above Milledgeville, and we laid in a beautiful cotton crop. I got it ginned and shipped to market by railroad, and made some decent money off of it. My Uncle Uriah even opened an account for me at the Maritime Bank."

"So what went wrong with your life?"

"The war. My cousin enlisted in a Confederate regiment in Virginia, and my fiancé's father thought me a coward for not enlisting. He attacked me, and I defended myself. I hit him with an ax handle, and broke his collarbone. He even broke off my engagement with Angela, the girl you saw at Libby Prison."

"Why did all that happen to you?"

"Because of my beliefs. I could not join the Confederate service, and my Uncle William threw me out for it. I went to live with my Uncle Uriah, and he helped me enlist in the Union Army. My fiancé went to Richmond and married my cousin Joseph."

"Why were you so hard on that provost guard back in Baltimore?"

I just decided that I had been pushed around enough in this war. The man was working for an absolute idiot who has never served in a fighting unit. I was not going to be arrested for only taking care of my personal business."

Another officer soon entered their car, holding his ration of hardtack and cheese, and clutching his canteen.

"Lieutenant Snelling, I'm Lieutenant William Ward of the Eightieth Illinois, may I join you for a while, sir?"

David's demeanor settled, and he extended Lieutenant Ward the hospitality of his passenger compartment. "Sure, please join us. This is First Sergeant Looney, of the First Middle Tennessee Cavalry."

The two men exchanged pleasantries, and then Lieutenant Ward began to initiate a conversation. David looked out the window of his car, and saw beautiful pastures, rolling green hills, livestock, and rail fences pass by, as they sped down the tracks.

"Some of the boys got to speak to the girls working with the Sanitary Commission. They all had either husbands or sweethearts in the Army of the Potomac. Whenever those men have had furloughs home, they have all bad-mouthed General Joe Hooker. They told how badly his army is run, and they even told salacious things about Hooker's headquarters."

David was now curious. "What things were those?"

Lieutenant Ward took a bite of cheese, a slug of water, and continued…"Well, they told me that all sorts of prostitutes and bad women are seen coming and going from the general's headquarters tent. It has gotten so bad, that the soldiers now refer to all whores as 'Hookers'".

David's face turned red with embarrassment. That was shameful behavior for any U.S. Army officer to engage in, much less a commanding general. "You know, I would think that the commanding general of an army would set a good example for all of his soldiers to follow, and not engage in such conduct. How can his own men respect him?"

Lieutenant Ward wolfed down more bread and cheese, and answered. "That's just it, sir, they don't. All of the soldiers have told those ladies with the Sanitary Commission that if General Hooker is in command in the next battle, that General Lee's army will whip them again.

And that's not all they said. They said that they were afraid that if they lost the next fight, we will lose the war."

Sergeant Looney then got upset. "Did you hear that, sir? Oh God, what would we do if that happened?"

David was concerned, but kept his composure. "Lieutenant Ward, can we assume that if opinion against General Hooker is so widespread, that his superiors in the War Department also know about his situation?"

"I would think so, sir."

"Well then, maybe General Hooker might get relieved, and some other general might be appointed to take his place. You also need to remember that General Grant's army is in front of Vicksburg, and General Rosecrans still has the Army of the Cumberland around Nashville. We still have a war to fight, if the War Department will get us back to Tennessee. Everyone has to do their duty, or the war is lost everywhere."

Lieutenant Ward ate the last of his hardtack, and stood up to take his leave.

"You're right, sir. This war can be won yet."

Lieutenant Ward exited the car, and David thought about the situation he could have faced in Richmond had the War Department discovered his service record from the 57th Georgia Regiment. He was certain that he would have been executed had his Confederate service history been discovered.

He then remembered what Colonel Streight and Captain Smith told him at Libby Prison. "Win the war." He was determined to help his commanders to do just that.

* * * * *

The B&O engine *Tom Thumb II* puffed on, and pulled them past the town of Mount Airy, Maryland, and on across the Potomac River into Harpers Ferry. Harpers Ferry was now located in the new state of West Virginia. The engine halted to take on coal and water, and B&O Railroad officials at the depot distributed additional food to the men for their trip west.

The hard tack and cheese were once again passed out, and the soldiers ate their evening meal while the engine took on coal and water. David noted the picturesque view of the town from the train depot. Mountains in the Blue Ridge range surrounded the town, and the Shenandoah River ran into the Potomac River just above the town.

The train was soon refueled, and pulled away from the station just before dusk. The men slept while the *Tom Thumb II* sped west over the B&O line, and into the Potomac River Valley.

They arrived near the end of the line at Wheeling, West Virginia. Wheeling was located on the Ohio River, and the river was over a half mile wide there, and was swift and deep. However, engineers had been unable to bridge the river there before the war. A steam ferry was tied below the end of the B&O line, and the cartel officers instructed the soldiers that a change of trains was required.

They left the cars in a cold, steady rain. David pulled on his oilskin that he kept rolled up in his haversack. Some of the men had no rubber raincoat or oilskins, because they were taken from them at their time of capture at Cedar Bluff.

They transferred to the large steam ferry, which was powered with large steam engines and a paddle wheel mounted on its rear. The ferry soon crossed the river in the cold rain, and the soldiers were directed to march uphill from the docks on the Ohio side of the river.

They walked up to a railroad siding, where another railroad engine and cars were parked and waiting. The engine and its tender bore the designation "U.S. Military Rail Road". The men were soon loaded into the waiting cars, and the train sped west toward Columbus.

The men grabbed some much needed sleep while the U.S. Military Rail Road engine and train sped by the small towns of Cambridge, Zanesville, and Reynoldsburg, and into the Ohio State Capital, Columbus.

The train pulled into the depot at three thirty a.m., and the men were soon dusting the coal soot of the train from their sleepy eyes, and were lined up in formation by the NCO's.

David stepped out of the train and onto a large wooden depot building, where he spied the familiar form of a Union Army officer. He now sported a Hardee hat and a set of major's oak leafs on his shoulder straps, but David recognized Major William Bankhead at once.

He walked over to the major and saluted. "It's really nice to see you again, sir. Lieutenant David Snelling. You enrolled us into the service down in Huntsville last summer."

"I remember you well, lieutenant. You were promoted from the ranks. Have your men form up over there, and I'll escort you down to Camp Chase. Welcome to the great State of Ohio."

"Thank you sir. We will form up directly, sir."

The men formed ranks on the quad opposite the train depot, and were soon marching up Lockbourne Road, past the Ohio State Capitol building.

They then turned down Livingston Avenue, and marched for another two miles to Camp Chase. Camp Chase was a series of brick and wooden frame buildings that served as a U.S. Army depot and barracks.

David also noticed that some wooden buildings were being constructed inside a stockade near the rear of the camp. A cartel officer soon emerged from a brick building, and saluted Major Bankhead, and began to address the men.

"Welcome to Camp Chase. I am Captain James Greene. In a few moments, Sergeant Shipley and myself will have you line up and give us your name, rank, and unit. We will then take you off the prisoner exchange list, and return you to active duty in the United States Volunteer Army.

You will be with us for a few days, where you will be issued new weapons. Your officers will be required to write monthly reports, and then you will be sent to Louisville and Nashville, and returned to active duty. Sergeant Shipley, go ahead and have the men line up for us."

Sergeant Shipley attended to his duty, and all of the former prisoners were soon accounted for and enrolled into active duty service. When David got to his enrolling officer's section, he asked the officer in his line, Lieutenant Mercer, what date it was.

"It's the twenty second of May, sir."

David thanked the lieutenant, and his troopers were soon led to their temporary quarters, a series of I houses and shotgun wooden buildings that were to be their barracks for a few days.

David then sat down and took out the letter he had promised to mail for Captain Smith. He was reminded that he had run out of ink. He sent Sergeant Looney over to headquarters to obtain some ink and paper. He then prepared a short letter to Sarah Smith, Captain Smith's wife.

Mrs. Sarah Smith

140 Ludlow Avenue
Cincinnati, Ohio

Camp Chase, Ohio
May 22, 1863

Dear Mrs. Smith:

I served with your husband in the First Middle Tennessee Cavalry. I commanded Company "D", and Captain David commanded Company "E". We surrendered with the rest of Colonel Streight's command to General Forrest at Cedar Bluff, Alabama.

David and Colonel Streight and most of his officers have been detained at Libby Prison. We were exchanged by the cartel and sent to City Point, and then by steamer to Baltimore.

Captain Smith asked me to send you a letter from him, which I am enclosing. He asked me to wish you and your children good health and happiness, and he wanted me to tell you that he is in good health and good spirits. David was brave and courageous in his handling of troops on this expedition. He served Colonel Streight's command well as a scout and rear guard commander for the column.

My hopes and prayers are for the safe return of Captain Smith from his confinement, and for his return to the bosom of his family.

Very Truly Yours,

David Snelling
First Lt., First Middle Tennessee Cavalry

Chapter Seventeen

David and the rest of the troopers in the First Middle Tennessee Cavalry were given their pay for the preceding month and the month of May by the paymaster. The men were reissued side arms and sabers and spurs. David was required to prepare monthly reports for both companies for April and May of 1863.

David was issued a Colt Police Revolver and a saber. He decided that he should purchase some field glasses to replace those that were taken from him after his capture. He went to a sutler that had set up shop on the grounds at Camp Chase, and purchased a decent pair of field glasses.

Near the sutler's tent, a representative from the Spencer Arms Company was demonstrating a newfangled Spencer Repeating Rifle to a group of infantry officers. David joined an infantry major and a colonel in observing the demonstration by Alex Hayes with the Spencer Arms Company.

Mr. Hayes was around forty years old, with long side whiskers, and was wearing a white linen duster over a brown tweed suit. He demonstrated the handling of the rifle to the on looking officers.

"Gentlemen, the Spencer Repeating Rifle is fifty two caliber. The rifle is loaded through a tubular magazine that inserts into the gunstock. One pump of the lever on the rifle feeds the brass encased cartridge into the firing chamber and cocks the hammer of the weapon. When the trigger is pulled, the rifle fires. When the lever is pumped after firing, the spent shell is ejected, and a new shell is chambered, and the gun is cocked and ready once again.

This rifle can fire seven rounds in thirty seconds, gentlemen."

The infantry officers were aghast. They could not believe such a performance. The major had a question. "What about percussion caps?"

Mr. Hayes responded quickly. "The brass shell contains a built – in percussion cap which ignites the powder charge inside when the hammer strikes the edge of the shell."

The colonel also had a question. "How much did each rifle cost?"

"Each rifle costs $75.00. However, if individual men want to purchase these fine guns, we can set up payments on military allotment from each soldier's pay. Are any of you gentlemen interested in the weapon? I just sent a large shipment of Spencer Rifles to Colonel John Wilder at Nashville."

David was quick to speak up. "If I purchase a rifle, could you put one into my hands today?"

The salesman looked as if he had been caught off guard. "Lieutenant, I sent the last Spencer Repeating Rifles down to Colonel Wilder's brigade in Tennessee. I have two Spencer Repeating Carbines in stock. Would you care to examine those? This one is a demonstration model."

David did not hesitate. "Yes, sir, if you don't mind."

Mr. Hayes opened a wooden case inside his tent, and emerged with a shorter, more compact version of the Spencer. He handed it to David, who immediately recognized the shorter version as a carbine.

"This is the Spencer Repeating Carbine. It is clip–fed with .52 caliber rimfire brass shells, just like the Repeating Rifle. It has open iron sights, and the rear sight is adjustable. It also has a ring on the bottom of the stock for a leather sling. These carbines have been issued to cavalry troopers back east. Here, it is unloaded. Handle it, get a feel for the action."

David took the carbine and noticed that it weighed more than eight pounds unloaded. He pulled the lever, and noticed the smooth movement of the carbine's lever action. He dry fired the weapon, while pointing it in a safe direction first.

"How does it load into the stock?"

Hayes took the weapon from David, and twisted the stock tube counterclockwise, and then lifted the loading tube from the stock.

"Then you feed the brass shells into the tube with the bullet end pointing out the end of the barrel. The magazine holds seven shots."

David did not need to be 'sold' on this new weapon. He reached for his wallet, and began to pull out U.S. greenback bills.

"Here is $80.00. Please sell me the carbine and a box of 100 shells, Mr. Hayes."

Mr. Hayes was delighted to make a cash sale on the spot. "Certainly. I will get you a receipt, lieutenant, but first, what is your name?"

"Snelling, David R. Snelling. First Lieutenant, First Middle Tennessee Cavalry."

* * * * *

Camp Chase, Ohio
May 25, 1863

Dear Uncle Uriah and Aunt Faith:

I was exchanged with the enlisted men and NCO's in Colonel Streight's command, and sent through the lines to City Point, and then by steamer to Baltimore. The War Department sent us west on the B&O Railroad to Ohio, and then here to Camp Chase.

They issued us new sabers and side arms, and I even bought a new Spencer Repeating Carbine from a Spencer Arms Company man. I also bought a new journal, and this is the first serial letter in my new book.

I hope that Angela was able to forward you my other journal, which I gave her at the Libby Prison. We are to board the cars for Indianapolis tomorrow. We will then go down to ferry over the Ohio near Louisville, and then down on the L&N to Nashville. We are to be returned to duty after receiving our remounts in Nashville.

The men are in good spirits, and are itching to be returned to duty. So am I.

I will write to you again when we reach our new post in Nashville.

Very Truly Yours,

David

David's Company "D" and Company "E" soon arrived in Nashville on June 13th, 1863, where they received their mounts. They were then ordered to Cripple Creek, Tennessee, just east of Murfreesboro. David's Company "D" and Company "E" were then reunited with Colonel Stokes' First Middle Tennessee Cavalry regiment.

General Rosecrans' Army of the Cumberland had been idle in the vicinity of Murfreesboro for over six months. General Rosecrans had stockpiled thousands upon thousands of rations, mules and horses, small arms and ammunition. He was not quite ready to attack General Bragg's Army of Tennessee, even after repeated prodding from the War Department in Washington.

Finally, near the end of June, General Rosecrans issued the necessary orders for his army to move, in accordance with a clever and well executed plan.

The Confederate troops were positioned to guard important mountain passes through the Cumberland Mountains. General Rosecrans' goal was Chattanooga, an important railroad junction and river crossing in southeast Tennessee.

Rosecrans would send Gordon Granger's Corps through Guy's Gap toward Shelbyville as a feint, in order to deceive the Rebels as to the true objective of his line of march. Another feint would be made by General Crittenden's Corps toward McMinnville.

* * * * *

On June 27th, the First Middle Tennessee Cavalry, under the command of Lt. Colonel Robert Galbraith, was ordered to Guy's Gap in support of an attack by Colonel Robert A. G. Minty's First Brigade of Cavalry.

The entire cavalry force totaled over 2,800 troopers, and they started down through Guy's Gap in support of General Gordon Granger's Corps of infantry.

The Confederate Army Corps of General Leonidas Polk was stationed at Shelbyville, but soon received an order from General Bragg to retreat to Tullahoma, some eighteen miles to the southeast.

General Bragg was informed by General Wheeler's Cavalry that Wilder's "Lightning Brigade" and General Thomas' Corps of the Army of the Cumberland had seized Hoover's Gap. They had also marched down the macadamized pike, and captured the town of Manchester, Tennessee.

Polk's infantry wasted little time in retreating from Shelbyville, through the rain and mud, and over to Tullahoma.

At Tullahoma, General Bragg held a council of war with his corps commanders, William Hardee and Leonidas Polk. General Hardee counseled Bragg to fight, while General Polk advocated an immediate retreat.

General Thomas had also marched his corps from Manchester to Hillsboro, less than a dozen miles from General Bragg's right flank. General Bragg then ordered his Army of Tennessee to retreat to Decherd, some twenty miles to the southeast, along the Nashville & Chattanooga Railroad. He posed a question to his corps commanders at Decherd: Should he fight on the line of the Elk River? (or) Fight at the foot of the Sewanee Mountain pass between Cowan and Sewanee?

General Bragg ordered a retreat of his entire army through the pass at Sewanee Mountain, and down to Bridgeport, and then over to Chattanooga.

* * * * *

At Shelbyville on June 27th, David's Company "D" rode on the flanks of Colonel Galbraith's brigade, and they had the advance on the pike through Guy's Gap.

David's spirits lifted as he heard the sounds of Federal buglers sounding "Charge", and he witnessed Rebel troops and troopers retreating before a Union advance. Several squads of Rebel Cavalry commanded by Joe Wheeler offered resistance on the pike into Shelbyville, but they were either shot down or driven off by the weight of the Federal advance.

They weather was rainy, soggy, and miserable. David noticed however, that his Spencer carbine could fire and operate effectively even in rainy weather, when other carbines were rendered useless.

Near Guy's Gap, two Confederate horsemen charged them from a screen of oak trees, and David shot them out of the saddle with his Spencer Carbine. They arrived at the outskirts of Shelbyville later that morning, only to find that the Rebel infantry under General Polk had retreated south.

Colonel Minty ordered his entire brigade of cavalry to pursue the enemy, and the troopers marched their horses to the southeast in the red mud and the rain.

David had his oilskin coat and oilskin cover on his kepi, but his breeches were soaked through from his thighs down to his knees. The other men in the brigade were soggy and miserable as well. The rain was unrelenting, and the roads that were not macadamized with crushed limestone were soon churned into muddy quagmires.

On the 28th, they continued their pursuit of Bragg's infantry toward Tullahoma, and then on to Decherd and Winchester. The troopers did manage to capture some Confederate soldiers that were too tired to retreat south with Bragg's main army. These men were either herded to the rear by provost guards, or paroled where they were encountered and captured.

On July 1st, Colonel Minty then ordered his brigade to Cowan, where they began to concentrate near the mountain pass of Sewanee Mountain on July 1st. General Bragg had left General Nathan Bedford Forrest's brigade of cavalry at Sewanee Mountain, with orders to hold off the Federal advance.

Forrest had several pieces of artillery, but he could not effectively use them in the constant driving rain. His cavalrymen had managed to keep most of their gunpowder dry, but their carbines and shotguns were not sufficient to hold the pass against the superior Federal force.

Colonel Minty and Lt. Colonel Galbraith ordered dismounted troopers forward as skirmishers, and soon ordered over eight hundred men forward to the pass that evening. They engaged the Confederate troopers slowly, as the Rebels contested every inch of ground. The Union attack was soon halted by the darkness, which came early in the evening because of the overcast skies.

The following morning, General Forrest received word that General Bragg's army had safely crossed the Sewanee Mountain, and was nearing Bridgeport. He then ordered his rear guard to fall back through the streets of Cowan, and to cross over Sewanee Mountain.

On July 4th, General Bragg's Army of Tennessee had reached Chattanooga. General Rosecrans' Army of the Cumberland had brilliantly thrown the Rebels out of Middle Tennessee.

Colonel Minty's brigade, and Lt. Colonel Galbraith's First Middle Tennessee Cavalry Regiment were then ordered back to Shelbyville, and then over to Franklin.

Near Franklin, David's mare stepped into a gopher hole and came up lame. After walking her for a couple of miles on foot, David decided he needed a remount. He placed Lieutenant Day in temporary command of the company, and asked Sergeant Looney to escort him back to Camp Campbell, where he could obtain a remount from the cavalry remount station.

They had walked several miles on the pike north of the town of Franklin, and were near a hedgerow of bushes at Roper's Knob, when they spied an overturned carriage by the hedgerow. They then thought they heard the muffled cry of a woman.

Using hand signals, David ordered Sergeant Looney to dismount, and to draw his pistol. David reached over near his saddle, and drew his Spencer Repeating Carbine from its leather holster. He led Sergeant Looney around the carriage, and up through a sunken lane that led by the hedgerow. As they eased by the carriage, they saw a woman's leather purse and horsewhip near the overturned buggy.

They heard the woman's muffled cry again, and they picked up their pace in the sunken road. They soon rounded a bend in the sunken road around the hedgerow, and saw what was happening.

A lovely red haired woman was on the ground before them, being held by a man in a Confederate uniform. She was twisting her lower body to the left and to the right, desperately trying to keep her pantalets and petticoats wrapped up above her knees.

Another man was standing at her feet holding a Bowie knife, and talking to her in a deep voice. "We don't want to hurt you, we just want a little lovin', honey..." The other man started tearing away the woman's blouse and bodice.

David saw that the man had on the uniform coat of a Union sergeant. He immediately cocked his Spencer carbine, and chambered a .52 caliber shell from its magazine. The Union sergeant then dropped his knife and spun around, reaching for a Colt Police pistol at the front of his belt.

David fired the carbine, and the bullet caught the sergeant in the chest, lifting him clean off his feet. The Confederate soldier spun around, drawing a Colt pistol from his belt, and attempted to shoot David.

Sergeant Looney shot him through the head, with the pistol round entering through his forehead, and exiting out the back of his skull.

The woman on the ground screamed in terror as David put down his carbine and took off his oilskin coat. David did his best to reassure her. "Please, ma'am, you have no need to fear us. We will take you home now, if we can get your buggy righted."

She let him ease her up onto her feet, and he covered her torn blouse and bodice with his oilskin coat. He then took her by the hand and led her up the sunken lane to her buggy, carefully stepping around the body of the Union sergeant. David and Sergeant Looney heaved and pulled, and righted the woman's buggy. David then picked up her handkerchief and purse, and boosted her up into the front seat of the spring buggy. He took the whip and handed it to the woman.

"If you will wait here for a moment, ma'am, Sergeant Looney and I will load these bodies on his horse, and escort you back to your home. Let me introduce myself. I am First Lieutenant David Snelling, commander of Company "D", First Middle Tennessee Cavalry."

The woman retied her bonnet.

"I am Mrs. James Riley. This sunken road leads over to my father's home. He is a physician in Franklin. Have you heard of Dr. Edward Mallory?"

David shook his head. "No ma'am, but we have not been here very long, either. Do you have a first name, Mrs. James Riley?"

The woman then batted her green eyes, and smiled. "Yes, my first name is Janet. I am really thankful that you and your sergeant came up on us when you did. Those men would have raped me."

She began to cry, and David offered the lovely young woman a shoulder to cry on. After she had her cry, David loaned her his handkerchief, and asked her to blow her nose. Sergeant Looney then appeared, having placed the bodies of the two soldiers over the back of his horse.

David drove Janet's buggy down the sunken lane, and Sergeant Looney followed them on foot, leading both horses. On the way, David asked Janet about the soldiers. "Mrs. Riley, where did you encounter those two soldiers?"

"Right where the buggy was overturned. They hailed me out on the pike, pretending to beg for food. When I refused to stop, they grabbed the halter on the mare. I tried to beat them off with my whip, but they pulled me out of the buggy. They then dragged me up the hedgerow there, away from the main road."

"You were fortunate that we came along when we did. I will need to send my sergeant down to Franklin for the provost marshal. Will you give him an affidavit or statement as to what took place here?"

"Oh yes, I certainly will. You are Southern men. Why are you fighting with the Yankees instead of against them?"

David expected to hear that question sooner or later. "Because of our beliefs. Why did your husband enlist in the Confederate Army?"

"Because he wanted to do his duty. He wanted to defend his home and his family. He's with Archer's Brigade, in the Army of Northern Virginia. He is a major. We were married just before his regiment left for Virginia. We lived on a farm near Carthage. After he left, our hired hands enlisted in the Confederate Army, and I could not work the farm by myself."

"So you moved back here with your parents?"

"Yes. They wrote me and told me that I would be safe here until James could return home. Maybe they were wrong."

They rounded a bend in the sunken lane, and David then saw a lovely two story house, built with hand sawn Loblolly Pine boards. The second story was framed with a porch surrounded by railings made of Red Oak. Huge oak pillars cut into square beams held up the front of the roof, and formed the corners of the first and second story porches.

They stopped at a brick walkway that led to the front porch, where a Negro servant named Claude walked out. He was forty years old, and wore a black coat with a white waistcoat, and black jean cloth pants. Janet asked Claude if Dr. Mallory had arrived home yet. Claude told her that he was coming from the barn, since he had returned from delivering a baby. She then asked if her mother was downstairs. Claude told her that she was in the front parlor.

She stepped down from the buggy, and told David that she would inform her family about what had occurred that afternoon. "I will send Claude to summon my father for you. He will want you to place those bodies back in the barn. I need to tell my mother about this first. I will then change clothes and join you inside."

David asked Janet to show them to the barn, and they led the horses down a cobblestone pathway around the house. On the way to the barn, they were joined by a tall and elderly man dressed in a white linen coat and cotton duck pants. His personal appearance was neat and flawless, and he wore a black waistcoat, and a gold watch chain was visible below his waistcoat pocket.

"Lieutenant, I am Dr. Edward Mallory. Why are you here, and where did those dead men come from?"

David knew that his news would be upsetting to the Doctor, so he asked him to walk with him toward the barn. "Sergeant Looney and I were heading north on the pike to the remount station in Nashville, when we encountered your daughter's overturned buggy near the end of your drive. We drew our weapons and investigated. We walked up your drive a ways, and saw this man in a Confederate uniform holding your daughter on the ground. The man in the Union sergeant's uniform turned and drew a pistol on me. I shot him in the chest with my carbine. The other one tried to pull a pistol on us, and my first sergeant shot him through the head."

Doctor Mallory was obviously disturbed. He placed his face in his hands, and then ran his fingers through his hair. He then turned and put his hand on David's shoulder. "Tell me something, lieutenant. This will just be between us. In the strictest confidence. Was my daughter...violated...in any way by these men?"

"No, sir. She was putting up quite a struggle when we got there. We killed them before they could proceed any further with the crime. But we need to ask a favor of you, Dr. Mallory."

"Anything you will ask, I will do for you. You have placed me forever in your debt. You have done a service for me that I can never repay you for."

"The provost marshal in Franklin will need a written report from a medical doctor that would confirm the cause of death for these men, the entry and exit wounds, and so forth. I personally would like such a report to corroborate our version of this incident."

"Then such an autopsy you shall have. Let's put these men out in the barn. I will examine them, and will send Claude to my study after pen and paper. You shall have a report prepared for you this very evening. In the meantime, you and your sergeant need to go ahead and wash up for supper. You will be spending the night with us here."

"Sir, we do not want to impose on you and your family."

"I will insist, lieutenant. By the way, I did not get your name."

David held out his right hand. "I'm David Snelling. My sergeant is Anderson Looney. We serve in the First Middle Tennessee Regiment of Cavalry."

"Welcome to our home. You may go ahead and put your animals in the barn. You will find water and forage their in the stables inside. When you are done there, Claude will show you where you may wash up for supper."

"Thank you, Doctor Mallory. You are too kind."

They put the bodies of the soldiers and their animals in the barn, where they fed and watered the animals as well. They then washed up for supper, and they were led into the dining room by Claude.

The dining room was paneled with Red Oak, and floored with White Oak boards. Mahogany sideboards and a large mahogany table awaited them, with several lovely place settings on a linen tablecloth.

They were greeted by Mrs. Mallory, a tall and willowy woman of forty and seven years, who was dressed in a dark blue dress, and had her blonde hair pinned back in a tight bun. Janet soon joined them, wearing a blue crinoline dress over a new starched petticoat. She had also pinned her hair back into a bun, and her red hair contrasted with the royal blue color of her Sunday dress.

They were waited on by a Negro woman that they called Abigail. Abigail was in her late thirties, and was tall and lovely. She was dressed in a black dress, but wore a white smock and a white cap that contrasted with her smooth ebony skin.

She was shapely and well bosomed, and served them a delicious meal of lamb stew, cabbage greens, field peas, and cornbread. Doctor Mallory soon joined them after the meal was served, and the conversation was light hearted and pleasant. They did not discuss politics or the war. Instead, they focused on the history of the area, and various plants and animals of the region.

After supper, Sergeant Looney and Dr. Mallory walked out on the front porch to smoke cigars. David and Mrs. Mallory and Janet took a stroll in the rose garden. The sun had set with an orange glow in the west, and the moon was climbing in the east in its full glowing splendor.

Janet led David around to various points in the garden. She showed him different rose plants and vegetable plants she had tended during the summer season. They outpaced Mrs. Mallory, who had stopped to crop off some red roses for an arrangement she had planned to make for her foyer.

While they were out of her mother's earshot, Janet broke one of her mother's rules by asking David about the progress of the war.

David told her what he knew, with some hesitation. "Grant has captured and occupied Vicksburg. General Banks has captured Port Hudson. General Rosecrans has possession of all of Tennessee except Chattanooga. General Lee's army, as far as we know, was defeated up in Pennsylvania, and has retreated south to the Potomac."

Janet did not appear to be upset, until David began to tell her about General Lee's retreat. "James is with Archer's Brigade. He sent me a letter about two months ago, and he told me that they were going to cross the Potomac into Maryland. He told me the men in his outfit were confident and ready to move north. He did not think General Lee's army could ever be beaten." Tears began to well up around her lovely green eyes.

David was as tactful as he could be in this situation. He admired this young woman's beauty and courage, and did not want to say anything to hurt her feelings. He took her by the hand, and did his best to reassure her. "I'm sure that your husband and his command are safe. The mail service to this part of Tennessee has been interrupted. You may receive a letter from your major any time, letting you know that he is safe." Her eyes lit up with the notion that her husband might be safe and sound. She kissed David on the cheek, and told him that he was the sweetest man she had ever met. Even if he had chosen to fight for the Yankees.

Dr. Mallory met them at the dog run at the rear of the house, and offered David and Sergeant Looney the use of the guest rooms upstairs. David thanked Dr. Mallory for his hospitality, and headed upstairs with Sergeant Looney after Abigail, who was holding a whale oil lantern.

Abigail turned down the bed in the first upstairs guest room, which Sergeant Looney offered to take. She bent over and asked Sergeant Looney if she could do anything else for him, and he answered her with a playful slap on her curvaceous behind.

She soon showed David to his room, where she also turned down the bed. He also noticed that his oilskin coat had been folded into a neat bundle in a corner chair. He said "Good night" to the lovely Abigail, pulled off his boots, and stripped down to his Union suit. He soon fell asleep quickly in the feather bed.

* * * * *

The next morning, Abigail fed them a breakfast of ham, biscuits, and fresh eggs. David had given them some real coffee from his daily ration, and it had been brewed for them in a tin pot.

They drove down to Franklin in the spring buggy, where the dead soldiers and the doctor's report were offered up to the provost marshal. The provost marshal interviewed Sergeant Looney and Janet Riley before he took David's statement. He asked David an obvious question right off the bat.

"Why did you kill those deserters, lieutenant?"

"Because they needed killin' at the time, sir. They were in the process of committing a forcible felony, and they attempted to draw their pistols on us. We had no choice."

"I believe you, son. No charges will be preferred against either one of you. You do need to report to Lt. Colonel Galbraith, though. I believe he has some transfer orders for you."

David then reported to headquarters, where he was told that his entire company had been ordered to march to Nashville. They were to leave out the next morning for Nashville.

Doctor Mallory obtained special permission to allow David to spend the evening away from the post, and he drove David and Janet back to his home in their spring buggy. David's lame horse was led behind, as he did not want to aggravate the mare's sore front leg.

Dr. Mallory led David to the rear of the barn, where he had a black horse stalled in a small paddock. The horse was sleek and muscular, about fifteen hands at the shoulder. He had a bright white star in the middle of his forehead, yet the rest of his body was jet black.

He neighed when the Doctor came up, and nodded his head at the familiar figure of Doctor Mallory. The Doctor pulled down his saddle and bridle, and the horse obediently allowed himself to be readied for riding. David noticed the fire in the animal's eyes as his master got him ready to ride. He asked Doctor Mallory if he could ride the splendid stallion, and what his name was.

"His name is Ajax. And you can ride him down the lane and up the pike a mile or two. He needs to burn some energy today."

David led Ajax out of the paddock and into the sunken lane. He flipped the reins over the saddle, and quickly pulled himself onto the stallion. He gently led him down the lane at first, letting the steed go at the walk by the hedgerow.

He then eased him out on the macadamized pike, where he brought Ajax to a canter. They had begun to take to one another, this young cavalryman and this race horse, and David put the spur to Ajax, to see what he could do.

The stallion began to go at the run, stretching out his front legs to catch the pike, and eating up yardage with each sleek movement of his legs. David hung on and enjoyed the thrill of riding such a surging mass of power.

He finally pulled back on the reins, after Ajax had eaten up two and one half miles of the pike. He walked the animal back home, and then dismounted at the end of the sunken drive. He rubbed Ajax's muzzle, and led him at the walk back to his stall. He rubbed the animal down carefully, fed him some dry oats, and gave him some water.

Dr. Mallory met him at the door of the barn as he was coming out. His breeches were wet with sweat of Ajax, but David had long since grown used to that aroma in the cavalry.

He asked Dr. Mallory if Ajax was a racehorse. The doctor scratched his forehead, and told David about Ajax.

"I raced Ajax just before the war down in Vicksburg, over at Louisville and at Baton Rouge. He was in the money on his first race when he was a two year old, and has won five or six races after that. I was offered $2600.00 for him down at Vicksburg in '59. His sire was a thoroughbred. At one time he was the most valuable possession I had.

After what happened the other day, though I now realize that material possessions do not compare to family. Lieutenant Snelling, do you agree with that statement?"

David was unsure as to what the old man was talking about, but he agreed. "Yes, sir."

"Well, son. When you saved my little girl the other day from being ravaged by those vile deserters, you did something for me that placed me forever in your debt."

"Now see here, Doctor Mallory, I was only doing my duty. It is an officer's duty to investigate unusual situations."

"I understand that. But I will nevertheless display my gratitude by giving you Ajax here as your remount."

"Oh, dear me, no. I could never take this valuable animal from you."

"Young man, I insist. Stay the night. Sleep on it. Think it over. You have a long war ahead of you. A splendid animal such as this would help you immensely in the cavalry."

David could not refuse the good doctor. "All right. I will sleep on it. I will let you know in the morning."

"I would have it no other way. Let's see what Abigail has cooked up for supper."

David enjoyed the meal of fried chicken, field peas, and mashed potatoes that Abigail prepared for their evening meal.

He also enjoyed the company of Janet Riley. She was dressed in a yellow crinoline dress that displayed her lovely bosom. He told her a funny story about a stubborn team of mules that refused to pull one of his cotton wagons before the war. He watched her eyes sparkle with amusement as he finished his story, and could not help but feel that he was infatuated with her.

He told himself that he was insane; that he was falling in love with another man's wife, but his emotions won the day. He listened to Janet as she read a few chapters of *Bleak House* to him and her parents, and he loathed the hour he had to take his leave of her and go upstairs to retire to bed.

* * * * *

The next morning, after an early breakfast, Dr. Mallory took David's cavalry saddle and saddled up Ajax for him. David shook his hand and thanked the Doctor for his generous gift. He left his lame mare with Doctor Mallory, who said he would treat her problem, and use her to pull his spring buggy on his medical calls.

David mounted Ajax, and rode up the path toward the main house. Janet came out on the brick path to greet him on the lane, with her blue calico dress streaming in the morning breeze. Her red hair streamed down below her shoulders, as she hurried to see David off.

David pulled back on the reins and halted Ajax, and Janet pulled his muzzle and told him good bye. She then asked David to return and see them whenever he got back to Nashville.

"You and Sergeant Looney will always be welcome in our home. Thank you so much for saving me." She pulled David down from the saddle and kissed him on the cheek.

David was smitten. He could only stammer a reply that indicated he would love to see her and her family again. He also told her that he hoped her Major was safe, and that he was sorry that she was exposed to the ruffian deserters in the manner that she was. He wished her good health and happiness, and placed his hand upon her cheek.

He then put the spur to Ajax, and they cantered down the sunken lane, and down the pike a mile toward Franklin.

They met Sergeant Looney and both companies "E" and "D" on the pike, heading north to Nashville. He took his place at the head of his company, and led them up the pike into the town limits of Nashville.

Both companies marched through the streets of town, and down to the Cumberland River landing. They boarded the large side wheeler steamer *Fitch*, where they led their horses into pens at the stern of the vessel.

They then stowed their gear on the second deck, while the men of Company "E" went to the galley below for evening mess. The steamer was soon untied and got underway, steaming downstream toward the Ohio River.

The officers and NCOs were given several recent newspapers and a *Harper's Weekly*, and David had an opportunity to catch up on recent news concerning the war. He also had the opportunity to make another entry in his journal, a serial letter to his aunt and uncle down in Georgia.

> Aboard the Steamer *Fitch*
> In the Cumberland River
> September 10, 1863
>
> Dear Uncle Uriah and Aunt Faith:
>
> We have been transferred back to our original regiment in Alabama by order of the War Department. General Dodge told us he wanted us back in his department, and his request was granted. There is hope among the men that the Union might be turning the tide, and gaining the upper hand in this war.
>
> General Lee's army was defeated in Pennsylvania, after a terrific and terrible three day battle. General Banks captured Port Hudson. General Grant has captured Vicksburg, and opened up the entire Mississippi River to Union traffic.
>
> General Rosecrans has kicked General Bragg's Army of Tennessee out of all of Tennessee save Chattanooga. His campaign was clever and masterful. We rode with his army from Shelbyville to Sewanee. All of the men in our outfit believe to a man that Rosecrans is the man to finish this war, and to completely defeat the Rebel army.
>
> After our summer campaign in southeast Tennessee, we were ordered to Franklin. Sergeant Looney and I were on the Nashville Pike, when we encountered a lovely woman who was being accosted by two deserters. We shot the blackguard

villains before they could rape her, and her father repaid me by giving me his valuable stallion.

I found myself becoming quite taken with this lovely woman, even though she is married to a major in Archer's Confederate brigade. They invited me to visit them when our unit returns to Nashville, but we are headed by steamer to Camp Davies, Mississippi, via Paducah, Cairo, and Memphis.

I have to go now, they are calling us down for evening mess. May the Lord bless and keep you.

Love,

David

Chapter Eighteen

They sailed down the Cumberland aboard the steam boat *Fitch*, heading toward the Ohio River. The weather had grown noticeably cooler, and the bottomland hardwood trees had begun to turn into their autumn colors. The third autumn of the war was rapidly approaching.

David went down to the stern of the steam boat to check on Ajax, and noticed flights of ducks and geese heading south in their familiar "V" formation. On his way back, Sergeant Looney greeted him, in the company of another officer whom he introduced as First Lieutenant Joseph Hornbach. David knew Hornbach, as he had transferred over to the regiment from the 21st Ohio Infantry in July of 1862. He had been captured at Stones River back in January, and had been exchanged while both companies were with Streight's command in Alabama.

Hornbach was thirty nine years old, but he was clean shaven and baby faced, and appeared to be much younger than his thirty nine years. David knew his vices, and knew that one of them was a love of liquor.

Nevertheless, Lt. Hornbach ranked him, since his commission predated David's commission.

David saluted him, and Sergeant Looney formally introduced them. Hornbach wasted no time in asking David for a favor.

"Lieutenant, I have been appointed to take command of Company "E". I have looked at the men's carbines, and they just will not do. The quartermaster in Nashville told me that we can requisition some Burnsides out of Cairo, but we don't have any forms. Do you have any requisition forms?"

"Yes, sir. Sergeant Looney has several requisition order forms."

"Would you be so kind as to fill one out for me, for arms for one officer and seventy eight men? They are to be shipped from Cairo to Memphis, which is our destination point."

David responded quickly. "Yes, sir. I'll fill it out right now. Are you going to send an orderly to the quartermaster in Cairo when we tie up there?"

"I'll send two men with the requisition to the supply depot once we tie up at Cairo. Thank you, David."

"Yes, sir. Anytime."

David waited until Lieutenant Hornbach had departed before he spoke to Sergeant Looney.

"Same old Joe Hornbach. Always getting someone else to do his work for him."

Sergeant Looney chimed in. "You know, they said he was drunk at Stones River, and failed to set up a proper picket post. Twenty five men got captured along with him."

David knew the reason for Hornbach's neglect of his duty. "It's the liquor. Some men get on it and just can't get off of it. Alcohol can ruin a good officer."

Sergeant Looney was even more philosophical. "Liquor has ruined many a good man. It has done it before, and it will do it again and again. It's one of the world's great vices, among other things."

"Just remember this, Anderson. If we ever are deployed on a mission, and Hornbach is called on to set up a picket, we need to set out our own picket posts. You understand?"

"Yes, sir. I get the message."

* * * * *

They soon steamed into the Ohio River at Smithland, and then steamed past Paducah, Kentucky, where the Tennessee River joined the waters of the Ohio. The Tennessee River was a much wider river than the Cumberland, and the Ohio River below its confluence with the Tennessee was consequently much wider. They steamed past Paducah on the Kentucky side, and continued downstream several miles until they reached the river port of Cairo, Illinois. Cairo was an important river port. The Union Army maintained a weapons and supply depot there. The town was situated at the end of a peninsula that separated the Ohio and Mississippi Rivers.

A railroad line ran down to Cairo, and that enabled the Union Army to maintain the supply depot there. Lieutenant Hornbach sent two corporals from the *Fitch* to the U.S. Army depot once the steamboat reached the river landing at Cairo. Captain Charles Eastman on the *Fitch* advised the corporals that they would need at least two hours to take on coal and wood, and water their steam boilers.

David walked down to the stern of the *Fitch* to give Ajax an apple he had saved from the wardroom mess. The stallion greeted him with a nod of his head, and a nuzzle against his sleeve.

David fed Ajax the apple, and the animal began to chew it immediately. David rubbed Ajax down, and then took a stroll out on the forward deck. Other cavalrymen saluted him as he walked by. He returned their salutes, and stood over by the railing on the port side. He looked out at the mile wide rushing river, and wondered about the status of the war, and the slavery system.

How could the south side of the river be a slave state, and his side remain a free state? Too much blood had been shed so far in the war for the status quo of the slave system to remain. The land should be all slave or all free, he thought. That was what the war was coming down to. America would be either all free soil, or the war would have been fought for nothing.

The steamer *Fitch* completed loading its stores of coal and firewood, so the river boat captain ordered the boat to slip its moorings, and head downstream. They soon entered the broad and flat Mississippi River, which was almost a mile wide. They passed General Grant's old battlefield at Belmont, and later that evening steamed past General Pope's place of victory at Island No. 10. David noticed that most of the fortifications at Island No. 10 had been washed away by the spring floods of the Mississippi River.

David went down to the galley and messed with Sergeant Looney and Lieutenant Day. He stepped back onto the main deck just after dark, and saw a sand bar off an island that the pilot referred to as Island Number 18. The *Fitch* later put out her deck lanterns, and the pilot tied her up off Island Number 21, on account of the dangerous logs and river snags being ahead down river on the Arkansas side. They would tie up the *Fitch* and wait for better visibility in the morning.

The horses were taken off the boat and fed early the following morning, and the stalls in the aft section of the boat were cleaned. The horses were then led up the gangway into the boat, and were locked back up into their stalls.

The river pilot soon signaled his readiness to the first mate, and the *Fitch* soon slipped her moorings and steamed south on the serpentine waters of the Mississippi River.

They soon passed Forked Deer Island and Island Number 28. Early that afternoon, they rounded a sharp bend in the river, and noticed the revetments of Fort Pillow on the bluffs overlooking the river. David got out his field glasses, and saw Negro troops in blue uniforms and red kepis manning the guns of the fort. The guns were heavy Columbiads, mounted on huge iron rotating carriages on steel half moon shaped tracks.

They passed the Hatchie River towhead and Island No. 35. Later that evening the *Fitch* rounded Loosahatchie Bar, and began to steam around Mud Island. The steamer then tied up on the main docks of Memphis. Lieutenant Hornbach ordered the men and horses off the steamboat. They were soon marching out Poplar Avenue toward the U.S. Cavalry depot, which was located on the east side of the City of Memphis.

When they arrived at the camp, David reported to General Hurlbut's adjutant, and the two companies were ordered to put up ten wedge tents and two wall tents for the men and officers of each company. David and Sergeant Looney supervised the placement of the tents, and had picket lines tied off for the horses.

Later that evening, David saddled Ajax, and took a ride around the outskirts of Memphis with Sergeant Looney.

Most of the men in town carried pistols, Bowie knives, or Arkansas toothpicks. They drank heavily, and were subject to drawing knives or guns when angered. The women were well dressed and sometimes courteous, but many of the ladies were open Confederate supporters.

They rode down Poplar Street near the City Hall and the docks off Mud Island, and noticed several hundred bales of cotton stacked out in the streets. A platoon of Negro soldiers and a white lieutenant were guarding the cotton with loaded muskets and fixed bayonets.

David could not help but stare at the unusual spectacle. "Sergeant Looney, I have raised and shipped and sold cotton all of my life, but I just can't get used to the cotton being guarded by Union troops."

"Well sir, it's contraband now. All of the cotton there under guard will be shipped up to Cairo, and will be sold by the Treasury Department. The adjutant general came by yesterday, and told us that the standing orders of the department require us to destroy any quantities of cotton that we find that cannot be shipped north."

David pulled back on Ajax's reins. "I know what our orders are, sergeant. What I'm saying is that it is just a sight that's hard to get used to. You never grew any cotton, did you?"

"No sir, we only grew corn. Cotton never did well in Lawrence County. We never had any hands to cultivate it and pick it anyway."

* * * * *

The following morning, the Burnside Carbines ordered by David from Cairo arrived in Memphis aboard the steamer *Wabash*. The Quartermaster sent the weapons and ammunition out to the camp in a wagon pulled by a team of strong gray mules. Lieutenant Hornbach was instructed to issue out the carbines to his company, and to collect the old arms from the men, and return them back to the Quartermaster in the same wagon. The men lined up and exchanged arms, while David's company "D" struck the tents and prepared to move out to the train station.

They drew one day's rations, and then rode down to the railroad station on the outskirts of Memphis, known as station number six. Lieutenant Hornbach ordered the men to dismount, and the horses were unsaddled and loaded on boxcars when the U.S. Military Railroad train pulled into the station.

Once the men were all aboard, the American Standard 4–4–0 engine belched a cloud of steam, and pulled away from the depot. Their route was the Memphis & Charleston Railroad, and their destination was Corinth, Mississippi.

The train took them east, through the richest part of the State of Tennessee. The land had been cleared in some areas to the point where it resembled Mid Western prairies. The plantation houses were all at least two stories high, with large majestic columns made of oak or Yellow Pine. David noticed that the plantations were all at least large enough to have 80 to 100 Negro hands on each estate.

David noticed that Lieutenant Hornbach had walked back to the caboose, where he was drinking heavily from a small bottle of whiskey. The engine pulled them through Collierville, Moscow, and into La Grange. At La Grange, the engine took on fuel and water, and then headed east to Grand Junction.

They soon passed through Saulsbury, where David noticed long lines of Negroes heading east along the railroad. He could not understand why they were moving in such large groups, and where they were headed. They soon eased through Pocahontas at dusk, and began to turn south and east toward Chewalla.

They soon crossed the Mississippi state line as it grew dark, and David noticed a half moon in the eastern sky as the train sped on. An hour later, the engine passed the outer Federal fortifications near the town of Corinth, Mississippi.

They soon pulled into the railway depot, which was covered with army wagons, tents, soldiers, and weapons. The huge Tishomingo Hotel dominated the view of town beyond the depot. It was two stories tall, built of brick, with two large verandahs on each floor. Wooden railings connected the verandahs to large Yellow Pine columns that ran from the ground to its roof. The hotel was built in 1850, and was the most spacious in town.

They unloaded their horses from the train, saddled them, and led them off from the depot where they could be fed and watered. David was engaged in unloading the horses, when Sergeant Reid met him near the station.

"A courier's here, sir. He has written orders from General Dodge. You and Lieutenant Hornbach are to report to the Curlee House right away." David took the written dispatch, read it, and then shoved it into his pocket.

"Sergeant, see if you can find Lieutenant Hornbach. If he is drunk, throw some water on him and sober him up. We have got to find our way to the Curlee House. Please get Ajax saddled and brought up for me."

"Yes sir, right away, sir." Sergeant Reid saluted David, and headed back to saddle Ajax. David walked over across the depot, and asked a sergeant in a Kansas regiment the directions to the Curlee House. The sergeant had a picket post of five men in black slouch hats, and they were guarding around thirty bales of cotton that was stacked out in the street. Negroes were seen everywhere, moving down to the depot, and begging food from several army units in the area of the depot.

David was told to ride up Jackson Street to the intersection of Childs Street. Sergeant Reid and Lieutenant Hornbach were nowhere to be found, and then Sergeant Looney appeared in the darkness with Ajax.

"Where's Lieutenant Hornbach? We have to report to General Dodge's headquarters."

"We can't find him, sir. We suspect he may be at a bar or some bawdy house, but will keep looking for him."

"No, there's no time now. You just come on with me."

They mounted their horses and rode from the area of the depot, up Jackson Street. They were guided by the light of coal gas street lamps, which were placed on the corner of every block.

They rode past Federal style clapboard frame houses, and some houses that were more elaborately constructed in the Greek Revival style. They finally stopped at a white house at the intersection of Jackson and Child Street, which was known as the Curlee House. It was a lovely Greek Revival style house, with two porches framed by square Corinthian Columns, hewn out of Yellow Pine, and painted white.

A white rail fence framed both sides of the porch. David could make out several sentries, which appeared to be General Dodge's escort, standing guard in front of the house. He dismounted, stated the nature of his business, and received a salute from the guard.

"Colonel Spencer and General Dodge are expecting you, sir, go on inside."

The corporal saluted David. David returned his salute, and entered the front of the Curlee House, while Sergeant Looney tied off their horses on the rail fence out front.

Hurricane lamps were hung out on the porch, and were also placed and lit in each of the rooms of the house.

A tall and handsome officer was seated at a desk in the front parlor, across from a sergeant major of infantry. David walked over to the officer's desk and saluted, and the young officer stood up and returned his salute.

"Lieutenant David Snelling reporting, Colonel Spencer." David saw the colonel's shoulder straps in the light of the hurricane lantern.

"It's really good to see you again, Colonel." Colonel Spencer introduced David to Sergeant Major Henry Wilson, who was acting chief of staff for General Dodge.

"It's good to have you back with us, Lieutenant Snelling. Especially after Colonel Streight's raid into Alabama."

"Do you know if Colonel Streight and his other officers were ever exchanged, sir?"

"I am sorry to say that they were not exchanged. The cartel was halted at the end of May because the Rebels refused to exchange Negro soldiers. Streight and his officers remain in Libby Prison, as far as we know."

"I am really sorry to hear that, sir. Especially for Captain David Smith."

"Where is Lieutenant Hornbach, Mr. Snelling?"

David could not lie for Hornbach any longer. "He disappeared somewhere around the area of the depot, sir. I have sent several men out to look for him once I received your dispatch."

"Then I shall have to place him on report. I may even speak to the Provost Marshal when he is done with his conference with General Dodge. I may even have him placed under arrest. The Provost Marshal may not want the extra work, though. He has his hands full enough, with all the refugees and Negroes running around here to police."

"Where are all the Negroes and refugees coming from, sir?"

"From southern Tennessee, Alabama, and Mississippi. The Negroes here heard about the Emancipation Proclamation, and now they seek out our lines. The refugees are people that live in the area of occupation of our forces. General Dodge now commands the left wing of the 16th Army Corps. He has 20,000 troops under command from here to Camp Davies to Decatur.

That many troops in one area will eat up livestock, forage, and provisions of many local farmers. Many times, receipts are issued for the forage and the livestock consumed. But some families can't just live on greenbacks. They pack their belongings and head north to find work. That places burdens on our transportation system. The Negro problem is being worked out somewhat, though."

"How is that, sir?"

"We have been given permission from the War Department to enlist Negro men into the Federal service. Several regiments of Negro troops are being raised and equipped here. We can send them into the infantry and heavy artillery companies. God knows we need the manpower, after Rosecrans got bested near Chattanooga last week."

"What happened to General Rosecrans' army near Chattanooga, sir? We have been in constant motion, and have heard no news about the progress of the war."

"General Longstreet's Corps was transferred by rail from Virginia to North Georgia. General Bragg then attacked Rosecrans' Army of the Cumberland near Chickamauga Creek, and routed two thirds of his army. Only General Thomas managed to make a stand against the Rebels. He fought off the whole Rebel Army, until he could withdraw his command after dark on the second day of the battle.

The Union Army is now under siege in Chattanooga, after being thrown into full retreat. I believe that General Sherman and General Dodge will be ordered to Bridgeport to their relief in the near future."

"Colonel, I really appreciate General Dodge transferring us back to our own unit. Most of our service was in Tennessee. Excuse me for my ignorance, but I know you served as General Dodge's Chief of staff. Colonel Streight told me something about General Dodge's reputation as an engineer. What was his service history, sir?"

"It is always good for a subordinate officer to learn more about his commander. General Dodge is a railroad engineer by trade. He does not run engines, mind you. Instead, he designs and builds railroads. He laid out the path of the Trans Continental Railroad through the Rocky Mountains from the Nebraska Territory three years ago.

He entered the service as colonel of the 4th Iowa Infantry in 1861. He commanded a brigade at Pea Ridge, where he was wounded, and had four horses shot out from under him.

He was promoted to brigadier general, and given command of the Department of Columbus. He rebuilt the Mobile and Ohio Railroad from Columbus, Kentucky to Trenton, Tennessee. He also commanded a brigade at Stone's River. He was assigned to command the District of West Tennessee until November of last year, when he was given command of the District of Corinth. I have formerly served him as chief of staff, but have been appointed as commander of the First Alabama Regiment of Cavalry."

The door to the dining room opened, and General Dodge emerged in a new blue uniform with black cuffs on his sleeves, and a Union Army major walked out of the room behind him. David saluted the officers at once, and they returned his salute.

It was hard to believe that General Dodge was only thirty two years old. He had short brown hair, a full beard with gray patches in the front, and he carried himself with the authority of a general commanding an entire Department.

He introduced David to Major Walter Phillips, the Provost Marshal for the Department of Corinth. Major Phillips was tall and thin, and wore a black slouch hat and long side whiskers. He was a red – haired and freckle faced man with piercing coal gray eyes. Major Philips saluted the general, and took his leave from the building.

The general led them back into the dining room, where he had set up a makeshift office on the dining room table. Several rolled–up maps were visible near the general's hurricane lamp.

They remained standing near the table until General Dodge told them to sit. The general then began to debrief David concerning Colonel Abel Streight's ill–fated raid into Alabama.

"Lieutenant Snelling, what, if anything did Colonel Streight accomplish on his mission?"

"Well, sir. We engaged General Forrest's command several times, and inflicted casualties on his command. Forrest's own brother was seriously wounded. We captured several enemy supply wagons at Day's Gap and at Blountsville and Gadsden. We destroyed a quantity of arms and uniforms and commissary stores in Gadsden.

Captain Milton Russell's men destroyed a large iron works near Centre, between there and Rome, Georgia."

"What, in your opinion, was the cause of Colonel Streight's capture by Forrest's command?"

"Well, two things, sir. Colonel Streight's command was poorly mounted to begin with. His entire mission proceeded under the assumption that he could mount his entire command from horses and mules captured out of enemy territory. Most of the animals were unshod, and became tender footed on the mountain trails that were rocky."

"I see. Go on, lieutenant."

"Secondly, most of the infantrymen in his command were armed with regular Springfield rifles, and their paper cartridges became damp and were ruined when we crossed several deep mountain streams. At Blount's plantation, we fought an engagement with Forrest's command, and many of Streight's infantry troops were unable to fire their weapons because their cartridges were ruined."

"Colonel Spencer, I hope you are taking notes. These lessons should be learned, and Colonel Streight's mistakes should not be repeated."

"Yes sir." "Do go on, Lieutenant Snelling."

"Well sir, when Colonel Streight surrendered, I was one of a group of officers that wanted to cut our way north toward Bridgeport. General Forrest convinced Colonel Streight that he was outnumbered, and the colonel surrendered us at Cedar Bluff."

"I appreciate your honesty and candor, lieutenant. I have taken notes of your account and comments, and will compare them to Colonel Streight's report once he returns from Libby Prison.

The war must go on."

Colonel Spencer then chimed in. "One of the items of business that we were going to discuss with you and Lieutenant Hornbach was your permanent transfer back to the First Alabama Regiment of Cavalry. Your Company "D" will be redesignated as Company "I". Hornbach's Company "E" will be redesignated as Company "K". General Dodge has a new assignment for all of us, commencing next month."

"That is correct, Colonel Spencer. The war must continue. General Rosecrans was badly whipped by Bragg's Army of Tennessee at Chickamauga Creek. His entire command is now under siege at Chattanooga. General Sherman has notified me by telegraph from Iuka to prepare to march my command to reinforce Chattanooga within the next month. I have been asked to rebuild the Nashville & Decatur Railroad all the way to Stevenson. I have established headquarters in Pulaski, Tennessee, and will march the left wing of the Sixteenth Army Corps through there toward Chattanooga in two weeks.

General Sherman has asked me to order some of my cavalry to raid the West Point Railroad somewhere below Atlanta, in order to disrupt General Bragg's line of supply. General Sherman believes a break in the West Point line would disrupt Bragg's ability to receive reinforcements from Montgomery and Mobile.

Colonel Spencer has volunteered to take his regiment of cavalry over to break this road. Your two companies have been across some of the same part of the state. You will assist Colonel Spencer as scouts for his command."

"Yes, sir. I'll do my best, sir."

"I know you will. Let me get my map. General Dodge reached for one of his rolled up maps, and unrolled the map, and placed rock paper weights on all four corners.

"You will march from Iuka to Russellville, then past Bull Mountain to Natural Bridge, and then to Jasper. From Jasper, you are to proceed to Columbiana, Alabama. You are to destroy the railroad and any rolling stock from Line Station to Elyton. This is a new line that was built for carrying iron that is being mined and milled in that area.

From Elyton, you are to proceed to the southeast, where you are to break the West Point Railroad somewhere between Opelika and Montgomery. You will have two steel six pounder guns and a little over 870 men in your regiment.

Your orders are to destroy a portion of the West Point Railroad, together with rolling stock, track, and depots, doing as much damage as possible."

Colonel Spencer wanted David to comment on the raid. "Lieutenant Snelling, what is your assessment of these order?"

David rubbed his chin for a moment, and then spoke his mind. "Well, Colonel, you are pretty much following the same general plan as Colonel Streight, except you seek to accomplish more damage to the railroad lines and rolling stock with less men than Colonel Streight started with. In essence, sir, your plan seeks to accomplish more, with less men."

"I understand your concerns, lieutenant, but our regiment will be better mounted and armed than Colonel Streight's men were."

General Dodge then had the last word.

"Colonel Spencer, I will have your orders drawn up and sent over to Camp Davies in the morning by Courier. I have some unfinished business with Lieutenant Snelling."

"Yes, sir. I'll see you off in the morning, sir. Lieutenant, I will need you to have your men in the saddle by seven a.m. tomorrow."

David saluted Colonel Spencer. "Yes, sir. We'll be ready to move out, sir."

Colonel Spencer saluted General Dodge, who returned his salute, and then left the dining room.

General Dodge reached for a canvas bag behind his desk.

"Now, Lieutenant Snelling. We have two items of business. I believe you have a pawn ticket to redeem"

David reached into his wallet, and retrieved the $20.00 pawn ticket for the Colt Navy revolver. He handed it to General Dodge, who produced the revolver from his bag.

"Let's see. You will owe me twenty one dollars. I will only charge you $1.00 for lugging this pistol around in my baggage for five and a half months."

"That's very kind of you, sir. Here is twenty one dollars." David reached into his wallet, counted out the greenback bills, and handed them to General Dodge.

"It was most kind of you to keep the Colt Navy pistol for me, sir."

"Under the circumstances, lieutenant, it was the appropriate thing to do. We have another item of business to discuss. I saw a mutual friend of ours three weeks ago, a peddler from Macon, Georgia by the name of James McBurney."

David's hairs stood on end. How much did General Dodge know about his past life?

"Yes, sir. He helped me enlist into the Union Army at Huntsville."

"Don't worry, lieutenant. Your secret is safe with me. I admire you for using all of your resources to get from Milledgeville to Huntsville to join our ranks without being shot or thrown into prison.

I sent Mr. McBurney to Line Station, and General Rousseau sent him to Yazoo City to get information on Rebel strength and troop movements in our Department. I have instructed him to journey through the lines, and to meet up with you on your mission. You are to take down Mr. McBurney's information, and in confidence, pass it on to Colonel Spencer.

Colonel Spencer will ultimately decide how to deploy his regiment, but I want him to have all of the latest intelligence on the enemy at his disposal."

"Yes, sir. I will do my best to help him, General Dodge."

"I know you will. I had your two companies transferred back here because I need veteran troops in this department. A good many of Colonel Spencer's troopers were recruited at Camp Davies this past summer, and they are new and undrilled. Many of them have never seen combat. You veterans need to show these greenhorns the ropes. Good luck, Lieutenant Snelling, and good hunting."

"Yes sir, thank you again, sir."

David saluted General Dodge, who returned his salute. He then put on his kepi and exited the dining room of the house.

He stepped through the front door and off the porch of the Curlee House, where he returned the salutes of General Dodge's sentries.

Sergeant Looney was there to meet him with Ajax. He handed David the reins, and both men mounted up and rode back toward the depot.

"Sergeant, you will need to have Sergeant Reid pass the word to both companies that "Boots and Saddles" will sound at six thirty in the morning. We are ordered to Camp Davies, and we have to pull out at seven a.m. The buglers will need to wake us at five a.m."

"Yes, sir."
"Did Sergeant Reid get us all a room at the Tishomingo Hotel?"
"Yes, sir, he did. But it is up on the second floor."
"That will have to do. Let's go back and get some sleep."

* * * * *

Camp Davies, Mississippi
October 10, 1863

Dear Uncle Uriah and Aunt Faith:

After traveling over 1000 miles, we have finally arrived at our new duty station.
Camp Davies is enclosed in a ten acre square, surrounded by a strong log stockade. The barracks are all log cabins, and the colonel's quarters is a large frame "I" house, which has a separate room for the adjutant. There are fire places and windows in all of the cabins, and most of the barracks have corn–shuck mattresses.

There is a theater, a bakery, and a hospital within the camp. We have drilled with the different companies of the First Alabama Cavalry Regiment almost daily. Our two companies have been reassigned as companies "I" and "K" of the First Alabama Cavalry Regiment.

Most of the new recruits are green and not well drilled, but we have orders to move out in a raid toward Elyton and Opelika next week. It could be like the ill–fated raid of Colonel Streight, but I can only put my trust and faith in God, and hope for the best. I bought your Colt Navy pistol out of pawn from General Dodge yesterday. He had faithfully kept the pistol for me these six months.

May the Lord bless you and keep you both.

Love,

David

Chapter Nineteen

On October 17th, David, Sergeant Anderson Looney, and ten other troopers rode out from Camp Davies toward Iuka, and then south across the Natchez Trace. Their scouting mission was to scout out the best line of march toward Jasper, and to procure guides that would take the First Alabama Regiment to Walker County.

They passed a beautiful plantation house near Vincent's Crossroads, and they rode on the south banks of Bear Creek. They camped near Bay Springs, Alabama for the night, and slept under the stars in the autumn chill.

They awoke at daylight the next morning, and arrived at a small farm just south of Bear Creek owned by Clement Kemp, a Union loyal man whom they wanted as a scout. They fed their horses at his corn crib, and paid him for the forage, and they persuaded him to accompany them back to Camp Davies, and then on to Jasper.

Mr. Kemp was forty five years old, and was tall and wiry. He wore a slouch hat, blue jean cloth pants, and a checkered shirt. He farmed twenty five acres of corn in an area that he had cut out of Sweetgum, Water Oak, and Loblolly Pine woods. He had built a large barn and corn crib, and a fine cabin of squared up logs. He farmed the place with the help of a younger wife and a fifteen year old nephew.

David persuaded him to scout for them for twenty dollars, and paid him with greenbacks given by Colonel Spencer for that purpose.

They soon mounted up and headed back north along Bear Creek, toward the Natchez Trace. Mrs. Kemp, an attractive brunette of around thirty years, packed them some fried chicken and biscuits to eat for their supper. Mr. Kemp donned his jean cloth coat, packed his single shot horse pistol, and rode his black mare north with the troopers.

They rode through a heavily wooded area along Bear Creek, and they soon crossed the Natchez Trace. The Trace at that point had been worn down to a sunken road in the limestone and clay hillsides.

Autumn had come to the Deep South, and they noticed the colors of trees as they rode back north. The Sycamore and Wild Grape leaves had turned golden, along with the Beech trees. The Sweetgum and Dogwood and Red Oak trees had turned scarlet to purple, and the Red Maples had turned a crimson color. All of the trees stood together on both sides of the road as a multi–colored autumn canvas for their view.

They rode past Woodall Mountain late that afternoon. That evening after dark, they joined the rest of the regiment, at an encampment near Walker Siding.

David reported directly to Colonel Spencer, who was pleased with the guide, and the selection of the route for their expedition. They were to convey two six pounder guns, and three wagons to carry forage and feed for their horses.

They were to cook and carry with them three days of rations. Any other food needed during the expedition would be obtained on the way. They were ordered to move out at nine o'clock the following morning.

The next morning, "Boots and Saddles" was blown at eight a.m., but the troopers could not get into line and move out of camp until nearly ten o'clock.

David and Mr. Kemp and Company I had the advance, and Colonel Spencer and some of the other officers rode with them.

On the road heading south, they passed the ruins of houses that were burned by the 7th Kansas Cavalry in retaliation for the shooting of two of their men by guerillas in the area.

They camped for the night at the farm of a Union man named Earl Pollard. Mr. Pollard had a forty acre farm near Cripple Deer Creek, where he grew corn and sorghum. Colonel Spencer and Captain Trammel bought some corn for the animals out of his corn crib, which they paid for with Federal greenbacks. Some men from Company H then took some of Mrs. Pollard's chickens, which they also paid for after she protested vigorously.

They started south for Vincent's Cross Roads the following morning, after feeding and watering their horses. The wagons brought up the rear of the column, as they made their way down the road, with two horses abreast. The woods on either side of the road were dense, and consisted of hickory and oak trees, Tupelo and pine trees, and tangles of Wild Grape Vines decorated the tops and sides of the trees. Patches of Water Locusts, and occasional briars and cane brakes added to the thick, lush under story of the forest, and made riding a horse difficult everywhere except the cleared roadway.

They road south as far as Vincent's Cross Roads, a small town above the Natchez Trace and near Bear Creek. They halted at noon and ate their rations on the grounds of a fabulous plantation owned by Robert McRae, a rich planter who claimed to be a Unionist.

Mr. McRae owned a large two story house, two or three general stores and dry–goods stores, and a cotton plantation. He shipped his cotton up the Tombigbee, or up the Natchez Trace up to the Tennessee River during the time before the war. Some of his slaves had gone north to Corinth, and others had just run away.

The colonel did not want to stay at Vincent's Cross Roads for the evening, so the column resumed its march, and headed south along Bear Creek.

That evening, they passed near Bay Springs, after crossing the Alabama state line. They stopped to feed their horses at a small farm near Bear Creek, owned by Mack Daniels, a thirty five year old farmer. That evening after nine o'clock, several men reported that their pistols and wallets had been stolen from their saddle bags.

Colonel Spencer ordered Mr. Daniel's house searched, where the stolen items were recovered. Colonel Spencer ordered some of his men to burn Mr. Daniel's house. Captain Trammel and a small detail piled up pine straw across Daniels' front porch, and lit the straw with Lucifer matches. Soon the entire house caught fire, and the entire structure burned to the ground in a matter of minutes.

They awoke the next morning under the blare of bugles, and tended to the needs of their animals. They boiled water for their coffee, cooked their rations of bacon, and ate their morning ration of bread or hardtack.

"Boots and Saddles" soon sounded, and the regiment mounted up and headed east across Bull Mountain. David's Company "I" was in the lead. Clement Kemp knew the country well, and kept the column on heavily wooded trails, away from Rebel Cavalry patrols in the small towns.

They continued on across Bull Mountain, noticing the spectacular view of the autumn leaves from the mountain trail.

They spent the night on the property of a Richard Crews, who had open Rebel sympathies. The men fed their horses hay and corn from Mr. Crews' amply stocked corn crib, and lieutenant William Gray, the colonel's adjutant, gave him quartermaster receipts for the forage.

The men killed one of Mr. Crews' sows, and soon the smell of fresh pork cooking in fry pans wafted from their campsite.

The following morning, the column pushed out after eight a.m., after the animals were watered and fed. They crossed the Buttahatchee River at ten o'clock, and headed southeast over Pea Ridge toward Jasper. The trail became rough and rocky, as they ascended Pea Ridge. They arrived that evening at the farm of Charley Kight, a Union man that lived on the side of a limestone mountain. Charley was fifty five years old, with silver hair, and was tall, thin, and wiry. He wore blue jean cloth trousers, and a buckskin jacket. He farmed corn on a narrow strip of land between two steep hills. His field of corn was 100 yards wide, and only 500 yards long.

Yet Charley made a living by farming corn. He lived in a limestone cave at the base of one of the hills. Inside the cave, Charley had built a series of interior rooms out of Red Oak and White Oak boards, and he had placed an iron wood burning stove in the cave for heat, and for cooking.

The other cave served as a forage bin and a corn crib. Sergeant Looney knew Mr. Kight, and vouched for his loyalty to Colonel Spencer. Colonel Spencer saw that Mr. Kight was paid cash for his corn crop, as the regiment needed almost all of his crop for ready forage. He agreed to accompany the regiment as a guide for another $20.00, and that sum was paid over to him promptly.

Later that evening, some men in Company C brought in ten Alabama men as new recruits for the regiment. One of the regiment's wagons broke an axle, and had to be burned that evening.

The colonel ordered a detachment of fifty men to ride south to Allen's Factory, and to burn the tent factory there. The factory made cotton canvas dog tents for the Confederate Army.

That evening after dark, a courier from Company "F" asked David to walk with him back to the colonel's tent. David walked back to the colonel's tent, and saw the colonel asleep on a wooden cot with a blanket wrapped around his body.

He was sweating profusely from his forehead, and was being administered to by Dr. John Stewart, the young assistant surgeon from Company F. David saluted Dr. Stewart, who wore a white coat, and carried the rank of a major.

"Lieutenant, the colonel sent for you, but he has some form of swamp fever. He just received a written message from a Union man down in Jasper. He wants you to read it and report back to him tomorrow evening."

David took the note and opened it. He then began to read it:

October 22, 1863
Near Jasper, Alabama

Lt. David Snelling
c/o Colonel George Spencer
1st Alabama Regiment Cavalry

Dear David:

I have specific information concerning Confederate troop movements in Mississippi and Alabama that are relevant to your expedition.

I am at a tavern about ten miles west of Jasper called the Boar's Head. Please meet me here tomorrow. It will be good to see you again.

Sincerely,

James McBurney

David looked up from the letter, and understood that this mission must be executed with some discretion.

"Doctor Stewart, please tell Colonel Spencer when he wakes up that I will take care of this."

"Thank you, lieutenant."

David saluted the doctor, and walked back to where Company "I" was encamped. He found Sergeant Looney, and began to fill him in on their new mission.

"Sergeant, go ahead and saddle our horses. We need to ride toward Jasper right away. Tell Lieutenant Day that he will be in command of the rest of the company until we return. The column will move out at dawn, and Lt. Colonel Dodds will probably be in command. Colonel Spencer has fallen ill."

"Yes, sir."

Soon, Ajax and Sergeant Looney's horse was saddled, and they rode past the pickets, and down toward Jasper on the old road.

The area was heavily wooded and hilly, with large oak and hickory trees. It soon began to rain, and they broke out their oilskins, slipped into them, and rode on.

Eight miles down the road, they saw a large building constructed of squared up pine logs. A shingle was hung out in front of the building, which bore the name of "Boar's Head" on both sides. A small stable was located at the side of the building.

The rain was steady, and soon turned the red clay road into a slippery stream of mud. They dismounted, and Sergeant Looney led the animals into the dry area sheltered by the stable's cedar shingle roof.

David stepped up to the door of the tavern, and noticed lit hurricane lamps near the windows. He checked his Adams revolver under his oilskin coat, and then unlatched the door.

In the dim light of the tavern, he saw James McBurney's familiar stumpy figure seated at a table near the rear of the room.

A slim old man in a buckskin shirt was at the bar, pouring beer into a glass from a keg. He raised his free hand when David walked in.

"Welcome young man. Mr. McBurney has been expecting you. I am George Leavell. Union men are welcome here."

David thanked Mr. Leavell for his hospitality, and sat in the chair next to his old friend, James McBurney. He shook Mr. McBurney's hand, and removed his dripping oilskin jacket, and laid it on the chair across from them at the pine board table.

The peddler from Macon looked David in the eyes, and immediately stated his business.

"I have just returned from Yazoo City. A spy has infiltrated General Dodge's headquarters. I overheard his report to General Ferguson a week ago.

General Stephen Lee was ordered to harass General Sherman's troops from near Florence to Decatur. General Lee soon learned that General Sherman's plans were to abandon the railroad at Decatur, and to use the river boats to supply the army at Stevenson.

General Lee's two thousand troopers have been ordered to Jasper to intercept your column. General Ferguson has been ordered east from Oxford, Mississippi, to hit your column from the rear. General Ferguson also has three brigades, around two thousand troopers, and four six pound horse artillery pieces. Where is your regiment at this time?"

"Most of them are ten miles west of Jasper, or around eight miles west of this tavern."

"You need to pass this information on to Colonel Spencer immediately."

"I will. Right now, though, I need to ask you some questions."

"Go ahead, lad. I am at your service."

"Where are you going from here?'

"I have two mules and a wagon load of merchandise at the livery in Jasper. I will go to Opelika for General Rousseau, and then over to Columbus and to Macon. I will go up to Milledgeville to deliver some merchandise the following week."

"Will you see Uncle Uriah, then?"

"Most certainly."

"Good. I have been working on a set of serial letters which I wanted to get to him and Aunt Faith somehow."

David tore the letters out of his journal, folded them lengthwise, and handed them to James McBurney.

"I will put these in my oilcloth envelope, and then in my haversack, David. I am sure that they will want to know that you are safe."

"Tell them that I miss them, and hope to see them soon."

David arose and donned his oilskin jacket.

"Duty calls, Mr. McBurney. You take care of yourself."

"You do the same, lad. Be careful out there." McBurney raised his glass to David, and finished his drink as David nodded to Mr. Leavell and left the tavern.

He walked out to the stalls in the rain, and saw Sergeant Looney lying on a haystack, fast asleep in his oilskin jacket. He gave Sergeant Looney a nudge, and told him that they needed to report back to Colonel Spencer at once.

They mounted up, and rode back down the road toward camp. The rain slacked off, and soon became nothing more than a heavy mist. They rode on until they encountered the picket line at three thirty in the morning.

David reported immediately to Colonel Spencer, who was wide awake when he arrived at his tent. David reported the intelligence he had obtained from James McBurney to Colonel Spencer, who decided to turn back and retrace their path back to Mississippi.

"We need to turn around and confront General Ferguson's force. We don't need to allow him to interpose his force between us and Camp Davies. I know the men will be disappointed about turning back, but I can't ignore this intelligence. Lieutenant Snelling, I am grateful. You just might have saved this command with that piece of information."

"Thank you sir. I was just following General Dodge's instructions."

Colonel Spencer called for his adjutant, Lt. Frank Tupper, and issued orders to Lt. Colonel Dodds and to Major Cramer to turn the regiment back at seven a.m.

David saluted Colonel Spencer, and led Ajax back to his encampment. He then grabbed two hours of much needed sleep.

* * * * *

The men were disappointed about turning back the next morning, and some units did not receive the order until after daylight. Company K had taken the advance and marched two miles up the road before they could be halted and notified of the change in the marching orders.

Dr. Stewart had also fallen ill, and was taken behind one of the horses in a travois, which had been rigged from Sweet Gum saplings and blankets.

Later that afternoon, David and Sergeant Looney were leading the advance, along with some men from Company "H". One of the NCO's from Company "H" was a young Sergeant Major, Francis Wayland Dunn. He was a dark haired, skinny 20 year old with long side whiskers and three "up" stripes on his chevron, and had three "down" stripes as well.

As they were riding together, Sergeant Looney rode by David, and asked him, "Who that boy with all the stripes was?"

David laughed out loud, and answered:

"That 'boy' is Wayland Dunn. He ranks you, Anderson. He is a sergeant major. When you address him, you must salute him. He ranks all other sergeants in this regiment. They just made him regimental sergeant major."

Anderson understood, and they rode on for another two miles in the woods, when they soon encountered four Rebel scouts on the edge of a pine thicket.

They spurred their horses, drew their pistols, and gave them chase.

However, the Rebel scouts fanned out and disappeared. Clement Kemp was with them, and Sergeant Major Dunn noted that he rode exceptionally well.

They stopped for the evening at the farm of George Underwood, a pretty farm on the edge of a high hill that he had planted in apple trees. They bought some apples from Mr. Underwood, who was identified as a Union man, and they took a couple of stray chickens, and obtained some corn for the animals. Mr. Underwood had a large barn, and a nice two story house covered in pine clap boards.

Companies "I" and "H" were to lead the advance, so they rode two miles beyond Mr. Underwood's to make camp. Sergeant Looney was adept at making apple sauce, and David cooked the chickens on an open fire with a long spit of green wood. The officers and NCO's of both companies enjoyed a good supper that night.

Lieutenant Day was sent to order up the picket lines for the night, and they enjoyed a full night of sleep for the first time in four days. They arose at four a.m., ate a quick breakfast, and tended the animals. Clement Kemp took them on an obscure trail that led through the pine and oak woods, and up to Bull Mountain.

They stopped for the evening at a small town named Wallace, at a crossroads near Bull Mountain. The town was tiny. It consisted of a store, two or three clapboard houses, a post office, and a large shed. The area around the town was hilly, and heavily wooded.

The men caught a number of chickens that were running around the shed. Later that evening, those chickens became part of the officer's mess. They ate the evening meal with Colonel Spencer, Lt. Colonel Dodds, and most of the officers. David noticed that Colonel Spencer was well spoken, and made an effort to learn about all of the officers serving in the regiment. Some of the officers sang songs after supper. "Sweet Rose of Alabama", "Hail Columbia", and "The Battle Hymn of the Republic."

Lt. Frank Tupper was an excellent baritone singer, and he carried a tune well without musical accompaniment from instruments. David and Sergeant Looney later took their leave, and spent the rest of the night sleeping in the back of a corn crib.

The next morning, the entire regiment pulled out, and headed to the west northwest through the forest below Bull Mountain. They soon crossed Bull Mountain Creek, where the column halted to refill their canteens, and to water their animals. They continued this path toward the Natchez Trace, crossing the Alabama state line once again. They were guided by Clement Kemp and Company "I", and they moved at such a grueling pace that the last three companies could not keep up. They soon halted at a plantation located two miles from Vincent's Crossroads, which was owned by August Patterson. It was a large cotton plantation that was formerly worked by 50 or 60 Negroes. The main house was a wooden clapboard structure painted white, with white painted columns and black wooden shutters. The plantation had a decent – sized cotton gin with 50 saws, a ginhouse, and a large cotton warehouse on the property.

They halted at the plantation to feed and rest their horses, and Colonel Spencer and his staff soon rode up and joined David and Sergeant Looney at the plantation house.

"Lieutenant Snelling, I have ordered some men from Company K and Lieutenant Hornbach to scout beyond Vincent's Crossroads for any sign of the enemy."

David did not like the fact that Lieutenant Hornbach was given this assignment, as the success or failure of their mission now depended on Lieutenant Hornbach. It would be insubordination to mention this to Colonel Spencer, however, so David held his silence.

Some of the men from Company H reported to Colonel Spencer that several bales of cotton had been found in the warehouse. Colonel Spencer sent Sergeant Major Wayland Dunn and ten other men over to guard the cotton. He ordered another officer down to burn the cotton.

A forty five year-old woman in a black crinoline dress, and a white cap and shawl walked out on the front porch, and asked to address the "commanding officer".

Colonel Spencer walked over to the wiry woman, and identified himself as the "commanding officer" of the regiment. Colonel Spencer removed his black slouch hat when he spoke to her, and was respectful to her when he addressed her.

She, on the other hand, was brazen and rude and outspoken. She identified herself as Mrs. Ruby Patterson. She wanted to personally rebuke the leader of this horde of thieving, dirty, no-account Yankees. The Southern people would never, ever be subdued and subjugated by such scum. Their way of life would never be destroyed and overcome by such soldiers as these. The Southern people were a different people, and could never live under the rule of a Black Republican president.

Colonel Spencer held his tongue, until he had heard as much of her bad mouthing as he could take. He told her that the First Alabama Cavalry and the Union Army were the children of Israel, coming to bring a plague on her and her husband's house.

"You fired on our forts and our ships, you made war on a peaceable people, your fellow countrymen. You will now feel the hard hand of war upon your land."

The Patterson woman remained defiant. "It is you sir, that will soon feel the hard hand of war fought by man against man, as opposed to man against woman."

David heard this exchange, and decided that they were about to be attacked. He went over to Colonel Spencer and saluted him, and offered up his explanation of the situation.

"Sir, I believe we are about to be attacked. This woman would not be this uppity and defiant around a whole Union regiment, unless Confederate troops were in the area. Lieutenant Hornbach has yet to return. Notice how quiet it is around the field over there. At this time of day, you should hear squirrels barking and birds singing. You can't hear anything out there, sir. I suggest we deploy for battle on one side of the field, sir."

Colonel Spencer rubbed his bearded chin for a moment, and came to a decision. "You are right to be cautious, Lieutenant Snelling." He then summoned Adjutant Frank Tupper, and issued orders for the immediate deployment of all of the companies in the regiment.

The colonel issued orders for deployment along both the Iuka Road and the Tupelo Road. On the right of the Iuka Road was a cornfield, which was 150 yards wide and one half mile long. It was surrounded by thick underbrush made of briars, Water Locust, Wax Myrtle, and Poison Oak. Companies "F", "B", and "G" were deployed to the left of the road, and companies "E" and "A" were deployed on the right of the Iuka Road. Company "H" was deployed in the field to the right of the Iuka Road, and Companies "I" and "K" were deployed in the field on the left of the same road. These companies were deployed in mounted positions.

A small white frame house occupied the center of the field, and that is where the regiment's horse guns were unlimbered. Not long after they were deployed with their pistols at the ready, the Rebel horsemen attacked their position.

Lieutenant James Lukens unlimbered the two gun battery on a hill near the white frame house, and began lobbing shells across the field at the Rebels.

Company "C" was posted behind the field and the white clapboard farmhouse as a rear guard. The pack mules with the rations and ammunition were tied up in the rear behind Company "C". Several score of Negroes who had taken up with the column also crowded to the rear, adding more confusion to the battle. They shrieked and groaned as the six pounder guns were loaded and fired.

David was at the center of his line with Company "I" in the cornfield, and saw the Rebel troopers move out. The corn had been harvested two months before, and most of the cornstalks had been cut and tied together in stacks across the field. Some of the troopers had been ordered to dismount, and to engage the Rebel troopers as skirmishers with their carbines from behind the tied up stalks of corn.

The Rebel troopers wore butternut colored uniforms, and were led by General Ferguson, who wore an ostrich feather in his gray slouch hat. He rode a gray mare that was around fifteen hands high. They came out of the dense forest at a trot, never moving faster than a canter.

Their line was composed of three brigades of cavalry, over 2200 troopers strong, and it overlapped the field and the entire line of the Union troopers. They then blew their bugles and sounded the charge, and the Rebel horsemen raced for the road near the center of the field.

Companies "E", "A", and "H" were soon driven back by the weight and force of the Confederate attack. The Union troopers in those companies took casualties, and gave up ground.

As the Rebel troopers pressed on, Colonel Spencer issued orders to Companies "B", "F", and "G" to fall back behind the white frame house, near the artillery batteries. Most of the new recruits in all of these companies had never been in combat, and they soon ran off the field. The veteran troopers in these companies also raced back.

David looked to the right of his line on the left portion of the cornfield, and saw that the Union troopers were being outflanked on the right side of the cornfield. David saw Captain Stenburg of Company "B" take a musket ball through the head, and was instantly killed.

Lieutenant Swift of the same company, a handsome twenty eight year old officer, tried to rally the men of his company, but soon took a shot in the stomach from a Rebel trooper's pistol.

David saw that he needed to buy his company some time, as the Rebel advance threatened to swamp his men. He drew the Spencer Repeating Carbine from its holster, and stood up high in the stirrups. He aimed at the color bearer of one of the Rebel regiments, and fired at the horse's chest.

The horse took the .52 caliber ball at full speed, and threw the color bearer, his Stars and Bars, and two other troopers in the advance guard in a somersault across the field. David fired two more quick rounds, killing two other Rebel troopers. He then ordered his troopers to draw their pistols and open fire. Saddles were emptied across the field, but the Rebel troopers gave a yell and kept coming.

David sent Sergeant Reid and two men after Lieutenant Swift, and they quickly bore him off to the rear. The artillery near the house then opened up on the Rebel troopers, and began to inflict casualties on horses and troopers. Horses and riders were wounded, killed, and disemboweled by solid shot from the six pounder guns. The Rebel riders were held up by the artillery fire, giving the Union troopers an opportunity to retreat. A small strip of Sweet Gum trees in the center of the field was used as cover by troopers in Company "L". They dismounted, and began to fire into the Rebel troopers with their Burnside carbines.

David received written orders to fall back behind the white frame house, and to lead the advance around the field, and on around toward Iuka. Most of the Regiment was ordered to reform at the crossroads, and Companies "D", "K", and "C" were left to check the advance of the Rebel troopers.

David and his Company "I" rode down to the cross roads, where he saw a group of officers and NCO's attempting to rally the men against the attackers. The refugees, Negroes, and shirkers from the regiment kept pushing the column forward. Clement Kemp, the guide, soon got separated from the column.

After a few minutes, he reappeared in the company of Sergeant Major Dunn. David then led them out with the advance column into the road.

Lieutenant Lukens had limbered his guns, and drove them up the road at the head of their column. Sergeant Major Dunn also rode after the pack train, and brought the pack mules out onto the Tupelo Road.

They moved to the south and west of the field, in the direction of Tupelo, where they crossed a small rocky stream. On the other side of the stream, as they rode up the Tulip Tree covered banks, the advance took fire from Rebel muskets.

Captain Chandler of Company "E" was killed, as he was shot through the heart while crossing the stream bed with the advance column.

The Rebel troopers then charged the rear guard companies, who had prepared for such an attack. The dismounted troopers fired several volleys from their carbines, and unhorsed many Rebel troopers.

David and the advance guard crossed a small field of broom straw, and then descended into a swamp bordered by Palmetto and Wax Myrtle bushes. The briars and Wild Grape vines grew thick between the trees, and greatly impeded the progress of the column.

The swamp soon narrowed into a small stream, and the Federal troopers traversed the stream in a single file. The guns were pulled behind the advance column, but one of the wheels on one of the guns became wedged between two large rocks at the stream bottom. The banks were a mixture of limestone and gumbo clay, and were coated in moss. The men pulling the guns tried desperately to free the first piece, but to no avail. The artillerymen cut the teams away, and mounted the pull horses and rode ahead with the troopers.

Captain Shurtleff and Sergeant McWright of Company "D", rode up to the opposite bank and tried to exhort the men and get them to halt. Sergeant McWright told Colonel Spencer that the guns had been left in the creek. Colonel Spencer did not want to report to his superiors that he had lost two guns to the Rebels.

He drew his pistol, and tried to form a line. He was joined by Sergeant McWright, and Sergeant Major Dunn. The Rebel horsemen then began to press the column, firing shots again at the advance guard.

The men began to run toward the rear, spurring their horses on. One man rode past Colonel Spencer, hatless and without his carbine. Colonel Spencer told him to halt, or he would blow his brains out.

The trooper stopped for a few seconds, and then said "It is only a bullet anyway." He then spurred his horse and lit out away from the colonel and through the woods.

Company "I" held together pretty well, joined by other groups of troopers from different companies. Sergeant Major Dunn rode with David and his men. The men basically divided into two columns. David's men and Colonel Spencer went toward the west, and were guided by Clement Kemp. They went a short distance through the woods, and then they were fired on in ten quick volleys from Rebel troopers from their right rear.

Lieutenant James Perry from Company "L" was instantly killed, and other men were also killed while encouraging the men to hold their ground. Captain Tramel and Captain Ford also attempted to get the men to halt and form ranks, but to no avail. David saw Union troopers flee a field in confusion; a sight he had not seen since Stones River.

They followed their guide, Clement Kemp, directly through the woods, and away from the main roads. They ran in a circular direction, away from the Tupelo Road, and in the general direction of the Iuka Road. They crossed a bridge over a small stream, and were fired on by three or four dismounted cavalryman.

One of the carbine balls clipped one of David's shoulder straps. A private in Company H rode with their column after he was shot through the hand and body. He rode with them for six or seven miles. He was bleeding, and soon weakened, however. He was forced to stop at the porch of a small house because of his wounds. He was simply too weak to keep pace with the rest of the column.

They had ridden for 15 miles, but were actually only seven miles from the battlefield, because of their circular route. Twenty miles above the battlefield, they stopped to feed and water their animals. They rode on until four o'clock that afternoon, halting just three miles short of the Union lines at Iuka. They made camp near Woodall Mountain, on Little Cripple Dear Creek. They had little food, but shared hardtack and coffee with each other. They numbered more than 120 men, consisting of Company "I", and men from Company "H" and Company "E".

David and Sergeant Looney messed with Sergeant Major Wayland Dunn. He told some funny stories about the battle from the time of their retreat.

Wayland described a trooper that had been thrown off near a creek, who then jumped on behind another trooper's horse. The fellow in front said: "Oh Lord, do get off." But he could not push the trooper off, or persuade him to get off.

He finally said "Well if anybody is shot in the back, it will be you!", and kept on riding. They laughed at Wayland's story, and posted pickets, and turned in for the night. They had ridden seventy five miles that day, and they needed to rest their animals.

* * * * *

The following morning, they arose and mounted their horses, and rode through the Union picket line into Iuka, Mississippi. David sent Sergeant Major Dunn to the quartermaster to draw rations for the men, and forage for the horses.

Sergeant Major Dunn drew rations and forage for 122 men from the regiment. Sergeant Looney and two other troopers took Lieutenant Swift to the field hospital, where he could be attended by the post surgeons.

David was ordered to report to General Sherman's headquarters to give an oral report of their raid. He rode over to a white frame house that served as the department commander's headquarters. Two sentries saluted David at the porch of the dwelling, as David dismounted and tied Ajax at the hitching post. He returned their salutes and entered the dwelling, where he came to attention and saluted a Major Nichols.

The major was tall, with a black slouch hat, and dark mutton chop side whiskers.

"At ease, Lieutenant. I am Major George Nichols, chief of staff for General Sherman. We are in the process of issuing orders for the resupply and relief of Federal troops in Chattanooga. General Rosecrans has been relieved, and General Grant has been ordered by the President to hold Chattanooga at all hazards.

General Sherman will see you, now. He wants you to brief him on your mission, and on the location and strength of Ferguson's cavalry."

"Yes, sir."

David was led into the dining room of the house, where a red haired and bearded officer was seated, wearing the two stars of a major general on his shoulder straps. He was writing furiously, while smoking a cigar. A plate of half eaten beans and bacon lay on the table, with half of a tin cup of hot coffee.

When they entered the room, Major Nichols introduced them, after David stood to attention and saluted the general. General William T. Sherman sat back in his chair, pulled on his suspenders, and puffed away on his cigar while he conversed with David.

"Lieutenant Snelling, give me your report as to what happened to your regiment. I take it that you command a company in the First Alabama Cavalry?"

"Yes, sir. I command Company "I", sir. We were ordered by General Dodge to march on the railroad at Elyton and break it. We were then to march to Opelika and break the Atlanta & West Point Railroad there, sir. We marched to Jasper, Alabama, where a detachment was sent out to destroy Allen's Factory. Allen's Factory was burned to the ground. General Dodge ordered me to make contact with a Union intelligence agent near Jasper, sir. He gave me information that indicated that General Ferguson was pursuing us with three regiments of Rebel cavalry.

We turned back and marched to Vincent's Cross Roads, where we were attacked by Ferguson's Rebel cavalry. They overpowered us, sir, and some of our green troopers ran from the battlefield. We were worsted, sir, I regret to say."

General Sherman took several puffs from his cigar, and then asked David a question.

"To what do you attribute this defeat, Lieutenant Snelling?"

Well, sir. The scouting company did a poor job of reconnoitering the enemy units and the position of these units. The field officers deployed the companies poorly, and failed to deploy the artillery batteries in a proper position to support a defense of our position."

"Well done. Officers need to learn from the mistakes of their superiors so that they will not be repeated. What were your casualties in the battle, Lieutenant Snelling?"

"None dead, none wounded, but three missing."

"Very well. I am going to issue orders through General Dodge that will place command of the First Alabama under Colonel Mizner. Some of the more experienced companies in your regiment will draw scouting duty. General Dodge has made his headquarters in Tennessee. Colonel Spencer is to return there as his chief of staff. We are in the process of relieving the siege of Chattanooga.

We can sure use some scouts and cavalry on our campaign. What is General Ferguson's present strength?"

"Sir, he has three regiments of cavalry. I would say he has 2000 men under his command. Sir, I need to send a confidential written communication to General Dodge at Pulaski. The intelligence agent at Jasper told me that a Rebel spy has infiltrated his headquarters."

"Certainly. Major Nichols, provide a pen and paper for Lieutenant Snelling. Lieutenant, I will see that General Dodge receives your communication at once. Well done, Lieutenant. You are dismissed."

David saluted General Sherman, and was shown to a small room, and was provided a pen and paper to write his dispatch to General Dodge:

Iuka, Mississippi
October 28, 1863

General Grenville Dodge
Commanding Dept. Of Corinth
Pulaski, Tennessee

General:

I made contact with Mr. James McBurney near Jasper, Alabama on the 23rd of this month. He gave me valuable information on the disposition of General Ferguson's Cavalry. His information may have saved our regiment from complete disaster.

McBurney also told me that you have a spy in your headquarters area. He is a Rebel officer disguised as a Union officer. This man has gone through our lines several times to convey our troop movements and dispositions to the Rebels. McBurney saw him in Yazoo City earlier this month. This man is dangerous, and should be arrested at once.

Mr. McBurney can confirm all of this information in detail, when he returns from Georgia.

Lt. David Snelling
Commanding Co. "I", First Alabama Cavalry.

* * * * * *

Glendale, Mississippi
November 20, 1863

Dear Uncle Uriah and Aunt Faith:

I hope and pray that Mr. McBurney was able to forward you the few pages of my journal that I gave him last month. I hope that you all are in good health, and wish I could see you in person, as opposed to you hearing from me indirectly.

Our regiment survived Colonel Spencer's debacle at Vincent's Cross Roads. Mr. McBurney gave me information that we were to be attacked by two Rebel cavalry brigades. We turned back at Jasper and retraced our route, only to run into General Ferguson's small brigade at Vincent's Cross Roads.

The green troopers in the regiment ran from the battlefield, and the veteran troopers could not quell their panic or keep them in check. I escaped from Vincent's Cross Roads to Iuka with most of Company "I", and part of Companies "H" and "E".

Lieutenant Swift and several other officers were shot and killed while trying to rally the men. Lieutenant Swift was gut shot, and we bore him off the field, and carried him on horseback with us to Iuka. He lingered on for six days after the battle, and died at the post hospital at Iuka.

The regiment was scattered into different groups, and groups of troopers made their way back to Glendale and Iuka for several days after the battle. Some troopers have yet to be heard from. All of the women hanging around the regiment have been ordered to move by Colonel Mizner, our new commander. Some of these women are actually married to our troopers. Others just say that they are 'married', as it appears that some of these young women are destitute, and use the troopers as a means of a daily sustenance.

The railroad to Corinth and Memphis is to be abandoned, and the Tennessee River is to be used as a means of supply at Eastport. A second major has been appointed to co–command the regiment in the place of Colonel Spencer.

Colonel Spencer has been reassigned as chief of staff for General Dodge at Pulaski, Tennessee. In a couple of days, our company and Company "K" have been ordered to ride out with Colonel Mizner and the Seventh Kansas Regiment and the Third Michigan Regiment. We will go out on a scouting expedition toward Okolona and Pontonoc. The men with decent horses from our regiment will go out on this scout with Colonel Mizner.

I will write you again once we return from this expedition.

Very Truly Yours,
David

* * * * *

At daylight on November 26, 1863, Colonel Mizner led 400 men from the Third Michigan Cavalry, 300 men from the Seventh Kansas, and 200 of the best mounted men from the First Alabama Cavalry out of Corinth, Mississippi.

They marched thirty one miles south, and encamped near Blackland, Mississippi. The brigade then rode southward to Chesterville, and then turned to the northwest, and marched past Pleasant Ridge near Molino, Mississippi.

Near Molino, the brigade got into a skirmish with Confederate cavalry under the command of General Stephen D. Lee. The Rebel troopers had blocked the road with a barricade of logs and cotton bales. They opened fire on Colonel Mizner's advance guard, and killed several Michigan troopers. The troopers of the Seventh Kansas regiment outflanked the Rebel trooper's barricade, and killed fifteen Rebels, and captured thirty five Rebel troopers.

The column then marched to Ripley, where Colonel Mizner ordered the 200 men from the First Alabama Regiment to escort the thirty five prisoners back to Corinth. Companies "K' and "E" had horses that were in too poor a condition to keep up with the rest of the brigade.

David and Sergeant Looney were excellent judges of horseflesh. They could examine an animal, and immediately determine if it was underfed, or suffering from a disease or infirmity. They accepted underfed animals as remounts, while rejecting the diseased animals.

Lieutenant Hornbach and other officers were not as skilled in selecting remounts for their companies. They selected horses in poor condition to serve as remounts, and now they simply could not keep pace with the rest of Mizner's brigade.

They were ordered to march from Ripley to Corinth, past Silver Springs Hill and Crow Mountain. They left Ripley early on the morning of November 29th accompanied by one company from the Third Michigan Cavalry.

At mid day, they marched past Ham Hill, and soon forded the Hatchie River near a hill know as Crow Mountain. At the base of the hill was a one room school house made of white painted clapboards, with a tall bell steeple.

They called a halt on the grounds of the school house to cook their rations, and to feed the horses and the Rebel prisoners. The school house had two large windows on each side of the building, and David noticed that children's faces were pressed up against the glass of one of the windows from one end to the other.

David rode Ajax up to the front porch of the schoolhouse, and tied him off at the hitching post. As he entered the door of the schoolhouse, he was greeted by a pretty black haired schoolteacher of nineteen years. She was dressed in a gray wool dress, and she sported a white straw hat with a blue ribbon at the brim. She had blue eyes, and stood around five feet eight inches in height. She had charge of thirty pupils, all varying in age from six to fourteen years. Half were girls, and the other half were boys.

The teacher took control of the situation. "Students, you are to take your seats immediately. I must now speak outside to this officer. Sir, I need to speak to you outside."

David did not believe that the schoolmarm was a day over nineteen years of age.

"At your service, ma'am." David removed his kepi, and followed the teacher out onto the porch outside.

"What are you doing here? What do you want with us?" David could see the alarm in the young woman's eyes.

"We mean you no harm ma'am. We have been ordered to escort these prisoners back to Corinth. We only aim to stop here to draw water from your well, and cook our rations, and feed our stock and our prisoners."

"You are a Southern man. What are you doing fighting with the Yankee army?"

David had heard that question before, and decided that he would be disarming.

"You are the second lovely Southern woman that has asked me that question this year. I fight for the Union because of my political and moral beliefs. I am opposed to disunion and secession."

The school teacher had blushed, and her cheeks had turned nearly red. "Forgive the question. Troops on both sides have visited this part of the state. I have thirty students here. It is almost time for me to ring the dinner bell. I will need to send the oldest children out to the well to draw water for their lunch. Would it be all right to allow the children to eat their lunches outside?"

"Yes, of course. They can gather under that big Sycamore tree near your well. I will post a guard near there so they will not be molested. I will also post a guard here at the schoolhouse. We will draw our water after your children draw theirs, and will cook our rations under that Water Oak across the way. Your children must not go near our prisoners, though."

"You are more than kind, lieutenant. What is your name?"

"David Snelling. What is your name, miss?"

"Amelia Wall."

"Well, Miss Wall, if you get a chance, I would like to share a cup of coffee with you, to repay your hospitality."

"That would be lovely. We have had no coffee here for more than two years. It is a chilly and blustery day out."

David bowed to Miss Wall, and then ordered Sergeant Looney to post a guard near the children, and around the schoolhouse.

Several tall young boys exited the rear of the schoolhouse with tin pails, and they took turns pumping water from the hand pump at the well head. The day was cool and windy, and the boys were bundled up in homespun wool jackets.

They pumped their water, and Amelia lined them up under a large Sycamore tree, where they sat down and began to eat their lunches from tin lunch pails.

David and his company watered their animals and began to cook their rations on the opposite end of the school yard. They shared their bacon and hardtack with the children, who gobbled down the hot food greedily. David took a hot tin cup of coffee over to Amelia, who was seated on a folding chair underneath the Sycamore tree.

She smiled as she took the hot cup of coffee from David. "I even got some sugar off of Sergeant Looney for your coffee."

"Thank you. It is very good. I normally don't drink it black, but it is wonderful to have real coffee again. I am so tired of this dreadful war. When will it all end?"

"I see it lasting at least another year or so. There is plenty of fight left on both sides. I suppose that you have a boyfriend off in the Confederate Army?"

"Not really, but several friends of the family went off and enlisted in General Barksdale's brigade."

"How do you like being a teacher?"

"It can get on your nerves, but these children are generally well–behaved. If I tell their parents that any of them have acted up, they are punished promptly at home. That really keeps them in line."

Sergeant Reid interrupted them at that moment, walking up with a sandy–haired freckle faced boy of ten years. "Lieutenant Snelling, this lad is Jason Patrick. He says that he always wanted to enlist in the cavalry. Whenever his pa and his ma go off to town, he goes out and rides around on all of their stock, cows and all."

They all laughed. "Well, it is a pleasure to meet you young Jason. My horse over there is called Ajax. He was a real racehorse before the war. You can go over there and pet him if you want. Sergeant Reid will go with you. Go ahead."

They shook hands, and Sergeant Reid led the boy over to greet Ajax, who was tied out at the hitching post.

Sergeant Looney came over and saluted David, and reported that the prisoners had all been fed. "I'm sorry that Sergeant Reid interrupted you while you were talking to the lady. I can see you were making some progress here." He gave David a wink, saluted, and walked over to where the guard was posted.

The wind kicked up again, and David realized that the lunch recess was probably over already. He also realized that his company needed to push on, in order to make Corinth by nightfall.

Amelia arose from her folding chair and handed David her tin cup. She donned her straw hat, and called the children to wash their lunch pails and line up for class.

"It was a pleasure to meet you, Lieutenant Snelling. You are a gentleman, even if you are riding with the Yankees."

David removed his kepi, bowed to Amelia, and then kissed her hand. "It was a pleasure to meet you Amelia. I would like to call on you if I ever ride through here again."

"My pa won't like that, but we'll see." Amelia smiled, and then stepped into the school house, as David mounted Ajax.

The rest of the company mounted up, and the trailing companies "K" and "E" soon followed, and they resumed their march toward Corinth. One of the companies of the Third Michigan cavalry had also joined them on the return trip, because some of their horses had thrown shoes, and were tender footed.

The sky soon cleared on the windy afternoon, and they spotted crows circling overhead. They moved on the pike at a steady pace, in spite of the poor condition of most of the horses.

They soon passed through the small town of Jonestown. An hour later, they crossed the Tuscumbia River, and they soon entered the outer defenses of the fortified town of Corinth, Mississippi. David noted to himself as they passed the fortifications that General Dodge and his engineers had designed and established all of the fortifications around Corinth.

They turned the prisoners over to the Provost Marshal when they got into town, and David reported to the Assistant Adjutant General, and began to make out his monthly reports.

* * * * *

December 5, 1863
Corinth, Mississippi

Dear Uncle Uriah and Aunt Faith:

We went out on a scout with Colonel Mizner last month toward Okolona, where we saw a large force of cavalry under the command of Confederate General Stephen Lee.

We avoided contact with the large cavalry force, but we had a fight with a smaller force that had barricaded the road near Molino. We killed fifteen, and captured over thirty Rebel prisoners.

We just received news that General Grant's Army of the Tennessee, and General Thomas' Army of the Cumberland attacked the Rebels at Missionary Ridge, and drove their army clean off of Lookout Mountain from Chattanooga.

We also heard that Grant killed or captured over 15,000 men. If this is correct, then General Grant is surely the man to win this war. McClellan, Hooker, Burnside, and even General Meade have obviously failed to win the war in the east. General Grant has proven himself time and time again, and his record cannot be ignored.

Grant has been nothing short of brilliant in his handling of the troops under his command. His success in this dire situation at Chattanooga most certainly will be noticed by the War Department in Washington

I have to go now. I need to kill and issue a beef cow out to the men. I make them draw lots for the division of the hindquarters cuts.

I hope you all are in good health and good spirits.

Love,

David

Chapter Twenty

On December 20th, the companies "I", "E", and "D" and "L" were ordered to Corinth to accompany the Third Michigan Cavalry and the Seventh Kansas Cavalry to Tennessee. They were to escort a brigade of infantry and two batteries of artillery from the 16th Army Corps under the command of Brigadier General Joseph Mower.

Major Francis Cramer was in command of the four First Alabama companies, and he was soon detailed as an assistant adjutant to General Mower. The brigade assembled and formed up at seven a.m., and they soon moved out into the cold and crisp December air.

They were ordered by General Dodge to West Tennessee. General Nathan B. Forrest had been given command of all Confederate forces in West Tennessee and North Mississippi, and Mower's column was sent to seek them out.

General Mower had intended to push over toward Memphis along the line of the Tuscumbia and Hatchie Rivers. However, heavy rains during the previous two weeks had caused extensive flooding on the Tuscumbia River and the Hatchie Bottom.

The entire column was forced to march east, and then north into Tennessee, crossing smaller streams that were also flooded from the recent rains.

They crossed Muddy Creek, Roland Creek, Turkey Creek, Snake Creek, and Tar Creek with the aid of General Mower's pontoon train. On December 23rd, the reached a small section of the Forked Deer River known as Jack's Creek, which was twenty five miles southwest of Jackson, Tennessee.

David rode at the head of Company "I" behind Major Francis Cramer, who had been detailed as an adjutant to General Mower. David found Major Cramer to be a decent officer, but his appearance was disarming. Major Cramer was a dead ringer for Robert Toombs, a noted Confederate statesman from Georgia.

Neither David nor the Union officers knew that General Mower's column was about to collide with the newly created command of General Nathan Bedford Forrest.

Forrest left Bragg's Army of Tennessee, and was soon given command of all Confederate forces in west Tennessee and north Mississippi. Forrest had around 150 troopers that had gone west with him, and he began to recruit and enlist troopers in west Tennessee. They were mostly deserters, "shirkers", bounty–jumpers, and men who had previously avoided military service.

Nevertheless, Forrest had a substantial force in the area of Jackson, Tennessee, when his scouts reported enemy activity south and west of the town. He ordered a force south to meet the Federal force, develop their strength, and retard their progress.

Before daylight on the morning of December 24, 1863, a detachment of recruits for General Forrest's command were moving south under the command of Lt. Colonel David M. Wisdom. Those troopers soon collided with Company "L" of the First Alabama Cavalry Regiment under the command of Lt. Alonson Edwards.

Company "L" had orders to drive in the enemy's pickets if resistance was encountered on the march. Company "L" began to drive in the pickets of the Confederate troopers near Jack's Creek. General Forrest had instructed some of the cavalry companies to dismount and entrench near Jack's Creek, in order to support the lead elements of the Rebel brigade.

Company "L" of the First Alabama Union Regiment soon drove the Rebel pickets back to their prepared positions on Jack's Creek. The Rebel troopers had entrenched themselves in well–hidden positions beneath Beech trees and canebrakes near the creek.

The entrenched Confederate troopers opened fire on Company "L", killing 18 year old Private Jesse Files.

Company "I" was directly behind Company "L", and David and Sergeant Looney heard the firing at their front, and moved forward at the trot. Other Rebel troopers had dismounted and hidden themselves in prepared positions along wooded areas near Jack's Creek.

As David's company rode up with their pistols drawn, the Rebel troopers opened fire on them. Nineteen year old Sergeant Henry Welch was shot through the head and killed, along with thirty year old Private William Pell. David ordered the men to take cover behind a nearby grove of Sweet Gum trees. Their training and experience soon took over, as every fourth man in the column held the horses of the other three men, so they could fight while dismounted.

David drew his Spencer Repeating Carbine, and crept forward near the front, leaning behind a Wax Myrtle bush. He chambered a .52 caliber round by moving the lever of the carbine forward. He saw a Rebel trooper expose himself to fire, and he aimed at the trooper and pulled the trigger. The carbine rocked his shoulder, and the Rebel trooper pitched forward almost before the report of the carbine could be heard.

The Rebel and Union troopers exchanged gunfire at the creek, and their skirmishing drew the attention of General Forrest and Lt. Colonel Wisdom. They ordered more Confederate troopers to dismount, move forward, and join the fray. David looked up through the hardwood bottoms of the creek bed, and saw many gray–clad troopers weaving their way forward through the trees. He summoned Sergeant John Reid, and sent him back to request reinforcements from Captain Shurtlef.

David began to shoot more Rebels with his Spencer Carbine, chambering and firing four rounds in less than forty seconds. Sergeant Looney and Sergeant Reid led more troopers forward, and pointed their Burnside Carbines toward the Rebels, aimed, and fired at will.

The Confederate troopers were mostly new recruits, and began to fall back in the face of resistance from veteran well–trained Union troopers.

General Forrest responded by feeding greater and greater numbers of dismounted troopers into the battle, which stepped up the pressure on the Union troopers. Even though the Rebel troopers were inexperienced, their numbers were hard to overcome.

David's Company "I", and Companies "L" and "E" were slowly forced back. David sent Sergeant James H. Murphree back to summon Major Cramer, to request reinforcements from General Mower's infantry brigade.

Sergeant Murphree was an experienced trooper, a forty four year old father of three children. He was born and raised in Blount County, Alabama. Several of his younger brothers had enlisted in the First Alabama Cavalry.

However, on the way back to summon Major Cramer, Sergeant Murphree took a Minie ball through his lungs. A Tennessee sharpshooter took careful aim at the good sergeant, fixing his peep sight between the yellow piping on the back of Murphree's uniform coat. He fired, and Sergeant Murphree was hit, and fell face forward into the edge of the creek bed. In fifteen minutes, Sergeant James Murphree bled to death on the banks of Jack's Creek.

The Confederate troopers began to drive the Union troopers back, and David called for a bugler, and asked him to sound "recall". "Recall" was sounded, and the men began to lay down covering fire at the Rebels, to allow different units to withdraw. It was skillfully done, and soon the Union troopers remounted and rode about one mile back toward the approaching infantry column.

The infantry column had taken the wrong road, however, and several men had to search for the column down different roads. Sergeant Reid and two other troopers finally got word to them, and reinforcements were soon sent out to Jack's Creek.

Three regiments of Indiana infantry, and several companies of the Seventh Kansas Cavalry were soon lined up and deployed down the road.

It was nearly nightfall before all of the reinforcements could deploy for the attack. They began to advance on General Forrest's Confederate troopers, who had begun to withdraw from the battlefield. General Forrest and most of his lead regiments had moved west and north of Jack's Creek, crossing the Forked Deer River above Henderson, with several wagons, several hundred horses, and some captured beef cattle and rifles.

Lt. Colonel Wisdom and several rear guard companies were encamped in a small corn field near Jack's Creek, when they were attacked by the Union troopers and infantrymen.

They were cooking their rations when they were hit, and they reeled back in total confusion. A bugler began to sound the alarm, but the Union troopers hit them hard, and began firing into their camp, dismounting and killing Rebel troopers.

The survivors broke off into small groups, and fled pell mell through the creek bottom. In less than thirty minutes, the Union troopers were in complete possession of the Rebel cavalrymen's encampment.

They cooked their rations over the same campfires. David then organized several burial details to locate the bodies of the fallen Union troopers. The troopers were buried the following morning near the edge of the cornfield.

The bodies were wrapped in their great coats, and on Christmas Day, Sergeant James H. Murphree of Company "I", Jesse Files of Company "L", William Pell of Company "I", and Private William Welch of Company "D" were laid to rest.

All of the available companies of the First Alabama lined up near the graves for the ceremony, which David performed. He opened his King James Bible that he carried in his haversack, cleared his throat, and began to read.

"In the Gospel of John, Chapter 14, verses one through three, Jesus said:

'In my Father's house are many mansions; if it were not so, I would have told you. I go to prepare a place for you.

And if I go and prepare a place for you, I will come again, and receive you unto myself; that where I am, there ye may be also.'"

He closed his Bible and began to address the troopers, who were standing before him in the cold, hatless, in their great coats.

"These men died so that their country, their nation might live. They volunteered to serve in this regiment because they loved the Union, and they pledged their lives to preserve and protect it.

It is now up to all of us to finish this war and win this war, so that their sacrifice will not have been in vain. As our Lord sent his son to deliver us from sin, we have been sent to deliver this country from secession."

Sergeant Reid then sang "Amazing Grace", in a fine baritone voice, and the bugler blew "Taps" over the graves of the fallen troopers.

They mounted up and moved out in pursuit of Forrest's troopers, as sleet began to fall from the overcast sky.

* * * * *

General Forrest marched his cavalry brigade north and west, crossing the Hatchie Bottom on the Estanaula Road below Brownsville. His brigade engaged and routed an Illinois cavalry regiment, and then headed southwest toward Somerville and Collierville.

The First Alabama Cavalry companies, and all of the troops under General Mower's command retreated south to Pocahontas. They then received orders to march west, through Saulsbury, and then on to LaGrange.

General Grierson had been ordered to load his cavalry brigade on the cars in Corinth, and to meet General Mower's command at LaGrange. The remaining companies of the First Alabama Cavalry were also ordered to travel with General Grierson's command on the cars to LaGrange.

The weather had turned horribly cold, freezing mud puddles on the ground hard enough to bear the weight of a horse. David and his men rode west toward Mount Pleasant. They arrived there around noon, and stopped to feed and water their horses. Colonel Mizner was in command of all the cavalry regiments in the brigade. The First Alabama Cavalry occupied the rear of the column, and was ordered to move up from the rear to the front of the column.

Mount Pleasant had once been a pretty town, with a gin house, white frame houses, a depot, and a large store. However, it was now almost entirely destroyed.

They marched to within a few miles of Collierville in a swamp along Russell Creek. They learned from an old timer who lived near the swamp that General Forrest had marched his entire command through there two days before. They camped that night in the swamp. While David and his company were setting up camp, a courier from Colonel Mizner brought him a dispatch from General Dodge at Pulaski:

Head Quarters
Pulaski, Tennessee
December 15, 1863

First Lt. David R. Snelling
First Alabama Cavalry
Corinth, Mississippi

Lieutenant Snelling:

I received your dispatch the first week of November, and ordered the Seventh Kansas Cavalry to actively seek out spies in our lines.

They captured a Joshua Brown and a Samuel Davis. Upon Davis were found letters from Captain Coleman, General Bragg's chief of scouts. He was dressed in a faded Federal soldier's coat when he was captured.

I tried to impress upon him the danger he was in, and that I knew he was only a messenger. He would not truthfully answer my questions, though, because he was protecting his superiors. I found large mail of value on him, and much of it was letters from friends and relatives of soldiers in the Confederate Army.

I had him brought before me again, and I made another direct appeal to him to give me the information I knew he had. He refused to do it, and I let him be tried and suffer the consequences.

Davis died a hero's death, as he was hung as a spy. Your timely dispatch helped me locate and break up this ring of spies that were working to disrupt my command.

I am indebted to you and to Mr. James McBurney for your timely information.

Very Respectfully,

Grenville M. Dodge
Brigadier General

* * * * *

The following morning, the entire brigade returned to Corinth. There was no need to stay in that area, since General Forrest had evaded them, and had slipped his command through to Panola, Mississippi.

Chapter Twenty One

Near the middle of January, orders were soon issued that required Camp Davies and Corinth to be evacuated.

The Seventh Kansas Cavalry had been ordered home to recruit new cavalrymen, and most of their horses were to be sent over to the First Alabama Cavalry. The government stores and sick and injured soldiers were soon loaded aboard railroad cars, and were sent to Memphis.

Orders to move were finally issued on January 23rd.

After the men marched out of the barracks and stables at Camp Davies, engineer details were sent in to fire the buildings. They were made mostly of Yellow Pine, and they caught fire and burned quickly, sending up torrid streams of flame, and columns of black smoke.

The next day, the evacuation and demolition process was repeated in Corinth on a larger scale. The large government buildings were fired, but fire spread from them to other private buildings. The Corinth House caught fire and burned, and the fires spread through barracks, warehouses and stables. Shells and munitions left around the camp also caught fire and exploded, adding their fireworks to the yellow conflagration. The next morning, there was little left of Corinth, Mississippi.

The men camped that night two miles north of Chewalla, Tennessee.

* * * * *

David's Company "I" was ordered on a scouting mission from Camp Davies, Mississippi to White Sulphur Springs, Tennessee, on January 12th. They marched a distance of sixty miles, and returned on January 14th.

On February 7, 1864, the entire First Alabama Cavalry Regiment was ordered to proceed south from Memphis, Tennessee, under the command of Colonel William McMillan.

Lieutenant Alonzo Edwards' Company "L" was ordered to ride the point at the head of the brigade on the march south from Memphis. They rode into a swamp, and did not march free from the Cypress swamp until mid day. Some of the troopers found some corn to feed their horses hidden in a wooded area near a small farmhouse. After feeding and watering the trooper's stock, the column pushed south. They halted for the night at Hernando, Mississippi, some twenty two miles south of the Tennessee line.

They camped just south of town, and moved out at nine o'clock the next morning after the infantry column had marched up. They had to stop and rebuild the wooden plank bridge over the Coldwater River, which included several extra spans across a Cypress swamp on each side of the true river bed.

They marched down to a small town named Coldwater, after the river, where they camped for the night. The weather was freezing, and the troopers had to take extra care of themselves and their animals under such extreme conditions.

The following morning, the troopers and infantrymen moved out before daylight. Two companies of infantry and the First Alabama Cavalry repaired the bridge across Hickahala Creek and its adjoining swamps, and then marched into the town of Senatobia. Around two miles from town on the main road from Memphis, 25 or 30 Rebel troopers had set up breastworks, and opened fire on Company "H".

First Lieutenant Peek had the bugler sound "charge", and pitched into the Rebel troopers, who fired a few fleeting shots, and vanished into the woods. Lt. Peek and Lt. Richard Turrentine led Companies "H" and "D" on the chase after the Rebel troopers, skirmishing with them for two miles. Infantry companies were then sent out beyond the road toward Senatobia, and picket posts were set up.

David's Company "I" cooked their rations in the field behind a physician's home, just outside of Senatobia. While they were eating their midday rations at one-thirty, there was heavy firing on the picket posts on the left side of the line. The "alarm" was sounded, and Companies "H" and "I" responded to the sound of the firing. Lt. Peek's company "D", and two infantry companies were engaged by the rebels, and had to fall back.

Company "I" came forward, and the men fired their carbines into 30 or 35 Rebel troopers that had turned to flee from the approaching troopers. Later that evening, Colonel McMillan ordered Senatobia abandoned, and all Federal troops had to recross Hickahala Creek before nightfall. Lt. Peek's horse was shot, and several other troopers lost horses that day.

The following morning, Colonel McMillan sent the wagon train back to Memphis, and ordered the bridge over Hickahala Creek burned. He also appointed David and Sergeant Looney as special couriers. They were to transmit dispatches back to General Hurlbut in Memphis. They were picked for the assignment of courier duty because they were better mounted than the other troopers.

That same morning, David and Sergeant Looney took dispatches from Colonel McMillan, and rode back north into Memphis.

Colonel McMillan's column then marched east northeast from Senatobia toward Holly Springs. They marched through the small towns of Bucksnort and Wyatte. The column then marched several miles to the east of Chulahoma, Mississippi, where it halted for the night on February 14th. David and Sergeant Looney had returned to Memphis on February 10th with dispatches, and they returned to catch up with the column at Cox's Plantation on February 14th. They delivered dispatches from General Hurlbut which indicated that General Smith's Cavalry column had departed from Collierville.

McMillan's command camped on the grounds of a fine plantation owned by Jeffrey Cox. The plantation was one of the finest David had ever seen. Mr. Cox had a large two story white clapboard house, with square columns on the front porch. The windows were adorned with black shutters.

Mr. Cox had a large red barn, and excellent quarters for his Negro slaves. They resided in double log houses, with wooden split rail floors. He had a fifty saw cotton gin and excellently built gin house facilities. None of Mr. Cox's slaves had ever left him, because he had treated them well. He had over forty five slaves on the plantation.

His wife was an attractive auburn haired woman with green eyes. She was gracious and kind to the soldiers, in spite of her home being inundated with the hated Yankee troops.

Colonel McMillan took 1400 pounds of meat from Mr. Cox, and gave him U.S. Army Quartermaster's receipts for the provisions. David saw a slave girl that was extremely light skinned there, with red cheeks and auburn hair. She was lovely, with green eyes and a pleasant smile. She had household duties only, and was treated differently from the other slaves. David spoke to a Negro woman that he thought was her nurse. He found out that she was her grandmother. The old woman also told him that Mr. Cox was the girl's father.

Two officers in Company H got horses from Mr. Cox's brother, Mark Cox. They paid him in U.S. greenbacks for the excellent animals. Early on February 15th, David and Sergeant Looney were ordered to return back to Memphis with dispatches. They led their horses out beside Cox's gin–house as infantry troops were firing it. Mr. Cox was out beside the gin house with a stone jug, lying back against his rail fence. He was highly intoxicated, and told anyone within earshot that the Union Army had ruined him, costing him at least $400,000.00. David and Anderson could smell the odor of whiskey on Mr. Cox as they mounted their horses, and retraced their route back to Memphis.

On the way back, David spoke to Anderson about Mr. Cox and his situation.

"You know, Anderson, Mr. Cox had a nice plantation over there. He had everything a man could ever want. He supported secession and the Confederate government, thinking that the war would be over with in a matter of weeks, and would never touch him. Now the war comes to him, and he says he is ruined financially."

Anderson got the point quickly. "So I wonder if he thinks Jeff Davis and the Rebel government should be supported right now?"

They rode back on the State Line Road in a steady rain. They broke out their oilskin coats, pulled them on, and rode back to Memphis with their dispatches.

* * * * *

On the 17th, Colonel McMillan gave the First Alabama Cavalry permission to move out, and they came into Memphis over the State Line Road, moving into camp outside of town at two p.m.

* * * * *

Memphis, Tennessee
March 6, 1864

Dear Uncle Uriah and Aunt Faith:

We went out with Colonel McMillan's brigade last month down to Senatobia, where we skirmished with some Confederate cavalry units.

Colonel McMillan ordered myself and Sergeant Looney to carry dispatches back to Memphis, so we made a round trip back to headquarters during McMillan's expedition to Chulahoma. We camped on a plantation owned by a well to do man named Jeffrey Cox. None of his slaves had ever left him, because he had treated them so well. His slave quarters were superbly built and maintained. I saw a sixteen year old girl with auburn hair and reddish cheeks that you would call a Mulatto Negro. Her grandmother told me that Mr. Cox was her father. She was really lovely.

It rained and then snowed here, and the snow has accumulated and stuck around for a couple of days. I got cleaned up and went to a sermon last Sunday at Union Church with Lieutenant Dunn. It was an excellent sermon, and I wish that Aunt Faith could have been here to hear it with me.

We have orders to move across the river to Arkansas next week. Rumor has it that we are to provide guards for a work gang of Irishmen who are going to work on a railroad over there. I hope we can get across the Mississippi River without any trouble.

I have to go now, as I need to finish the tri–monthly reports.

Yours Truly,

David

On the night of March 11, 1864, the First Alabama Regiment received orders to move with ten day's of cooked rations the next morning.
    At 8:00 o'clock, Colonel Dodds marched the entire regiment down to Mud Island, where the troopers began to load their horses and equipment aboard the steamer *Crab*. The *Crab* was poorly maintained, and was attended to by several long bearded sailors, and a red–faced river pilot, who was dressed in a black broadcloth jacket, with worn twill trousers.
    The steamer was only large enough to ferry twenty troopers at a time, along with their horses. One of the paddle wheels on the steamer was broken, so the steamer had to veer hard to the starboard side to hold her course against the Mississippi River current.
    The spring flood had not yet come down the Mississippi, so the stricken craft could navigate across the mile wide stream without too much difficulty. The *Crab* took all day to ferry the regiment over the mile wide Mississippi, but the men finally assembled at Hopefield Point right after dark.
    They moved along a narrow road through Cottonwood trees and canebrakes to Lakes, Arkansas. Lakes was six miles from Hopefield Point, and was only 500 yards from the Mississippi River, which made a sharp bend west at that point. Here they met a group of 100 Irishmen, who had been hired by the U.S. Military Rail Roads to tear up a five mile portion of railroad track. The workmen were to tear up the rails, and move them to another railroad bed on a line that ran to Little Rock and the Arkansas River.

The Irishmen were hard drinking, well muscled men, and were all dressed in twill pants, checkered shirts, and jean cloth jackets. David saw that they were all cheerful and light hearted, but were probably clothed uniformly by their employer, who had brought them down from New York City.

The next morning after roll call, Lieutenant Peek and Lieutenant Wayland Dunn took their company out to guard the Irish railroad hands while they pulled heavy iron gun trucks out of river mud with strong draft horses.

David saddled Ajax, and rode out with Sergeant Looney to scout the countryside beyond the area of the railroad cut. The land was completely flat, and was often flooded by the Mississippi River during the winter and spring. The banks of the river beyond the railroad cut were only twenty feet above the stream bed. There were small Cottonwood trees and River Birch trees everywhere, mixed in between thick and tall canebrakes.

There were bayous and oxbow lakes all over the flood plain, where water had pooled from seasonal flooding from the Mississippi. David had earlier noted to Lieutenant Dunn that the flood plain soil was very rich, and could easily yield a bale of cotton to the acre if planted and tended properly.

The regiment went out with them on a scout the same afternoon, and returned from a ten mile sortie without finding any Rebel troops. They marched back to Hopefield with the Irishmen, the gun trucks, and their work wagons.

The next morning, Companies "H" and "F" went out with several work gangs of Irishmen, who rode out on heavy work cars that were pulled by four mule teams. The workmen pulled up one half mile of railroad iron, and pulled it over to Lakes.

The next morning, David, Sergeant Looney, and fifty men from Company "I" went out on a scouting mission, and saw 25 Rebel guerillas hidden in a cane brake. They fired on them and charged them, only to see the gray clad soldiers split up and scatter through the cane brake.

They split up and followed the guerillas, who separated even further, and headed deeper and deeper into the cane brakes and surrounding bayous.

They were not worth capturing, in David's opinion, so he had a bugler sound "recall". The company soon assembled, and they marched back down the dirt road back to Lakes.

The sky seemed much wider on the flood plain, and the sun began to set in the west before they could get back to camp. A violet line could be seen on the horizon, bordered by a grayish – purple band above it. David noticed that this type of sky could only be seen in the winter months when the sun set away at an angle, rather than overhead.

The natural beauty of the flood plain was deceptive, as the troopers had been warned by their scouts that 200 Rebel Guerillas were hidden several miles out in these canebrakes. They got into camp as the rest of the troopers were cooking their beans and bacon rations. David could hear the Irishmen singing, and saw them swinging their knit caps and dancing jigs by the campfire.

David ate a quick supper of bacon, biscuits, and coffee. He wrapped himself in his blanket, and slept under the stars on the cold, clear night.

The next morning, Company "I" rode out and stood guard over the Irishmen while they ripped up rails with their nip bars, and loaded them onto heavy wagons drawn by draft horses.

At twelve o'clock, Major Godfrey ordered Lieutenant Hornbach and twenty men out to relieve David and Company "I" from guard duty. The railroad workers sat down and ate their midday meal at twelve–thirty while David and his company were being relieved.

David looked up at Lieutenant Hornbach, and noticed that he appeared to be inebriated. He saw Sergeant John Smith of Company "K" come in at the head of a column of Company "K" troopers. He went up to the sergeant, and reminded him that guerillas had been known to be in the area, and he should put out several strong picket posts to protect them and the workers.

Sergeant Smith gave David a half hearted reply, and David ordered his company to mount and return to camp. He was uneasy about Hornbach's condition, and hoped that the Rebels would not attack the workers during his shift.

They arrived in camp around one fifteen, and the men rubbed down their horses and began to cook their mid day rations. David remained uneasy though, and kept Ajax saddled and close by him at the camp. He began to cook his ration of bacon and canned beans, and sat on an old log with Lieutenant Wayland Dunn.

Lieutenant Dunn's father was an ordained minister back in Michigan, and Wayland was a devout Christian and a Bible scholar.

They were discussing their reading of the Book of Luke when they heard gunfire out near the picket posts. David asked Sergeant Looney to have the bugler sound the alarm, while he and Lieutenant Dunn both mounted Ajax, who was saddled and ready.

David rode Lieutenant Dunn out to where his Company "H" was bivouacked, and dropped him off. Lieutenant Dunn had his company bugler sound the alarm, while David marched most of Company "I" out to the cars on foot.

He put the spurs to Ajax, and rode hard down the dirt road that ran alongside the old railroad cut. He rode at top speed, letting Ajax stretch out his front legs and eat up the road with his huge stride.

He topped the hill above the work area, and saw the Irishmen walking back toward him, away from their heavy wagons. He stopped the lead man, and asked him what had happened. He told David that the Rebel guerillas had fired on Company "K" from behind two canebrakes near their work area. Lieutenant Hornbach had been drinking, and failed to put out any guards or pickets for the work party. David asked him about the captured men, and also asked him if any horses or equipment had been taken.

The lead man told him that 17 troopers and one officer had been captured, together with their arms, and nineteen heavy work horses had been taken. David instructed the Irishman to hike back down the road to camp. He then turned Ajax around, and spurred him hard, beating a path back to camp.

He got into camp a few minutes later, and reported to Major Godfrey what the lead man had told him. David and all of the company commanders wanted to turn out and follow the Rebels and recapture the horses, and liberate the captured troopers.

David tried to convince Major Godfrey that they could run down the Rebels and out shoot them with their carbines. However, Major Godfrey was concerned about being attacked by more Rebel guerillas. He and Major Cramer wanted to place a strong guard of four picket posts, with 25 troopers per post. Lieutenant Peek, who was serving as Adjutant for Major Godfrey, induced him to put out 10 troopers at each picket post. Other troopers were sent out into the canebrakes to look for the Rebels, but they had no success on the cold and foggy afternoon.

The next morning, several patrols were sent out to track down the Rebel guerillas. Lieutenant Dunn was sent six miles north to Marion with troopers from Company "H".

Lieutenant Cheney with Company "F" was sent west to Lakes, Arkansas. David and Company "I" were sent out to track the path of the captured troopers from "K" Company. Later that afternoon, Major Cramer thought Lieutenant Cheney and his men were overdue, so he sent David and 21 troopers from Company "I" to find him.

David met Lieutenant Cheney's column coming back near a grove of Cottonwood trees along side an oxbow lake. They returned to camp, and reported to Major Cramer that 60 Rebel guerillas had attacked the column, and they had quickly marched the captured troopers at least 18 miles.

They also reported to Major Godfrey that an immediate pursuit by the regiment would have allowed the recapture of the troopers and the work horses. What David did not tell Major Godfrey was that he and Lieutenant Hornbach were both blamed for the capture of the 17 men and the loss of the work horses.

Major Godfrey and Major Cramer both decided to ferry the regiment across the river the next morning. The Irishmen had completed most of their work, and another regiment could be ferried across to guard them later. The spring floods of the Mississippi were soon coming, and the Irish work crews would be unable to work out in the flooded bayous anyway. They would probably have to wait until September before their work could be finished.

The *Crab* once again ferried the men across the mile wide Mississippi River, and onto the state docks at Memphis. They marched into camp at seven o'clock in the evening, and ate cold rations and sacked out for the night.

The next morning, a courier came into camp to notify Major Godfrey and Colonel Dodds that they had been ordered back to Decatur, Alabama. Their method of returning to Decatur was unusual, though, because they were to return back by water. The steamer *Westmoreland* was to take them upriver to Cairo, Paducah, and then to Smithland.

The next day, they struck their tents, packed them into bundles on their pack mules, and headed them down to the state docks across from Mud Island. When David and Company "I" finally moved out and got to the docks, David recognized the familiar lines and decks of the side wheeled steamer *Westmoreland*. He rode down to the water front, and boarded the steamer by walking up the gang plank. He soon greeted Captain Ward, and exchanged pleasantries with his river pilot as well.

The men and horses were loaded aboard the *Westmoreland* during the afternoon. The pack mules had to be left behind, though. They would be loaded and sent to Camp Campbell aboard the next northbound steamer. Major Cramer's horse soon developed seizures from a severe case of horse distemper. He began to kick against the wooden stalls on the stern end of the steamboat. Lieutenant Dunn and Captain Shurtleff attempted to restrain the plunging stallion, but to no avail. David recommended that the animal be thrown overboard. Five troopers grabbed his bridle, and guided him off the stern end of the boat. Three men rushed him, and shoved him over the side.

The horse struggled with the Mississippi River current, and let the current carry him down several hundred yards below the state docks. He struggled to shore though, out of eyeshot of the troopers aboard the *Westmoreland*. Out of sight and out of mind.

The *Westmoreland* slipped her moorings and steamed around Mud Island the following morning at daylight. The spring flood of the river had just begun, but the powerful engines of the steamer pushed it upstream without difficulty.

Spring was beginning to show around the banks of the Mississippi. It was the fourth spring of the war. Rosebud trees were in full bloom, and some new small green leaves were beginning to appear on hardwood trees. The *Westmoreland* stopped and took on coal in Cairo, and then steamed upriver to Paducah, where the army detained the First Alabama for one day.

They steamed twenty miles up the Ohio River from Paducah to Smithland, and then they steamed up the Cumberland River to Clarksville, where the steamer took on coal. The horses were run out of the steamer and fed and watered, and their pens were cleaned before they were led back in . They arrived in Nashville on April 3rd, where they were reunited with Colonel George Spencer. He called the officers to an officer's conference when the regiment arrived at Camp Campbell. The horses were reshod, and remounts were obtained at the cavalry remount station at Camp Campbell. David and Lieutenant Dunn managed to "borrow" a smoked Boston Butt and two pounds of coffee from the quartermaster on April 8th, and he sent them down to Franklin by Frank Kellogg's young son Mark, with a note to Dr. Edward Mallory:

Camp Campbell, Tennessee
April 8, 1864

Dr. Edward Mallory
Franklin, Tennessee

Dear Dr. Mallory:

Our regiment steamed into Nashville aboard the *Westmoreland* a few days ago. Some of our officers have never been to Roper's Knob, and would like the opportunity of a visit.

Please accept this smoked ham and the enclosed coffee as a gift from a Union officer that describes himself as nothing less than your friend. Ajax is in splendid health, and would like to see his old master, if you so desire.

This may be ill-mannered and in slightly poor taste, but I would like to call on you tomorrow evening with Sergeant Looney, Doctor Swaving, our regimental surgeon, and Lieutenant Wayland Dunn, a gentlemen and Bible scholar. We are seeking a hot meal, some musical entertainment, and the fellowship of a wonderful family such as yours.

If we can come tomorrow, please acknowledge on the bottom of this note, and return it back to me by Master Mark Kellogg.

Yours truly,

Lt. David Snelling
1st Alabama Cav., USA

* * * * *

Mark Kellogg delivered David's note on the evening of April 8th, and Doctor Mallory acknowledged it and penciled an immediate and hasty reply. David and his officers were always welcome in his home, as long as he lived. He also thanked David for the coffee and the ham.

The next morning, David obtained permission from Colonel Spencer to attend the dinner party at Dr. Mallory's residence. The regiment mounted up at ten o'clock, and began to ride south on the Franklin Pike. Signs of the coming spring were visible all around them. The Dogwood trees and Redbud trees were in full bloom, and the hardwood trees had begun putting out tiny leaves on their branches. The weather was cool in the morning, but temperatures had become more pleasant in the afternoons.

They marched down the macadamized pike, moving at a brisk pace on the good road. Ajax was in familiar territory, and his ears pricked up as he noticed that he was very close to his old home.

At one o'clock, the regiment bivouacked in the town of Franklin. David bought Lieutenant Dunn a small meal at a tavern in the village, and then they met Doctor Swaving and Sergeant Looney, and rode up toward Roper's Knob.

They soon arrived at the sunken road that led to the beautiful home of Doctor Mallory, where Claude met them near the barn. David then had the men lead their animals over into the large and spacious barn, where they were fed, watered, and rubbed down.

They walked along a brick path through the back porch of the house, where they were greeted by Abigail and Mrs. Mallory. Janet Riley soon walked in from the parlor in a pretty blue crinoline dress. She was in the company of a lovely young woman of nineteen years with strawberry blonde hair and green eyes. The blonde haired girl was in an emerald green dress made of taffeta that emphasized her lovely green eyes.

Janet introduced the girl to David and the officers as her younger sister, Katherine Mallory.

"Katherine was off visiting our cousin Gladys in McMinnville when you were last here, Lieutenant."

David walked up and kissed Katherine's hand, and her response was cool, but polite. He introduced them to Lieutenant Wayland Dunn, Lieutenant William Cheney, and Doctor John Swaving.

All of the men except Anderson Looney and Doctor Swaving were in their mid–twenties. Anderson was thirty years old. Doctor Swaving was a tall forty year old, with graying dark hair. He was dressed in a white frock coat with the insignia of a Union Army Major. Unlike his younger trooper friends, he carried no side arms, being a regimental surgeon, as required by the U.S. Army regulations.

They made their way down to the rose garden, where Claude had set up a small table with a punch bowl. They enjoyed the punch while Mrs. Rose Mallory gave them a tour of her garden, which featured several pink and red and purple azaleas in full bloom, in all of their spring glory.

They went up to the house shortly thereafter, where they were soon joined by Dr. Mallory. He had just arrived from Franklin, where he had set the broken leg of a carpenter who had fallen from a scaffold.

Doctor Swaving exchanged pleasantries with Dr. Mallory after David introduced them, and they soon began to talk about various fractures, and how difficult some broken bones were to set and reset. They then began to discuss other difficult medical cases.

The younger men were naturally drawn to the lovely ladies, and they formed a semi circle around the lovely Katherine, and her beautiful sister, Janet. Mrs. Mallory joined in on their conversations with the troopers, informing all of the men about David's and Anderson's heroism the previous year. They had saved Janet from being ravished by deserters, and she poured out her praise for David and Anderson, and their heroism.

Abigail came into the parlor to announce that dinner was ready in the dining room. Mrs. Mallory led them into the large dining room, where she carefully seated the troopers and her daughters. Janet was seated next to her and Lieutenant Dunn. Katherine was seated between David and Lieutenant Cheney. Abigail served them the roasted Boston Butt with black eyed peas, baked yams, cornbread, and boiled pinto beans. They washed their splendid meal down with the coffee that David had sent them by Mark Kellogg the day before.

After they had finished their meal, Anderson volunteered to help Claude and Abigail with the dishes, while Doctor Swaving and Doctor Mallory went out onto the back porch to smoke cigars.

A few minutes later, Mrs. Mallory led them all back into the parlor, where Janet had laid out an arrangement of sheet music on the piano. Katherine was going to sing for them, and she began to sing "Lorena" in a lovely, sweet voice. She then sang "Sweet Rose from Alabama", "My Country 'Tis of Thee", and "Clementine" in the same sweet voice. The men were fixated on the lovely Katherine. David should have been taken with her, too, but he could not shake the infatuation he had with Janet. While his comrades were mooning over Katherine, David was watching Janet at the piano, staring at the gleam of the candlelight as it danced across her red hair. He tried to tell himself that it was madness to continue this infatuation with her, because she belonged to another man, a major in the Rebel army.

He could not bring himself to transfer his infatuation from Janet to Katherine, even though Katherine was an unmarried and available woman. To David, Janet was the sun, and Katherine was the moon, and the brilliance of the moon could not compare to the brilliance of the sun.

Katherine sang several hymns, including "Amazing Grace", and "A Mighty Fortress is our God" before Doctor Swaving reminded them that they had to rejoin the regiment on the march south.

Katherine had not yet completed her arrangement of songs when Dr. Mallory asked David if he could see Ajax, and visit with him a short while. David, Dr. Mallory, and Dr. Swaving slipped out of the parlor, and walked back to the barn over the brick walkway.

They had Ajax in his old stall, which was the first one in the spacious barn. Ajax pumped his head up and down when he saw Dr. Mallory approach him. Dr. Mallory scratched the white blaze on Ajax's forehead, and the mighty stallion muzzled him gently with his mouth.

"I love you too, old friend. Let me visit with him a little while, please, David."

"Certainly, Dr. Mallory. We will wait on the other side of the barn."

David and Dr. Swaving walked past the rows of stalls in the large barn, until they neared the last stall. They began to hear a peculiar grunting and moaning sound that was not just one sound, but was a series of sounds.

David knew that no one animal could make noise like that, so he drew his Adams revolver, and crept closer in to investigate. Dr. Swaving put an arm on David's shoulder.

"You can put your revolver away, lieutenant. I think I know what is generating that noise."

David complied, and they stepped forward toward a large haystack in the last stall of the barn. What they saw was shocking.

Abigail was completely naked, and was seated on top of Sergeant Looney, who was having sexual relations with her. The sergeant had removed his trousers and drawers, and Abigail had removed her dress, petticoat, and stockings. Her ebony breasts pulsated up and down as she moved up and down on the sergeant. She would moan, and he would grunt with each up and down movement of her behind.

She was lovely, and her ebony body was graceful in its movements during their lovemaking. She had her eyes closed, and was perfectly absorbed in her activity. Sergeant Looney saw them though, and he pulled Abigail off of him and stood up, covering his private parts with his drawers. Abigail gave a shriek and ran behind the haystack with her clothing.

Sergeant Looney did the same. Dr. Swaving took control of the situation at once. "Sergeant Looney, get dressed, and report to me on the other side of the barn in five minutes." "Yes, sir."

Dr. Mallory had heard the ruckus, and walked to the end of the barn to find out the nature of the problem also. "Oh, it is just a minor disciplinary matter with the Sergeant that we will need to attend to. We have it taken care of, Dr. Mallory." Dr. Mallory could not see Abigail, who was hiding behind the haystack.

That seemed to satisfy Dr. Mallory, who went back and renewed his visit with Ajax after being joined by Katherine and Janet.

David was presented the opportunity to speak to Janet alone, and he did not waste it. "How is your major? Have you heard from him since the summer?"

"I got two letters from him in September and October. He got shot through the left leg during Pickett's charge at Gettysburg. It was just a flesh wound, though. He healed up quickly and rejoined his regiment inside of a month."

"That is really good news. I wish you nothing less than pure happiness, Janet."

David took her hand, and Janet knew that he was sincere. "You are a sweet man, Lieutenant Snelling. You take care of yourself." She laid her hand upon his cheek, and fireworks went off in David's head. He was totally taken with her, yet she was another man's wife.

A moment later, Dr. Swaving walked up with Ajax and his horse, which had already been saddled.

"Lieutenant, I have placed Sergeant Looney under arrest. Lieutenant Dunn has his side arm. Please thank Dr. Mallory for his gracious hospitality, and thank Mrs. Mallory for the wonderful meal."

Janet was also gracious. "You and Lieutenant Snelling, and even Sergeant Looney are welcome here anytime, Doctor."

David mounted Ajax, and waved a quick goodbye to Janet Riley. He glanced over his shoulder at her as Ajax stepped down the sunken lane, and saw her smiling up at him.

They trotted down the lane, and out onto the pike, toward Franklin. Once they got out onto the pike, Doctor Swaving questioned Sergeant Looney, while they were riding along.

"Why did you violate the good Doctor's hospitality and generosity by having sex with his maid servant?"

Sergeant Looney was forthright and unashamed in giving his answers to Doctor Swaving's questions.

"She has lived there with Dr. Mallory since she was fifteen years old. She has never had a chance to go out and spark men, or get married. Claude is just too old for her, and she saw a chance to have relations with a younger man.

She was quick to seize the opportunity, and she planned our get together right after supper."

Doctor Swaving was shocked. "Aren't you married, Sergeant Looney?"

"Yes, sir. I have been married over five years. But I ain't seen my wife in over two years. I get no letters from her, and I don't know if she is dead or alive."

"Why did you have carnal relations with that woman?'

"To be honest, sir, I was tempted. She is a lovely girl, and man, she was more than willing. We already did it once before ya'll got out there. You saw us while we were having our second go."

Doctor Swaving had heard enough. "I will tell you, Sergeant, that you have committed an offense which will require you to stand a court martial."

"What offense would that be, sir?"

"Conduct unbecoming an officer. You will be charged and tried once we get down to Decatur. I don't know what your punishment will be, but the members will find you guilty, I am sure."

Chapter Twenty Two

The First Alabama Cavalry Regiment marched south from Franklin, Tennessee to Columbia, Tennessee on April 10th. The regiment camped overnight in Columbia, and then marched south along the railroad to Pulaski, Tennessee. General Dodge had rebuilt the railroad from Nashville to Decatur the year before, and the route was lined with small block houses, containing guards of Union troops.

The regiment saddled up and rode south to Athens, Alabama, where they acquired around forty decent horses from the cavalry remount station. Since there was at least six lieutenants available, Sergeant Looney's court martial was quickly convened in Athens at the City Hall. Doctor Swaving testified first, giving evidence as to their status as guests in Doctor Mallory's home. He gave explicit testimony which clearly indicated that Sergeant Looney had sexual relations with Dr. Mallory's maid servant on the premises in broad daylight. Dr. Swaving also testified that Sergeant Looney and Abigail were caught in the act of fornication, and the act was done while Dr. Mallory was in the barn with them.

David was called to testify in the proceeding, and his direct testimony corroborated the testimony of Dr. Swaving.

The charges were then read again to Sergeant Looney, and he admitted to the charges and specifications made against him. When asked if he wanted to offer anything in mitigation prior to sentencing, David asked to speak for him. He addressed the members in a clear and passionate voice:

"I have served with Sergeant Looney since we both enlisted at Huntsville in August of '62. He has served as First Sergeant in our company since September of the same year. He has served in action and distinguished himself in many engagements, from Stones River to Streight's Raid to Jack's Creek. He has been captured and exchanged, shot at, and has survived all of the hardships of war.

What he has confessed to you now is that he is human, and that he has succumbed to temptation. He has been a good and faithful soldier. He has been honest with the members and with the Court. Please be as lenient on him as you can. I need him to continue to serve his company, this regiment, and his country, thank you."

David sat down on a makeshift bench behind Sergeant Looney. The members were then read the charges and specifications by the Judge Advocate, Major Micah Fairfield, and the members went out to deliberate.

An hour later, the members emerged from the anteroom with a verdict which had been reduced to writing. An orderly passed the verdict to Major Fairfield, who read it aloud, after instructing the defendant to rise.

"Sergeant Anderson Looney, it is in the sentence of the members that upon a finding of guilt, you are to be reduced in rank to private, commencing on April 14, 1864, and continuing. This Court is adjourned."

The major banged the gavel upon the city council table, and the court martial concluded.

Outside City Hall, Sergeant Looney's three stripes were removed from his uniform coat, and he was returned to duty.

The court martial reconvened a short while later, as a James Barnett was being tried for stealing and selling horses from the regiment. All of the men believed he was guilty, and hoped that he would hang.

* * * * *

May 2, 1864
Decatur, Alabama

Dear Uncle Uriah and Aunt Faith:

Our regiment has been ordered to join General Sherman's army on his campaign in north Georgia. We have learned that General Grant has been promoted and sent east to fight General Robert Lee's army. We are now attacking the Rebel forces in concert, both in the east and the west.

We will move out in the morning with the 64th Illinois Infantry, and the tail end of the entire 16th Army Corps. It will be wonderful to be back on Georgia soil again, in a Union Army uniform.

We have been detailed to guard the wagon train of the 16th Army Corps. We will march through Bridgeport, and across Lookout Mountain with the infantry.

I hope you are in good health and good spirits. May the Lord bless and keep you. I have to go now, as we are issuing rations to the troopers before we move out.

Yours truly,
David

* * * * *

On May 4, 1864, the First Alabama Cavalry left Woodville, Alabama, guarding 269 wagons of the 16th Army Corps train. They reached Belfonte, Alabama on the Tennessee River, where they camped at mid day. The rear of the wagon train made it up to Belfonte over the rough mountain roads at five o'clock.

The next morning, "Boots and Saddles" was sounded at four a.m., and the entire column moved northeastward along the Tennessee River toward Bridgeport. They crossed a portion of the Tennessee River on a wooden railroad bridge that General Dodge's troops had rebuilt several months before.

Colonel Spencer sent David and Lieutenant Dunn ahead of the column to find a campground for the night. They camped on Long Island, the same place where David had deserted the 57th Georgia Infantry in July of 1862.

The area was not as heavily wooded as it was then. Many of the oak and hickory trees had been cut and burned for firewood and bridge timbers by the thousands of Union and Confederate troops that had passed through Bridgeport over the past two years.

They left their campground the next morning, marching at the head of the column. They rode the flanks of the 9th Illinois Infantry, of General Veatch's division of General Dodge's 16th Army Corps. David was saddened by the demotion of Anderson Looney, but he was happy to now rejoin General Dodge's corps for the coming campaign in Georgia. Up to now, their action as cavalry troopers had been limited to scouting raids and minor skirmishes. David considered their duties important, but also realized that their operations to date had been mostly side–shows.

General Sherman's campaign in Georgia was the war. His Grand Army totaled over 102,000 men, and he was assembling his forces for an attack on the Confederate Army of Tennessee, commanded by Joe Johnston. Johnston had 45,000 men dug into the north Georgia mountains around Rocky Face Ridge, between Dalton and Tunnel Hill.

The First Alabama only marched eight miles that day, up an extremely rocky and hilly road across the edge of Racoon Mountain, near the Tennessee River. The mountain came down so close to the river that the rock had to blasted to construct the wagon road and the railroad tracks above. The regiment passed broken wagons and dead mules that had been left behind by the 15th Army Corps.

They camped on the other side of the Obar Spring, which ran out of the foot of Lookout Mountain. The spring ran wide and deep, and was swift. Its current was swift enough to drive a grist mill or a saw mill. David set pickets from Company "I", and then he and Lieutenant Cheney were detailed to butcher three of the last of the beef cows they had been driving, to issue out fresh beef rations to the regiment.

The next morning, they began to climb the famed Lookout Mountain, just below Chattanooga. As they climbed the mountain, David looked back toward Alabama, and could see the broad and shiny Tennessee River, as it wound its way around Mocassin Bend.

They rode past some of the old fortifications and battle lines from the battles that had occurred back in November. The veterans of the 9th Illinois pointed out the lines of the Union and Confederate positions on the day of the Battle of Missionary Ridge.

They showed David and Sergeant Reid where two Union regiments had attacked up a steep cliff that required climbing, rather than walking. All of the men agreed that it hardly seemed possible that the Rebel positions could have been taken. They all agreed that the battle was extremely important, because of the strength of the position that was captured.

They continued to climb Lookout Mountain, which was the highest peak in the northwest Georgia chain of mountains. They marched underneath a canopy of small green leaves that were emerging from hickory, oak, and oak trees.

They camped for the night at Lee and Gordon's Mill, which was just on the other side of the Chickamauga battlefield, where a titanic battle had been fought the previous September. As they crossed the heavily wooded area of the battlefield, David noticed that some of the shallow graves of the soldiers had been washed down by the spring rains. They could see more than a few bleached bones of the dead soldiers protruding through some of the sod.

It turned cold the following day, an extremely unusual cold snap for early May. They donned their oilskins and heavy coats, and pushed on. They escorted the wagon train, and they drove 400 head of cattle from Lee and Gordon's Mill down to Ship's Gap.

The Army of the Tennessee, commanded by Major General James McPherson, had been ordered to go around to the rear of Joe Johnston's army. They were ordered to march through Ship's Gap, Villanow, and then through Snake Creek Gap, where they were to advance to Resaca, on the Oostanaula River.

General Sherman's other two armies, the Army of the Cumberland under General George Thomas, and the Army of the Ohio under the command of Major General Schofield were ordered to demonstrate against the Rebel troops at Rocky Face Ridge, in order to keep them fixed in position. Meanwhile, General McPherson and his Army of the Tennessee would quickly outflank General Joe Johnston's troops, and get behind his army by taking Resaca. General Dodge and his 16th Army Corps had pushed ahead with the Army of the Tennessee, and was also closing in on Resaca.

The First Alabama Cavalry began to drive the cattle through Ship's Gap early in the morning, but was held up by the slow progress of the wagon train ahead of them.

They paused at several intervals while the cattle drank from several mountain streams. They dined on cold water and hardtack in the saddle, and they heard cannon fire from the general area of Rocky Face at different times in the afternoon.

* * * * *

Once General Joe Johnston learned that McPherson's Army of the Tennessee had got into his rear at Resaca, be began to issue orders that would culminate in one of his "clean retreats" back toward Atlanta. The Confederate positions on Rocky Face Ridge near Dalton were abandoned, and his Army of Tennessee retreated back toward Resaca.

Johnston's forces and General McPherson's Union forces skirmished with each other at Resaca, but General McPherson had blown a golden opportunity to encircle and capture Johnston's entire force. General Johnston soon realized that his position at Resaca was untenable, and issued orders for the Army of Tennessee to retreat south to Kingston.

General McPherson's Army of the Tennessee and General Schofield's Army of the Ohio were sent south in direct pursuit of Joe Johnston's Confederate forces.

The First Alabama Cavalry was ordered up to Ringgold, Georgia for the purpose of escorting General Schofield's wagon train down to Resaca. They left for Ringgold on May 13th, and returned to Resaca on May 17th. David and Lieutenant Dunn saw General George Thomas pass by with his Army of the Cumberland near Resaca. He was a portly man, with an iron gray beard and a full face, and appeared to be fifty years old...

The next morning, the regiment moved south through Calhoun along the Adairsville Road. They marched south at a slow pace, hindered by the long columns of Federal troops marching down the road before them, and their long wagon trains.

David and Lieutenant Frank Tupper selected a campground for the regiment on a hill with a grove of tall Blackjack Oak trees. The troopers gave their horses a good feed of fresh clover they had brought down from Resaca.

Just before dark, David and Frank Tupper saddled their horses, and rode up to the top of a tall hill a few miles above Adairsville.

As the sun was beginning to set, they saw the wagon train of General Sherman's army spread out on three parallel roads before them.

Each wagon was pulled by four mule teams, and they were strung out on each of the red clay roads as far as they could see. From one end of the long valley to the other, the U.S. Army wagons were lined up one behind the other, moving south.

David opened up his field glasses, and took in the spectacular sight. He handed the glasses to Frank Tupper, a dark haired mustachioed lieutenant who was serving as adjutant.

David swatted a large horsefly on Ajax's neck. It was rather warm, and he had unbuttoned his uniform jacket, exposing a blue checkered cotton shirt. "So far, General Johnston had rather retreat south than fight. But at some point between here and Atlanta, he'll fight." They rode down from the top of the hill, and returned to the camp.

* * * * *

The next morning, the Army of the Tennessee occupied Adairsville. On the same morning, May 19th, lead elements from the Army of the Tennessee and the Army of the Cumberland also marched south and captured Kingston without a fight.

General Schofield marched his Army of the Ohio through Cassville, and planned to link up with the rest of the Federal army at Kingston.

Confederate General John Bell Hood's corps was in position near Cassville to spring his trap on the Army of the Ohio, when a wayward division of Federal troops wound up in the Confederate rear, around five miles east of Cassville. Their unlikely presence unnerved General Hood, who canceled his planned attack.

General Johnston then ordered General Hood to fall back from Cassville. That afternoon, all of the corps of the Army of Tennessee, and all three Federal armies were arrayed against each other in a broad valley between Kingston and Cassville. The Federal and Rebel guns began booming away at each other.

That night, General Johnston held a council of war with his corps commanders, General William Hardee, General John B. Hood, and General Leonidas Polk. After hearing arguments in support of an attack, and arguments that the army should retreat, General Johnston chose to retreat. Orders were issued that night for the Army of Tennessee to retreat to prepared positions at Allatoona Pass.

General Sherman, when he discovered that General Johnston had retreated down to Allatoona Pass, realized that the position there was too strong to take by direct assault.

Instead, General Sherman ordered a general flanking movement with all three of his armies...General McPherson and the Army of the Tennessee were ordered to march to Dallas, Georgia.

General Sherman's plan was to outflank General Johnston and the Army of Tennessee from their powerful position at Allatoona Pass.

General Joe Wheeler's Confederate cavalry quickly discovered the flanking movements of General Sherman's forces, and General Johnston was soon alerted about the Federal flanking movements. Orders were issued to Confederate forces at Allatoona Pass to retreat to the southwest, and to dig in before the advancing Federal troops near New Hope Church.

General "Fighting Joe" Hooker launched a Federal attack against the right wing of Johnston's army at New Hope Church. The attack was commenced with Hooker's entire 20th Corps of the Union Army. His guns boomed and rumbled, and a real thunderstorm rained down lightning, hail and rain on the troops as they struggled in the springtime weather. The scenes were so fiendish, and fighting so intense, that the area around New Hope Church was nicknamed the "Hell Hole" by the veterans there.

The Army of Tennessee was ordered to march around the left flank of the Confederate forces, and to concentrate around Dallas, Georgia, which was just to the southwest of New Hope Church. On May 26th, the First Alabama Cavalry Regiment had marched to within five miles of Dallas, near Willow Springs Road, on the Dallas side of Brushy Mountain.

On the other side of Dallas, the Confederate troops of the Army of Tennessee had constructed their defensive lines across two twin small peaks, Ray Mountain and Elsberry Mountain.

The Rebels had placed a strong line of sharpshooters at the peak of both mountains, and their artillery was sighted at sharp angles to give enfilading fire against any attacking column of infantry.

The First Alabama followed the 64th Illinois Infantry into battle lines near Dallas. The 64th Illinois could be heard exchanging musket fire with the Rebels from dawn until dusk. The cavalrymen were encamped in a wooded ravine that was sheltered from enemy fire by a large hill opposite Elsberry Mountain. David also heard cannon fire from the other side of Elsberry Mountain, over near New Hope Church.

The next evening, General William Hardee ordered Confederate General William Bate and his division to attack the Federal troops under

General McPherson near Dallas. The Rebels assaulted the Union lines, only to be repulsed at a cost of 400 casualties.

On May 29th, the First Alabama escorted the wagon train of the 16th Corps into Kingston for forage and supplies. While in Kingston, the men noticed a large railroad train being loaded with wounded soldiers, and the orderlies advised them that the train was headed back to unload the wounded at hospitals in Chattanooga.

On the way back to camp near Dallas, the troopers passed 150 ambulances heading into Kingston with wounded men. David counted at least five hundred walking wounded headed back toward Kingston as well. The fighting around Dallas was fierce and intense, and the casualties on both sides there reminded David of the Battle of Stones River.

David and Sergeant Reid spoke to a captain in the 64th Illinois Regiment that told them about the Rebel attack on McPherson's lines the day before. He told them that the forefront of the Rebel attack was made against two regiments that were armed with Spencer and Henry carbines. The captain told them that 123 Rebel attackers were shot down in front of those two regiments in ten minutes.

The captain also told them that their Rebel prisoners told them that the governor of Georgia demanded General Johnston to attack the Union Army before it reached Atlanta, so that the city would be spared any destruction.

The following morning, the First Alabama pulled out with the 16th Army Corps, setting up their camp around three or four miles northeast of Dallas.

May 29, 1864
Near Dallas, Georgia

Dear Uncle Uriah and Aunt Faith:

Our regiment now serves as escort to General Grenville Dodge, who commands the left wing of the 16th Army Corps. We have heard skirmishing and cannonading all down the lines, which have been laid out in heavily wooded, hilly country. The Confederate main battle lines are laid out across two small twin mountains between Dallas and New Hope Church.

Dodge's infantry has successfully repulsed no less than four Rebel attacks on their ranks. The 16th Corps is so well skilled at for fortifying their lines, that several Rebel prisoners have claimed that they bring their fortifications with them to battle.

There was a hard attack made on the infantry's lines yesterday that was repulsed by the 66th Indiana Regiment, and by artillery fire from the 39th Iowa Infantry's batteries. The grape shot and canister fire from the batteries, and the volley fire from their muskets turned back the Rebel attacks.

We had coffee with a colonel from the 66th Indiana Infantry, who said they counted 53 dead Rebels in their front last night. The 16th Corps has been ordered to move to the left, over to near New Hope Church. We are now three or four miles northeast of Dallas.

Pow! Pow! Pow! Some of our boys are now skirmishing with the Rebels near the front lines. Company "H" has been detailed to move General Dodge's headquarters. Our company and Company "L" have been ordered to move out tomorrow and file into line as skirmishes. It is good to be on Georgia soil again. I have to go now, "Boots and Saddles" is sounding.

Yours Truly,

David

* * * * *

On June 3, 1864, Companies "I" and "L" were ordered out on the skirmish line near General Sweeney's division. At ten o'clock, some firing broke out along the line of the Confederate works, which were located across a large hill over one half mile away. Some sharpshooters had crawled forward of the Rebel works, and began firing at the troops from across the way. The troopers had been ordered to dismount, and every fourth trooper held the horses in a ravine at the rear of the skirmish line.

David crouched behind a fallen Loblolly Pine tree, and peered through his field glasses at the Rebel sharpshooters. They were working in two man teams, firing at the Indiana infantrymen in line on their immediate left. David could see puffs of smoke bloom out from their positions as they fired. He could hear their bullets whiz past the space between the Union and Rebel lines. He heard one or two of the bullets strike their marks, and saw troops fall back as they were hit.

David decided that the sharpshooters should not be allowed to conduct their business without fear of reprisal.

He sent for Sergeant Reid and four of the best marksmen in the company, and asked them to open fire on the sharpshooters with their .54 Caliber Burnside Carbines. The men crouched behind the large Loblolly Pine log, adjusted their gun sights, and began to open fire on the sharpshooters.

David got his Spencer Repeating Carbine, adjusted its peep sight, and chambered a .52 caliber round into the firing chamber. He peered through his field glasses at a sharpshooter who was reloading his special rifle, and then quickly pulled up his carbine, sighted the target, and fired.

He then peered through his field glasses, and saw dust kick up around four feet below the sharpshooter. The Rebel marksman was dressed in a butternut coat and had a gray kepi. He took aim and fired at David's smoke, and David heard the bullet whiz over his head.

He chambered another round in his Spencer, aimed higher, and fired. He looked through his glasses, and saw the Rebel marksman pitch forward.

This process was repeated when David spied another sharpshooter, except he asked to use Sergeant Reid's Burnside Carbine the next time. He noticed that the .54 caliber Burnside Carbine threw a ball further than his Spencer.

He killed two more sharpshooters that day, and the company got five, but one of the Rebel marksmen fired a shot that hit one of their horses in the rump.

At four p.m., they pulled off the main skirmish line, and reported back to camp at General Dodge's headquarters.

* * * * *

On June 1st, Union cavalry under Major General George Stoneman and Brigadier General Kenner Garrard captured Allatoona Pass. This gave General Sherman's railroad repair gangs a golden opportunity. When the repair gangs were finished, Sherman's army had an all–weather railroad supply line from Chattanooga to within seven miles of the front lines.

On June 10th, it began to rain, and rain hard for two straight days. The red clay roads from Kennesaw Mountain through New Hope Church and Dallas became muddy quagmires. Footing for the mule trains became slippery. It became difficult to pull artillery guns and caissons in the muddy clay roads.

On June 4th, General Johnston had the Army of Tennessee pull out from the fortifications around Dallas, and move to the north and east.

General Hardee's corps occupied 1520 foot Lost Mountain, which was to the left of the Confederate line. General Polk's corps occupied an area from 1300 foot Pine Mountain over to the Western & Atlantic Railroad. General Hood's Corps was anchored to the left on the Western & Atlantic Railroad over toward Brushy Mountain on the right.

On June 11th, Union Army railroad crews had repaired the Western & Atlantic Railroad all the way down to Big Shanty. Sherman's Army had shifted its position to the left, in order to oppose Johnston's army as it shifted toward the Western & Atlantic Railroad.

David and Company "I" of the First Alabama were in the process of escorting wagons from the front lines back to the quartermaster depot at Big Shanty. There in the valley below Big Kennesaw Mountain, they spied a locomotive and a supply train pulling into the station.

The engine and its train had pulled almost all of the way to the skirmish line of the 17th Corps, when the engineer let out a blast from the engine's steam whistle. When the men of the 17th Army Corps saw the American Standard 4-4-0 engine with its balloon shaped smokestack, they let out a chorus of cheers and shouts that could be heard for miles. Twenty five thousand troops and troopers shouted and lustily cheered in unison at the arrival of fresh food and supplies from Chattanooga.

* * * * *

General Thomas massed 130 guns below Big Kennesaw Mountain, and sighted them on the Rebel works near the summit of the peak. On June 15th, the 17th Army Corps had shifted their lines near the front face of Kennesaw Mountain. Their lines connected with the 15th Army Corps at right angles to the mountain. The 16th Corp's lines were to the right, and joined the lines of the 15th Army Corps.

The 17th Corps also set up artillery to bombard the Rebel position on Kennesaw Mountain. David, Lieutenant Dunn, and Sergeant Reid rode over to the artillery park of the 17th Corps.

The Parrott Rifles were unlimbered, and the gun crews were working the guns in their shirt sleeves in the heat of the summer morning. The scene was fascinating to David, who had studied the science of artillery projectiles at Franklin College.

The twenty pounder Parrott Rifle was elevated at maximum height, to slant their fire up the side of the heavily wooded Kennesaw Mountain. Artillery officers wearing red kepis, red shoulder straps, or red corded blue slouch hats were mounted, and observed the firing of the batteries.

One or two of the officers would send orders to the gun crews through sergeants and sergeant majors, who wore blue uniforms with red chevrons and red piping on their jackets and uniform trousers.

Smoke and fire erupted from the guns as the gun crews fired and serviced the weapons. The projectiles emerged from the various weapons and made different noises, from a shriek, to a sucking sound, to a whiz. David supposed that the noises were related to the size of the shell, and the amount of the powder charge in each different gun.

David and Lieutenant Dunn saw several of the generals from the various army corps there. General McPherson was a heavy set, young, dark whiskered man. General Logan had long mustaches, and was a savage looking man, with weathered facial features.

He was unusually cross that morning because the army mules had bit the tail off of his big black stallion. They sat on their horses on a hill overlooking the Union guns, watching the mountain with their field glasses. The Union shells all detonated upon impact, raining hell and death upon the Confederate fortifications on the mountain.

The generals all believed that if they could not take the Rebel fortifications by assault, maybe they could destroy them with iron shot from their guns.

David and Lieutenant Dunn and some of the other officers watched the artillery bombardment for the rest of the day. Wild rumors had circulated through the army the week before about General Grant's success in Virginia. Some rumors had Grant capturing Richmond, and all but winning the war.

This week, though, the truth had filtered down about Grant's defeat. It was soon known that the Army of the Potomac had received a whipping at the hands of Robert E. Lee's Army of Northern Virginia.

Most of the officers agreed that Grant was badly whipped at the Wilderness. However, the men were encouraged to hear that the Army of the Potomac was heading south, not north, after receiving a defeat in pitched battle with Lee's army. The troopers prepared their evening mess, and bedded down to the sounds of cannon fire and musketry coming from Kennesaw Mountain.

* * * * *

Every officer at some point in their career makes a bone headed move, according to Sergeant Reid. He had served in the cavalry for over three years, and had observed many officers in the U.S. Army make mistakes. On the morning of June 19, 1864, Sergeant Reid saw Colonel George Spencer make a very large mistake.

At eight a.m., Colonel Spencer ordered the bugler to sound "Boots and Saddles", and he then ordered the regiment to mount up and move out toward Marietta.

Colonel Spencer, however, did not order the regiment to move to the rear of the line toward the railroad. Instead, he ordered the regiment to march through the skirmish line between the armies, until they were in range of Rebel artillery. Confederate gunners began to open fire on them from Kennesaw Mountain. Rebel skirmishers in front of their main battle lines began to open fire on them as well.

Bullets and artillery shells began to rain down to their right, and sailed over their heads.

General Sherman was out on his horse, Duke, observing the Rebel lines, when he noticed the faux pas of Colonel Spencer. He waved his black slouch hat at Colonel Spencer, and ordered him to pull his regiment out of the dangerous area between the two skirmish lines.

Colonel Spencer saw General Sherman's waving, and ordered the regiment to angle toward a wooded area inside the Union lines. The entire regiment made it back unscathed, though, and they managed to move General Dodge's headquarters that evening. David and Sergeant Reid observed that same evening that Colonel Spencer had come close to doing his regiment some serious damage, taking it through an infantry skirmish line.

They both agreed that Colonel Spencer was just inexperienced, but they hoped his inexperience would not cost their lives in the future.

General Sherman became impatient with his army's progress in front of Kennesaw Mountain, and he ordered a general attack all along his lines for the morning of June 27th. At 8:00 a.m., 200 Union guns shelled the Confederate positions on and around Kennesaw Mountain for one hour. At nine a.m., the Union troops began to advance on the Confederate positions all along the line.

The attacks were beaten back and stopped by Confederate troops in their prepared entrenchments who fired their muskets and artillery as quickly as they could in the summer heat. At eleven a.m., the attack had fizzled out, and the army commanders had canceled the attack orders for Sherman's troops.

General Sherman canceled his plans for further assaults on the strong Confederate lines around Kennesaw Mountain; and began to write orders that called for his troops to outflank Johnston's troops just above the Chattahoochie River.

* * * * *

Just a day or so after the Battle of Kennesaw Mountain, most of the First Alabama Cavalry Regiment received orders to relocate to Rome, Georgia, where they would form part of the garrison of Federal troops there. David's Company "I" was ordered to remain with the 16th Army Corps as General Dodge's escort cavalry.

On July 1st, General Sherman ordered McPherson's Army of Tennessee to move around General Johnston's left flank, and on the other side of Smyrna, Georgia. When General Sherman's troops began their flanking movement again on the left of Johnston's lines, General Johnston ordered his army to evacuate their positions on Kennesaw Mountain.

David and his Company "I" moved with General Grenville Dodge's headquarters along with McPherson's troops to Nickajack Creek, in order to threaten the Confederate left rear.

General Sherman hoped to catch the Confederate army out in the open, with its back to the Chattahoochie River. When the Union troops approached the Confederate forces about two miles beyond Vinings Station, General Sherman saw them occupying: "the best line of field entrenchments I have ever seen"

David and his troopers climbed a hill just beyond Vinings Station, though, and could see the church steeples and roof tops of Atlanta, a mere eight miles away. A courier soon sent for David and Lieutenant James Day, and asked them to immediately report to General Dodge's headquarters.

David and Lt. Day immediately obeyed, and found General Dodge's headquarters a half hour later in a tent under a Water Oak tree near Nickajack Creek.

David recognized General Dodge, and he and Lt. Day immediately saluted him, and Captain Henry Horn, a bearded Assistant Adjutant General on his staff. David and Lt. Day were introduced to Captain George Hickenlooper, an engineer with the U.S. Army Topographic Engineers. Captain Hickenlooper wore a black slouch hat with a castle insignia on its front. He was short and squat, and had a bushy mustache.

General Dodge was to the point. "David, I have a job for you. I want you to find Colonel Abram Miller, of the brigade known as the "Lightning Brigade", the 3rd Brigade, 2nd Cavalry Division; and report to him at Sope Creek. From there, you are to march up to Roswell, and down to Shallow Ford. You have been ordered to ford the Chattahoochie at Shallow Ford, and hold the river crossing until my command can march up and join you. Captain Hickenlooper, please get out your map, and show these troopers the relative positions and their objective."

"Yes, sir." Hickenlooper unrolled his map upon a makeshift table set up on two saw horses. "Gentlemen, here we are at Nickajack Creek. You are to ride north by east, and cross the Western & Atlantic Railroad between Smyrna and Vinings Station. From that point, you will ride north and east to some paper mills on Sope Creek. That is where you will rendezvous with Colonel Abe Miller and his brigade. From there, you will march up to Roswell, and then down to Shallow Ford, which is here. Your command and Colonel Miller's brigade will then capture Shallow Ford and hold it until all of General Dodge's command can march up from here. Do you have any questions?"

"Yes sir, Captain. Will we have a scout to help us get to Sope Creek in the dark?"

"Yes, Lieutenant. Captain Audenried of General Sherman's staff will meet you and your command here in two hours."

"We will be here, sir, and will be ready."

"I knew you would, Lieutenant Snelling. That is why I sent for you for this assignment. You are dismissed."

David saluted General Dodge, and he and Lt. Day rode back to the company, and had the company bugler blow "Boots and Saddles".

Ninety five minutes later, all of Company "I" had marched to General Dodge's headquarters on Nickajack Creek. There they met Captain Audenried, a clean shaven man of thirty years, who sported long brown hair, and a tall forage cap.

He led them on a march in a column of twos on the road toward Smyrna, and then off the main road and through thick woods, until they crossed the Western & Atlantic Railroad. They pushed on in the moonlight in their column of twos, and they crossed Rottenwood Creek just above Moore's Mill. They swam their horses across the narrow stream, and turned north by east, crossing through several small farms, until they reached the Roswell–Marietta road.

They continued on toward the northeast in the darkness, until they reached some old paper mills on the banks of Sope Creek. There they were challenged by Federal Cavalry pickets of the 3rd Brigade of General Garrard's 2nd Cavalry Division.

Captain Audenried identified himself, and received directions to Colonel Abram Miller's headquarters. They found Colonel Miller was stretched out on a makeshift cot in a large tent just above one of the paper mills on Sope Creek.

Captain Audenried introduced David to Colonel Miller. Colonel Miller was tall and dark haired, with blue eyes, and a beard of dark brown hair that was bushy, but well trimmed.

He had been a country doctor before the war, and his easy going manner impressed David. He commanded a brigade of mounted infantry troops from Indiana and Illinois. The 17th and 72nd Indiana Regiments, and the 98th and 123rd Illinois Regiments were formerly known as Wilder's "Lightning Brigade", because they were armed with Spencer Repeating Rifles.

Colonel Miller told them that they were to march to Roswell at 3:30 a.m., and would then march south to the Chattahoochie River, and Shallow Ford. David was instructed to follow Captain Audenried and the 72nd Indiana Regiment to Shallow Ford, where they would attempt a nighttime river crossing.

"Boots and Saddles" soon sounded for all troopers at 3:00 a.m., and the men mounted up in a column of twos, and headed along Sope Creek until they reached the Marietta Road. They then rode north by east for four miles, until they reached the little mill village of Roswell, Georgia. The moon had set and it was so dark, the men had trouble finding their way.

They soon came to a large fork in the road, where they chose the road heading south. They rode below the town around three quarters of a mile until they reached a road that ran parallel with the Chattahoochie River. They deployed along a bluff that was overlooking the river at Shallow Ford.

The 1st and 2nd Sections of the Chicago Board of Trade Battery followed them and unlimbered at the top of the bluff.

The river at that point was two hundred and fifty yards wide, and was swollen from recent rains. A dense fog covered the river, and a large white house could be seen on the south side of the river, where Rebel sentries were seen asleep on the porch. David could make them out clearly with his field glasses.

Captain Audenried then passed the word down to David that every fourth trooper was to hold horses at the rear of the bluff, while the rest of the troopers in the company were to cross the river.

The horses were quickly sent to the rear, and Captain Audenried instructed David to order his men across with their carbines at the ready. "You will cross when the artillery opens up." "Yes, sir." David passed the appropriate instructions to Sergeant John Reid, who got the troopers ready.

Thirty minutes later, the batteries on the bluff opened fire, sending 10 pound Parrott Rifle shells across the river.

The 200 picked men from Miller's brigade, and David's Company "I", headed down the bluff and into the cool, swift waters of the Chattahoochie River. The bottom at Shallow Ford was rocky and slick with moss, but the water was waist and shoulder deep.

David struggled across the rocky river bottom, occasionally getting himself pulled sideways by the steady river current. Rebel riflemen up at the house began to shoot over their heads, missing their targets on the moonless morning.

David would stop occasionally, pour water out the end of his Spencer Carbine barrel, and would fire a .52 caliber round up toward the white frame house on the opposite bank.

Other troopers from Miller's brigade repeated the firing process with their Spencer Repeating Rifles, sending shots and volleys at the Rebel defenders on the south bank. Some troopers would raise up, pour water from their barrels, and fire off a round, and then drop back down low into the water, while slowly easing across the rocky river bottom.

Soon, all of the 200 troopers had reached the south bank of the Chattahoochie, and they overran the white frame house, capturing the 40 or so Rebel sentries that had picketed the area. David and Sgt. John Reid captured a Rebel prisoner in a butternut colored uniform that told them they were the "God–damndest fellas they ever seed, loading their guns under water like that."

Captain Chester Thomson of the 72nd Indiana Regiment soon ordered all of the men to build breastworks around their bridgehead at Shallow Ford. They soon piled up fence rails, rocks, and dirt, and had a workable defense line in place by daylight.

The rest of Miller's brigade waded the river to join them, and other troopers from Minty's cavalry brigade soon followed.

General Kenner Garrard, the commander of the Second Division of the Cavalry Corps of the Army of the Cumberland, rode up to the bluff at Shallow Ford, and summoned Major James McCoy of General Sherman's staff to the bluff for a conference. He needed a dependable officer and two dependable troopers to carry a message to General Dodge and General Sherman that Shallow Ford had been taken.

Major McCoy sent a trooper across the river at Shallow Ford to summon David and Sergeant Reid, and they were asked to report to General Garrard at the top of the bluff. He introduced David to General Garrard, and David promptly saluted him.

General Kenner Garrard returned David's salute, and then explained why he had been summoned.

"I need you to ride hard to General Dodge, and take this dispatch to him. I have another copy here for General Sherman. Please mount up and ride out at once. I want them to get these dispatches as soon as possible."

"Yes, sir." David took one of the dispatches and asked Sergeant Reid to get Ajax for him. Ajax was led out, and David took the dispatch and mounted up. He instructed Sergeant Reid to direct Lieutenant Day to take command of Company "I" while he was gone. Major McCoy took another copy of the dispatch from General Garrard, and rode out for General Sherman's headquarters.

David rode hard for General Dodge's command, which was rumored to be on the march between Marietta and Roswell. He rode up through the mill town of Roswell, and then turned west onto the road leading into Marietta.

He gave Ajax the spur when he hit the road leading toward Marietta. It was eleven miles to Marietta, and General Dodge's XVI Corps was supposed to be marching up to Marietta from Nickajack Creek. David pulled Ajax back to a canter, allowing him to rest, but the horse continued to eat up the road.

He rounded a bend in the road near Blackjack Mountain, and spied the head column of troops in the vanguard of Dodge's 16th Corps. He was hailed by pickets in the advance guard, and told them he had an important message for General Dodge.

He was soon led to General Dodge, who was riding a white stallion. He saluted General Dodge, and handed him the dispatch from General Kenner Garrard.

General Dodge read the dispatch from General Garrard, and ordered his men to march faster up the road toward Roswell. The men grunted and sweated in the mid summer heat of the afternoon, but picked up their pace on the march. David was ordered to return to Shallow Ford, and to locate nearby buildings that could be demolished for lumber for bridge construction.

General Grenville Dodge graduated from engineering school, and he had a knack for constructing bridges with the use of available materials.

David and Sergeant Reid located an old barn and two frame houses above Shallow Ford, and led some of General Dodge's staff officers to them once the 16th Corps had marched below Roswell. Major McCoy of General Sherman's staff also sent word through Lieutenant James Day that General Dodge wanted work horses from the cavalry companies bivouacked near Shallow Ford.

"I don't know what he could be talking about, sir. We ride our horses. We don't work 'em."

"What the general is talking about is a horse that we now ride, that has also been broken in as a work animal. Get Anderson Looney down here with twelve other troopers, and we'll find animals that were also broken in as work horses."

* * * * *

General Dodge soon brought up the bulk of his command, and they began to tear down barns and buildings on the north bank of the Chattahoochie River. The expert carpenters and craftsmen in Dodge's command soon put a foot bridge across the river at Shallow Ford.

One half mile up river above Shallow Ford was a railroad bridge that had been burned by Rebel cavalry a week before. All that remained of the old bridge were scorched piers and stone pilings that had been driven into the river bottom.

General Dodge organized a work gang of blacksmiths, carpenters, and laborers around 1,000 men strong to rebuild this burned railroad bridge. David ran a work gang of laborers and horses and mules. Their job was to pull down nearby buildings, and to pull the salvaged timber from the buildings down to the bridge site.

The quartermaster had sent them hammers and saws, and the blacksmiths made them pry bars to use in their demolition efforts. They went after a large barn that was located a quarter mile from the bridge, and began to pry all of the outside boards loose. Several troopers then piled the loose boards aboard wagons, and they then drove the wagons down to the bridge site.

Large saw pits were dug near the banks of the river on the bluff above the bridge. Crews of lumberjacks and mule teams went into the nearby forest, felling tall Loblolly Pine trees. The trees were then skidded to the saw pits, where they were sawed into long square boards by the cross-cut saws of the men at the saw pits. Fires were kindled near the saw pits, where the saw work was done both day and night.

During daylight hours, engineers and carpenters began framing out the bridge with the long green pine boards. Large boards from the demolished buildings were then brought down and nailed to the bridge frame of long green pine boards.

The work was done quickly, but was perfectly done. General Dodge's men had built and rebuild block houses and bridges from south Tennessee through north Alabama, and were thus highly skilled and experienced.

Railroad work crews laid railroad track across the wooden bridge, once the bridge spans across the river were rebuilt. At dusk on July 13, 1864, General Dodge had completed his most impressive engineering feat of the war. A double tracked trestle bridge over the Chattahoochie River, eighteen feet wide, and 710 feet long. The work crews had completed this terrific feat in less than three and one-half days.

General McPherson then wired General Sherman at Vining's Station on July 14th: "The bridge is finished, and the Fifteenth Corps will cross the river this afternoon…"

Chapter Twenty Three

Rome, Georgia
July 20, 1864

Dear Uncle Uriah and Aunt Faith:

Our company has been ordered to Rome, and we have rejoined our regiment here on the plantation of a Colonel Shorter. The house is large and beautiful, and I was told cost $10,000.00 to build. It has two stories, two kitchens, and large and substantial outbuildings. The grounds are covered with ornamental shrubs and different fruit trees. There is a spring at the center of the plantation, and our camp is near the Coosa River. Rome is a pretty town, with wide and spacious streets.

Two Illinois regiments and one Iowa regiment, all of infantry, and one Michigan battery guard the town. I go out swimming almost every day with Lieutenant Dunn in the Coosa River. We picked a great many blackberries yesterday.

Last week, when we were with General Dodge near Roswell, we build a seven hundred foot double tracked trestle bridge over the Chattahoochie River. It was put up over a burned out set of pilings in three days. It was a remarkable feat of engineering. As commander of his escort cavalry, I had the opportunity to work on the bridge, and to help round up timber from nearby buildings and barns.

We captured several Rebel cavalry pickets when we captured the bridge head at Shallow Ford. All of the prisoners had been told that General Joe Johnston was going to be relieved of command, because he had failed to give General Sherman a major battle on the north side of the Chattahoochie River.

I hate being transferred away from the main action in this war, which is near Atlanta. I can only bide my time here, and obey orders, in hopes that we will be ordered back to the main army soon.

My thoughts and prayers are with you now in Putnam County. May the Lord bless and keep you.

Love,
David

David was in camp on the grounds of Colonel Shorter's mansion, when a courier summoned him to Colonel Spencer's headquarters. He combed his hair, trimmed his mustache, and rode Ajax up to the front porch of the splendid Shorter Mansion. He saluted the guards posted at the door as they saluted him, and he entered the entrance hall of the mansion.

He spied Henry Peek in front of the parlor, and noticed that he now had captain's bars on his shoulder straps. "Hello Henry, congratulations on your promotion." He saluted Captain Peek, who returned his salute at once.

"It should have been your promotion, David. You should have been promoted months ago. Go on in. Colonel Spencer is expecting you."

David entered the parlor, and saluted Colonel Spencer, who returned his salute, and asked David to sit down in front of his desk.

"Snelling, you should have received a promotion to captain. I lobbied hard for you with the War Department. Someone in Washington questions your loyalty, on account of your Deep South upbringing. Tramel and Shurtleff got appointed as majors without any difficulty.

I think though, that there is another way for you to get promoted, and I want you to have every advantage."

"How is that, sir?"

"General Dodge is about to be sent home with the 7th Iowa Regiment to recruit as veterans. He is also going to stump the state for votes for President Lincoln. You know that George McClellan is running against the President as a Democratic candidate?"

"Yes, sir, I had heard that."

"This war is not won yet. The Army of the Tennessee just fought a terrific battle near Bald Hill outside of Atlanta last month. The Rebels got beat up bad, but Atlanta was not taken. General McPherson was killed, and our army lost around three thousand men.

The people back home are finding it harder and harder to support the war. If President Lincoln loses the election, the war will be lost."

"I understand that, sir, but what does that have to do with me?"

"The War Department will give General Dodge the authority to promote one soldier from this regiment once he goes on his leave. If you could go down to his headquarters and do some act that would please him, that promotion would be yours."

"What can I do for General Dodge, sir?"

"Ajax is by far the most splendid piece of horse flesh I have ever seen. If General Dodge were astride Ajax, it would draw the immediate attention of voters and potential recruits. He would stump his own home state in a way that would get him noticed. You need that sort of thing in politics, David. What do you say?"

David had been put on the spot. Ajax was a gift from a man that respected him, the father of a woman that he was infatuated with. On the other hand, if Ajax could help General Dodge stump for votes in Iowa for President Lincoln, that would help his country more than him keeping Ajax.

"In order to make your decision easier, David, I have acquired a very fine mare from Colonel Shorter which I would give you in lieu of Ajax."

"I appreciate that, Colonel. I will gladly give Ajax to General Dodge. Of all of the men in this Army, I appreciate and respect General Dodge the most. I will need written pass for myself and both animals to get to General Dodge's headquarters, though. I would not want to get arrested for desertion by the Provost Guard."

"I shall write you a pass this very minute. David, you shall not regret this. There is a promotion in this for you. I will have the mare brought around for you now. Colonel Shorter calls her 'Sally'. You need to leave at once for Atlanta, David. I will send word to Sergeant Reid to have Lieutenant Day take command of your company while you are gone."

"Yes, sir." David took the pass from Colonel Spencer, saluted him, and started to leave the Shorter mansion. He then mounted Ajax, took Sally in tow, and went over to the regiment's quartermaster. He drew four day's rations of coffee, hardtack, and bacon, and then set out on the pike for Kingston.

He trotted into Kingston in two hours, and watered his animals and fed them at Two Run Creek. He then mounted up and rode south along the Western & Atlantic Railroad to Allatoona Station. He was briefly detained there by a provost guard, who reviewed his pass before letting him by. He camped for the night a few miles further south at Big Shanty.

He arose the next morning, fed and watered the animals, and rode past Kennesaw Mountain, Marietta, and down to Vining's Station. He halted for a time near the Chattahoochie River to water the stock, and bought a couple of catfish off a private who had spent a productive morning fishing in the river.

He fried his catfish for his dinner with some makeshift hush puppies of army hardtack. He crossed the river over a railroad bridge that had been built by General Thomas at Defoor's Ferry. He rode five miles south, and located General George Thomas' headquarters. He was told at Thomas' headquarters that General Oliver Howard had been given command of McPherson's Army of the Tennessee, and the entire Army was on the march south toward Ezra Church.

He received directions from an artillery captain on the Lickskillet Road, and soon found General Dodge's headquarters that evening. He tied up the horses near a large Sycamore tree, and gave his pass to troopers of the 7th Iowa, who were serving as General Dodge's escort.

David was once again greeted by Captain Henry Horn of General Dodge's staff. The staff officers were seated with General Dodge eating beef stew. Captain Horn handed David a pewter plate, and began spooning stew on David's plate. "Get your tin cup and pour yourself some coffee, there. General Dodge is about to describe the Battle of Atlanta for Major George Nichols of General Sherman's staff."

"On the evening of July 21st, our Army had advanced to within two miles of Atlanta. Leggett's Division of Blair's 17th Army Corps carried a large hill, known as Leggett's Hill.

On July 22nd, the Army of Tennessee had its right resting near the Howard House, north of the Augusta Railroad, and over to Leggett's Hill. Giles A Smith's Division of the 17th Army Corps held this hill, with a weak flank in air.

I was ordered by General McPherson on the evening of the 21st to send one brigade of Fuller's Division to the left of the line, and they bivouacked at right angles to Blair's lines. Early on July 22nd, General McPherson rode to my headquarters, and ordered me to send General Sweeney's Division over to the left of General Blair's lines. I ordered General Sweeney to march his command from the Augusta Railroad to Sugar Creek. He marched his division up the road until he met Fuller's command, and there he halted his division.

The enemy approached our lines from a heavily wooded area from the south and west.

General Hardee's Corps was ordered out of their works around Atlanta to attack us from the south, and the battle began within fifteen minutes of 12 o'clock, and lasted until midnight.

There was around 21,000 Union troops in line of battle at 12 o'clock noon, and they were attacked by Hardee's Corps and Cheatham's Corp's, and Georgia Militia under General Smith.

Where I stood just at the rear of the 16th Army Corps, I could see their entire line, and could see that both of my flanks were being enveloped by the enemy attack. I sent a staff officer to General Giles Smith, requesting him to refuse his left and protect the gap between the 17th Corps and my right. The Divisions of General Fuller and Sweeney were formed in a single line of battle in the open fields, and were warmly engaged. The enemy, massed in columns three and four lines deep, halted and opened a rapid fire on the 16th Corps. They fell back after taking initial fire from our lines, and then reformed and attacked us again."

General Dodge picked up his tin cup, took two sips of hot coffee, and continued his narrative:

"The Rebels reformed their columns, and their regimental colors waved and fluttered in advance of their lines. Our artillery then opened up on them at once.

As Hardee's attack fell upon the 16th Army Corps, his left division commanded by Patrick Cleburne lapped over and beyond Blair's left, and poured down through the gap between the left of the 17th and the right of the 16th Corps. Blair was attacked in front, flank, and rear.

As Cleburne's Division advanced along the open space between the 16th and 17th Corps, they cut off and captured a portion of two regiments under Blair's command. Hardee attacked them in the rear, and Cheatham attacked them in the front until 3:30 p.m.

At 3:30, after a lull, an extraordinary effort was made by the Rebels to wipe out Giles Smith's Division and capture Leggett's Hill. Around this position, the fighting was desperate. Fighting was done hand to hand, until it grew so dark that nothing could be seen but gun flashes on both sides. The ground was literally covered here with the dead of both sides.

Around 4:00 o'clock, Cheatham's Corps attacked again in front of the 15th Corps, and Lightburn's division became panic stricken and fell back. General Logan at that time was in command of the Army of the Tennessee, and he asked for assistance at that point on the line.

I sent Mersey's Brigade from the Second Division, and they recaptured the works and the guns that had been lost to Cheatham's men.

We lost 3500 men killed and wounded, ten guns, and 1,800 men taken prisoner. The Rebels lost at least 8,000 men in the battle.

I will tell all of you this about that great battle: Every man was at his post; every man did a hero's duty. They proved that they might be wiped out, but they were never made to run."

When it was clear that General Dodge was finished with his account, some of the officers cheered and said "Bravo!", and the men clapped.

Others said "Well done!", or "An excellent tribute!", or words to that effect.

General Dodge then drank a slug of coffee, and then turned his attention to David. "Lieutenant Snelling, what brings you down to this headquarters?"

David knew that all eyes around the campfire were now trained on him. He then began to speak, delivering his unrehearsed lines as if he had rehearsed them all the way down from Camp Shorter.

"General Dodge, in honor of your glorious victory at Leggett's Hill, and in recognition of your stellar career as an engineer and soldier, our regiment presents you Ajax, a glorious Thoroughbred stallion. His owner paid over $3,000.00 for him before the war. We heard you are going home to Iowa to recruit for new soldiers and campaign for President Lincoln, and we wanted you to do it in grand style."

David walked around to the other side of the Sycamore tree, untied Ajax, and led him over to General Dodge.

The general rubbed Ajax's white star on his forehead. "He is a magnificent animal. Thank you very much, David. When you return to your regiment, please thank Colonel Spencer for me also. Captain Horn, please go tie Ajax up behind my headquarters tent. I need to discuss a personnel matter with Lieutenant Snelling."

"Yes, sir. I will take his reins, now, sir." Captain Horn led Ajax around to the rear of the headquarters tent, while David and General Dodge went inside the tent. General Dodge had a small writing desk set up behind a cracker box, and a newfangled kerosene lantern provided his light inside. He pulled some spectacles from his uniform coat pocket, and hunted for his order book and pencil. He sat down on a small folding chair, and offered David a seat on a hardtack box. David sat down across from General Dodge, and loosened his necktie.

"The War Department has given me authority to make an at large promotion within my regiment of escort cavalry before I go on leave. You, David, are worthy of such a promotion. What do you have to say about that?"

David was now on the spot. "Well...sir, I have thought about it quite a bit. An officer is only as effective as the men who serve under him. I once was a very effective first lieutenant, but now, I can no longer say that."

"Why so, David?"

"Well, sir, my First Sergeant, Anderson Looney, was caught diddling with a physician's servant girl over in Franklin, and Doctor Swaving preferred charges against him. He was court martialed and lost his stripes. I would rather be an effective first lieutenant than a mediocre captain, sir. If you only have one promotion to make, sir, I would want you to promote Anderson Looney back as my first sergeant."

General Dodge smiled, took another sip of coffee, and began to speak.

"David, you have learned one of the greatest lessons about being an officer. You are only as effective as those who serve under you. If you want Anderson Looney back, then you shall have him back as a first sergeant. I will have Captain Horn write out a warrant for him tonight. Is he really that good, David?"

"Sir, he is the best judge of horseflesh that I have ever seen in this life."

"You know, David, the Rebels know that they are whipped. It's just a matter of time before Atlanta falls."

"I guess, though, one of your tasks, sir, is to convince the people back in Iowa and in other states that the Lincoln Administration can win the war."

"Absolutely. Your gift of that magnificent animal will help greatly in that department. David, I know that the paymaster has held up your pay these last two months. Please do me a favor, and let me give you $200.00 for Ajax. I know that he was your horse, and he was given to you by a physician in Franklin. Hold that sum of money for me, and maybe you can do something again for me later. I know that animal is worth more than ten times that amount, anyway."

"If you insist, sir." David took a roll of bills from General Dodge.

"Maybe that will be enough to square away some of your debts, if you have any in your regiment. You take care of yourself, David. We will meet again, I assure you."

David knew then it was time for him to leave.

"Thank you, General Dodge. Good luck to you in all your ventures." He saluted the general, and took his leave from his headquarters tent. He walked out to the campfire, said his good byes to the staff officers, and picked up his saddle and blanket. He saddled Sally, put his bridle on her, and mounted her with his saddle bags and carbine.

He then rode back toward the river, away from the Army of the Tennessee, and away from the main action in the war, and back toward Rome.

* * * * *

On the way back to camp, David realized quickly that Colonel Spencer was no judge of horseflesh. Sally just would not do. She could not eat up the road the way Ajax could. She needed rest quite frequently. She did not respond to the spur as rapidly as Ajax did. In short, David decided to replace her as soon as he could.

He stopped by the quartermaster, and drew a set of first sergeant's stripes, and had the pleasure of pinning them on Sergeant Anderson Looney. Major Tramel and some of the other officers thought David had been crazy not to accept the promotion for himself as offered by General Dodge.

The men in the ranks heard about David's generosity, though, and loved him for it.

They received orders to go on a three day scout to Jacksonville, Alabama. On the way back, near Hollingsworth, Private Samuel Winters of Company H got two nice stallions from a pasture, and then David saw an opportunity.

He bought a black stallion from Winters by giving him Sally, and $100.00 of the cash General Dodge had given him for Ajax. The regiment returned to Rome on August 16th. They learned in camp on the 17th that they were to be ordered out the next day for a scout down to Cedar Bluff, Alabama. Companies "I" and "K" would have the advance.

* * * * *

August 25, 1864
Camp Shorter, Georgia

Dear Uncle Uriah and Aunt Faith:

We had a recent scout down to Cedar Bluff, Alabama, where General Forrest captured us last year. We went over Lookout Mountain to Alpine, looking for General Clanton's First Alabama Confederate cavalry. We captured some Rebel officers home on a furlough, and borrowed their coats to use for our scouting mission. We found that Colonel Weatherspoon and 100 men had been in the valley earlier, and we met a judge on Cider Mountain that claimed to have voted against the Alabama secession ordinance.

We went back over the mountain at Prices, and camped in the yard of a large farm. All of the regiment's horses were tied to picket lines set up in the yard. The farmer was Wyman Creel, who had several bee hives set up on the side yard near his house.

Private William Duffel of "A" Company turned over one of the beehives that afternoon, looking for honey. The bees swarmed out, and began to sting the horses with a fury. The horses went crazy, kicking and bucking. Dr. Swaving tried to untie Colonel Spencer's horse, and it kicked him, breaking his leg below the knee.

We got the doctor out, set his leg, and put him on the wagon. I started to slap Private Duffel for his stupidity, but Colonel Spencer would not allow me to do it. He instead pulled on his gauntlet, and hit Duffel in the jaw with his fist.

On the way back, Sergeant Looney asked me if Dr. Swaving's injury was delayed justice being measured out to him. Dr. Swaving had charges preferred against Sergeant Looney, you see, and had him reduced to the ranks. I told Sergeant Looney that the Bible teaches us to live in the present, not the past, and that we must forgive our enemies.

We returned safely to Rome on the 23rd without incident.

I have to go now, as I need to detail some of the men to issue out the day's ration.

Very Truly Yours,

David.

* * * * *

General John Bell Hood had been placed in command of the Confederate Army of Tennessee in July of 1864, when General Sherman's forces were just outside of Atlanta.

He had issued attack orders to his corps commanders almost immediately, causing attacks to be made against Sherman's forces in three sorties.

The first sortie was directed against General George Thomas and the Army of the Cumberland at Peachtree Creek. It ended in failure.

The second sortie was against General McPherson and the Army of the Tennessee at Leggett's Hill, and it also failed to drive the invaders away. The last sortie was at Ezra Church, against the Army of the Tennessee, and it was an even greater failure. In all three sorties, Hood's

Army sustained 13,000 casualties, against General Sherman's 8,000 casualties.

At Ezra Church, General Sherman issued orders to his three armies to cut the Macon & Western Railroad and the Atlanta & West Point Railroad below Atlanta with a grand left wheel maneuver.

On August 31st, General Hood ascertained the danger to his army's main supply line, and he ordered Hardee's corps and Stephen D. Lee's Corps to Jonesboro to attack the Federals there.

Both sides lost around 2,000 men each in over two days of fighting around Jonesboro. In the end, Hood's forces withdrew to Lovejoy Station, and Sherman's forces occupied Jonesboro.

General Hood ordered Atlanta evacuated, and on September 3rd, General Sherman's Federal forces entered Atlanta. General Schofield sent a telegram to the War Department: "General Sherman has taken Atlanta." General Sherman later wired General Henry Halleck in Washington: "Atlanta is ours, and fairly won."

Chapter Twenty Four

One month after the fall of Atlanta, General Hood and the Army of Tennessee laid a pontoon bridge across the Chattahoochie near Campbelltown, and then marched north to Powder Springs.

General Sherman left one corps to hold Atlanta and marched north to pursue Hood's army. He rushed a division of the Army of the Tennessee under Brigadier General John Corse north by rail to hold Rome. When General Sherman learned that Hood's troops had captured Big Shanty, he ordered General Corse to defend the large Federal supply base at Allatoona.

General Corse moved 2000 men to Allatoona, leaving the First Alabama Cavalry to hold Rome. French's division of Stewart's Confederate troops attacked Allatoona with 3000 men, and a savage fight was conducted on October 5th.

The Rebels withdrew from Allatoona after the bloody fight that cost 706 Federal soldiers, and 799 Confederate soldiers.

General Hood then marched north again, crossing the Coosa River near Rome, and moving up the Oostanaula River to Resaca, where his troops broke the railroad for five miles. General Hood left a rear guard of cavalry under Colonel Clanton and General Joe Wheeler near Cave Spring.

General Corse was ordered with the First Alabama and the 9th Illinois Mounted Infantry to attack the Rebel troops near Cave Spring. Troopers with the First Alabama and the Ninth Illinois attacked the Rebel Cavalry about five miles out of town, on the side of a small mountain.

The Federal cavalry drove the Rebels out of a heavily wooded area, and into several rocky and hilly fields, where they were attacked by General Corse's infantry of the 15th Army Corps.

The Rebel troops used the hills and the rocky and wooded slopes for cover, and escaped capture at the hands of the superior and more mobile Federal cavalry. David's Company "I", and Captain Peek's Company "H" drove Clanton's Rebel cavalry down the river road, before orders were issued recalling them back to Rome.

General Sherman's army pursued Hood's army to LaFayette, Georgia on October 17th, but Hood's troops escaped into Alabama. General Sherman then decided that pursuing Hood was fruitless.

On October 29th, orders were issued to divide the Federal forces in Georgia. All troops located north of Resaca were sent to Nashville, to make up part of a new command under General Thomas with the 4th and the 23rd Corps.

The remainder of the Federal troops would constitute the Army of Georgia under General Sherman, and would make up around 60,000 men.

General Sherman issued orders to abandon all points south of Dalton. All sick and wounded, and baggage and equipment not needed in future campaigns were sent by rail to Chattanooga.

* * * * *

On October 31st, David was summoned to Colonel George Spencer's headquarters tent, which was located in the rear of Shorter's mansion at Rome. General Corse and General Sherman had selected the Shorter mansion itself as their headquarters.

David reported to Colonel Spencer, who asked him to sit down on a box of hardtack, as he had a new assignment for him.

"You have been selected for a very special assignment, Lieutenant Snelling. You are to select twenty one men from your company, and you are to report to the headquarters of the Military Division of the Mississippi. You are to command the escort cavalry of the commanding general."

David had a puzzled look on his face.

"Uh…where would these headquarters be, sir?"

Colonel Spencer removed his slouch hat and wiped his face with his handkerchief. He then began to laugh, and then addressed David again. "That would be wherever General Sherman desires to go, from Rome to Atlanta, or down to the Atlantic Ocean. You, young sir, are to command General Sherman's escort. You caught the eye of General Corse the other day, and General John Corse has caught General Sherman's eye of late. Captain Audenried and Major McCoy already know you, and you met Major George Nichols at General Dodge's headquarters.

Go select twenty one of your best troopers, and report to General Sherman at 1:00 o'clock."

"Yes, sir. Thank you for the opportunity, sir."

David saluted Colonel Spencer. Colonel Spencer returned his salute. "David, you will do just fine. You are marching through the same country where you were born and reared. Carry on. Lieutenant Day will command the rest of your company while you are on detached service. Go on and select your men."

David left Colonel Spencer's tent, and rode back to Company "I", which was camped on the edge of a paddock behind the Shorter Mansion.

* * * * *

Kingston, Georgia
November 9, 1864

Dear Uncle Uriah and Aunt Faith:

I have been chosen, along with twenty one men from Company "I", to command the cavalry escort of General William T. Sherman. I, of all people, command the security force for the second most ranking officer in the whole army! I was summoned to the general's headquarters this past week when we were at Camp Shorter, and got briefed by Major Nichols as to my orders and duties. I am to provide security and escort services to the commanding general. I will also be ordered to ride on scouting and foraging missions from time to time.

We have gone with the bulk of the infantry of General Sherman's army to Kingston, in a belated effort to catch General Hood's Rebel army. General Hood has marched his troops into Alabama, and appears to have escaped us.

The good news, dear aunt and uncle, I am saving for last. We are now marching south, and will march your way, to either Savannah or Augusta. I may get the coveted opportunity to see you in the flesh before this cruel war is over. Please take care of yourselves.
I have to go now. We have to be ready for inspection in twenty minutes. Until next time, I am

Very truly yours,

David

* * * * *

On November 15, 1864, General Sherman's Army of Georgia marched into Atlanta from Kingston, Georgia. General Corse and the Fourth Division of the 15th Army Corps burned the mills and factories at Rome, and joined General Sherman's headquarters staff on the march into Atlanta.

General Sherman was 45 years old, with red hair, a close cropped beard, and a receding hairline. He talked and smoked cigars almost constantly while he was off his horse and in camp during the evenings. During the day, they rode with General Sherman's aides, Captain Audenried, Major Henry Hitchcock, a lawyer from St. Louis, Major McCoy, and Major George Nichols. None of General Sherman's aides were above the rank of Major. They rode the flanks of the infantry, riding off the side of the road to allow the columns of infantry to pass. General Sherman always said that the troops had the right of way, and his headquarters staff honored his wishes. They would ride into mud holes and briar thickets and plum tree thickets on the edge of roadways to avoid the marching infantrymen.

They crossed the Chattahoochie River at Powers Ferry over the bridge that General Thomas had built back in June. David saw some of Captain Poe's men setting charges and preparing to fire the bridge the next day. Captain Poe was General Sherman's chief of engineers, and General Sherman had ordered him and another engineer detail down to Atlanta, to destroy railroad depots there.

They rode into Atlanta down Whitehall Street late that day, and camped near the court house. David dined with Major Hitchcock that evening, and they ate boiled eggs, hardtack, bacon, and beans.

The following morning, David, Sergeant Looney, and ten troopers escorted General Sherman down to the Car Shed, which was a large brick depot at the terminus of the Western & Atlantic Railroad, the Georgia Railroad, and the Atlanta & West Point Railroad.

David and General Sherman watched Captain Poe and his men destroy the Car Shed with iron and steel rams. All the walls were destroyed, and all of the depot rails were ripped up. Fires were built out of cross ties, and rails were heated, and the ends grabbed with wrenches. The rails were then twisted around wooden posts, ruining them for future use.

David helped Captain Poe lay powder charges around several locomotives stranded at the depot, and he watched the explosion of the engines from a safe distance near the courthouse.

Other soldiers were detailed to set fires at warehouses and munitions houses, and the vivid fires and explosions lit up the sky that evening, and all night long. Shells left in the warehouses would explode in the fires, contributing spectacular fireworks to the autumn sky.

They camped again near the courthouse, where David put a guard of ten troopers on General Sherman, while he dined with Major McCoy and Captain Audenried. His escort troopers were all armed to a man with Spencer Repeating Carbines, and were the best shots in the company. They were all serenaded by a band from the 33rd Massachusetts Volunteers, which played a collection of pieces for them until ten p.m., when tattoo was sounded.

They arose at 6:00 a.m. for the march to the sea, with General Sherman mounting a fast walking bay stallion named Sam, and issuing the orders to move out across from the court house.

His Army of Georgia was divided into a right wing, commanded by Major General O.O. Howard, which consisted of the 15th Corps under Major General P.J. Osterhaus, and the 17th Corps, commanded by Major General Frank P. Blair.

The left wing of the army was commanded by Major General H.W. Slocum, and consisted of the 20th Corps, commanded by Brig. General Altheus Williams, and the 14th Corps, commanded by Major General Jeff C. Davis. The cavalry division was commanded by an eccentric officer, Brigadier General Judson Kilpatrick, who had the nickname "Kill Cavalry".

General Sherman and his headquarters followed the left wing of the army, marching out the Augusta Railroad, and into Decatur.

They stopped at a house near the court house square, after passing the earth works and battle lines where the Battle of Bald Hill had been fought in July of 1864.

They rode east along the Five Forks Trickum Road past the looming granite face of Stone Mountain, a huge 600 foot granite mountain that dominated the skyline east of Decatur. David and the escort troopers all believed that Stone Mountain resembled a piece of the moon.

The halted an hour at Lithonia, where Captain Poe's men pulled up railroad track with a steel hook, and then set fire to the ties, heating the rails, and twisting them with Captain Poe's special wrenches. The pioneer companies were very efficient, and several miles of track were torn up, and the depot was destroyed by the time the column had resumed the march.

They rode through dense thickets of oak and pine after crossing the Yellow River, and they camped for the evening at Conyers. They spoke to a woman in Conyers that evening, who told them that Confederate currency was 27 for 1 for gold dollars, and 26 to 1 for silver. Freed blacks could be seen moving through town, speaking to General Sherman occasionally. General Sherman would explain to them that they were free to come and go, and he warned them against doing violence to their former masters or their families.

They camped at Conyers that night, and arose and marched across pontoon bridges over the Alcovy River the following morning. They crossed the outskirts of Covington, the county seat of Newton County, and halted about two miles south of town, on the farm of a Judge Harris. Judge Harris and his family actually lived in a large white frame house in Covington. His farm had only Spartan–style living quarters of large log cabins built of squared–up logs. They rode up to the well and horse trough, where the escort and headquarters staff watered their animals.

They spied soldiers from the advance guard pulling hams and bacon sides out of the smokehouse, and pouring sorghum molasses into their tin cups. They rounded the corner of one building with General Sherman, and saw a bearded sergeant of infantry with a ham slung in a burlap bag over his shoulder, a roll of strung sausages slung across his rifle, and a face buried into a cup of molasses.

When he saw General Sherman, he stood at attention and saluted, and quoted part of his Special Field Order No. 120: "Forage liberally on the country", while molasses streamed down his face.

The men on the staff erupted in laughter at the order being quoted sotto voce by the soldier, but General Sherman and Major McCoy gave the soldier a somber lecture. Foraging was to be done only to feed entire regiments, and by men that were properly detailed for the purpose.

They camped for the night near the barn of Judge Harris, and David ate supper with Major Hitchcock and Major Nichols. They dined on freshly killed chicken and sausages from Judge Harris' smokehouse. Away from the camp fire, in the nearby woods, they heard gunshots all around. Major Hitchcock was thirty five years old, of medium build, but stocky. He jumped at the gunshots, and was not accustomed to hearing that kind of noise at supper time. David assured him that the gunfire was from other soldiers "foraging liberally on the country", by shooting pigs and chickens and livestock for their supper.

Major Nichols then began to discuss the South, and the peculiar institution of slavery with David. He particularly assailed slavery as being un–American, or being contrary to the American traditions of self reliance and upward mobility.

"David, you were born and raised on a cotton plantation near Milledgeville, is that correct?"

"Yes, sir. That is true. My uncle owned the plantation, but I ran several gangs of Negroes. I ran the cotton gin and the steam saw mill. I left home because I was kicked out."

"Tell us more, David. Why did you leave?"

"My Uncle William despised the fact that I was a Union man, and would not enlist in the Confederate Army. He forced me out at gunpoint."

Major Hitchcock then joined in on the conversation. "Well then, his loss was the Union Army's gain, eh David?"

"Yes, sir, I guess it was."

"Tell me then, David, let us résumé our discussion of the slave and plantation system."

Major Hitchcock then began to interrogate David, using his training as a trial lawyer.

"When you were doing all of this work for your uncle, did he ever make you a partner on his plantation?"

"Well, he said he would, but it never really worked out that way."

"If your uncle would have died, say in 1861, who would have inherited his plantation?"

"His son, Joseph."

"Did Joseph ever really do any real work on your uncle's plantation, David? My question is, did he ever do anything to deserve his inheritance?"

"No sir. He was a poor worker, even when he was at his best."

"Yet your uncle had willed everything to him?"

"Yes, sir."

Major Nichols then joined in. "You see, David, that is a closed society. The only way wealth is transferred down South is through inheritance. Up North, fortunes are made by the work and sweat of free enterprise. Men work in small shops and small businesses all over the North, and fortunes can be made in ten or twenty years, if one works hard and saves his money. Down South, everything in the way of wealth is tied to plantations, and inheritance determines the transfer of capital, unless you are a cotton factor or a railroad agent."

David took a sip of coffee. "That about sums it up, sir."

Major Hitchcock then offered a cigar to David, who politely declined. He lit one up with a Lucifer match, and Major Nichols lit up a pipe as well. Major Nichols then looked at the stars, and spoke. "David, did you have those kinds of heady discussions back at the First Alabama Cavalry?"

"Uh, no sir, although Lieutenant Frank Dunn and I would speak on topics such as the Bible. He was a great man with live stock, sir. He would say things like 'The mule train would be better served if they would cut two mules off the six mule teams and double their rations. A strong mule pulls twice as well as a weak, underfed mule.'"

Major Nichols face lit up. "That is a capital idea! I will write that up and submit it to General Sherman, and he will probably issue an order to the regiments to change the teams on the mule trains, and give the mules extra forage. I will get the general's order book, and will draft the order right now. Major Hitchcock, will you review my language after I write the order out?"

"Certainly."

"Then I shall proceed. David, we have a copy of the *Augusta Constitutionalist* over there if you would like to read it. It doesn't compare to the *New York Tribune*, but it will do."

"Yes, sir. Good night, sir. Good night to you too, Major Hitchcock."

"See you in the morning, David."

* * * * *

They marched out the next day in a heavy mist of rain, over muddy red clay roads of the Piedmont area of Georgia that David knew quite well. They marched fifteen miles, according to Captain Poe's odometer, and camped for the night near Newborn, on the Eatonton Factory Road. That night at camp, the shooting of livestock and the stealing of foodstuffs from the houses and farms around Newborn got so bad, that Captain Audenried and Major McCoy issued orders to attempt to put such conduct to a halt.

The next morning, Major McCoy came by, and asked David to take a foraging party out after some horses and mules. Some of the headquarters horses had come up lame, and some of the mules in the supply train had broken down from fatigue. David was issued quartermaster receipts, and was instructed to issue them to any farmer that had the livestock in his possession. If the stock could be cut out in open paddocks or fields, though, it was to be taken at once.

David picked Sergeant Looney and eight other men, and they crossed the Little River around five miles west of Shady Dale at dawn. They rode in a fine mist, in forty degree temperatures, among the fiery red and gold autumn leaves of the hardwood trees.

They rode along the Little River toward Martin's Mill, where David knew of several small plantations. One of the plantations was owned by James Willard, a man that had excoriated him for refusing to enlist in a Confederate regiment.

Sergeant Looney cut out two of his fine horses, while David wrote Mr. Willard a quartermaster's receipt. Mr. Willard accepted the receipt at the point of a Spencer Repeating Carbine, after protesting the seizure of his stock.

They rode closer to Eatonton Factory, ahead of the approaching columns of infantry, and discovered more mules and horses on a large plantation. The owner had fled before the large Federal army, and David rode into camp that night near Mr. James Vann's farm with eleven mules and six horses. They easily found their way back to General Sherman's headquarters, as the valley below where they had traveled was lined with thousands of burning campfires set by the marching hosts of the left wing of General Sherman's army.

The weather turned rainy and even colder, though, and it soon rained hard and long enough to turn the red clay below them to slippery mud. Infantry soldiers, mules and wagons, and horses had a hard time navigating the slippery mud the next day.

They marched down to Murder Creek the middle of the day, after the rain had passed, and a bitter cold wind had begun to blow in from the west.

David had longed for the opportunity to see his Uncle Uriah and Aunt Faith, and his opportunity came on November 21, 1864, at 2:00 o'clock. He rode to the head of the General's column, and informed General Sherman that they had arrived at Uriah's mill. General Sherman had known Uriah Snelling during the Mexican War, and wanted to visit with him a short while. They spied him out in the yard around his mill, engaged in building ovens of brick on his grounds.

David dismounted and hugged his Uncle Uriah, who looked a little older, and a little more gray headed than when he had last laid eyes on him. David's Aunt Faith came out and hugged him, too, and then David properly introduced them to the members of General Sherman's staff.

They were all then served a dinner of baked ham, black eyed peas, yams, and corn bread. Uriah asked General Sherman if he had any millers in the ranks, and several men came forward. "I have constructed these ovens with metal racks, so that they would accept iron hardtack molds. I have prepared flour for you to bake hardtack. All you have to do is put your men to work for a few hours, and you will have thousands of hardtack rations."

General Sherman pulled an unlit cigar from his mouth, and sent for Major McCoy.

"Major McCoy, send out a detail to round up around fifty or so millers from some of the regiments crossing over the creek yonder. Tell them that I want them to man the grist mill here, and to run it out all day, making wheat flour. I also want some men to start boiling water, and others who have worked in bakeries to bake the hardtack in these ovens out here in Uriah's yard."

"Yes, sir, right away, sir." Major McCoy saluted General Sherman and left. They had a little time to visit after dinner, and David presented his Uncle Uriah with his serial letter to him and Aunt Faith. Aunt Faith gave David back his old journal, the one that Angela had mailed down from

Richmond the year before. It was inked on the side "First Lieutenant David R. Snelling, First Alabama Cavalry."

Uriah knew that David would be pressed for time, as the general's column was going to move out that afternoon. "David, I just want to tell you how proud we are of you. It is an extreme honor to command the escort of the commanding general. I do need to give you some recent news, though."

"What is that, sir?"

"Joseph was captured this summer at Spotsylvania. He is in prison now at Point Lookout, Maryland. William has gone mad with grief. He attempted to get up a large sum of money, and to bribe a high Confederate official to get him released through a medical discharge and or prisoner exchange. In order to raise the cash he needed, he sold a number of servants off of Greenbrier. Joe Buck was sold to Howell Cobb."

"Oh, God, not him. He always treated his blacks like dirt. Joe Buck was nothing but good to Uncle William. It disgusts me that he was treated that way."

"Well, son, you can free him tonight. Cobb's second plantation is on your direct line of march. That is assuming you are headed to Milledgeville."

"Your assumption is correct. Getting back to Joseph, did he really have a medical condition that would warrant his release?"

"They said he had consumption, but I don't know if that was true or not." "Uncle Uriah, I would love to stay, but we have to move out."

"I know son. I was a soldier once, too. Come kiss your Aunt Faith goodbye, and saddle up in a few minutes. I do need to tell you this before you go. You don't need to think that you have to return back here after the war. After you left the 57th Georgia, Julia Bonner raised a big stink around here about you. You might consider moving to North Georgia or even to Nashville or Alabama after the war. You can start a new life in any of those places with the friends you have made in the army. The army is a brotherhood, David. Never forget that. Keep up your journal and your serial letter to us, as they have made some interesting reading."

"I will, sir."

David saddled his horse, and kissed his Aunt Faith goodbye. She gave him a boiled fruit cake to present to General Sherman, who had been delighted with her cooking. David ordered the escort out after General Sherman, and looked back at his Uncle's grist mill as his horse trotted down the road. Men from General Morgan's division were running the mill and baking hardtack outside in the brick ovens. Other men were loading baked hardtack in boxes, and were stacking the boxes in wagons lined up near the road. This war had changed this part of the world in a hurry. He bundled up his blue wool greatcoat against the cold wind, and trotted his horse to the southeast.

They made ten miles in the bitter cold wind, and made camp at one of Howell Cobb's plantations on the Monticello Road. They stopped at Howell Cobb's 6000 acre plantation, all but deserted, except for a few old Negroes. Oats and corn and peanuts had been left, though, along with salt and 500 gallons of sorghum molasses.

Major Nichols dismounted his horse in front of one of several log cabins that had served as slave quarters, and was complaining to David about the cold weather. "If this is your sunny South, sir, then I say damn your sunny South!"

"Well, sir, you have to understand that the high humidity here makes hot weather hotter and cold weather colder."

David looked around, and saw several groups of Negroes very poorly dressed. He saw a number of crude wooden furnishings in the cabins that were built from green wood with poor hand tools. David believed that Joe Buck had been given the job of constructing the furnishings, but had been given crude tools and no assistance in his duties.

He found Jo Buck huddled in a nearby cabin, with huge holes in his shoes, keeping himself warm with a blanket. His hair had turned completely white, and the arthritis in his hands kept them from moving freely. Howell Cobb had worn him completely out.

When he saw David, he did not recognize him at first. David removed his forage cap, got down on one knee, and began to speak to him, slowly. "Joe Buck, before I left here, I told you that the next time you saw me, that I would be wearing a blue uniform. I also told you that the next time I saw you, you would be free."

A gleam of recognition went over Joe Buck's eyes, and he fell down to his knees, and hugged David's boots. "God Almighty bless you, master Dave. You have come home at last!"

David hugged him, and spoke to him again.

"By order of the President of the United States, you are a free man. Please get up and come with me."

David found an old uniform and pair of drawers in his saddlebags, and he put them on Joe Buck, along with an old pair of brogans. His anger at his Uncle William had reached the boiling point, and he knew what he had to do.

He went to General Sherman, who was seated by the fire, eating toasted peanuts. He told him that he wanted to ride eight miles to the southwest to visit his rich uncle, who forced him to leave his plantation because of his Unionist views.

General Sherman gave him permission to ride over to Greenbrier that evening, along with five other men. He did admonish David before he left to remember that he was a sworn volunteer officer in the United States Army, and he should govern his behavior accordingly.

David ordered Sergeant Looney to mount up with four troopers, and he found an extra horse for Joe Buck to ride.

They mounted up that evening, and rode west, finally arriving at Greenbrier at nearly six o'clock. Joe Buck had told him on the way that most of the slaves at Greenbrier had run off, except Zack Dawson and Savannah.

They eased down the pea gravel covered drive, and David soon noticed signs of decay. Nut grass had grown up knee high around the boxwoods, and the boxwoods had suffered from a lack of pruning. The brass lamp fittings had tarnished almost beyond recognition. David remembered that Joe Buck and Zack Dawson used to scrub them down with baking soda and vinegar to keep them new looking and shiny.

Sand spurs had sprouted up along the chinks between the mortar joints on the brick walk, and the front porch really needed another coat of paint.

David and Sergeant Looney walked up to the front porch with their carbines in hand, and David rapped on the front door.

Zack Dawson answered the door a few moments later, and he was surprised to see David, and even more surprised to see Joe Buck McGee in a Federal officer's uniform.

David asked for his Uncle William. Zack said he was in the parlor, but that he would bring him out to the door. David asked Sergeant Reid and two other troopers to dismount, draw their carbines, and take station at the end of the front porch.

Five minutes later, William Floyd walked up to the front door, still in his dressing gown and carpet slippers. He had not shaven that day, and David smelled the odor of whiskey on his breath. William was shocked to see David, and the sight of the armed troopers on his porch struck terror in his heart.

"David, is that you, boy? What are you doing here?"

"I command General Sherman's cavalry escort, Uncle William. I saw Joe Buck over at Howell Cobb's place last night, and got very upset."

"Why is that?"

"He was a loyal and devoted servant to you for many years. He did skilled work for you. He has performed labor and services for you far in excess of his purchase price. Yet you sold him to that no-account Howell Cobb."

"What is he doing here?"

"The President of the United States issued a proclamation last year that freed servants such as Joe Buck. Last night, General Sherman set him free. The last time I was here, you ran me off at gunpoint. I came back here to let you know that there is a God in heaven, and there is justice in this world."

"General Sherman, David, is the greatest general, and is the meanest man in the world."

"After I get done here, Uncle William, you just might think that I am the meanest man in the world. We have just passed a column of soldiers from General Jackson's division. They have detailed a party to come down and destroy your gin house and cotton gin."

"Oh, God, no."

"I did persuade General Jackson that your steam saw mill should be spared. Georgia and the rest of the South will need to rebuild and rejoin the Union after this war is finished. There are many acres of pine and hardwood timber around here that could be cut into lumber. I obtained an order from the general that your saw mill is to be spared. I will post that order in front of the mill before I leave, and it will be spared. But only on one condition."

"What is that?"

"You need to hire Joe Buck on as your foreman, and either pay him an honest day's wage, or agree to divide a percentage of your profits with him. You need to agree to those conditions now, or I will destroy this order."

"...I have no choice, David. I need the capital desperately. I agree to your terms."

"Uncle William, I heard about Joseph being captured, and taken prisoner in Maryland. I promise you that when I get up that way, if I get up that way, I will see that Joseph is released. He is like a brother to me."

Tears began to roll down William's face. "David, please forgive me. You have to understand that I am proud of you, in spite of what I have said."

"There is one more thing. Here is $200.00 in U.S. greenbacks. I need a remount, and I need one now. I am going to take Hercules, and I will send you another $250.00 once I get paid next month."

"Please don't take Hercules, David."

"Would you rather I got him, and paid you for him, or would you rather a Yankee bummer come down and steal him outright?"

"I see your point. Give me the money."

David handed him the $200.00, and stepped down off the porch. "Good bye, Uncle William."

"Goodbye, David."

He asked Joe Buck to unsaddle his horse, and he left him in the paddock for his Uncle William. "You will need a decent horse to help you work the mill, Joe Buck."

Joe Buck caught Hercules, and put David's saddle, saddlebags, blanket, and bridle on him. David stepped into the stirrups, and Hercules responded to him immediately.

Joe Buck walked up to see him off. "Thank you for everything, old friend. You take care not to get killed."

"I will do just fine, Joe Buck. This war has filed a hard edge onto me. You cut some lumber, and try your best to rebuild things around here when we are gone."

"I will, David. I will never forget what you did for me. Ever."

"Good bye, Joe Buck." David felt the tears well up in his eyes as he put the spurs to Hercules. The other troopers had mounted up, and they brought their horses to a canter on the pike, as the smoke began to rise from William's large gin house.

Chapter Twenty Five

William Lovett Harrell was a veteran Confederate solder, thirty two years of age, with a tall and muscular build, and dark eyes and dark hair. He had enlisted in the Pulaski Greys in May of 1861, one month after he had married lovely twenty year old Elizabeth McCranie. They had just settled down on a small farm in Telfair County when the war broke out, and his buddies pressured him into joining a company of the 49th Georgia Infantry that was being raised over in Hawkinsville.

He went to Virginia and fought in the Seven Days Campaign, and the battles of Sharpsburg, Fredericksburg, and Gettysburg, without even receiving a flesh wound. He had seen Yankee soldiers run, and he had seen men die in battle.

He got a furlough during the Mine Run campaign, and he took the train cars down to Macon, and hired a horse at the livery, and rode down to see Elizabeth on their farm in Telfair County.

He was deeply in love with his curvaceous young wife, and he made love to her day and night on his furlough. He could not erase the image of her in his mind, her lovely hair and skin, her beautiful eyes, or the curve of her breasts.

He never reported back to the Army of Northern Virginia, and the Provost Guard was sent out in April of 1864 to look for him. He was luckily in the house eating his dinner after plowing the fields, and he crawled down a trap door inside the house, down into the root cellar. Elizabeth threw the day's washing onto the floor to cover the opening.

The provost guard knocked on her front door, made an inquiry about the whereabouts of William, and then mounted up to leave. The blue tick hound on the porch did not like the looks or the smell of the Provost Marshall, and began to bark angrily at him. The Provost Marshall pulled out his Colt pistol, and shot the dog dead.

William heard the gunshot, and poked his head above the trap door. "Did they shoot the dog, Liz?"

"Yeah, they did. And if you don't keep your head down, they'll shoot you, too."

* * * * *

William soon learned from the postmaster that if he were to enlist in the Georgia Militia, that the governor of the State of Georgia would grant him an immediate exemption from Confederate military service.

William promptly enlisted in Company "I" of the 7th Georgia Militia. For a while, he was able to live a blissful existence as a militia private, continuing to farm and to set up housekeeping with Elizabeth in Telfair County.

After Sherman's capture of Atlanta, though, the 7th Georgia Militia was called up, and was marched to Hawkinsville, Perry, and on to Fort Valley, where they were carried on the cars to Macon.

On November 23rd, 1864, on a cold day, a full division of Georgia State Line troops and Georgia Militia troops were assembled under the command of General Gustavus Smith, and were marched out around eight miles east on the Georgia Central Railroad to a small town near the Twiggs and Jones county lines. Griswoldville was named after Samuel Griswold, the famous cotton gin builder and designer. The town consisted of a post office, a series of shops, and Samuel Griswold's house, and the Griswold & Gunn Pistol factory.

General Judson Kilpatrick's Federal Cavalry had attacked Joe Wheeler's Confederate cavalry the day before there, and had driven them out of town. The troopers then burned the pistol factory, post office, and Griswold's shops, as well as rail cars backed onto a siding there.

When the Georgia State Line troops and Georgia Militia arrived at Griswoldville, they saw the level of destruction laid onto the town by the Yankees, and they were enraged.

At that moment, the rear guard of the 15th U.S. Army Corp was encamped near the Duncan Farm on the edge of Big Sandy Creek, with the flanks supported by cavalry, who were also guarding the wagon train of the 15th Corps. The Federal troops were under the command of Brigadier General Charles C. Walcutt, and were veteran troops. They had fought and defeated Rebels at Champion's Hill, Vicksburg, Dallas and New Hope Church, and Leggett's Hill.

They were armed mostly with Spencer Repeating Carbines. General Smith's scouts discovered the Federal troops outside Big Sandy Creek, and deployed his four brigades in attack formation. His troops were mostly old men and young boys, who had not experienced the shock of battle, and did not know what to expect from combat.

They attacked the entrenched Federals in a field near the Duncan Farm, and on no less than three occasions, the Federal veteran troops blasted them back with their repeating rifles. William's Company "I" charged the Federal works twice, and William saw their colonel and their captain get shot through the head on the second attack.

Young Johnny Stevens was with him, and Johnny foolishly attempted to get up and charge the Federal works for a third time. He grabbed him by the seat of his pants, and forced him down behind a Wax Myrtle bush. "Get down, boy, you can't take those works. These officers here are damn fools. Those men have repeating rifles, and they all have fought battles before."

The Georgia Militia attack failed miserably, at a cost of 750 killed and wounded. The Federal troops had lost 125 men, including General Walcutt, who was wounded in the leg, and had to travel to Savannah in an ambulance.

General Smith ordered his beaten forces back to Macon. William Harrell decided that his militia officers were all damn fools. He would do his duty and stick with his outfit for one more fight. If his officers were to needlessly throw away lives again, though, he planned to light out and head back home to his pretty wife and farm in Telfair County.

* * * * *

The left wing of the Army of Georgia soon approached the Georgia State Capital, which was Milledgeville. The Georgia General Assembly was in session, all of the members claiming to be stalwart foes of the tyranny of the Black Republican Government of Abraham Lincoln.

Once the Federal troops were detected on the north end of Baldwin County, though, a mad scramble ensued among the stalwart foes of tyranny to simply get out of town. Horses and carriages dashed madly about, some even running into other wagons and carriages on the streets, in a mad rush to flee the Yankee army.

Some legislators of the General Assembly offered to hire buggies and horses at $500.00 and even $1,000.00 per carriage. Governor Joe Brown packed up all the furniture in the beautiful governor's mansion, and loaded it on a wagon for Macon. He lit out on the Garrison Road in great haste, not wanting to be captured by Federal troops in his own Executive Mansion.

General Sherman's Twentieth Corps had previously entered Milledgeville from Madison, Georgia. General Slocum established his headquarters in the Milledgeville Hotel. General Sherman moved into the Governor's Mansion that had been stripped and vacated by Governor Brown the evening before.

The Georgia State Arsenal near the State Capitol was destroyed by Captain Poe's engineers. David journeyed over to the State Capitol later that evening, as some of General Sherman's officers staged a mock legislative session that evening. They stood on the paper streamed floor of the Hall of Representatives, and they passed several mock bills of legislation.

Captain Audenried stood up on the floor, and proposed a bill to repeal the ordinance of secession for the State of Georgia. It passed, by a wide margin. Major McCoy arose, and proposed a resolution that Jefferson Davis, President of the so-called Confederacy, be promptly and immediately kicked in the pants.

David saw an opportunity to make some more fun, and remembered some of the parliamentary procedures used by the 1861 Georgia General Assembly:

"Would the distinguished Senator from...uh...Atlanta yield the floor?"

"Why, of course." Major McCoy did not yet understand what David was up to.

"I propose that Senator McCoy's measure be amended, so that the kick across Jeff Davis' rumpus be placed not on one side, or the other side of his rumpus, but be given right down the middle."

There were shouts and laughter and applause from the "Legislators", who adopted David's amendment by a wide margin.

Later that afternoon, David and Major McCoy were walking out to the Capitol Gate, when David noticed several Union troops of the Provost Guard, the 125th New York Regiment, ransacking the Georgia State Library, throwing books out of the second story window.

David was horrified that public property was being destroyed in that manner.

"Oh, sir, please order those people over there to stop destroying the State Library. That type of destruction does no good, it doesn't win the war. It will only bring a reputation of infamy and disgrace to this army. Please stop them, sir."

Major McCoy observed their activities, and agreed with David. He called to a sergeant major in the 125th New York, and asked him over.

"Sergeant Major, I am issuing orders to all troops not to burn or destroy public library books or public archives here. I will send Lieutenant Snelling back with a written order that you are to post on this building.

You are ordered to post an armed guard of six men around this building. Go in there and order your men to stop ransacking this library at once. Do you understand me, man?"

"Yes, sir. Right away, sir."

The sergeant major entered the library, and David heard yelling throughout the library, and the book tossing stopped. He turned back to Major McCoy.

"Thank you, Major. I was here in January of '61 when the Union flag was hauled down in this square. It flies here again now, and one day soon, it will fly here for good. Georgia will need her records when she returns back to the Union."

Major McCoy began to walk out the Capitol Gate, near to the picket line where their horses were tied. He stopped and turned toward David before he mounted up.

"I'll have the appropriate orders drawn for you to take back in one hour. You will need to report to the Governor's Mansion then. That is where General Sherman has set up his headquarters." "Thank you, sir." David saluted Major McCoy, and walked down the street to get Hercules, where he had tied him at the Milledgeville Hotel.

David rode up Greene Street from the Capitol, up toward the Garrison Road, to the large Greek Revival Executive Mansion of the State of Georgia.

He tied his horse Hercules out on the side yard of the mansion, and walked past Federal First Alabama pickets that were set by Sergeant Looney.

David entered the building, and saw that Governor Brown had emptied it of furnishings completely. He stepped out past the foyer, and saw the rotunda above him, looming up above the front staircase.

He then spied Major McCoy seated in the next room near General Sherman, who was seated on a hardtack box, with a roll of blankets and haversack full of hardtack nearby.

David saluted General Sherman, who greeted him in his usually cheerful manner. Major McCoy handed David the order to post at the State library, when a rider in a Union Army colonel's uniform rode up. He was led to Major McCoy, who promptly introduced him to General Sherman.

"General Sherman, this is Colonel Charles Howard, who is just up from Gordon. He has news of a battle that was fought near Griswoldville on the 22nd."

"Where the hell is Griswoldville?" said General Sherman.

David knew the area well, and rapidly supplied the information. "It is about eight miles east of Macon on the Georgia Central Railroad. It is at the Jones and Twiggs County line."

"Thank you, David. Go on, Colonel, brief us on the battle."

"Well, sir, Walcutt's brigade had the duty to guard the trains that were parked near a large log church. I think they called it the Mountain

Springs Church. Walcutt had most of his brigade deployed east of the little town, across a field, near a swampy creek.

The Rebels sent a whole division of militia against 'em, and they were beaten off after they had charged our boys two and three times."

"Did you get any report as to casualties?"

"Yes, sir. They hit us with 5000 men, and left 300 dead on the field. We wounded 1200 of their men, and they only got 100 of our soldiers. General Walcutt was wounded in the leg, though."

"Where is he now?"

"They are marching over to Gordon and over toward Irwinton, sir. General Walcutt is in an ambulance."

"I may just decorate him for this. Tell him 'well done' for me when you next see him, colonel. Major McCoy, bring us Captain Poe's map of the middle part of Georgia."

"Yes, sir."

General Sherman lit another cigar, and began pulling on his beard, while Major McCoy spread the map out over a hardtack box.

"Lieutenant Snelling, come over here and show me some points on this map where we need to be vigilant. I don't want any more surprises. We will cross the Oconee over the toll bridge here, and march down the Kings Road to the Sandersville Road. What does Howard's Corps need to look out for, Lieutenant?"

David studied the map for just a moment.

"Well, sir, there is Ball's Ferry, which is on General Howard's line of march. The Oconee River current is swift there sir, about nine knots, and that is the only decent ferry point for fifty miles.

The Oconee Bridge of the Georgia Central Railroad is above there, just below Toomsboro. There is trestle work for two miles on the west bank of the river, and for one half mile on the east bank of the river."

General Sherman was swift to size up the situation, and issue the appropriate orders.

"Colonel Howard, I am going to have Major McCoy prepare written orders for Colonel George Spencer and the First Alabama Cavalry. He is to send at least fifty men to capture and hold Ball's Ferry on the Oconee River. I will also issue orders for General Howard to capture and burn Oconee Bridge and the causeway trestles below Toomsboro. You will ride down and transmit the orders after they are written."

"Yes, sir."

"Lieutenant Snelling, you will ride out on another scout after we get down to Sandersville, say around Tennille Station. We might need some more horses by then, and I want to scout well between here and the Oconee.

We have perused some Augusta newspapers that say that General William Hardee has been given command of all Rebel troops in the state. I think he only has coastal defense forces under his control. He is a very good soldier, though, and because of that, we must be vigilant."

"Yes, sir. I will go out whenever you want me to, General."

* * * * *

They moved out of Milledgeville across the toll bridge over the Oconee the next day. They marched out in clear, cool weather down the Kings Road toward Sandersville.

They crossed over some large hills and through steep and narrow roads, and then crossed the fall line, where the red clay gave way to sandy, loamy soil. They marched through pine forests of Loblolly and Shortleaf Pines, and saw occasional cleared areas containing cabins and small cornfields.

They halted near Gumm Creek and made camp at the home of a Widow Oxley. General Sherman used her parlor as his headquarters, and David and some of the staff officers camped out in the widow's back yard.

While David was engaged in cooking cornmeal hoecakes over the campfire, General Sherman came out of the house, smacking his lips on Aunt Faith's boiled fruitcake.

"David, tell me son, why do they call this delectable morsel a boiled fruitcake? And what all is in it, anyway?"

David flipped the hoecake over in the iron skillet as it browned.

"General, she put cut and preserved cherries and preserved pears from her orchard into that fruitcake, along with shelled pecans and Black Walnuts. She sweetened the cake with honey and sorghum molasses."

"Yeah, but how was it boiled?"

"It was mixed up and poured into a metal pan and cooked in a hot oven. Aunt Faith would remove the cake every ten or twenty minutes and stir it, until most of the water was boiled out of it. Then she spooned the cake into a smaller metal pan, and set it in the spring house to cool. That is how it took its shape."

General Sherman ate the last bite of cake, smacking his lips all the while. "It is just a culinary masterpiece. It was even better than the wonderful beefsteak I had tonight. Major Hitchcock, where was the best beefsteak prepared in St. Louis?"

The major finished his hoecake, and walked over to the campfire. "I don't know about St. Louis, sir, but the best beefsteak I ever enjoyed was at the Maxwell House in Louisville. It just melted in my mouth. A large Porterhouse steak, wrapped in bacon."

Major McCoy decided that it was time to play a little joke on Major Hitchcock.

"Major Hitchcock, go ask Lieutenant Snelling where his best 'beefsteak' was had."

Major Nichols removed his kepi and began to chuckle, and Major Hitchcock then knew he had been had. He walked into their joke anyway, and asked David the loaded question.

"Lieutenant Snelling, where did you have the best beefsteak of your life?"

David finished his corn hoecake, took a sip of hot coffee, and addressed Major Hitchcock. "Well, sir. We were at Stones River on the night of the first day of the battle. It was cold, cold, weather, in the twenties, sir, much colder than what we saw last week above the Little River.

Wheeler's cavalry had captured all of our supply wagons on our side of Stones River, and we were on short rations. We ran out of rations near dark, when Wheeler's Cavalry attacked us. We fought hard from our breastworks and beat 'em off of us twice, and they left their dead and wounded on the field.

We shot up a good number of their horses and mules, and near midnight, we were very hungry. Lieutenant Day comes up to me and says. 'Sir, I'm so hungry I could eat a horse.' My eyes got big as saucers, and I organized some parties, and we carved up the haunches of those dead horses and mules, and we cooked 'em on the wheels of smashed caissons.

I had one 'beefsteak' from the rump of a dead horse, and I tell you sir, it was marvelous. General Crittenden came over to tell us to put out our fires, and we gave him a 'first rate beefsteak' To this day, I still think the General thought he had eaten cow meat that night."

The staff officers all laughed, and Major Hitchcock was taken aback. "Lieutenant Snelling, you are a hard man, sir. A hard man, indeed."

General Sherman lit a cigar with a Lucifer match, and threw the spent match into the campfire. "It takes hard men like Lieutenant Snelling to win this war, Major. You need to remember that."

David took his leave of the officers, and stood his watch on the picket line near the General's headquarters that night.

* * * * *

Two days later, they entered Sandersville behind the advance guard of General Sherman's first brigade. Wheeler's cavalry began firing at the advance guard in the streets of Sandersville, some men even firing down from the windows of the court house. David heard several rifle bullets whiz past them as they advanced up the street. The Rebel horsemen were driven out of town quickly, and David spied a dead Rebel trooper on the portico of the brick court house.

General Sherman set up headquarters in a large frame house on the other side of the square, and immediately began issuing orders at once.

The court house was to be burned, because it had been used as a fortification. Two or three stores would be burned in retaliation for Confederate troopers burning the bridge over Buffalo Creek. They were delayed a full day at Buffalo Creek, until Captain Poe brought up the pontoon train.

After the midday meal, they marched four miles south out to Tennille Station. They marched through pine forests over a sandy road, in the cool, crisp autumn air. The Army's cattle driven behind the column had increased, even though the men were shooting and consuming fresh beef daily.

David was halted with part of the column by an attractive forty five year old woman who sought a guard for her house and smokehouse. She was dark haired and well mannered, and David brought her to Major Nichols, who ordered a guard posted around her house. Her husband was an officer in the Army of Northern Virginia.

David also passed details briskly engaged in ripping up tracks and destroying rails by heating and bending them. They marched out again at midday, past the Widow Peacock's. That evening, an old black man approached General Sherman, and told him that he wanted to be sure that they were really "Yankees". He told the General: "This nigger can't sleep dis night."

On some former occasion, General Wheeler's Confederate cavalry had donned light blue overcoats, and had impersonated Union soldiers. When the Negroes had shown them sympathy, they were beaten by the Rebel troopers.

He told the General that he wanted to be sure before he committed himself. General Sherman stepped out with him on the porch of the building he was using for his headquarters, and asked the Negro to look across the horizon.

As far as he could see, campfires were burning, and they appeared to be almost as numerous as the stars in the sky.

General Sherman asked the old man if he had ever seen such a sight before in his life, and the old man was convinced that the "Yankees" had arrived in force.

* * * * *

On November 29th, near the middle of the day, General Sherman's party rode into Tarver's Mill on Limestone Creek.

The mill was below a creek that was backed into a cypress swamp by the dam, which contained a decent flume which turned a sound grist mill. The men appropriated the corn meal, and prepared corn bread for their mid day meals. A large Live Oak shaded the mill, and Spanish Moss hung down from all of the trees.

Judge Tarver owned the mill, and the white two–story frame house nearby. He had been gone for two weeks, and had left his womenfolk at the mill. David caught the eye of a lovely girl of sixteen or seventeen years named Kathleen that was dressed in a simple homespun dress. She had black hair and blue eyes, and was greatly agitated about the presence of all of the soldiers at the mill.

General Sherman told them to get buckets, and to save as much meat and salt and meal as they could. He then posted a guard on their house day and night, consisting of no less than six armed soldiers.

They moved out after dinner, and David was ordered east to scout, and to pick up some fresh horses for the staff officers. He took Sergeant Looney and four other men, heading south and east into Emanuel County.

They were going down into Emanuel County to scout for Rebel cavalry, and to steal horses. David always thought that he was being ordered to do something he could hang for in civilian life, and that was stealing horses.

They rode into the little town of Cross and Green, where they got four horses at a livery stable. They took five more fine animals from a paddock near Summertown, and then turned north to rejoin the main column.

They were riding ahead in a column along the road, when they were fired on by Rebel troopers, who gave them chase. David put the spur to Hercules, and the fabulous horse leaped across ditches and ravines, tearing away from their pursuers. David purposely led the Rebel troops in his direction through the forest, and they began to close in on him. He then spied three deer in a meadow off the road, a buck and two does. He spurred Hercules in their direction, and the deer bolted back into the Rebel column, confusing David's pursuers.

David doubled back and rode nearly fifty miles back to camp, where he rejoined General Sherman's headquarters near Midville. His backside ached, and his joints throbbed, as he dismounted from the saddle and rejoined the headquarters camp. Some of the staff officers of General

Sherman had thought David had been captured, or "gone up", and some wagers had been made over his fate when he did not return by noon on the second day. David did not care about the wagers, he was only glad to be back, and only sought relief for his aching backside.

* * * * *

On December 3, 1864, General Sherman's vanguard put pontoon bridges over Buckhead Creek, and entered the important railroad town of Millen. The general declared a three hour halt in Millen, so its warehouses and substantial train depot could be destroyed.

The depot was constructed of wood, mostly Slash Pine and Longleaf Pine, and the car shed was support by a series of graceful wooden arches.

The downtown area contained a hotel, and three large frame storehouses. Two of the storehouses had been used to store grain and foodstuffs for the Confederacy. One of the storehouses had recently been used as a prison for Union officers. The hotel was constructed as a white frame two-story structure, and had a large dining hall, and several outbuildings.

When General Sherman's headquarters party arrived in town, soldiers of the 17th Corps were already hard at work tearing up railroad track.

The hotel had been abandoned by its tenants, except for a number of Negro women and small children. There was one resident of the hotel that was described as crazy white woman, who had lived there for several years. The owners of the establishment fed her as a charitable gesture, and she lived there free of charge. David posted a guard of ten well armed men around General Sherman near the hotel, and went toward the outbuildings to find some forage for the horses.

As he rounded the rear entrance way of the hotel, he noticed that straggling soldiers were setting fire to the rear of the structure. The soldiers had been angered because the owners had refused them service in the dining hall for the midday meal.

The heart pine around the rear of the hotel building began to catch fire and burn, assisted by turpentine the soldiers tossed onto the clap boards of the hotel.

David and Captain Dayton rushed to where the headquarters horses were tied, near a picket fence at the rear of the hotel. They dashed across the railroad tracks with the horses in tow, and retied them under a Swamp Oak tree at a house located three hundred yards from the depot.

When they arrived back at the hotel, the dining hall was engulfed in flames. Someone suggested that the crazy woman was still inside the burning hotel. David, Captain Dayton, and Major Hitchcock rushed through the burning structure, dodging smoke, searching for the crazy white woman.

She was soon located in the garden, where she was found holding a gray "Hong Kong" goose. She was over fifty years old, and looked to be out of her mind. Major Hitchcock found a Negro woman that said she would take care of her, and gave her $5.00 U.S. to hold, until she could make arrangements for the woman. Negro children piled out of the hotel with salvaged bed clothing and bedding. Major McCoy appropriated a wagon for them, and the refugees were transported to a nearby church.

General Sherman had set up headquarters in a large frame house located up hill from the Millen railroad depot. At 1:00 p.m., an old man by the name of Paul Myers attempted to speak to General Sherman concerning his cabin. He complained that soldiers were about to burn it down for no reason.

Captain Dayton sent a courier over to General Leggett to determine why Myers' cabin was burned. General Leggett sent a note back within the hour, indicating that the cabin was burned because 100 bales of cotton had been discovered concealed in a vault underneath it.

Major Hitchcock cross-examined and sharply questioned the old man, who admitted that he had claimed to be a citizen of Philadelphia, but had lived in Georgia since 1861. He admitted that the cotton was purchased in March of 1861 at eight cents per pound, and was being held by him and his son–in–law for resale at a future date.

Major Hitchcock lectured Myers on cotton being declared contraband by the Federal Government, and that he could not speculate in cotton without taking certain risks. Myers soon left in disgust.

The headquarters officers soon had a grand view of the burning of the railroad depot, storehouses, and ticket office.

T.R. Davis of *Harper's Weekly* walked out with them toward the opposite side of the depot, and sketched the burning depot for his publication. Flames rose up the Longleaf Pine pillars, and soon engulfed the entire structure, as the heart pine heated up, and was engulfed in the flames.

General Howard rode up to confer with General Sherman, and he complained about the utter lack of discipline among the soldiers in the ranks. A nearby store had been completely and totally looted of all its wares and foodstuffs.

The town of Millen had been partially destroyed out of military necessity. It had almost been completely destroyed due to the avaricious plundering of some undisciplined troops. General Sherman was persuaded to issue a standing order through Captain Dayton, A.A.G., to the division commanders and to the headquarters guard and provost guard, which would allow the arrest and /or the shooting of soldiers who willfully set fire to public or private dwellings without orders.

* * * * *

December 8, 1864
Below Eden, Georgia

Dear Uncle Uriah and Aunt Faith:

General Sherman has pushed his army ever closer to the gates of Savannah itself. General Corse and the 4th Division of the 15th Corps pushed out thirteen miles ahead of the main army yesterday. His division put pontoon bridges across the Savannah Canal, and his whole division has entrenched between the Ogeechee and Little Ogeechee Rivers.

General Hardee had McLaw's Rebel Division dug in above them at Ogeechee Church, and they had to rapidly withdraw during the night back into their prepared defenses around Savannah.

We move out today toward Station No. 1 on the Georgia Central Road, or toward Pooler, as the little town is called. We have had very good weather during our march south, and hope to complete our investment of Savannah before the winter rains commence.

It was wonderful to get to see you again, and I hope to see you again soon following the close of this war. I have to go now, and direct a party as they unload General Sherman's headquarters' stores.

Yours very truly,

David

* * * * *

On December 9, 1864, General Sherman's headquarters party began to march southeast toward Savannah, along the road leading into Pooler.

Cannonading soon commenced that morning, and David noted the sound of the Rebel guns as they fired from General Hardee's lines. David then heard an explosion of two separate rounds in the road ahead, which did not sound at all like cannon fire.

He and Major Hitchcock and Major Nichols rode up with General Sherman to see what the explosion was.

Adjutant Frank Tupper of the First Alabama Cavalry had been leading his horse down the road, when the animal stepped on two torpedoes buried in the road. The torpedoes exploded, killing his horse, and blowing off his right foot just above the ankle. A piece of the shell penetrated his same leg below his knee, and he had another fragment enter his right hand.

Other troopers applied a tourniquet to his leg, and had him covered with a blanket. David dismounted and took Frank Tupper by the hand, and gave him some words of encouragement.

A gang of Rebel prisoners were being marched across the field, when a Rebel sergeant observed them and stopped to comment. "Looks like you found some dangerous ground there, Yank." The sergeant began to laugh, and pointed over at Frank Tupper, who continued to lie on the ground. He was in excruciating pain, but uttered no word of complaint.

David became enraged. He ran over to the Rebel sergeant, drew his Colt revolver, and hit him across the face with the gun barrel. He then turned the gun around, and whipped the butt end of the pistol handle across the sergeant's face, breaking his nose. He pulled the sergeant to the ground, cocked the pistol, and shoved the end of the pistol barrel up into the sergeant's bleeding nostril.

"You little Son of a Bitch, you refuse to come out and fight like men, so you resort to planting bombs in the road. You will tell me where you have planted them here and now, or I will plant you, do you understand?"

At that moment, Major Hitchcock rode up and called David down. "See here, Lieutenant, your methods are barbaric and violate the laws of war. You have gone to excess here."

At that moment, General Sherman rode up. "I approve of his methods, Major Hitchcock. He had the right idea, he just did not have the necessary numbers of men to accomplish our objective. Major Nichols."

"Yes, sir."

"Who has the Provost Guard duty today?"

"The Second Wisconsin Regiment, sir."

"Have them bring up all of the Rebel prisoners captured over the past three days. Give them a pick and a shovel each, and then order them to uncover their own torpedoes out in the road. Major Hitchcock, I told you that it will take hard men like Lieutenant Snelling to win this war. Carry on, Lieutenant. Snelling"

"Yes, sir."

The Rebel prisoners were soon brought out, and they very carefully uncovered seven more buried torpedoes in the road. Some of the torpedoes were 12 lb shells with a friction tube that was set to trigger an explosion when the shell was stepped on. An entire battalion of First Alabama Cavalry had passed over the shells without incident, until Frank Tupper had stepped onto two of the shells some time later. General Sherman then rode back to camp near Pooler, where he prepared general orders to General Slocum and General Howard to invest the City of Savannah.

* * * * *

The next morning, December 10, 1864, General Sherman issued Special Field Order No. 130, ordering all of the Corps Commanders to invest the City of Savannah.

General Sherman's 20th Corps and the 14th Corps occupied the left part of the line to the Savannah River. The Army of Tennessee (17th and 15th Corps) extended to the right, and down to the Ogeechee River below the City of Savannah. General Howard sent out scouts in small boats to open communication with the Union blockading fleet in Ossabaw Sound.

The weather was cloudy, foggy, and rainy. General Mower's division began their advance down the Louisville Road below Pooler, and General Leggett's division followed.

General Sherman and some of his staff officers had taken breakfast at a white frame house on the Louisville Road. General Sherman later mounted Sam, and trotted down the road in the direction of Savannah. David was required to follow, along with Sergeant Looney and twelve First Alabama troopers.

They then heard the report of cannon fire, and heard a rushing noise overhead. A solid shot had been fired over their heads, and struck the road above them back toward the frame house. David saw that General Sherman was in immediate danger, and he put the spur to Hercules, and caught up with General Sherman near a Water Oak tree.

"General, they have the range on us. I saw two Whitworth Rifles up the road. It is my job to protect you, sir."

General Sherman nodded his head. "You are right, I will go back. Those shells are from 32 pounders, though. We need to go behind the railroad cut. That will be the safest place in this cannonade."

They rode back past the white frame house behind a culvert near the railroad cut, which was four feet deep.

Solid shots continued to hurl at them, and shot bounced off the road every four minutes.

A Negro was standing out near the road, and the shot had taken off the back of his skull as it passed by. The Negro slumped over, instantly dead, as the 32 pound ball bounced up the Louisville Road. General Sherman and his staff officers prudently marched back beyond the railroad cut, putting a little more distance between themselves and the Rebel works.

* * * * *

On December 11, 1864, General Sherman decided that Fort McAllister had to be taken. The army was running rapidly out of supplies, and contact had to be made with the U.S. Fleet. General Howard had sent a regiment of engineers to rebuild King's Bridge over the Ogeechee River below Savannah.

On the evening of December 12, 1864, General Sherman, his cavalry escort, and his headquarters staff rode over the rebuilt King's Bridge, and spent the night with General Howard at Mr. King's house. Late that night, General Sherman ordered General Hazen and his division to assault and carry Fort McAllister by storm.

The fort was made of an unusual series of mounded earthworks that resisted even the concentrated fire of rifled Union naval guns. It was considered a formidable fort from the direction of the sea, because it could withstand heavy fire, and because of the heavy artillery emplaced inside the fortifications. The land front of the fort had a good parapet, ditch, fraise, and chevaux–de–frise, cut out of the large branches of Live Oak trees.

The fort commanded the approaches to the Ogeechee River, and was garrisoned by 250 Confederate troops, under the command of a Major Anderson.

General Sherman, his staff, and his escort cavalry rode down the river to the rice plantation of a Jeffrey Cheeves, where General Howard had established a signal station from the roof of a rice mill.

Captain Samuel Bachtel of the U.S. Signal Corps was in command of the wig wag station, and General Sherman rode up and began to issue orders to him directly. The captain was dressed in a regulation blue Union Army uniform, with crossed signal flag insignia on his coat sleeve. That denoted his duty as an officer in the U.S. Signal Corps.

They left their horses behind stacks of rice straw behind the mill, and they climbed onto the roof of the rice mill. David got out his field glasses and began to scan the horizon. From the rice mill roof, they could see out toward Ossabaw Sound, and across the Ogeechee River at Fort McAllister.

At two p.m., David saw a column of smoke out in the sound, and they saw a gunboat approach their position. As the boat approached from Ossabaw Sound, David could make out several officers on deck. He could also make out the Stars and Stripes flying from the masthead of the vessel. Naval officers in the vessel began to wig wag signal the signal station on top of the rice mill.

They signaled, "Who are you?" General Sherman had Captain Bachtel reply "General Sherman". The boat officers asked: "Is Fort McAllister taken?" General Sherman replied: "Not yet, but it will be in a minute!"

General Hazen's division then emerged from the woods, lining up as if on parade, their U.S. colors and regimental colors flying. They then formed up into lines, their bayonets fixed and gleaming in the sun, and they marched in toward the fort at the double quick.

The Confederate troops in the fort began to pour musket fire and some cannon fire into the assaulting Federal column. Some of the Union troops encountered buried torpedoes, that exploded on contact, killing some of the attackers instantly. The parapets filled with smoke as the lines of blue coated troops swept forward and swarmed over the parapets.

A few moments later, the Battle Flag of the Confederacy was hauled down, and Old Glory was raised above Fort McAllister. The observers on top of the rice mill let out a series of cheers.

General Sherman was anxious to make contact with the fleet that night. He commandeered a skiff at Cheeves Mill, and called for a volunteer crew. David, Captain Merritt, and Major Nichols told him that they were good oarsmen, and General Sherman took a seat in the stern sheets, and asked them to shove off. The tide was running in, and the men had a hard pull around the bend in the river, and rowed hard for three miles over to Fort McAllister.

General Howard asked to come along, and he joined General Sherman in the stern sheets of the skiff.

On the way down, they passed the wreck of a Union Navy steamer that had been sunk years before in an attack on Fort McAllister. They soon encountered a picket on the beach, who guided them to McAllister's plantation, where General Hazen had established his headquarters.

He was in the process of eating a meager supper of canned beans, bacon, hardtack, and coffee when General Sherman's party came calling. General Hazen graciously invited all of the officers to join him, Sherman and his staff officers congratulated General Hazen and his division on his brilliant victory.

General Hazen reported his losses to General Sherman at ninety two killed and wounded. He reported that his men killed fifty men of the Rebel garrison inside the fort, and they captured 250 men.

They went down to the fort after dark, and inspected the works, and David noticed the dead bodies of the attackers and the defenders in the moonlight of the full moon. They were lying near where they had fallen in battle. Burial parties would inter them the following morning in proper graves.

The rising moon gleamed across the sound, and General Sherman was determined to make contact with the Union Fleet immediately. They piled back into the skiff, and pulled down the river toward the sound. They rowed in unison with each other, and the four oars pulling through the water allowed them to double their speed with that of the Ogeechee River current.

Six miles downstream from Fort McAllister, on the other side of Shed Island, they saw a light, and they hailed the gunboat at anchor in the river.

They were welcomed aboard the vessel by a naval officer wearing eagles on his shoulder patches, and sporting long side whiskers and a cylindrical cap. He identified himself as a Captain Williamson of the U.S. Navy, captain of the gunboat *Dandelion*.

Captain Williamson informed them that Admiral Dahlgren was in command of the South Atlantic Squadron, and his flag vessel *Harvest Moon* was presently lying in Wassaw Sound. General J.G. Foster was in command of the Department of the South, with his headquarters at Hilton Head.

General Sherman immediately asked for pen and paper, and he penned several dispatches at once. One was addressed to the Secretary of War. The other dispatches were addressed to General U.S. Grant at Petersburg, and to Admiral Dahlgren and General Foster.

Captain Williamson took them back upriver to Fort McAllister, where General Sherman and his party pulled over in their skiff.

Late that night, Admiral Dahlgren sent a steamer to Fort McAllister after General Sherman, and he and his party steamed down river to Admiral Dahlgren's flagship, the *Harvest Moon*.

Admiral Dahlgren was a pleasant and courteous officer, and told General Sherman that there was nothing he would not do to assist his army. He offered to send demolition parties to Fort McAllister to remove any unexploded bombs or torpedoes from the works. He went to work immediately, and ordered vessels of light draught to carry mail and supplies to General Sherman's troops at Cheeves' Mill and King's Bridge, from Port Royal.

General Foster immediately arranged a shipment of six hundred thousand rations from Port Royal, and for the transport of 30 pounder Parrot Rifles to King's Bridge.

General Sherman's army would use the Parrot Rifles to open fire on the City of Savannah.

When General Sherman and his party returned from Admiral Dahlgren and the *Harvest Moon*, the general issued orders to prepare the wharf and depot at King's Bridge for receipt of the guns and supplies.

David was asked to run a number of horses and mules down from the Louisville Road to King's Bridge, and to assist the second Michigan Engineers and Captain Poe in repairing the depot at King's Bridge. All roads heading into Savannah were corduroyed with heavy split logs, in anticipation of the arrival of the heavy siege guns.

* * * * *

David was later sent out to help some of Captain Poe's men dig a gun emplacement for a heavy thirty pound Parrot Rifle. Their work was arduous in the swampy region below Savannah. They had to cut through vine tangles and briars, and Gallberry bushes in order to dig the gun emplacement, and move the Parrot Gun into position.

At daylight on December 21st, General Sherman's men found the City of Savannah evacuated, and sent word to General Sherman that General Hardee's forces had evacuated the city.

David and the First Alabama Cavalry escort rode with General Sherman down Bull Street to the customs house, where they observed the wreck of the ironclad ram Savannah still smoldering. General Hardee's forces had set fire to the navy yard, and scuttled several ships to keep them out of Federal hands.

They rode over to the Pulaski Hotel, where General Sherman attempted to establish his headquarters. He was approached there by a Charles Green, an English gentleman that offered his spacious house and stables up for his headquarters instead of the Pulaski Hotel.

Admiral Dahlgren was once again asked to clear torpedoes and barrier obstructions from the river above and below Savannah, and the U.S. Navy responded with heavy working parties and steamboats.

One hour after taking up quarters in the Green House, General Sherman was visited by a U. S. Treasury Agent, one A. G. Browne. The agent claimed in the name of the Treasury Department all captured cotton, rice, and stores in the public buildings.

General Sherman told him that the army had captured most of the stores, and they would mostly be distributed to and by army quartermasters. However, any excess materials would be given to the Treasury Agent. Mr. Browne suggested that General Sherman send a Christmas gift to President Lincoln, who enjoyed such things.

General Sherman took a scrap of paper, and wrote out a note for the telegraph operator at Fortress Monroe:

Savannah, Georgia December 23, 1864
To His Excellency President Lincoln, Washington, D.C.,

I beg to present you as a Christmas gift the City of Savannah, with one hundred and fifty heavy guns and plenty of ammunition, also about twenty five thousand bales of cotton.

W.T. Sherman, Major–General

* * * * *

December 25, 1864
Savannah, Georgia

Dear Uncle Uriah and Aunt Faith:

Merry Christmas from beautiful Savannah, Georgia. General Hardee evacuated his forces across the river the night of the 20th, and scuttled all of the vessels in the navy yard.

General Sherman's troops entered the city the next morning, and General Geary was named acting military governor of Savannah. Order has been restored here, and our army has secured the warehouses and wharves along River Street and Bay Street.

Savannah will be turned into a Union depot. Major Nichols has been charged with maintaining the headquarters mess, and he has sent me out to procure delicacies such as oysters and flounder for General Sherman's mess table. General Sherman has set up his headquarters in a fabulous house off of Bull Street, owned by an Englishman named Green. Major Nichols had a huge tray of turkeys prepared for Christmas, and we had all of the oyster dressing we could eat.

Negroes by the hundreds have been by the general's headquarters to see him. The general has even given the freed men the opportunity to farm on the barrier islands off the Georgia coast. I doubt that these people have the resources needed to farm anything different from subsistence farming. Preparations are about to be made for the invasion of South Carolina. We all are in hopes that this will be the final campaign of the war.

May the Lord bless and keep you.

David

Chapter Twenty Six

Just after Christmas, General Sherman had all of the soldiers of the Army of Georgia assemble and march down Bay Street in Savannah for a grand review. A viewing stand was constructed in front of the Cotton Exchange on West Bay Street, and General Sherman and his staff officers reviewed the troops of the Army of Georgia.

The men marched by in their regimental groups, by division. The foot soldiers marched by with their rifles, haversacks, and forage caps. Some of the regiments had dogs as mascots, who walked behind their regimental colors. Some soldiers had stolen gamecocks from several plantations along the way, and cages of gamecock crates on carts and wagons followed some of the regiments.

Wholesale promotions were handed out after Savannah was taken. Captain Poe had been promoted to colonel. General Judson Kilpatrick had been promoted to division commander. General George Spencer of the First Alabama Cavalry was promoted to brigade commander.

David had been named General Sherman's permanent escort cavalry commander. The infantry, being jealous of David's role as a cavalryman, convinced General Sherman to include a headquarters guard of sharpshooters that would rotate the duty every fourth week from infantry units. David welcomed the extra help in guarding General Sherman.

David stood by General Sherman's box with his Spencer carbine at the ready, watching the First Alabama Cavalry march by on Bay Street. Five years before, he had stood under those same Live Oak trees, pondering his devotion to the Union, and agonizing over whether he could serve in the Confederate Army.

He now stood on the same street, watching a triumphant Union Army march through the streets of Savannah. He knew in his heart that he had been right to hold out for the Union cause, in spite of the personal loss he experienced as a result.

They were winning the war now, and it was only a matter of time before the remaining Confederate forces would be compelled to surrender.

The 33rd Massachusetts band marched by, playing the tune of Julia Ward Howe, The Battle Hymn of the Republic.

David saw the rows of polished bayonets go by, and was reminded of her lyrics:

I have seen His fiery vengeance
Gleaming rows of burnished steel
As you deal with my contenders
With my mercy ye shall deal...
Let the man born of woman crush the Serpent with his heal...
While God is marching on...
Glory, glory,
hallelujah...

* * * * *

The second of January, 1865, involved a concerted movement of General Sherman's forces. The 17th Corps transported from Savannah to Beaufort, South Carolina, aboard the ships *Harvest Moon*, the *Pontiac*, and the *Coit*. The crossed onto the mainland via a pontoon bridge, and marched on Pocotaligo, which was twenty five miles inland. Many of the soldiers of the 17th Army Corps became seasick during their short voyage, and complained that they would never again be transported by sea.

General Sherman and his headquarters staff left Savannah for Hilton Head by steamer on January 21st. Heavy rains soon came, flooding creeks, oxbow lakes, and marshes along their line of march. The Savannah River soon left its banks and flooded low lying areas, presenting innumerable difficulties in moving an army.

General Slocum was ordered to cross his wing at Sister's Ferry, which was forty miles above Savannah. Captain S. B. Luce of the U. S. Navy gunboat *Pontiac* was assigned the task of ferrying Union troops across the Savannah River. General Slocum soon sent word to General Sherman via the navy that the Savannah River was three miles wide at Sister's Ferry, and could not be bridged with his pontoon train. General Sherman then rested his troops at Pocotaligo until the weather turned clear and cold, and the river level fell to more normal levels. After two divisions of the 20th Corps were across the river, General Sherman issued orders to march north from Pocotaligo.

General Schofield's 23rd Army Corps was ordered east from Nashville, Tennessee, and would transport to Beaufort, North Carolina via Baltimore, by sea. Schofield's troops were ordered to march up the railroad from Beaufort to Goldsboro, and to rebuild the railroad line along their march route.

On January 14th, nine regiments of the 17th Corps crossed a 600 foot bridge at Whale Branch. They soon ran into a force composed of three regiments of South Carolina Cavalry and infantry that were dug in on a road above them. Their position was surrounded by a swamp, and included at least five pieces of artillery.

Leggett's Division flanked the position, as the Union troops waded through swamps, and set up a skirmish line in an area that enfiladed the Confederate position.

The Rebels soon realized that they had been "flanked" at dark, and pulled out of their prepared lines near Pocotaligo before sunrise the next morning.

The First Brigade of the Third Division of the 20th Army Corps dislodged Confederate Cavalry from Lawtonville Crossroads with a similar flanking movement. In three successive days, the Confederate troops were turned out of strong positions that seemed to be impregnable on flooded swamp causeways.

The 20th and 14th Army Corps, on the other hand, had been ordered to cross the Savannah River at Sister's Ferry, and make the appearance of threatening Augusta, Georgia.

The Third Cavalry Brigade, consisting of the First Alabama, the Fifth Kentucky, the Fifth Ohio, and the Thirteenth Pennsylvania Cavalries, crossed the Savannah River, and occupied the town of Barnwell. Many of the men in the brigade believed that South Carolina brought about the war, and were determined to punish the state for its role in commencing the secession process among the Southern States.

They forced the Confederate cavalry out of the small town of Barnwell. After sunset, Kilpatrick's troopers began to set fires which destroyed most of Barnwell. Many of Kilpatrick's troopers soon nicknamed the town of Barnwell "Burnwell", instead.

* * * * *

February 8, 1865
Bamberg, South Carolina

Dear Uncle Uriah and Aunt Faith:

I have been retained as the commander of General Sherman's Cavalry escort, even after we reached and captured Savannah. We transported to Beaufort by steamers of the U.S. Navy, and then we marched up to Pocotaligo with the 17th Army Corps.

We marched from Pocotaligo to Ficklin's Plantation, Hickory Hill Post Office, and then to Duck Creek. Mower's Division and G. A. Smith's Division captured River's Bridge on the

Salkahatchie, and got us through a long and dismal swamp without great loss to the army. Some of the men waded through waist deep water to outflank the Rebel troops in the Salkahatchie Swamp.

The army's maneuvers in this state have fit into a typical pattern, viz, the troops reach a Rebel obstruction of artillery and earthworks mounted on a causeway in a swamp. Union troops invariably wade through water and mud and flank the Rebel position, and capture or turn the Rebel position by their flanking movement.

The army has a Corps of Pioneers of nearly 5,000 men that carry axes, saws, and picks. They have cut down trees and saplings, built bridges, and corduroyed roads all along our route from Beaufort. Some of the Rebels have felled trees and erected obstructions before us, and the Pioneers have cleared them away almost as fast as they were initially erected before us.

We have struck the South Carolina Railroad here at Bamberg, cutting Charleston off from Augusta and Columbia off from direct rail communication with both cities.

We aim now for the South Fork of the Edisto River, and Orangeburg. From Orangeburg, the state capital of Columbia is within easy striking distance.

We march out in the morning. I wish you all the best of health, and you are always in my thoughts and prayers.

Very Truly Yours,

David

On February 14, 1865, the division of Charles R. Woods of the 15th Army Corps crossed the Little Congaree River, and repaired the bridge so the rest of the army could cross over.

They were later attacked on the edge of a pine forest by a force of Confederate cavalry. General Wood's skirmishers soon advanced into the pine woods and drove the Rebel troopers back.

General Sherman, his staff officers, and cavalry escort crossed the Little Congaree, and camped in the cotton fields of an old plantation. There, General Sherman issued his orders for the investment and occupation of Columbia.

On February 16, 1865, General Sherman's lead corps arrived on the Congaree River, opposite the city of Columbia. General Sherman issued orders to Captain De Gres not to shell the town itself.

The next morning, General Howard's column marched into Columbia, astride a pontoon bridge that had been laid the night before. The Mayor of Columbia soon came out and surrendered the city, and asked for orders from the Federal troops.

General Sherman, General Howard and General John A. Logan entered the town with the 15th Army Corps. The city streets were filled with curious people milling about, and with smouldering bales of burning cotton. The wind had whipped up to a constant gale, blowing the cotton into trees, and onto roof tops. Cotton bales in the street had been set on fire and left by the Rebel Cavalry.

The town of Columbia was spacious and attractive, with three story brick buildings and tall churches with narrow steeples. Many citizens of Columbia were out in the streets, milling about, and were terrified that the feared Yankee Army had invaded their city in lieu of Charleston. Many state records and public stores had been removed from Charleston, and had been moved to Columbia to keep them out of reach of General Sherman's army. As fate would have it, General Sherman's Army feigned an attack on Augusta and Charleston, and drove through the middle of the state into Columbia.

David rode past saloons and hotels with General Sherman's staff officers, and was mortified when he saw local town owners handing out liquor to Union soldiers.

General Sherman selected a large two story house owned by Blanton Duncan as his headquarters, and ordered General Howard to post guards all around Columbia.

The 15th Corps marched through the town all that day, and marched out the Camden road. The 17th Corps placed a pontoon bridge over the Broad River above town, and did not enter Columbia.

General Sherman and Major Nichols then rode over to the residence of a Margaret Poyas, who had known General Sherman in 1845 when he was a First Lieutenant at Fort Moultrie. The general visited with Miss Poyas for a long while, and he then returned to the Duncan house to take a long nap later that afternoon. David and Major Dayton established quarters at the Nickerson's Hotel, where they dined and had some hot water drawn in their rooms, where they bathed. At eight p.m., as David was dressing, he noticed a bright light shining on the walls, which flickered and moved. It was a fire!

He completed his dressing, and ran down to the lobby of the hotel, where he saw Major Nichols. Major Nichols told him that Columbia was on fire, and high winds were spreading the flames beyond control. He told David that General Hazen's division and General Wood's division were actively fighting the fire, but the wind was fanning the fire across town. He ordered David to arm all twenty one of his escort troopers with Spencer carbines, and to report to the Duncan House at the double quick.

Flames and smoke poured from different buildings, as David and Sergeant Looney rounded up their men, armed them, and reported to the Duncan house. General Sherman personally ordered David to patrol the streets of Columbia from the market house to the Camden Road. He was to assist General Wood's troops and General Hazen's troops in fighting fires. He was to arrest any Union soldier that he saw deliberately setting fires. If the offender did not cease and desist after being hailed two times, the offending soldier was to be shot. General Sherman gave clear instructions to David, who acknowledged that he understood them.

David and his command then set out down the streets of Columbia. Near the market house, they stopped and assisted General Wood's troops in fighting a blaze at a two story house. They manned a bucket brigade, and threw water on the side of the clap boards until the house fire was extinguished.

They stopped and assisted some refugees in relocating to a safer area, and they protected some army rations and stores from looters that passed by the Duncan house.

Near the other side of the Camden road, they spotted three cavalrymen of the 9th Pennsylvania Cavalry, dismounted near two frame houses. The nearest trooper was a sergeant major, and was firing a porch with a lit pine knot when David hailed him. "Halt!, stop setting fire this instant! You are under arrest."

The sergeant looked up at David and began to laugh, and his comrades dismounted and lit pine knots with Lucifer matches.

As the Sergeant Major began to fire the porch of the house, he and his buddies began to sing:

"Hail Columbia, Happy land...
If I don't burn you...
I'll be damned..."

David pulled up his Spencer Carbine, and chambered a round. "I'll give you one more chance, Sergeant Major, halt! You are under arrest!"

The Sergeant Major took a swig of whiskey from a flask in his back pocket, and spit on the ground toward David. "Bugger off, you goody toad! We're busy here." He began to set fire to the other end of the porch as well.

David brought up his carbine, aimed at the Sergeant Major's chest, and fired. He was caught near his breastbone, and the .52 caliber round knocked him up against the front post of the porch.

The other trooper reached for his pistol, and Sergeant Looney fired, catching him behind the left temple. Both troopers were shot dead with their fire brands in their hands.

The third trooper bolted away, and rode his horse hard up the Camden Road. David immediately located a well behind the house, and buckets were brought out, and the fire was doused completely thirty minutes later. Most of the front porch had burned, but the house had been saved. The women and children that occupied the house were grateful that their home had been saved.

General Judson Kilpatrick and his staff officers soon rode up, in the company of the 9th Pennsylvania trooper that escaped earlier from the house. The general was dressed in high leather knee boots, a short blue coat with gold braid on the sleeve, and a purple waistcoat. Topping off his non regulation uniform was a large black hat. He had red hair, with long side whiskers, and he was only twenty six years old. However, he was a brigadier general in the Union Army, and had made a series of powerful friends in Washington. He hated everything Southern, and he had ordered his men to burn houses and barns in South Carolina along their line of march.

"Lieutenant, my man Sharp here says you shot down two of my troopers like dogs tonight. I ordered these men to burn all of the stinking Rebel houses, and you shot them for it! Whose side are you on? I am going to arrest you, and court martial you, buddy boy."

David knew that reasoning with the general was useless. He smoothly chambered another shell in his Spencer carbine, and pointed it at the general.

"General, I was following the orders of our commanding officer, General William Sherman, when I commanded these men to halt. They refused to halt, and I called them twice to do so. You are obstructing me from carrying out my lawful orders, sir. Your orders, on the other hand, are illegal, and you know it. This army does not deliberately burn out women and children. That does not win the war."

General Kilpatrick saw the Spencer Carbine pointed at him, and began to get enraged.

"Sergeant Locket, look at that insolent little bastard point that carbine at me! Go arrest him, now."

The sergeant began to climb down off his horse, and David fired a round that took off the sergeant's forage cap. He swiftly chambered another round into the Spencer, and aimed at the general. "The next round will be for you, general. Flying lead knows no rank. You had better leave me alone, or your men will plant you in South Carolina, tonight."

Kilpatrick's face turned red, and he was visibly enraged. "I'll see you hang for this mutiny, Snelling!"

At that moment, General Sherman, Major Hitchcock, Major Dayton and Major Nichols rode up. General Sherman's face was half covered in soot and grime. General Sherman was straightforward and to the point. "What in hell is going on here? General Kilpatrick, what is the meaning of this?"

Kilpatrick removed his black slouch hat, and mopped his forehead with his red handkerchief.

"General, this officer shot and killed two of my men. I want him brought up on charges and court martialed for murder and mutiny. Those men were acting under my orders."

"Lieutenant Snelling, tell me what happened here."

"General Sherman, we were patrolling the streets of town as per your orders, when we spotted two troopers attempting to fire this house. We shouted them down and ordered them to halt, but they instead set more fires.

We shot them when they refused to obey me, and attempted to burn out this family of women and children. We only followed your standing orders, sir."

"Did you order your men to burn out families here, General?"

Kilpatrick was backed into a corner. He could only confirm or deny that he had ordered his troopers to burn out private citizens in the town.

"Uh, sir, we have burned out only those who supported secession and disunion. Our men have it in for South Carolina, as they believe that this State caused us to go to civil war."

General Sherman then spied a four year old little girl, standing near the front porch of the dwelling, wide eyed with fear. "General, what type of politics does this child adhere to? We do not make war on women and children. Your men were shot because they disobeyed my orders. You have no business here. Get your command up to Winnsboro and Chesterfield at once. There will be no more talk of court martials.

Lieutenant Snelling simply obeyed my orders. Leave here at once, General."

General Sherman then gave David his lecture.

"David, remember that General Kilpatrick has some powerful friends in Washington."

David uncocked his carbine, and slid it into a leather holster on Hercules' saddle. "He's nothing but a little snot–nosed bastard, General Sherman."

General Sherman took two puffs from his cigar. "Just remember that snot nosed bastard ranks you. But if you and Kilpatrick ever go head to head, my money will be on you. Carry on, Lieutenant.

"Yes, sir."

General Kilpatrick and his men rode off, down the Camden Road. They turned north and rode above Winnsboro, up into a pine forest of Slash and Longleaf Pine trees. General Kilpatrick knew that the infantry had orders to march through the forest, and he set fire to the pine trees, causing a huge forest fire to burn for miles.

The burnt forest had to be traversed by the 17th Army Corps, and these men would have to march through miles of burned out woods. General Kilpatrick smiled to himself as he saw the forest burn. General Sherman and his men would have to eat a little dirt and soot to get to Winnsboro. They could eat the dirt and soot after him for a change.

* * * * *

The next morning, David rode out and surveyed a mostly burned and ruined city of Columbia. General Sherman ordered Colonel Poe to destroy the state arsenal, and some details were assembled to throw guns and ordinance into the Broad River. David rode by the South Carolina State Capitol building, and saw the Stars and Stripes waving proudly from its dome. The state capitol of the first state to secede from the Union was now in the hands of Union forces. Only two more capitals were left to be captured in all of the Confederacy east of Alabama. Surely the end of the war was near.

Some of the shells exploded while they were being unloaded at the arsenal, killing five men, and wounding several others. Details from the 17th and 15th Corps tore up miles of strap iron railroad track up the South Carolina Railroad.

Colonel Poe sent another detail out to destroy the Confederate Treasury Department engraving and printing presses that printed Confederate notes. Other public property and other supplies of cotton were also rounded up in the city, and were destroyed.

* * * * *

Two days later, the 17th Corps marched up to Winnsboro, and marched through the pine forest burned by Judson Kilpatrick. The men slogged through burned pine straw and leaves, leaving smutty feet, smutty trousers, and blackened faces at the end of their day's march. The 20th Corps arrived in Winsboro, just in time to put out a fire that was set by some of Kilpatrick's Cavalry. On February 23rd, the army had made the banks of the Catawba River, near Rocky Mount Ferry. Strong rumors had begun to circulate in camp that night that Charleston had been evacuated and captured by Union troops.

The men were relieved that the hot bed of secession had fallen after all the years of war.

* * * * *

Up in North Carolina, General Joe Johnston had applied to Jefferson Davis for reinstatement of the command of the Army of Tennessee. Jeff Davis had fired Joe Johnston in July of 1864, because he would not give a decisive battle to Sherman's forces. General Hood wrecked the Army of Tennessee in a series of futile attacks around Atlanta. He encamped the remainder of his army before Nashville in the dead of winter. General Thomas and his Federal troops attacked and routed the Army of Tennessee, and a beaten General Hood later resigned his crippled command.

The survivors of the Army of Tennessee were returned to South Carolina via Alabama and South Georgia, on the last remaining railroads available to move troops in the Confederacy.

Johnston had McLaw's Division and Kershaw's Brigade from the Army of Northern Virginia, along with Hampton's South Carolina Legion. The Confederacy had too little men to send him, though, and his only hope was to unite with the Army of Northern Virginia, and to defeat General Sherman's approaching army before the Army of the Potomac could react.

* * * * *

March 3, 1865
Near Thompson's Creek, South Carolina

Dear Uncle Uriah and Aunt Faith:

We have marched up below Chesterfield, South Carolina, in the historic hills of the Piedmont district of the state. The army made a great right wheel maneuver at Chesterfield, and we are heading straight for Cheraw. General Schofield is to land troops at the port of Wilmington, and his command has orders to join us in the interior of North Carolina.

Spring is in the air here in South Carolina. Plum, Peach, and Pear trees are in full bloom. I even spotted a few Honeysuckle Trees in the swamps near Lynches Creek. Hopefully, this will be the last spring of the war.

We have a resident artist in camp from *Harper's Weekly*, Mr. Ted Davis. General Sherman ordered him to draw three pictures of a 'ubiquitous' part of South Carolina life, to send north for the perusal of readers of *Harper's* and the *New York Times*. He told him to draw, as follows: (1) A palm tree, (2) A Nigger, and (3) a gamecock, in that order.

We are anxious to get through Cheraw and into North Carolina, where this army can fight the last desperate battle, and win the war.

I sit here in camp and see the beauty of the early blooms and greenery of spring. What I am reminded of, though, are the thoughts that the war can end way before summer, if all of us do our allotted work.

I hope and pray that you are in good health and good spirits, and long for the day when I may see you again.

Love,

David.

* * * * *

On March 9, 1865, General Sherman had learned that Joe Johnston had been given command of all Confederate forces in and about North Carolina. He knew that Joe Johnston was an able and skilled soldier, so orders were issued for all of the army wings to close up with one another along the line of march. David was summoned to General Sherman's tent on March 9th, and was ordered to take written orders to Colonel George

Spencer. Colonel Spencer was to order his brigade of cavalry to move closer in toward the existing infantry units, so both units could support one another in the event of Rebel attack.

David was to hand pick five men and a bugler, and carry dispatches to Colonel George Spencer. His brigade was ordered to close up with the 17th and 15th Army Corps, which had been ordered to invest and capture Fayetteville.

David round up his men and got an early start near Rockingham, but that evening a deluge of rain began to fall in torrents. David broke out his oilskin and waterproof kepi cover, while the other men broke out rubber raincoats. It soon became impossible to ascertain the proper path to take, or as to whether they were moving along a road or a deer trail.

David halted them under some tall Slash Pine trees, and drew his pocket compass. A check of his bearings indicated that they were moving in the right direction. They moved to the northwest, past Fayetteville, and over toward Monroe's Cross Roads. The rain had subsided about three thirty a.m., when they arrived at Monroe's Cross Roads. The whole town consisted of a post office, a store, and several decent sized log cabins.

David stopped before one of the cabins where he saw a light, and he called a halt. He was greeted at the cabin by a captain of the 13th Pennsylvania Cavalry, who identified himself as James Rice. Captain Rice was a by-the-book type of soldier, who was disappointed in his commanding general, Judson Kilpatrick. He had drunk a strong slug of whisky, and was somewhat under the influence of alcohol. David wanted to question him and obtain information as to movements of the cavalry, and their dispositions.

They were all too cold and wet to sleep, so they kindled a fire out in the yard near the cabin, and began to boil water for coffee. Captain Rice was short and compact, but had a powerful muscular build. He had black hair and blue eyes, and wore a tall forage cap. He had a bushy mustache that covered his entire top lip, all around the corners of his mouth.

Captain Rice was well versed on the antics and quirks of General Judson Kilpatrick. He was, in the colorful words of the Captain: "A whore monger and a whore hopper; a coward; a buffoon, an egotistical fool." Captain Rice, when he thought David was not looking, began pouring whiskey into his coffee from a metal flask he had in his coat pocket. When the whiskey began to take effect on him, he became even more talkative.

All of the cavalry brigade was deployed around a swamp about one mile down the road. General Judson Kilpatrick, at that moment, was at another cabin just up the road, making love to a beautiful woman named Marie Boozer.

Mrs. Boozer was a refugee from down near Columbia who was burned out of her house. Rather than curse the Federal cavalry that destroyed her home, she chose to be General Kilpatrick's consort.

She was according to Captain Rice "the most beautiful piece of woman flesh I ever beheld". Her skin was an alabaster color, her hair was black, and her eyes were a blue sapphire color. She was perfect in all of her features, and had the bearing of royalty.

General Kilpatrick rode into North Carolina in her carriage, and they had settled down for the evening in a cabin up the road from the cavalry encampment. David asked Captain Rice if General Kilpatrick had posted pickets around the swamp and up the road, and Captain Rice indicated that he thought that the picket party set up was woefully inadequate.

David immediately asked Sergeant Looney to send out two scouts up the road, and two additional scouts near the edge of the swamp. The bugler was to remain close by, to alert the encampment in the event of an enemy attack. The night had blown up cold after the rain shower, and there was a possibility that frost would be on the grass by seven a.m. the following morning. The daffodils and Red Bud trees were in full bloom, but Old Man Winter still had his grip on that part of North Carolina for the time being.

David listened to Captain Rice complain and belly ache about General Kilpatrick until he could stand it no longer, and then he excused himself and walked down to a nearby spring to clean up his mess kit and his coffee pot.

A reddish streak had appeared across the horizon indicating that dawn would soon come, and the sunrise would soon break over the eastern sky. Around ten minutes later, one of the pickets came riding hard from up the road, and halted and reported immediately to Sergeant Looney. Sergeant Looney then ran to David and indicated that the scout had spotted a sizable force of Rebel cavalry moving up the road in attack formation, with their regimental colors flying. David immediately ordered the bugler to ride into the Union cavalry encampment, and to sound the alarm. He then ordered Sergeant Looney to recall the other scouts from the swamp, and to report directly to Lieutenant Stetson, who commanded the artillery battery of the First Alabama Cavalry Regiment.

David then mounted Hercules, and rode over to Anderson Looney, with a wry look on his face.

"Anderson, we are presented an opportunity here that will only come around just once. I am going to ride over to the cabin where General Kilpatrick and Ms. Boozer are having sport, but I will only stay there for a moment. Please come with me at once."

They then rode up the road in the mud and in the puddles of rain water to a small frame house that some would call a cabin, but others would call a house, because some of the clapboards were whitewashed. A cavalry orderly from the 9th Pennsylvania Cavalry had been posted as a guard on the porch of the house, and David alerted him to the fact that an enemy force was approaching. He then told the cavalryman that he would go in and tell General Kilpatrick personally that a Rebel attack was forthcoming. The guard nodded his head, but had a terrified look on his face as David entered the small cabin, and entered a narrow hallway behind the main great room of the house. At the end of the hallway was a bedroom, which was covered by a hand hewn pine door, which was closed. David could hear General Kilpatrick and Ms. Boozer in the bedroom, in the act of passionate love making. David knocked on the door twice, and announced "The Philistines are upon thee, general."

The noise in the room stopped at once, and General Kilpatrick soon replied. "Is that you, Snelling? You little bastard, what do you want? Can't you see I'm not, uh, finished?"

"There's Reb cavalry coming up the road, general. I can see however, that you have better things to do this moment than fight the war."

David then left the house immediately, and looked up the road, only to see Reb cavalry flying at them at a smart trot, around 200 yards away. David leaped across the porch, and grabbed Hercules' bridle, and hefted himself into the saddle. Anderson came riding up behind him exhorting him to move with all haste, in a most respectful manner.

They thundered down the road toward the swamp with their horses' hooves flying, slinging mud over their shoulders with each stride of their horses in the soft North Carolina mud.

David and Corporal Bain and Anderson Looney arrived at the cavalry encampment near the swamp while it was being charged by Butler's, Hume's, and Allen's cavalry divisions which were being led by General Wade Hampton and General Joe Wheeler. The Rebs charged one side of the encampment, while David and Anderson and Corporal Bain arrived on the other side of the encampment. David immediately ordered Sergeant Looney, and Corporal Bain to locate Lieutenant Stetson's artillery battery. They drew their carbines, tied off their horses to trees, and walked into the camp with their heads down.

The Rebel cavalryman, clad in butternut jackets and slouch hats, succeeded in driving the Union troopers from their breakfast fires, and began to rout the Union troopers, and drove them into the heavily wooded area in confusion. David found Lieutenant Stetson at the foot of a Black Gum tree, taking shelter from the Rebel cavalry fire. Lieutenant Stetson pointed out the location of his six pounder gun, and the limber chest, which was nearby.

Pistol bullets flew past them as they took shelter near the foot of the tree, which was approximately 40 inches across at the stump. David had his Spencer Repeating Carbine, and chambered a shell immediately, and fired a round on the other side of the tree, killing a Rebel cavalryman who was charging their immediate vicinity. The only hope for rallying the regiment was to get the gun in action, as the Rebel cavalrymen had succeeded in driving most of the Union troopers away from the camp entirely. David asked Lieutenant Stetson if he could unlimber the gun and bring it to bear against the rebel troopers. Lieutenant Stetson indicated that he would need assistance to get the gun into action.

David ordered Corporal Bain to use his carbine to keep rebel troopers away from Lieutenant Stetson while he worked the gun. He then ordered Sergeant Looney to assist Lieutenant Stetson in unlimbering the gun and bring it to bear against the rebel troopers. Anderson began to protest: "But sir, I have never worked an artillery piece before."

David replied, "There is a first time for everything, Anderson." The gunfire from the Rebel troopers became more intense, and David had to crawl on his belly to avoid being hit by musket balls. He crawled past the Black Gum tree, and toward the limber chest of the section of artillery. He arose long enough to shoot a Rebel cavalryman out of the saddle with his carbine. He then took another position next to a White Oak tree, where he could comfortably cover the limber chest and gun within easy range of his carbine. Sergeant Looney and Lieutenant Stetson crawled toward the gun, and on their knees, unlimbered the piece, and began to load it with shot and canister. Lieutenant Stetson instructed Sergeant Looney to throw three bags of gun powder down the barrel of the gun, where Lieutenant Stetson immediately packed the powder home with a rammer. A solid shot and canister shot was loaded in immediately behind the gun powder, and a long quill was used to prick the bag of the gunpowder through the touch hole. Lieutenant Stetson then ran a friction primer into position, and asked Sergeant Looney to cover his ears. Two rebel troopers immediately charged the gun, and David shot them both dead with his carbine.

Lieutenant Stetson pulled the lanyard of the piece and the gun discharged, rocking back on its wheels and sending acrid smoke about the camp. Horses and men were bowled over, and the canister shot disemboweled man and beast alike.

The Rebel troopers understood the threat posed by the artillery piece, and began to direct their gunfire in efforts in the direction of Lieutenant Stetson's battery. Lieutenant Stetson and Anderson reloaded the gun carefully, but quickly. Anderson rammed a sponge rammer in a bucket of water, and swabbed out the gun to suppress any sparks left over from the earlier discharge of the weapon. New powder bags were inserted into the piece, and were rammed home with a tampion. Double shotted canister was then loaded into the gun, and rammed into position. A friction primer was then replaced, and Lieutenant Stetson elevated the gun slightly, and then pulled the lanyard again

Once again, the gun rocked back upon discharge, sending another cloud of acrid smoke across the camp. Horses and men were once again disemboweled, bushes and trees were clipped off by force of canister, which had the effect of a huge shotgun.

The Rebel attack was beginning to become more costly in men and animals, as other Union troopers used the gun as a rallying point, and began to rally around David and Sergeant Looney, offering the covering fire of their carbines against the Rebel attackers.

The additional troopers provided a covering gunfire against the attacking Rebel troopers, and gave Anderson and Lieutenant Stetson additional time to reload the weapon and service the piece.

Hume's cavalrymen then made an effort to charge the artillery piece in a column of twos. Lieutenant Stetson loaded the six pounder with canister, and calmly serviced the weapon while Rebel troopers began to bear down on them from across the camp. David and Corporal Bain fired five successive shots with their carbines, and emptied five saddles apiece. David soon ran out of ammunition in the carbine, and had to draw his Colt revolver. Hume's cavalrymen approached them within thirty yards, when Lieutenant Stetson pulled the lanyard of the piece. The gun rocked back again, and smoke once again billowed around the piece after it was discharged. The grape shot had an effect on the Rebel troopers that was incredible and devastating. Horses were crushed and disemboweled, men were thrown and blown to bits, and the first charge was broken in blood.

General Wheeler's men soon attempted a second charge at the artillery piece from across the camp, and David saw them coming, and ordered Corporal Bain to redirect his fire at Wheeler's troopers at the other side of the camp. David pulled the spherical tube from the stock of the Spencer carbine, and quickly slid seven shells into the tube.

He replaced the tube, and smoothly cocked the Spencer Repeating Carbine, and took aim at a major leading a second charge against them. David fired at the chest of the major's horse, causing the horse to somersault and throw its rider. Two other rebel cavalrymen were also thrown after making contact with the thrown major's animal. Lieutenant Stetson had one round of grape shot remaining, and he immediately and promptly loaded it into the six pounder. At the opportune moment, when the Rebel cavalrymen closed within forty yards, Lieutenant Stetson once again pulled the lanyard on the six pounder. The gun rocked back on its wheels and exploded another spray of fire and death at the charging Rebel troopers. A second attempt to take the weapon was once again broken in blood.

Ten minutes later, another more concerted effort was made to charge Lieutenant Stetson's battery. A more determined group of Rebel troopers made a charge from an area near the swamp, with some troopers zigzagging in between large trees between the battery and the swamp. David fired at those men with his carbine, until his ammunition was once again exhausted. He then drew his Colt revolver, and continued taking the Rebel troopers under fire. Lieutenant Stetson and Sergeant Looney had become frantic, as they had run out of grape shot and canister to fire at the Rebel troopers. However, David spied a large tin of round hard tack biscuits which had been newly opened for the morning breakfast, and had been abandoned by some of the Union troopers.

He walked over and picked up the tin of hardtack and handed it to Sergeant Looney and asked him to fire the tin of hardtack at the attackers, as that hardtack was certainly almost as hard as a lead canister ball, if not harder. Sergeant Looney gave an incredulous look at David, but David told him to pour them into the end of the barrel anyway, as they should have a similar devastating effect when fired at close range.

Anderson complied, and when the Rebel troopers closed to within thirty yards, Lieutenant Stetson pulled the lanyard on the artillery piece. The artillery piece once again recoiled and shot flame and smoke, and the hardtack biscuits maimed horses, and killed men.

At nearly seven thirty, the Rebel attack was withdrawn, as the three successive charges against Lieutenant Stetson's battery had utterly failed.

Later than morning, David went with Lieutenant Stetson on burial details to bury the dead that had fallen at Monroe's Crossroads. They counted 103 Confederate dead, and the 3rd Brigade of the Union troopers lost 18 killed, and had 70 wounded. Major Cramer of the First Alabama was wounded and taken prisoner, and Major Trammel was missing. David even sent a detail back to the small frame house to see about the welfare of Ms. Marie Boozer. Corporal Bain returned, and advised David that a party of the 5th Kentucky Cavalry had rescued Mrs. Boozer during the battle.

* * * * *

March 14, 1865
Fayetteville, North Carolina

Dear Uncle Uriah and Aunt Faith

The army has now captured Fayetteville, along with the large Federal arsenal which had been used to manufacture Confederate rifles and the other arms. The arsenal has been completely destroyed by the army. The machine shops and foundries have been pushed down with battering rams, and Colonel Poe has fired the buildings, so that even a foundation is not left to build upon. Several transports have arrived from Wilmington on the Cape Fear River, bringing supplies for the army. General Sherman has also ordered Negroes and other refugees that have been trailing this army back down to Wilmington, in the charge of a competent officer. These refugees totaled over 25,000 people, and they consumed a great number of our supplies. We are now crossing the Cape Fear River on the army's pontoon trains, and will be in the vicinity of Averysboro tomorrow. We are to move in the direction of Averysboro over to Goldsboro, and then from Goldsboro, on to Raleigh.

We were involved in a pretty sharp engagement at Monroe's Crossroads last week, and General Judson Kilpatrick was almost captured in the fight. He barely escaped with his uniform coat, his drawers, and a pair of boots on, and the 5th Kentucky Cavalry had to recapture his headquarters in order for him to finish dressing that morning.

The Rebel cavalry left a number of dead and wounded on the field, and Joe Wheeler and Wade Hampton personally led the charges against us. We used a six pounder horse gun with great effectiveness against them, and our men rallied and drove the attackers out of the camp. Our couriers have reached General Terry's troops at Wilmington, and General Terry sent a steam boat up the Cape Fear River with mail and news from the fleet.

We march now for Goldsboro and Raleigh, and hope to end the war as soon as possible. I long for the day when I may see you again, and hope that the Lord may bless you and keep you.

Very Truly Yours,
David

* * * * *

On March 16, 1865, General Hardee had placed his command near a strong position near Averysboro. They ran into Federal troops under the command of General Slocum. General Slocum deployed General Jackson's division of the 20th Corps in a rapid flank march, and the first line of the rear guard Confederate troops was completely captured. A large part of Rhett's brigade, and 217 Confederate soldiers were captured, along with a three gun battery. The Confederates lost 108 dead. A division of the 14th Corps was ordered up at noon, and then found that the Rebel line of works stretched from Black Creek to the Cape Fear River, at which point the river made a bend to the east. Their force was composed of three divisions, Butler's Division, Rhett's Division, and McLaw's Division, which consisted of around 10,000 troops. Hampton and Wheeler's cavalry were posted on the left flank of the enemy. It rained hard that night, and the Confederate troops evacuated their entrenchments under the cover of darkness back through Averysboro.

On March 17th, the entire army made a right wheel, marching in the direction of Smithfield and Bentonville. The country was found to be rich with forage and oats for the animals, as well as corn and hay. The peach and apple trees were in full bloom, and the army marched through a well cultivated country, cultivated by men who may own Negroes, but who are were not afraid to work beside them in the fields.

The Union troops appreciate this fact, and also appreciate the fact that the Old North State was the last to secede from the Union. For this reason, the usual deprivations that accompanied their line of march through South Carolina were not visited upon the Old North State. On March 19th, the army halted, and General Sherman's headquarters camp was pitched in the midst of soldiers of the 20th Corps. David arose on a cold March morning in the pine forest, to observe infantry soldiers frying potatoes in skillets, cooking chickens and other fowl on the red hot coals of their cooking fires. He smelled the aroma of coffee boiling in various coffee pots around the camp. He walked out of the fly tent that he shared with Major Hitchcock, and saw the sun beginning to show red in the eastern sky, under thin clouds. He walked out and rubbed down Hercules, and saw than he had grain and forage to eat, and water to drink. He then cooked his breakfast of bacon, coffee, and hardtack, devoured his breakfast, and prepared to move out with the rest of the headquarters party.

As the headquarters party saddled up and prepared to move out, David observed the infantryman breaking camp and marching out in files out into the road. All their knapsacks were strapped, their weapons were slung and ready, and the men fell into line as bugles blared. The bugle calls summoned the various infantry companies into position along the roadway. David looked at the blue coated soldiers, and recalled that he would soon miss this sight if the war were to end within the next month or so. He had grown accustomed to being near the infantry troops, and would miss his life in the army. The average person living in a happy home in a city away from the conflict, or in a farm away from the conflict would wonder why such things were to be missed. However, David considered himself part of a brotherhood, and he would miss this time he was spending in the service, strange as it might seem. At that point, they were breaking camp approximately five miles from Bentonville, where the road from Clinton to Smithfield crosses the Goldsboro Road. General Howard was at Lee's Store, two miles to the south, and both columns had pickets thrown forward for three miles forward of their position.

General Sherman's headquarters party began to move down to the New Goldsboro Road near Falling Creek Church, in an effort to join General Howard's column which was well strung out on the bad roads between there and Falling Creek Church. They had gone about six miles when they began to hear artillery booming off toward the north. Staff officers soon rode up and advised General Sherman that General Schofield had run into the entire Rebel army under the command of Joe Johnston himself. General Sherman then ordered up Hazen's division of the 15th Corps, which was back at Lee's Store, to fight a defensive battle until he could call up reinforcements from Blair's Corps near Mount Olive Station. A courier from General Terry rode up and indicated that his corps was at Faison's Depot, and General Schofield sent a courier indicating that his corps was near Goldsboro. General Sherman issued orders ordering the corps commanders to concentrate their forces at or near Bentonville as soon as possible.

Joe Johnston had attacked General Slocum's column aggressively and vigorously, capturing three guns and caissons from General Carlin's division, and driving two brigades of troops back on the main body.

General Slocum promptly deployed two divisions of the 14th Corps and two divisions of the 20th Corps on a defensive line, and he received immediate assistance from Kilpatrick's two brigades of cavalry. The combined forces of Hoke, Hardee, and Cheatham made successive assaults upon the Federal troops entrenched in front of Bentonville. General Howard soon brought his wing up the New Goldsboro Road, until his troops connected with the troops of General Slocum.

In the meantime, Hazen's division had reinforced Slocum's troops near the front lines, and sufficient barricades and entrenchments were constructed to make their position nearly impregnable from Rebel attack. General Sherman ordered artillery to shell the Confederate positions near Bentonville, and General Sherman ordered David to carry messages to the artillery commander, Captain De Gres. David returned from carrying the dispatch from General Sherman to Captain De Gres, only to spot T.R. Davis sitting on a hilltop with his sketch pad, sketching the artillery in action.

David peered over at T.R. Davis' work, which depicted a 12 gun battery in action on a small hilltop partially covered with Long Leaf Pines. The caissons and limber chests were pulled forward by the six mule teams hauling the wagons for each of the guns. The smoke and dust generated by the firing and recoiling of the guns were also depicted as hazes in T.R. Davis' sketch. The Rebel positions were depicted out in the edge of the large pine forest, and the panoramic sight was nothing short of breathtaking. David realized that the view was nothing short of spectacular, and hoped that the readers of *Harper's Weekly* could appreciate the spectacle presented by such a scene.

On March 21st, General Joseph Mower's division of the 17th Corps rashly attacked Confederate troops near a bridge across Mill Creek, which was the only line of retreat open to General Johnston's troops. Several of General Mower's troops were killed within a few feet of General Joe Johnston's headquarters. General Sherman knew that General Mower was impetuous, and had exposed his division too rashly, so he ordered a general attack along the line, which allowed General Mower to withdraw his division back to the 17th Corps' positions of the previous morning. At daylight the following morning, the Federal pickets encountered the lines deserted, and had determined that General Johnston had retreated back to Smithville, leaving his dead and wounded in the hands of the Federal troops.

The losses of the Federal troops around Bentonville was 1500 men dead and wounded. The Confederate losses were 250 dead, over 600 wounded, and over 1000 Confederates were taken prisoner. By March 21st, Goldsboro had been captured, along with its two railroad lines leading back to the seaports of Wilmington and Beaufort, North Carolina. The railroads had been repaired by Colonel W. W. Wright of the railroad department, and a large number of supplies therefore reached the army at Goldsboro on the 22nd. On the 25th of March, the New Bern Railroad was completed by Colonel Wright, and the first train of cars came in, giving the army a direct supply link from the depot at Morehead City back to Goldsboro.

The war was rapidly drawing to a close, and General Sherman was summoned for a conference with General Ulysses Grant, the general in chief of the armies of the United States.

On the evening of March 25th, David was summoned by a Major L. M. Dayton, and was ordered to arm five men with carbines, and to report to the railroad depot at Goldsboro to guard General Sherman as he made his way by railroad locomotive from Goldsboro to New Bern. Major Hitchcock and Major Dayton accompanied General Sherman, and met David at the depot at Goldsboro. Shortly after they boarded the railroad car, the train began to steam southeastward. There they boarded the railroad car, and the train began to steam southeastward through Kinston, and on to New Bern. During the trip south, Major Hitchcock sat with David and Sergeant Looney, and the topic of the reorganization of the army came up in the conversation. Major Hitchcock advised David that General Joseph Mower had been given command of the 20th Corps, and General Schofield had been left in temporary command of the army until General Sherman could return from City Point, Virginia. General Sherman was to travel by rail from New Bern to Morehead City, where he was to travel by way of the captured steamer *Russia* from Morehead City to Fortress Monroe, and from Fortress Monroe to City Point, Virginia.

Supplies of clothing and food for the army were to be shipped by rail from Morehead City to New Bern and on to Goldsboro. The army was to rest and refit at Goldsboro for the next campaign, which was believed to involve a final showdown battle with General Johnston's army somewhere in the neighborhood of Raleigh, North Carolina. All of the officers in the railroad car were in agreement that the status of the Rebel army was desperate, and that the Rebels would be ordered to fight one last desperate battle before the war could be put to an end.

For this reason, General Sherman issued orders reorganizing the army and refitting the army with supplies and ammunition, so that it would be properly equipped to fight the last great battle of the war. With the addition of the 23rd and 24th Corps under General Schofield and Terry, the army now constituted a body of roughly 80,000 men, together with General Kilpatrick's division of cavalry. They arrived a New Bern just at dark, and General Sherman and his accompanying guard and staff spent the night in a hotel near the railroad depot.

The next morning, they boarded the same railroad car behind the same locomotive, and the railroad car was off again in a south by southeasterly direction to the seacoast, to the port of Morehead City, across from Beaufort, North Carolina. At the railroad station at Morehead City, General Sherman was met by several wagons that were provided by

General Easton, where he was conveyed to the captured side wheel steamer *Russia*, commanded by Captain Smith. General Sherman, Major Hitchcock, and Major Dayton boarded the *Russia*, and the steamer put to sea at once, headed for Fortress Monroe, and City Point, Virginia. There at City Point, Virginia, General Ulysses Grant awaited General Sherman, and the President of the United States, Abraham Lincoln was also awaiting in a steamer known as the *River Queen*. David was instructed to remain at Morehead City until General Sherman could return, and to escort him back to Goldsboro upon his return from City Point, Virginia.

The few days that General Sherman was away at City Point with General Grant, David and Anderson Looney spent down at the docks fishing at Morehead City.

David found some excellent canes in a canebrake up the road from town, and they found some fishhooks at a general store, along with some decent fishing line.

They seized a few shrimp for bait at high tide, and they caught several mullet over the next two days. They invited all of the First Alabama bodyguard to partake of the mullet, which they fried up in a large iron wash pot.

On the morning of March 30th, General Sherman arrived back at Morehead City aboard the steamer *Bat*, commanded by Captain Barnes. Admiral David Porter loaned the *Bat* to General Sherman to return to his command.

They boarded the same locomotive and rail car that morning at Morehead City, and steamed on to New Bern. From New Bern, they ran up to Goldsboro, where the combined army was encamped. They army had been refitted and reorganized, as General Mower had been appointed Commander of the 20th Corps.

The Army of the Ohio under General John Schofield had united with the Army of Georgia at Goldsboro, giving General Sherman a combined force of over eighty thousand men.

On the way up from New Bern, David asked Major Hitchcock if he had heard anything about the war at City Point. Major Hitchcock explained that General Sherman had an audience with President Lincoln, who told him that too much blood had been shed in the war. General Sherman told President Lincoln that his troops would probably fight a final showdown battle. Mr. Lincoln expressed regret that such a battle should have to be fought, as it was his opinion that too much blood had been shed in the war.

General Sherman, though, was not convinced that a final showdown battle was not going to take place. He issued orders and prepared his forces for an attack from both Joe Johnston's troops, and the Army of Northern Virginia.

The railroads had by now been fully repaired from Morehead City and Wilmington, and the ground was so level there that 25 to 30 cars could be hauled by a single steam locomotive. Stores therefore arrived very fast, and the men were rested and reequipped for the final campaign.

General Sherman issued orders to move out on April 5th, but the army soon learned on April 6th that Richmond had fallen. The Confederate Army and Government had abandoned Richmond, and had fled west. General Grant's army was in close pursuit of the Army of Northern Virginia.

After receiving a dispatch from General Ulysses Grant, General Sherman set his troops in motion toward Raleigh. On April 11th, they marched into Smithfield, and on toward Raleigh. General Johnston's troops had burned the bridges over the Neuse River, however, and the Federal armies halted while the bridges over the Neuse River were rebuilt.

* * * * *

The Federal vanguard soon entered and occupied Raleigh, the capital city of North Carolina. General Kilpatrick and his cavalry division pushed on twenty miles up to Durham Station, where they skirmished with Joe Wheeler's Confederate cavalry.

On April 17, 1865, Sherman had arranged a meeting with General Joe Johnston to effectuate terms for the surrender of Johnston's forces. General Johnston had met earlier with Jefferson Davis, and had advised him that the continuation of hostilities would be 'nothing short of murder', since Robert E. Lee had surrendered the Army of Northern Virginia.

General Sherman was about to board a railroad car for Durham Station, when he was met by a telegraph operator with a coded message from the War Department. It was from the Secretary of War, Edwin Stanton, and the news it contained was shocking.

"President Lincoln was murdered about 10 o'clock last night in his private box at Ford's Theater in this city, by an assassin who shot him through the head by a pistol ball..."

General Sherman swore the telegraph operator to secrecy, and took his staff and escort with him to Durham Station.

They arrived at Durham Station on a train set up for the General and his staff, and there they mounted horses left there by Judson Kilpatrick's troopers. They rode forward to the Rebel lines with white flags of truce, where General Sherman and Joe Johnston met each other for the first time in person.

They met at the white frame farmhouse of a Mr. Bennett, who allowed the generals the use of his parlor for the surrender negotiations.

General Joe Johnston and General Sherman were professional soldiers. Both men knew that the war was over. General Johnston had met with Jefferson Davis earlier, and had attempted to convince him that further resistance was futile, as all Confederate forces to the Rio Grande should be surrendered.

General Sherman had met with President Lincoln some three weeks before on the *River Queen*, where the President had expressed a desire that the Southern men get back to work in their shops and in their farms, and that all further bloodshed cease.

At once, General Johnston was shown the telegram from the War Department concerning President Lincoln's assassination. General Johnston at once knew that the South had lost its best friend upon the death of President Lincoln. Both generals were determined to not only effectuate the surrender of General Johnston's forces, but to draft an instrument that could be used as a surrender vehicle for all remaining Confederate troops. General Johnston professed a desire to 'make one job of it.'

General Sherman then sat down and drafted a "Memorandum, or Basis of Agreement", which was much broader in scope than the terms General Grant offered Lee's army at Appomattox.

General Sherman gave the executed instrument to Major Henry Hitchcock, a noted constitutional lawyer and officer on his staff, and asked him to board the train to Morehead City, and to deliver the instrument to the War Department in Washington for approval. He ordered a strong guard for Major Hitchcock, and he ordered David to accompany him with Corporal Bain and five guards, armed with Spencer carbines.

They rode south in the General's special train to Morehead City, where the steamer *Bat* was waiting to take them to Washington. They quickly steamed north, up past Fortress Monroe, and up the Potomac River, and tied up on the Sixth Street docks the morning of the 21st. A buggy from the War Department picked them up, and drove them down Independence Avenue to Pennsylvania Avenue, and to the Executive Office Building, where Major Hitchcock reported to General Grant.

David was ordered to remain at the War Department, while General Grant and Major Hitchcock reported to President Johnson and the Cabinet at the Executive Mansion.

David had some business of his own at the War Department. He wanted to know the fate of his cousin Joseph, of Captain David Smith, and of Major James Riley, in the Confederate Army. He got a War Department civilian clerk to check the rolls of Union prisoners being held at the Libby Prison. David was informed the Captain David Smith had recently died of pneumonia, and the War Department was in the process of notifying his widow in Ohio. He had died at a hospital in Annapolis of pneumonia.

David was saddened by the loss of Captain Smith, but he was directed to a staff officer in the War Department concerning records on Confederate prisoners.

He went to the office of a Major Peck of the Army of the Potomac, and requested information on Confederate Major Joseph Floyd of Evans' Brigade of Ewell's Corps of the Army of Northern Virginia.

The major looked through several lists, and then found a list of prisoners from the Point Lookout, Maryland, Union prison camp. The major told David that Major Joseph Floyd had died on December 20, 1864, at Point Lookout, Maryland, of consumption.

David was staggered. He dropped to one knee, and began to blink back tears. He had loved Joseph like a brother, and the news of his death shocked him and staggered him. He begged the major's pardon, it was just the fact that Joseph was like a brother to him that made him react without discipline.

He asked the major to please look on the list of prisoners and recent casualties of the Army of Northern Virginia. He wanted to ascertain the fate of Major James Riley, Archer's Brigade, Hill's Corps of the Army of Northern Virginia.

Major Peck looked through another list which contained the names of paroled Confederate officers from Appomattox Court House. He then looked through the casualty returns of Archer's Brigade, and found an entry and copied it onto a separate sheet of paper.

"Lieutenant Colonel James Riley was killed at Five Forks, Virginia, this past March."

David took the information from Major Peck, saluted him, and thanked him for his time. He had loved two women in his life, and both of those women were now widows. He then realized that his love for Angela had not really been a mature love, but his love for Janet was with his whole heart.

More than anything, he wanted to marry Janet, to make love to her, and to spend the rest of his life with her. He would somehow make his way back to Franklin, and find an appropriate way to woo her. He knew that she would go through a period of mourning for one year, but he could call on her and her family, and he could assure her that his intentions toward her were honorable.

Angela was another matter. Her son Matthew now stood to inherit Greenbrier, should William Floyd die. Some effort had to be made to get Angela and her son back to Georgia.

He took his leave of the War Department, and went down to the Sixth Street docks. He found some representatives of some of the steamship companies there, and learned that he could purchase a round trip steamer ticket from Savannah to Richmond.

A number of northern steamship companies had established service down to Richmond, as a number of curious people had demanded to see the captured Rebel capital.

David then bought one ticket from Savannah to Richmond round trip, and composed a letter to Uriah:

April 21, 1865
Washington City

Dear Uncle Uriah:

I am sending this first to Savannah by regular steamer, and am hoping that the regular mails have resumed from Savannah to Milledgeville.

Enclosed please find one round trip steamer ticket from Savannah to Richmond, along with additional Federal greenbacks for the purchase of other steamship tickets. I have ascertained at the War Department while here on business as to the fate of cousin Joseph Floyd, and was deeply saddened to learn that he had died at Point Lookout, Maryland this past December.

I assume that you will agree that Angela and her son Matthew belong at Greenbrier, as opposed to living in Richmond. Since I am under duty to General Sherman and cannot leave my post, I am hoping that either you or some other reliable person can journey to Richmond and escort Miss Angela and her son back to Greenbrier.

My duties will require me to rapidly return to North Carolina shortly. You may write me at General Sherman's headquarters, Military Division of the Mississippi.

Yours Truly,

David

* * * * *

David enquired as to which steamers on the dock which would be heading to Savannah. He then paid the captain of the vessel a modest sum to carry his parcel to the U.S. Post Office in Savannah.

David then paid a cab to transport him back to the Executive Mansion on Pennsylvania Avenue. He was met at the back entrance of the White House by Major Hitchcock, who was on his way out.

They had been ordered to return to Morehead City by the steamer *Bat*, and to report to General Sherman immediately.

David summoned Corporal Bain and the balance of the headquarters guard, who escorted them down to the Sixth Street docks in buggies provided by the War Department.

A buggy followed them that was loaded with staff officers, and a short, bearded man who smoked a cigar, and had three stars on his shoulder straps.

David at once knew that was General Grant. He began to ask questions of Major Hitchcock when their buggy pulled off for the docks. The surrender negotiated by General Sherman had been presented to the Secretary of War and to President Johnson and the Cabinet, and it had been rejected.

It was rejected because it contained too many provisions that guaranteed the rights of the Southern belligerents. Too many political points were addressed in the surrender instrument, and there were issues in the agreement that should have been addressed by the Congress itself.

General Grant was being sent down to order General Sherman to prepare a new article of surrender for General Johnston that would be similar to the surrender terms agreed upon by General Lee at Appomattox Court House.

They left that afternoon aboard the steamer *Bat*, where they were joined by Lieutenant General Ulysses Grant and General James Rawlings, General Grant's chief of staff. After the evening mess, David joined Major Hitchcock at the taffrail of the steamer, where he was smoking a cigar. David had noticed that the major was angry, and had something on his mind. He had been seeking an appropriate time to speak to the major, so he walked up and asked him what was bothering him.

Major Hitchcock told him that the Secretary of War, Edwin Stanton, had openly accused General Sherman of being disloyal to the Government, on account of the extremely generous surrender terms he had offered Johnston's army.

The major indicated that he believed that General Sherman was acting to accept Johnston's surrender under the professed desire of President Lincoln to end the war quickly, and in such a way as to avoid useless bloodshed.

General Sherman had done just that, and in the process, was accused of disloyalty by a politician who never served in war as a soldier.

David did not understand the nature of the political infighting that had pervaded Washington after the assassination of President Lincoln. The conspirators had stabbed Secretary of State Seward, though not fatally, and had made attempts on other government officials.

Edwin Stanton, the Secretary of War, was now running the government de facto, and recently issued a number of orders to countermand General Sherman's authority as commander of the Department of the Mississippi. General Sherman was being ordered to resubmit the instrument of surrender to General Johnston on terms similar to the terms offered the Army of Northern Virginia.

On the way down Chesapeake Bay, the steamer met some Atlantic rollers, and most of the party became seasick. The weather was pleasant, and the ride was exhilarating, but the gloom of the political battle that General Grant witnessed at the Cabinet meeting was cast over them all.

* * * * *

They arrived the following Sunday evening at Morehead City, where they boarded a train to New Bern. The ride was quick and delightful up to Goldsboro and Raleigh. The Dogwood trees, Azaleas, and Wisteria were in full bloom, and the air was filled with the perfume of Honeysuckle and wild flowers along the way.

They arrived at General Sherman's headquarters the next morning before he was even dressed. General Grant broke the news to General Sherman, who arranged another conference with General Joe Johnston.

David and his small command were instructed to remain at headquarters, while the generals renewed their conference at Dunham Station.

The talk among the officers gravitated around employment or pursuits to be obtained after the war. David was slightly amused at the conversations he overheard. Before the war, men asked other men if they were going to join the army. Near the very end of the war, soldiers were asking each other about what occupation they would pursue after the war.

David met with Colonel George Spencer concerning a position in Decatur, Alabama, which involved school teaching, and newspaper publishing. He wanted to go work in North Alabama after the war, as it would present an opportunity to visit and court Janet Riley up at Franklin, Tennessee.

David knew that if he accepted a position created by Colonel Spencer, that he would be expected to help him politically. He did not care about that. He only wanted to be close to Janet. Decatur, Alabama was not that close to Franklin, Tennessee, but it was close enough. He planned to accept the position and move to Decatur after he resigned the service.

On the 20th of April, 1865, General Johnston and General Sherman executed a rewritten military convention which was executed and approved by General Grant. General Sherman, his escort and his staff returned to Raleigh by rail. General Grant returned to Washington, carrying the original surrender documents to the War Department with him.

General Schofield was ordered to take the paroles of the Confederate soldiers, and to inventory their arms and public property.

On return to Raleigh, General Sherman summoned all the army commanders together at his headquarters. Generals Schofield and Terry and Kilpatrick were to occupy North Carolina with their commands. The two other wings of the army were to march to Rocky Mount and to Weldon, and then on to Richmond, to await further orders.

On the 29th, General Sherman, one half of his escort, and part of his staff officers took a special train to Wilmington, North Carolina. David went with General Sherman, along with Major Hitchcock and Major Dayton. There in Wilmington, the steamer *Russia* awaited, and Captain James Smith cast them off at high tide, setting a course for Port Royal.

That evening, after a fine dinner served in the wardroom, David was summoned up on deck to speak to General Sherman, who was up on the railing smoking a cigar.

"David, General Grant brought me several dispatches from Washington. I received a letter from General Grenville Dodge, who now commands the Department of the Missouri. He is fighting Indians out on the plains, and he has specifically asked for you. He says that you and Sergeant Looney are the best judges of horseflesh he has ever seen. David, if you want to go out West, I will write you out a commission as a major in the Regular Army. God knows you should have been promoted to a major already."

David was taken aback by the General's offer. He was honored and thrilled deep inside of him, but he knew that if he accepted a western posting that he would never see Janet again. He struggled with his answer to General Sherman.

"Sir, I am deeply honored that you think so highly of me. However, I have accepted a position as a school teacher in Decatur, Alabama. I am also deeply interested in a woman up in Tennessee, and I don't think I could seriously court her if I were out on the plains fighting Indians."

General Sherman took two puffs from his cigar, and pulled on his beard a couple of tugs. "I don't blame you for wanting to leave the army, son. After this week, I may leave the service myself."

David saluted General Sherman, and reported to Major Hitchcock down at the galley. He was in the process of writing out orders for the resupply of the Federal arsenal at Augusta, Georgia. David was asked to recopy General Sherman's orders to General Gillmore's troops at Port Royal.

The next afternoon, they rounded Cape Hatteras, and the following morning, the *Russia* tied up at Port Royal, where General Sherman and his party greeted the Department Commander, General Quincy Gillmore.

There to meet them was an officer that had been dispatched from Macon, Georgia, a tall and lanky captain George Hosea.

Captain Hosea was a member of General James Wilson's staff. He gave an oral report to General Sherman of General Wilson's cavalry column. General Wilson had armed 13,000 cavalrymen to a man with Spencer carbines and Henry rifles, and had marched south eastward from Eastport, Mississippi.

On the way south, they had defeated Bedford Forrest's cavalry, wrecked dozens of railroads, and had captured Columbus, Georgia and Macon, Georgia. Captain Hosea had been sent south from Macon by General Wilson to procure supplies from the Union Navy.

General Sherman at once ordered David to form a guard, and to guard the captured steamer Jeff Davis while it was being loaded with supplies. The steamer was to travel from Port Royal to Savannah, and on to the Federal arsenal at Augusta, Georgia.

The steamer was to be loaded with coffee, hardtack, sugar, and other supplies for General Wilson's cavalry in Macon. While they were guarding the supplies during the loading operation, a sergeant in General Gillmore's command delivered a letter to David. It was from his Uncle Uriah:

April 29, 1865
Savannah, Georgia

Dear David:

I received your letter from Washington City, and promptly made arrangements to have Angela and little Matthew returned here by steamer from Richmond. We are now on our way back to Greenbrier, thanks to Joe Buck McGee.

Your letter had greater significance than you realized. Your Uncle William died this past December, and now Matthew has inherited all of Greenbrier.

The Court of the Ordinary has appointed me Executor of William's Estate, and I will seek an appointment as legal guardian of Matthew. I have set Joe Buck McGee up in the lumber mill, and business will be booming shortly.

David, if you have any notions of returning to Milledgeville after you leave the service, please think again. Julia Bonner saw you in your Federal uniform when you came through Milledgeville last November.
You have been excoriated to my face no less than ten times, and some of the men around here speak of bushwhacking you. If you return to Milledgeville and try to start a business, I assure you that it would suffer badly on account of your Federal service during the war.

I suggest that you relocate to Tennessee or northern Alabama after the war. Angela and her son are heading safely home, thanks to you. Please stay in contact with us.

Sincerely,

Uriah

* * * * *

David read Uriah's letter, and was thankful that Angela and Matthew were now safely on their way home to Greenbrier. He was also grateful that the sawmill there would provide them with a way to make a decent living, as railroads would now need cross ties, and lumber would be in very high demand now.

General Sherman ordered the captain of the *Russia* to convey them to Charleston Harbor, where they saw the Stars and Stripes flying over Fort Sumter.

They tied up at the docks, and walked down Broad and Meeting streets. The city of Charleston had been heavily damaged by Federal bombardments, and had been partially burned when the Confederate garrison set fire to the railroad depots at the time they evacuated the city.

The *Russia* again steamed out the same afternoon, passing into the Cape Fear River after a voyage north. On May 4th, they reached Morehead City, where David and his guards received orders to report to Salisbury, North Carolina.

David said his good byes to Major Dayton and Major Hitchcock, and he reported to General Sherman in Morehead City for the last time. He found the general on the pier, cutting off the ends of new cigars. He saluted the general, who returned his salute.

"David, you are a damn fine officer. I applaud and respect your loyalty to the Union, son. If you should change your mind about reporting to General Dodge, send me a telegram. I'll write you out a commission at once. Good luck to you."

"Good luck to you, General Sherman. Thank you for the opportunity, sir."

David took his leave of the general, and he and his guard detail took a train from Morehead City to Goldsboro, and then to Raleigh, where they rejoined the regiment.

When they arrived at Raleigh, they learned that the entire regiment had received orders to report to General George Thomas at Knoxville, Tennessee. David was overjoyed. He was at last heading back to Janet Riley, his true love.

Chapter Twenty Eight

The First Alabama Regiment left Hillsboro and marched to Greensboro, and then to Salisbury, where the troopers' horses were reshod. They then proceeded west through Lincolnton, Rutherford, Asheville, and Bull's Gap.

On May 31st, they arrived at Knoxville, Tennessee, having marched another 450 miles. The regiment was then ordered to Huntsville, Alabama on June 9th, and they reported to Major General Robert S. Granger on June 14th in Huntsville. David used the opportunity at that time to call on the school where he had accepted a position as a teacher of history and English, and to call on the newspaper where he was to work as an editor.

He drew a great deal of back pay, as he had acted as a company commander since 1862, and had only been paid a First Lieutenant's pay scale since that time.

Companies "I" and "K", having served the longest in active duty, were ordered to report to Nashville, Tennessee, in order to muster out their men.

They marched north up through Fayetteville and Shelbyville, and on to Murfreesboro, and over the pike into Nashville, where a great battle had been fought in December.

They once again reported to the cavalry depot at Camp Campbell, where the men received their orders to muster out by July 19th.

He lined up his company at assembly the following morning, and shook the hand of each trooper in his company. It was hard to part with the men he had served with for three full years. His Uncle Uriah had been correct. He was part of a brotherhood, and he would never forget the troopers that served with him.

He spoke to Sergeant Reid, Lieutenant James Day, and finally, to Sergeant Anderson Looney. Sergeant Looney was one of a few men who planned on going west, and would enlist to fight Indians under General Dodge.

Anderson was sincere when he addressed David: "Good bye, sir. It has been an honor serving under you. I hope that you become half the school teacher that you were a soldier, sir."

David shook Sergeant Looney's hand.

"Thank you, sergeant. Coming from as fine a soldier as you, it means a lot. Make General Dodge proud of you again when you go out west."

"Yes, sir."

David dismissed his company, who presented arms in a full salute to their departing company commander. He then went up to the temporary army headquarters where he submitted an affidavit to Lt. Colonel Bankhead.

David resigned his commission as a First Lieutenant in the First Alabama Cavalry Regiment, U.S. Volunteers. He sold his Spencer Repeating Carbine back to the quartermaster, since he would have little use for it in civilian life, and made an affidavit that he had rendered all returns of public property for which he had been accountable.

He then saluted Lt. Colonel Bankhead, and shook his hand, and walked outside of the headquarters offices and mounted Hercules.

He began to ride south on the Franklin Pike, through areas that had been cleared and fortified by the opposing armies that past December. Some of the area that he was supposed to be familiar with was unrecognizable, on account of the fortification activity by both armies.

He rode south, thinking only of Janet Riley. He now knew that he was deeply in love with her. He was saddened for her loss of her husband, but was thrilled in that it presented an opportunity for him to marry Janet.

He rode south that entire afternoon, noting the familiar landmarks as he drew closer and closer to Franklin. It had been some time since he had been around the area, but the old landmarks remained familiar to him. He saw Ropers' Knob and noted that the Mallory residence was nearby.

He spied the sunken lane where he and Anderson Looney first met Janet, and he now became excited. His heart was now leaping for joy in the anticipation of seeing her that same evening. He knew that he would have to control himself, as he knew that Janet would be required to show all of the necessary proprieties of a widow who had only recently been widowed by the war.

He gave Hercules the spur though, near the end of the sunken lane, because he was too impatient to get there. He noticed a black funeral wreath on the front door, and noted to himself that it was only appropriate for her to display such an arrangement after ascertaining her husband's death.

He turned Hercules into the barn, and greeted Claude as he was walking down the brick path from the main house.

Claude told him that Abigail had run off with a sergeant in the Union Army. Mrs. Mallory and Dr. Mallory were in good health, considering. David noted that the black wreath made of dyed black ribbon was on prominent display in their house.

David was once again announced by Claude, and Dr. Mallory arose to greet him. David shook his hand, and asked them where Janet was, that he would like to speak to her also.

A strange look came over Dr. Mallory's face. He was dressed in a black suit, with a white shirt, and he wore a black waistcoat. Mrs. Mallory was seated on the opposite end of the table, and she was wearing a black dress, with a white cameo broach. She began to sob when she heard David's last question.

David's heart sank. Oh no. Oh God No!

Mr. Mallory began to speak. "David, I need to tell you something. Just after the Battle of Franklin, we were completely swamped with all numbers of shot up and wounded Confederate and Union soldiers. I sent...for...Janet, and she helped us nurse the men, and she even assisted us with some of the operations.

We turned Mr. McGavock's home into a field hospital. A week later, Janet took ill...she was sick from Typhoid Fever. I did everything I could to save her David, but she died before Christmas.

We have her buried out back..."

Mrs. Mallory began to openly cry. David began to cry, the wet tears began to flood down his cheeks, and he went down on one knee, and wept and sobbed for a few moments.

He then found some self composure, and he reached down and found the strength to push himself upright. He reached into his coat pocket, found his handkerchief, and wiped his eyes and face.

"Please forgive me, sir. First, I learned recently of the death of my cousin Joseph in prison. Then, I learned my Uncle William had died in December. Now I learn that Janet, too, has died. We all have lost too much in that damn War."

Doctor Mallory came across the room, and placed his arm around David. "I know, son. We both feel the same way. Come with me to the rose garden, and I'll show you her stone. We got her a beautiful stone marker."

David went out to the garden with his friend, Dr. Mallory, to view the grave of his lost love. On the way to her grave site, his thoughts were only on the life and times that he could have had with her, had she lived.

End of Book One

Epilogue

The Search for David R. Snelling

In the fall of 1903, in a large brick Pension building in Washington, D.C., Wendell Willis was summoned to appear before George S. Ware, Commissioner of the United States Department of the Interior, Bureau of Pensions.

Commissioner Ware had telephoned him the day before, and requested a meeting with him that afternoon. He had packed his suitcase and took an express from Richmond to Union Station late that same afternoon.

He had sufficient time to have his best suit pressed at Williard's Hotel, and he hired a cab to take him up to the Pension Building.

Commissioner Ware's secretary, a lovely young woman who introduced herself as Betty Parker, led him into Commissioner Ware's office. She was blue eyed and blonde haired, and wore a straw hat and a pretty blue dress with white ruffles on both sleeves.

Wendell closed the heavy office door behind him, and heard Commissioner Ware washing his hands in his water closet next door.

He soon emerged from the water closet, and Wendell stood up and greeted his chief.

"Good afternoon, Commissioner. I came in last night on the seven o'clock express, and hope to help you in any way possible."

Commissioner Ware was tall and lean, and dark haired, with streaks of gray around his temples. He was forty two years old, and wore a navy blue pinstripe suit with a waistcoat. He wore a pair of wire–rimmed spectacles, and always appeared serious, in situation after situation.

Wendell knew that he had a special assignment, or he would not have been summoned as he was. Commissioner Ware loosened his bow tie, and shook Wendell's hand.

"Wendell, it is good to see you again. I got a telephone call about a veteran's pension claim last week from President Roosevelt. I had the file pulled from the records section, and had it cross checked at the Record and Pension office of the War Department."

He handed Wendell a claim file in the name of a 'David R. Snelling', No. 742036.

"This claimant was awarded a monthly veteran's pension for a partial disability under the Act of June 27, 1890. He has hired counsel and has sought increases in 1897 and 1898, through counsel, claiming that his disability and infirmity had increased."

"Where is he from?"

"Ozark, Franklin County, Arkansas. He went to the Post Surgeon at Fort Smith in '91, where he was examined. It was determined that he suffered from bleeding piles, and he got his right hand caught in a cotton gin in 1876. He claims a total disability as a result of the combination of the two conditions."

"With all due respect, Commissioner, this is a small potatoes claim. Why am I being called in to review this file?"

"Because General Grenville Dodge called President Roosevelt last week, and he demanded that Snelling's widow's claim be reopened."

"Commissioner Ware, I don't understand fully the situation here. He was awarded a pension and attendant increases, and yet his widow has been declined a widow's pension after his death. Is that a correct statement?"

"Yes it is. Snelling died in April of 1901. He left six children and a wife. Congressman James Blount made inquiry into the case, alleging that David Snelling's prior Confederate service disqualified Mrs. Snelling from receiving a widow's pension."

"What about the Joint Resolution of July 1, 1902?"

"That act does not apply here, because the pensioner died before the bill was enacted by Congress. Even though Congress removed the disabilities of prior Confederate service in Federal pension matters, the Act was prospective only. Snelling died before the law could be signed by the President.

General Dodge was told about the widow's recent denial, and he got mad as a hornet. He telephoned President Roosevelt and everyone in the cabinet. They in turn have put heat on me about this claim. I in turn am putting heat on you to resolve it. Please try to resolve this case quickly. Time is of the essence here, Wendell."

Wendell knew the appropriate response to this challenge. "Sir, I shall put my best field examiners from the South East and Southern Divisions on this case. They will go out and get affidavits from witnesses, and they will pursue all leads. I take it that Congressman Blount has furnished you with leads concerning the Confederate service issue?

"Yes, he has. Those witnesses reside in Georgia. He has also furnished us names and addresses of persons in Decatur, Alabama who can give affidavits."

"How old is the widow?"

"She claims that she was twenty two years old when they married in 1880, so that would make her forty three years old. They had seven children, I believe, and most of them are grown.

You need to instruct your field examiners to look for prior marriages and any other children from any prior marriages that may claim an entitlement. I am not implying any immorality here, but they also need to look out for any other women that may claim to be his widow. This man moved around quite a bit, and did not marry this woman until he was forty two."

"Sir, what is the widow's name? And did she tender a marriage license?"

"Her name is Margaret I. Snelling, formerly Margaret I. Nelson. She tendered a duplicate copy of a marriage license dated March 8, 1880. They have five children who would qualify as dependents under the Act. They have hired an attorney here in Washington, M.V. Tierney & Co., as a claim agent."

"How much was his original pension, if I might ask?"

"Six dollars per month. He drew this from 1895 for piles that he claimed he contracted while commanding General William Sherman's cavalry escort on his march through Georgia. General Grenville Dodge claims to have known this man well, and has pulled a lot of strings so far for his widow's claim."

"Does the War Department acknowledge or confirm his prior service record?"

"Yes. He enlisted in the Union Army on August 5, 1862, and was discharged on July 19, 1865. He served in the First Alabama Regiment of Cavalry. He was a cavalryman like us, Wendell, even though we fought dismounted at San Juan Heights. We don't need to let him down. Let's give his widow's claim every fair consideration."

Commissioner Ware handed a copy of the claim file to Wendell, who took it and placed it inside his brief case. "Commissioner, I shall immediately return to Richmond, and telephone two of my best examiners, and get them on this claim at once." Wendell stood up and shook Commissioner Ware's hand.

"You were a good First Sergeant, and a fine soldier in Cuba, Wendell. You are making a fine administrator, too."

Wendell left the Commissioner's office, and took an electric cable car over to Union Station. He boarded a 3:05 train to Richmond, and went back to the dining car with the Snelling claim file. He ordered a whiskey sour before dinner, and began to nose through the file in the Pullman dining car.

Snelling died on April 23, 1901 of bronchial pneumonia. His death record was filed in Ozark, Franklin County, Arkansas. His original claim was filed out of Fort Smith, Arkansas in 1891, where he was examined by the post physician. He reported there on August 26, 1891, where he was examined by a board of surgeons on part of his claim for a Federal pension.

He claimed that he contracted bleeding piles during General Sherman's March to the Sea in 1864. The claimant reported on his affidavit that he told General Sherman's chief of staff, Major L.M. Dayton, about his bleeding piles, but that he told no other officer about his problem. The physician's report of his examination confirmed the fact that Snelling indeed was suffering from a diseased rectum.

He had also injured his right hand in 1876, after getting it caught in a cotton gin saw. Wendell took a sip of his whiskey sour and smiled. One of the men that brought down King Cotton in the Civil War became a cripple while farming cotton twelve years later. Snelling's injury carried a touch of irony indeed.

Snelling had drawn a partial pension under the Act of June 27, 1890, commencing in 1891.

The basis for Snelling's pension claim was the partial inability to earn support by normal labor. His claim was dropped in August of 1901 on account of Snelling's death, but had been refiled by the attorneys as a widow's claim.

He reviewed an affidavit of John Grant from Ozark, Arkansas in the file, and the straightforward language in the affidavit got Wendell's attention directed to the plight of Snelling's widow:

STATE OF ARKANSAS
COUNTY OF FRANKLIN

Personally appeared, John F. Grant, age 53 years, before the undersigned officer duly authorized to administer oaths, who, after being duly sworn, does depose and state the following:

I was acquainted with David R. Snelling, knew him from the time he first arrived in this County. While I can't find the dates, I know it has been about twenty five years. I knew Margaret Snelling for about one year before she and David R. Snelling were married. My understanding at the time I first knew her was that she was single and had never been married. David and Margaret Snelling lived together continuously as husband and wife from their marriage until his death, and never divorced.

Margaret I. Snelling has not remarried since his death. The property owned by Margaret I. Snelling is one acre of land with poor improvements and household and kitchen furniture and wearing apparel all located at Ozark, Arkansas. All of her property is not worth over three hundred dollars, and she has no income.

John F. Grant
Affiant

Sworn to and subscribed
before me, N.A. McPherson,
County Clerk, this 10th day of June, 1901.

Wendell was moved by the plight of Mrs. Snelling, and became determined to help her. He reviewed her application for a widow's pension which was filed on May 20, 1901. He had been paid by the pension agent out of Knoxville, Tennessee up to February 4, 1901, under Certificate Number 883.149. She attached the affidavits of a number of neighbors and acquaintances in support of her claim for a widow's pension. David had drawn six dollars per month under the Act of June 27, 1890.

Wendell began to review other materials in the claim file, as he enjoyed a dinner of steak and potatoes.

David Snelling married Margaret Isabel Nelson on March 7, 1880, and they had seven children. Paul was born September 18, 1882, Bertha was born November 11, 1886, Grace was born March 18, 1889, Anna was born on November 1, 1891, Lois was born on September 13, 1893, and Julia was born on September 5, 1896. The second oldest child, Harriet, was born on November 23, 1884.

Wendell recognized the immediate need of David's family, and was determined to obey his chief and the President, and try to sneak Margaret's claim through.

* * * * *

The following morning at his offices in Richmond, Wendell Willis, Chief of the Southern Division of the U.S. Bureau of Pensions, telephoned two special field examiners. He called Abner Parkman in Macon, Georgia, and Marvin R. King in Birmingham, Alabama.

Wendell instructed the examiners as to the legal issues to be determined in the examination of the Snelling claim. The legal widowhood of Margaret Snelling had been established through submission of her marriage license and supporting affidavits.

The second issues to be determined were whether David Snelling had ever served voluntarily in the Confederate Army, and whether he was involved in a prior marriage.

Parkman was ordered out to conduct a field examination first, since David R. Snelling originally hailed from Milledgeville, Georgia.

Parkman was thirty two years old, having secured his position through the Federal Civil Service Commission. He was tall and lean, and he loved the ladies and the bar rooms. He was a dedicated public servant during the work week, but he liked to kick up some dust on the weekends.

Footloose and fancy free, he had never met a woman that he did not like. Maybe that was the reason that he never married, since he could never settle for just one woman. On the other hand, he found fault with several women that he had courted.

The Chief of the Southern Division had phoned him about an old goat who had recently died in Arkansas, leaving a wife and seven children. The old man claimed to have prior Federal service in William T. Sherman's army during the Civil War.

One of the legal rules that had made Abner's job easy over the years was a prohibition by law of a Federal pension, if the claimant was found to have a prior Confederate service history.

One of Parkman's favorite sources of information was former Senator John B. Gordon's office. As President of the United Confederate Veterans, General Gordon became acquainted with a number of ex–Confederate soldiers from all over the South. Those people had led Parkman to many a prior Confederate service record, and a speedy resolution to many Federal service claims by Southern born men.

Parkman telephoned General Gordon's office, and gave them the name of the decedent soldier, and his place of birth. Two names were immediately brought to his attention as potential contacts, Captain John Bonner, and William Wood.

Wood lived on Orange Street in Macon, which was just a short distance from Abner's office. Abner caught the electric cable car up Second Street, and then walked a couple of blocks up to Orange Street, where he caught another electric trolley car up to the top of the hill. The address given him was 107 Orange Street, and he soon located the new two story Victorian clapboard house. It was painted powder blue, and had navy blue shutters. He ducked his head to walk around the blooming Crepe

Myrtle bushes in the yard. A yellow dog was lying on the front porch, and lazily lifted his head as he walked up.

Abner removed his bowler hat, set his briefcase down, and knocked on the front door. A pretty red haired girl of twenty years answered the door. She was dressed in a yellow smock, and had her red hair pinned up in a neat bun underneath her straw hat. Abner spoke first.

"You must be Caroline. I spoke to you over the telephone on Monday. Allow me to introduce myself. I am Abner Parkman, Special Field Examiner with the United States Department of Interior. He opened his wallet, and showed the blue–eyed Caroline his credentials. She took a quick look at his credentials, and then stepped back and let him in the house.

"Do come in, Mr. Parkman. My mother has gone down to the farmers' market, but grandpa is back in the living room. He has been expecting you."

"Thank you, Miss Wood."

Parkman liked what he saw in Caroline Wood. He followed her down the hall, and into a large and spacious dining room. The room was floored with hardwood planks, and papered with a floral pattern wallpaper. The dining room table was long, and made of a fine mahogany.

A short and wiry gray haired and bearded man in a denim shirt and twill pants was seated at the end of the table.

Parkman introduced himself, and Caroline took her leave of them once he had stated the nature of his business.

"I am here to investigate a Union veteran's claim for benefits, Mr. Wood. Actually, it was a claim made by his widow. Do you recall or remember a soldier by the name of David Snelling?"

The old man scratched his beard, and sat back in his chair.

"Yeah, I do remember such a man. His Uncle William lived on a plantation below me about fifteen miles. I ran a cotton plantation up in Putnam County. That boy refused to join a Confederate regiment, and his uncle kicked him off of his place. I did not see him again until November of '64."

"Under what circumstances did you see him in November of 1864?"

"He was wearing a cavalryman's uniform, a blue Yankee uniform, and he was with several other troopers. I had just put the bridle on my big bay horse, and I was bent over reaching for the saddle. When I turned around, the horse was gone. All I saw was a cloud of dust, I swear.

I ran out of the barn, and saw Snelling riding away from me, leading my horse along. I shouted and cussed at him, but it did me no good. That man was a hell of a real horse thief. I have not seen him since. His Uncle

The Unionist 418

William died on that plantation, though. William's son died in a Yankee prison. William's grandson came home after the War, and did all right in the lumber business there later."

"Had Snelling gotten married before the war?"

"No, I do not believe he was married then."

"Was it clear to you that he was serving in the Union Army in 1864?"

"Yes, he was. No doubt of that."

"Do you know if he had previously served in the Confederate Army?"

"No, I do not recall that. His cousin, Julia Bonner, is still alive, though. She could probably answer that question for you. She lives over in Haddock, Georgia with her husband, John."

Parkman rose and thanked Mr. Wood, and then told him that he would mail out an affidavit for him to review and sign.

It had to be notarized, and a notary public was required for him to execute the affidavit. The old man advised him that a notary had an office up the street, and that he would execute and return the affidavit.

Parkman advised Mr. Wood that he would show himself out. He wanted to be alone with Caroline, and use that opportunity to ask her to the church social the following Friday. Such opportunities were not to be lost.

The next July morning, Parkman arose and donned his number two seersucker suit, and took the electric trolley down to the train station. He bought a train ticket from Macon to Gray, Georgia. The steam engine pulled out at 7:45 a.m., and pulled into the depot in Gray one hour later. The little town named after James Madison Gray had done well since the railroad was routed there.

Parkman walked over to the livery stables, where he rented a small buggy and a large red mule named Clyde. He loaded his briefcase onto the buggy, paid a deposit to the livery, and soon had Clyde trotting toward Haddock.

He had called former Congressman Joe Wheeler in connection with the lead he was furnished on Julia Bonner. Congressman Wheeler's son, James Wheeler, promptly called him back.

Julia Bonner's husband was John Bonner, who was a captain in the 57th Georgia Confederate Infantry. He had information on David Snelling on the issue of prior Confederate service.

Parkman thanked Mr. Wheeler for the timely lead and information. Mr. Wheeler thanked him for his careful inspection of the claim. Congressman Wheeler did not want any "homemade Yankees" drawing a Federal pension, or their widows.

The hot and hazy July heat began to chafe him as Clyde trotted up the road, so he stopped and pulled off his seersucker jacket. The deer flies began to buzz him and bite his neck, and he gave Clyde a crack across his rump. Clyde lurched forward, and began to trot up the red clay road toward Haddock.

Around five miles east of Haddock, near an old community known as Fortville, Parkman spied a series of frame houses on the edge of a large cotton field. It was almost noon, and he soon spotted a Negro woman seated on an oak rocking chair on the porch of an old farm house.

The house was built of gray weathered clapboards, and had double hung windows, a tin roof, and a fireplace made of hand made bricks. The house was at least forty years old, and could use a bit of maintenance work, thought Parkman, as he tied up his mule. He removed his hat, and approached the woman in a respectful manner.

She was dressed in a loose fitting cotton dress, and a pair of leather slippers. She was holding an infant son, who was around four months old. He began to cry, and the woman automatically unbuttoned the front of her dress, and pulled out a light brown breast, and directed her nipple toward the mouth of the child. Her breast was large and firm, and her areola was larger than a silver dollar. The baby was naked down to his waist, and was clad only in a diaper made of cotton cloth. He began to squirm and fuss, and his mother spoke out to him.

"Quit fussing and take 'diz thang, or I will give it to the nice white man over there. What can I do for you, sir?"

Parkman was polite and to the point. "Please forgive my intrusion, ma'am, but I was looking for Captain John Bonner. I was told that he could be found in these parts."

"I wash for him, sir. I do his washin' and a lot of his cookin' for him and for Miss Julia. My husband Fred used to sharecrop cotton with him, but he left me to go look for work up in Detroit."

"Where would his house be located?"

The woman used her left hand to point out a large white frame house across the field. "They stay in that big house over there, sir."

"Thank you, ma'am. You have been more than kind. What is your name?"

"Eula Mae Hill. And who might you be?"

"My name is Abner Parkman, ma'am. I work for the United States Department of the Interior, Bureau of Pensions. I have official business with Captain Bonner." He looked over at Eula Mae, as she was nursing her son. She had straight hair, unusual for a Negro woman. She had straight lips and clear, chocolate colored skin. She was a beauty as far as Parkman could see, a real find. Opportunities only come around once, so Parkman seized the moment.

"How long has your husband been gone to Detroit, Miss Eula Mae?"

She continued to nurse her son. "He's been gone about eight months. I ain't heard a damn thing from him, one way or the other."

That was the answer Parkman wanted to hear.

"It must get lonely 'round here, with your husband gone off and all. Could you use some company in the evenings, every now and then?" He was too bold, and he knew it.

"Yes, sir. You come over after dark most anytime, but bring me some whiskey and some victuals when you come, if you don't mind."

"I will be by here tonight, after I take a run into Gray, Miss Eula. I have some business to take care of now, but I will be back. It was a pleasure to meet you, ma'am. A real pleasure."

"It was good to meet you, too, sir. Please call again."

Abner could not believe his luck. Married women were the most grateful and the most lonely whenever he approached them. This girl was a real beauty. He would go and buy some whiskey, rent the mule and buggy for another day, and bring Eula Mae some groceries right after dark. He would probably spend the night with her. He was on a run of good fortune.

* * * * *

Two hours later, Parkman was seated at the dining room table of John R. Bonner and Julia L. Bonner. Captain Bonner was a sixty three year old farmer, who sharecropped 200 acres near Haddock. He was thin and wiry, about six feet tall, and had silver hair. His wife, Julia, was fifty three years old, and had a girlish figure and salt and pepper black hair, tied up in a tight bun.

She wore a calico dress, and the Captain wore denim overalls and a red checkered shirt.

They had given their signed written affidavits to Parkman, who began to read them back, to verify their accuracy; commencing with Julia's affidavit:

"I was born and reared here and have resided here all of my life. I do not know the claimant Margaret I. Snelling. I did know the soldier, David R. Snelling. I knew him from my childhood. He was partly reared in the house with me. He was my second cousin. I knew him up to the beginning of the war. He first enlisted in the Confederate Army, in Co. H, 57th Ga. Vol. Inf. My husband was the captain of the company. He enlisted during the early part of the war, but I do not remember the year, month, or day of his enlistment.

I do not know how long he served in the Confederate Army, but it was not a good while. He was a Union man all the while. I do not know whether he volunteered into Confederate service, or was conscripted. He was unmarried before the war, and he was, as far as I know, married only once after the war. I never saw him after the war. He went to Huntsville, Alabama, and there edited a newspaper. He wrote us several times, and sent us several copies of his paper, but because he deserted the South, we did not reply to his communications. After a while, he ceased to write and to send us his paper, and we lost sight of him, and had not heard of him for some time prior to his death. I did not know he had married, until his wife wrote us after his death. I have no interest in this case. I have read the foregoing affidavit, and it is true and correct, this 16th day of July, 1903."

"Is that your statement, Mrs. Bonner?"

"Yes sir, that is an accurate reading of my written statement."

"Very well. I shall go ahead and read out Captain Bonner's affidavit, then." Parkman began to read again:

"I am 63 years of age. I am a farmer, my address is General Delivery, Haddock, Jones County, Georgia. I have resided near here all of my life.

I was a Confederate officer during the late war. I served as captain, Co. H, 57th Ga. Vol. Infantry. I served from May 10, 1862 to the close of the war. I do not know the claimant, Margaret I. Snelling, but knew her late husband, David R. Snelling from about 1851 or 1852. He and I were school boys together. I knew him well up to the war. He first enlisted in the C.S.A. as a private in Co. H, 57th Ga. Vol. Inf. He enlisted at the same time I did. We went up to Chattanooga. Snelling deserted us near Chattanooga, at Bridgeport, Alabama, about July 1862. He was on picket duty at said place and under pretenses of putting a Confederate soldier across the Tennessee River he crossed the river in a small boat and left us, and I have not seen him since. Later during the war, he came through here as an escort of General Sherman and was then a lieutenant in the U.S. Cavalry. He came to our house with Sherman's Yankee soldiers. He was then a U.S. soldier and held the rank of lieutenant, and claimed to be serving on General Sherman's staff. I suppose he was 25 years of age when the war commenced.

Soldier was a Union man of heart and would have been conscripted with the C.S.A. under pressure, had he not volunteered, which he did, into the Confederate Army.

Our regiment was first drawn as the 54th Ga. Vol. Infantry, and was redesignated as the 57th Ga. Vol. Inf. in October, 1862. That is why Snelling's name cannot be found on the official roster of our regiment.

Soldier was never married before he went into the C.S.A. I knew that the soldier resided in Huntsville, Alabama after the war, and edited a paper. He sent several copies of his paper back here once to his uncle, who is now dead. I have no interest in the claim.

This statement is true and correct, to the best of my knowledge and belief."

"Is that a fair reading of your statement, Captain Bonner?"

"Yes, sir, it is."

"Very well, I will prepare a memo to the Commissioner of Pensions, and the examiner in Alabama will have some additional work to do. Congressman Joe Wheeler gave us some leads over there, and each person must be contacted. Thank you. Thank you for your kindness and your assistance."

"You are welcome. Good day to you, Mr. Parkman."

Parkman arose and went back to buy some items in Gray. He returned at dark to call on Eula Mae that evening.

The following morning, he arose and drove the buggy with Clyde into Gray, where he purchased a train ticket back to Macon. When he got to his office in Macon, he had his secretary type the following memo on her typewriter:

Macon, Ga. July 16, 1903

Hon. Commissioner of Pensions
Washington, D.C.

Sir:

Herewith I have the honor to return, with report, the papers in pension claim no. 742,036, of Margaret I. Snelling, widow of David R. Snelling, late Lieutenant, Co. I, First Alabama Vol. Cav., Post office address, Ozark, Franklin County, Arkansas.

The papers in this claim were referred to the field for special examination concerning prior service of the soldier in the Confederate Army, legal widowhood and dates of birth of children, and come to me, with notice waived, for further examination as to Confederate service and legal widowhood.

I recommend further examination as to prior marriage of soldier, as follows:

Col. C.P. Sheets, Decatur, Morgan County, Alabama,
Captain J.B. Stewart, Decatur, Morgan County, Alabama,
W.A. Raney, Decatur, Morgan County, Alabama.

Very Respectfully,
A. B. Parkman
Special examiner

Marvin King was a special examiner with the Southeastern Division of the Bureau of Pensions. His offices were located in Birmingham, Alabama. He received a telephone call from Wendell Willis in Washington concerning the Snelling pension matter, and he was mailed a copy of the documents the following week.

He was required to interview Christopher Sheets, William A. Raney, and Robert P. Baker. He was able to contact each of the witnesses over the telephone, and he set up a meeting with each of the men at the Morgan County Courthouse in Decatur. The meetings were scheduled for October 15, 1903.

The issues to be determined concerned legal widowhood of the Claimant, disqualification of benefits due to prior Confederate service, the voluntary nature of Confederate service, if any, and whether the decedent had any other children or a previous marriage.

Marvin was forty one years old, was married for ten years, and had two small little girls at home. He had served as an assistant comptroller in the Alabama Treasury, and secured his Federal position through the United States Civil Service Commission. He was a devout Christian, and believed that Federal veterans pensions should be paid even though prior Confederate service acted to disqualify claimants from benefits. He had found a number of situations in his investigation of claims where prior Confederate service was not a disqualifying factor, because the service was coerced.

Marvin packed his suitcase on October 14th, and took the 8:00 a.m. train from Birmingham to Decatur. He rented a horse and buggy at the livery, and drove over to the Decatur Hotel, where he got himself a room, and where he meticulously reviewed the Margaret Snelling claim file.

He was scheduled to interview only three local men, but two other men who were not on his list should be interviewed as well. General

Grenville Dodge was in Cuba, rebuilding railroads for the new Cuban national government. Major Henry Hitchcock, who mentioned the claimant in his memoirs on Sherman's March to the Sea, was a practicing attorney in St. Louis, Missouri. He had been informed though, that Attorney Hitchcock had died the previous year.

Marvin would schedule the depositions of one of these witnesses by written interrogatories once he made contact with him by way of telephone.

Marvin rented a buggy and a strong black horse at the livery, and drove down to the Morgan County Courthouse near the center of town. He hitched up the horse on the courthouse square, and buttoned his wool jacket against the early fall chill.

He climbed the stairs and made his way to the Grand Jury room, checking his pocket watch for the correct time. It was 8:58 a.m. He looked out in the hall in front of the glass window of the door to the Grand Jury room, and spied three old men in dark suits sitting on a pine bench.

All of the men were bearded, had white hair, and appeared to be over sixty years of age. A tall man that Marvin knew as Christopher Sheets introduced himself, and then Robert D. Baker, a retired 65 year old, and then William A. Raney, a thin and frail old man of 77 years; as the men in their Sunday clothes took turns introducing themselves to Marvin.

Marvin had them go into the Grand Jury room, where they each gave their sworn statements. Marvin then reduced their statements to written affidavit form, and read each of the affidavits back to the deponents.

"Mr. Baker, we will start with you." Marvin began to read:

"Personally appeared, Robert P. Baker, before me, M.R. King, a special examiner of the Bureau of Pensions, who, after being duly sworn, does depose and state the following:

I knew David Snelling very well. I knew him from the time he came here until he left. I should guess that he came here about 1868 or 1870 and he left here in 1874 or 75. He was under indictment for some irregularity in pension matters, and I was a United States Marshal at the time.

He left here to evade arrest, and I did not know what had become of him for a long time.
Question: Had David R. Snelling ever been married when you knew him?

Answer: Not to my knowledge. He had no wife while here and claimed never to have been married. Yes sir, I knew him very well and I am satisfied in my mind that he had never been married. After Snelling left here, I got a telegram from Washington telling me to send a Deputy Marshal to Chicago to arrest Snelling.

I send a deputy there, and he found where Snelling had been spending much of his time playing pool and billiards, but Snelling was gone.

I suspected that the telegraph operator here through whom the message was sent me from the Department of Justice was a special friend of Snelling. He wired him ahead of time, to keep him out of the way.

I never heard of Snelling any more until I heard through Congressman Sheets that Snelling had died, and that his widow had filed a pension claim.

    Robert D. Baker
    Deponent
    Sworn to and subscribed before me this 15th day of October, 1903, and I certify that the contents were fully made known to deponent before signing.
    M. R. King
    Special Examiner."

"Mr. Baker, is that your complete deposition, sir?"

"Yes, sir, it is." The ex-marshal had given many affidavits before, and he began to leave the room.

"I will send you a conformed copy of your affidavit in the mail, sir. Thank you for coming."

Marvin next took a sworn statement from Christopher Sheets, a former U.S. Congressman from Alabama. After taking the affidavit, Marvin read it back to him:

    "Personally appeared, Chris P. Sheets, who, being duly sworn to answer truly all interrogatories propounded to him during this special examination, does depose and state the following: I am 64 years of age, and I am an invalid. I reside in Decatur, Alabama.

    I never served in either army. I raised the First Alabama Cavalry for service in the Union Army. I would have been colonel of that regiment, but the Confederate officers arrested and kept me in jail for two years. I draw a pension of $30.00 per month by reason of Special Act of Congress.

    Yes, sir I knew David R. Snelling very well. He was a Lieutenant in the same company of the First Alabama Cavalry. I saw him once at Atlanta with Sherman's Army in November 1864. Snelling was a Georgian, and was first with the Rebel Army. There he deserted and joined the First

Alabama Cavalry. He commanded General Sherman's escort on the Georgia campaign. He was selected by Sherman because he knew all that Georgia country, and is complimented by Gen. Sherman in his memoirs. I first met Snelling at Atlanta and after the surrender, I got to know him very well.

Snelling came here right after the war and lived in and around Decatur here until about 1871 or 1872. He acted as claim agent and taught school. He got into trouble here with the court officials and skipped out.

The next I heard of him he was running a paper at Ozark, Arkansas. Somebody who had known him here was over there in Arkansas and ran across Snelling there in the newspaper business.

Question: Did you know or ever hear that Snelling had been married?

Answer: No, I never did. I did not know that he had ever been married. I knew him very well, and he has told me all about his past life and I am sure in my mind that he had never been married. I was not married then and we used to go to see the girls together, and I am sure that he would have told me had he ever been married.

I have understood your questions and my answers are correctly recorded herein.

C.P. Sheets
Deponent."

Marvin thanked former Congressman Sheets for his time and his statement, and promised him that he would send him a copy of his affidavit in the mail.

Sheets left the room, and an older man, who appeared to be over 75 years of age stepped forward to the table where Marvin was seated, and offered up his written statement.

The old man was dressed in a blue broadcloth suit of clothes, as for a Sunday church meeting. He pulled up a chair, and began to speak, as Marvin began to fill out a form affidavit with his pencil.

"I am 77 years of age. I have no occupation now. I remember David R. Snelling, who used to live here. He came here about 1866 or 1867, and lived here around three or four years. He was a Georgian. After the war, Colonel George Spencer became U. S. Bankruptcy Referee in this part of Alabama. He and Captain Jerome Hinds got control of Republican patronage for the State of Alabama. All of the officers of the First

Alabama Cavalry attended meetings before the end of the war, where this was discussed.

David got named Federal claim agent, and Colonel Spencer secured him a position as a school teacher. He also ran a weekly newspaper, The Huntsville Sentinel. Around 1872, General Grenville Dodge came into town, after he had been named Chief Engineer of the Union Pacific Railroad, and after he was elected president of the Society of the Army of the Tennessee. General Dodge was very critical of the U.S. Government Indian policy, and he spoke out against corruption, and against Secretary of War Belknap in the Grant Administration.

David attended the same rally, and covered General Dodge's comments, and reported them in his weekly paper. He also wrote an editorial which supported General Dodge, and denounced the Government's policy of issuing liquor licenses to Indian traders who traded liquor and modern rifles to Indians that would later attack our soldiers in the field.

Not two weeks after David denounced Secretary Belknap, a warrant was issued for his arrest by the Justice Department. David Snelling left town, but lost all of his possessions on account of the arrest warrant. In my opinion, he was not guilty of any wrongdoing.

Question: Had he been married prior?

Answer: No, I believe not."

Marvin wrote out a deposition, and had Mr. Raney sign it. He then notarized the statement, and he thanked Mr. Raney for his time. He did ask him if he knew of anyone else that had any more information on the claimant.

He answered as follows:

Yes, Attorney Henry Hitchcock had mentioned Snelling in his memoirs, and General Dodge knew him personally. A Melvin Thompson, a county commissioner in Aberdeen, Mississippi, also knew him.

Marvin thanked Mr. Raney for his participation in the process. He then rode back to the hotel, where he prepared a letter to Commissioner Ware, which he sent to Washington later that month:

Hon. E.F. Ware
Birmingham, Ala
Commissioner of Pensions
October 30, 1903

Washington, D.C.

Sir:

I have the honor to return with report of special examination all the papers in the above cited claim which was referred to the S.E. Div. to determine whether the soldier served voluntarily in the Confederate Army, legal widowhood of the Claimant, no prior marriage of the soldier and dates of birth of children and came to me with notice waived for testimony as to legal widowhood.

Captain J.J. Hinds is a resident of Philadelphia, and has an office at 115 Old Fellows Temple.

I deposed C.P. Sheets, W.A. Raney, and Robert Baker. In addition to those whose depositions are herewith, I interviewed Calvin Brown and W.C. Preston who knew the soldier but never knew or heard that he was or had been married.

The soldier was an intelligent man who engaged in school teaching, newspaper work, and working up pension and other claims and is said to have always secured more than he was entitled by law as his fee.

I wrote a Captain Thompson of Monroe County, Mississippi, who was County Supt. of Education soon after the time the soldier is alleged to have lived at Aberdeen, Mississippi, he knows nearly everybody in the county. He had some information on the soldier, but his information is not relevant to the issues left to be determined. His letter is attached.

J.B. Day of Flint, Morgan County, Alabama was not seen for the reason that it would have caused the loss of a day's time, and a livery bill that was regarded as useless. Examiner recommends telephone contact be made with General Grenville Dodge in Miami, Florida and with Major Jerome J. Hinds in Philadelphia, Pennsylvania, on the issue of prior voluntary Confederate Service.

Reference to the chief of the Board of Review is respectfully recommended.

Marvin R. King
Special Examiner

* * * * *

Department of the Interior
Bureau of Divisions

Birmingham, Ala. Oct. 16, 1903

Capt. E. P. Thompson
Aberdeen, Mississippi

Dear Captain:

David R. Snelling, late Lt. Co. I 1st Alabama Cav. U.S. Vols during the Civil War, who was a school teacher, claim agt. and newspaper man at Decatur, AL from 1865 or 66 to about 1874 is said to have lived in Aberdeen a portion of the time between 1874 and 1880, when he went to Arkansas where he died. I desire to know whether he had a wife while in Monroe County or whether he was supposed to have been married.

Would you kindly make inquiry of this man, if not personally known to you, and advise me by endorsement herein as to whether he was or had been married, and if so to whom and where.

An early response under cover of the enclosed envelope which requires no postage will be very much appreciated.

Very Truly Yours,
M.R. King
Special Claim Examiner

* * * * *

Aberdeen, Mississippi
October 25, 1903

Hon. M.R. King
Special Claim Examiner
U.S. Dept. Of Interior
Bureau of Pensions
Birmingham, Alabama
Dear Mr. King:

I am in receipt of your letter of October 16th, and had to consult one of my school teachers in the south end of the county about the soldier, David Snelling. I was reminded of a fellow with a newspaper background being posted as a preacher down at the Methodist Church near Bartahatchie, and discussed this matter with a high school teacher from that area last week. The teacher's name was Earl Sylvester.

He told me that they had a preacher at the New Prospect Methodist Church, who was a tall, thin single man who preached there around four years, from 1874 to 1880.

The name he used then was Robert Snelling. This man also claimed to have served in the 1st Alabama Union Cavalry, and it was also known that he had been formerly employed as a school teacher and newspaper editor.

My friend informed me that Robert was a wonderful preacher, and worked hard to win souls for Jesus Christ. He worked hard to keep his flock, and he held many a tent revival, and baptized many souls during his tenure there.

Earl told me that Robert professed a desire to go into cotton sharecropping in Arkansas, and told his congregation that he needed to farm and go back to his old profession, since he had worked on a cotton plantation in Georgia when he was a very young man.

This man was never married in Aberdeen when he was here, although Earl says that many a widow and many a single woman in that congregation tried to spark Snelling, but he never made it to the altar while he was there. Many a chicken was fried up on Sundays in vain, from what I was told.

I hope that the information obtained was of some assistance to you, and I greatly appreciate your fine efforts at pursuing Federal pension claims of my constituents here.

Very Truly Yours,
E.P. Thompson
Spt. Monroe County Board
Of Education

* * * * *

Commissioner Ware received Marvin's package from Birmingham on November 1st, and he immediately telephoned Wendell Willis in Richmond, and asked him to contact General Grenville Dodge in Santiago, Cuba.

Wendell sent a telegram to General Dodge in Santiago the next day:

November 3, 1903

General Grenville Dodge
President, Cuban Railroad Company
Santiago, Cuba

I am inquiring as to whether you knew a David R. Snelling of the First Alabama Union Cavalry Stop His widow has filed a pension claim with our office Stop General Wheeler's office gave us your address as possibly having knowledge of soldier's Civil War service record Stop

Please telephone me at Park 394 Richmond Virginia to discuss this claim in detail on your return to Miami Stop

Wendell Willis
Deputy Commissioner
Bureau of Pensions

General Dodge telephoned Wendell Willis when he returned to Miami the following week. He remembered David Snelling quite well, and was willing to write out answers to a set of written interrogatories concerning the widow's claim. He would answer the typewritten interrogatory questions, and have his answers notarized and returned. He also suggested that Wendell telephone a former law partner of Attorney Henry Hitchcock in St. Louis about the claim, and Wendell told him he would do so. The written interrogatories were received and completed, and returned to Wendell on November 17th. They were as follows:

Department of the Interior
Bureau of Pensions
Office of Deputy Commissioner
Richmond, Virginia

State of Florida
County of Dade

Case of Margaret Snelling, No. 742,036.

Personally appeared, Grenville Dodge, before the undersigned officer duly authorized to administer oaths, who, after being duly sworn, does depose and state the following:

1. Affiant is the chief engineer and president of Cuban Railroad Company. Affiant was formerly employed as Chief Engineer of the Union Pacific Railroad.

2. I was commander of the 16th Corps of the Union Army during 1863 and 1864 in the late Civil War. I commanded the Department of Mississippi and North Alabama in 1863, with my headquarters being located at Corinth, Mississippi. I knew Lieutenant David Snelling, as he commanded a company in the First Alabama Regiment of Cavalry. My Chief of Staff, Colonel George Spencer, assumed command of the First Alabama Cavalry in 1863. I knew many of the officers in said cavalry regiment. The solder at issue was a resourceful and brave and loyal Union officer. He was, in my opinion, denied advancement and promotion because of suspicion concerning his Deep South upbringing.

3. Was the soldier a married man during the Civil War? *Answer*: No.

4. Did the soldier serve previously in the Confederate Service prior to his enlistment?

Answer: Yes. I became president of the Society of the Army of the Tennessee in 1873. In 1874, I spoke at a soldiers' seminar of the Society at Corinth, Mississippi. David Snelling covered the event for his weekly newspaper. He came to my hotel room after my lecture, and had a drink with me. There in the hotel room, he confessed to me that his Uncle had persuaded him to enlist in the 57th Georgia Infantry Regiment in order for him to obtain transportation to Bridgeport, Alabama. He confessed that it was his plan to join the Rebel regiment in order to use its deployment as a means of getting near the Union lines. He told me that he would have been conscripted into the Army of Northern Virginia had he not enlisted in the 57th Georgia Infantry.

5. Was his Confederate service voluntary?
Answer: Yes, but only for a specified purpose. He had no intentions of ever serving in the 57th Georgia Regiment. He only used his deployment as a means of getting closer to Federal lines. In that respect, it cannot be proven that his prior Confederate service was voluntary, since it was also apparent that he had joined to avoid conscription into the Army of Northern Virginia.

6. Should his prior Confederate Service history operate as a disqualifying factor in the pension being considered for the widow?
Answer: No. Snelling's prior Confederate service did not involve a situation where arms were taken up against the Union, and where a significant role was played in the rebellion. In this case, enlistment in the Rebel regiment was done as a pretext, in order to put the soldier in a position where he could desert, and enlist in a Union Army regiment.

I hereby certify that I have given true and correct answers to the foregoing written interrogatories, this 11th day of November, 1903.

Grenville Dodge
Affiant

Sworn to and subscribed before me this 11th day of November, 1903.

Richard Hatch
Notary Public
Dade County, Florida

 Wendell telephoned Attorney Henry Hitchcock's office in St. Louis, and ascertained that attorney Hitchcock had died the previous year.
 He spoke to Mr. Hitchcock's law partner, who indicated that Mr. Hitchcock's law clerk, Henry Abrams, had recently gone through the Major's personal papers, and had found a previous affidavit Mr. Hitchcock had submitted in support of Margaret Snelling's claim in 1901.
 Wendell asked him to see if he could forward him a copy of the same affidavit, as he could present it to the Board of Review along with the other evidence.
 The affidavit was located, and was sent to Wendell the following week from St. Louis:

Department of the Interior
Bureau of Pensions
Office of Deputy Commissioners
Richmond, Virginia

State of Missouri
County of St. Louis

Case of Margaret Snelling, No. 742,036.

Personally appeared, Henry Hitchcock, before the undersigned officer duly authorized to administer oaths, who, after being duly sworn, does depose and state the following:

1. *Question*: What is your name and current profession?
   Answer: Henry Hitchcock. I am a former dean of the St. Louis Law School. I am a past president of the American Bar Association. I practice law currently in St. Louis.

2. *Question*: What were your duties during the late Civil War?
   Answer: I served as Assistant Adjutant General on the staff of Major General William Sherman during the March to the Sea, and the Campaign of the Carolinas. I held the rank of major, U.S. Volunteers.

3. *Question*: Did you know the soldier at issue, David R. Snelling?
   Answer: Yes. I knew him quite well. We shared a tent a many a night during the many miles the army traveled from Atlanta to Durham Station. Snelling was a lieutenant in the First Alabama Regiment of Cavalry, and he was appointed commander of General Sherman's escort cavalry.

4. *Question*: Had he ever been married during the time you knew him?
   Answer: No.

5. *Question*: Did you know whether or not the soldier had ever served in the Confederate army previous to his Union service?
   Answer: I was recently told about the soldier's alleged period of Confederate service in the 57th Georgia Regiment by General Grenville Dodge.

6. *Question*: In your opinion, was the soldier's prior Confederate service voluntary?
   Answer: No. I have had my associate counsel in Washington research the Official Records of the War of the Rebellion, and General Dodge has allowed me access to his old charts and records in Council Bluffs, Iowa. From the geographic deployment of the 57th Georgia Regiment in July of 1862, it appears that the soldier either enlisted in the Confederate regiment to get access to Union held territory to desert, or to avoid conscription into another C.S.A. Unit. In my legal opinion, the soldier's prior Confederate service was not voluntary.

7. I was with the soldier on a routine basis from the beginning of General Sherman's March to the Sea in October of 1864, to after the end of the war, May of 1865. He was a loyal and brave officer, who faithfully discharged his duties as a volunteer officer in the Union Army. I never saw this officer give anything less than his best for his country in the field. In the opinion of this affiant, the soldier's widow should receive her pension due her as a result of her husband's volunteer service.

Henry Hitchcock
AFFIANT

Sworn to and subscribed
before me this 15th day of June, 1901.

Beth Picard
Notary Public
County of St. Louis
State of Missouri

* * * * *

On December 3, 1903, Wendell Willis boarded a train for Washington, and the quarterly meeting of the Board of Review of the Bureau of Pensions.

He carried several case files with him, and each of the Board of Review members had case files from their districts that would also be reviewed the next day.

On the way up, after finishing a plate of steak and potatoes in the Pullman dining car, Wendell reviewed Margaret Snelling's claim file again. This woman had five minor children to support, and apparently lived dirt poor on a farm in Ozark, Arkansas.

Wendell reviewed the claim file again, noting the fact that officials in the U.S. Justice Department ran David out of Alabama with a bogus arrest warrant because he had publicly criticized Secretary of War Belknap's Indian Policy in 1872. He lost everything he had ever worked for, and then started over as an itinerant preacher in Aberdeen, Mississippi. He resurfaced later in Arkansas, where he got his hand caught in a cotton gin in Scott County, Arkansas on October 24, 1876.

Snelling turned in an affidavit in 1891 outlining his prior injuries, and stating his middle name as "Rodolfrus". Wendell found it rather ironic that a man who played a significant part in dethroning King Cotton during the Civil War was seriously injured farming cotton in 1876.

He would do what he could for his widow, but David's prior confirmed Confederate service would probably disqualify his widow's claim for a pension.

* * * * *

On December 4, 1903, the Board of Review met and rejected Margaret Snelling's claim by a vote of four board members to one.

The claim was opposed for rejection by the Board on the following grounds:

"Claimant has no title to accrued pension as soldier had a prior service in the Confederate Army and died prior to passage of Joint Resolution of July 1, 1902, and was therefore never entitled to pension."

* * * * *

On March 3, 1908, the new director of the Southern Division of the Bureau of Pensions, John T. Clements, received a letter from Washington D.C. pension attorney Milo B. Stevens, concerning claim no. 742,036, the claim of Margaret I. Snelling. The letter read in part as follows:

Dear Deputy Commissioner Clements:

I have been retained to represent Margaret I. Snelling, widow of David R. Snelling, who was a First Lieutenant in the First Alabama Cavalry, U.S. Volunteers, during the late Civil War.

Her claim for a pension was denied by your Board of Review in 1903, on the grounds that the soldier had a prior Confederate service history, and had died prior to the passage of the Joint Resolution of July 1902, and was therefore not entitled to said widow's pension.

My question, sir, is how you can reconcile this decision to an adverse ruling of your Honorable Assistant Secretary of the Interior in the case of Rebecca Medlock, 4 Bureau 96 (claim no. 4221), which was favorably decided for the claimant on April 11, 1904?

Does this not deny my client Equal Protection under the Laws in violation of her rights under the Fourteenth Amendment of the United States Constitution? It was my understanding that the Medlock claim also involved a soldier with a prior Confederate service history, who died before the Joint Resolution of 1902. This letter is to respectfully request you to reopen my client's claim for a pension at once, and to award her a pension as she has previously requested.

Very Truly Yours,
Milo B. Stevens
Attorney at Law

* * * * *

Deputy Commissioner Clements reviewed the favorable claimant's decision in Rebecca Medlock's case, and decided that Margaret Snelling's claim was no different than Rebecca Medlock's claim, which also involved the issue of prior Confederate Service. He prepared a memo to his claim examiner in the Richmond office:

March 4, 1908

Department of the Interior
Deputy Commissioner
Bureau of Pensions

To: Honorable Horace Selnick

Please prepare a Brief for Reopening on the claim of Margaret I. Snelling, Claim No. 742,036, which was a widow's claim for pension benefits, which was denied in December 1903.

The grounds of rejection is no longer tenable under the decision of the Honorable Asst. Secretary of the Interior of April 11, 1904 in the claim of Rebecca Medlock Vol. 4 Bureau 96, Case No. 4221. Reopen Margaret Snelling's claim for further consideration under the above administrative decision.

John T. Clements

Chief of Division

On May 8, 1908, the Board of Review approved Margaret Snelling's claim for a widow's pension under the Joint Resolution of July 11, 1902.

Margaret Snelling received her first widow's pension check in 1908. Her children under the age of 16 years each received an additional $4.00 per month.

In 1923, Margaret's monthly widow's benefit increased to $30.00 per month. In 1930, her monthly benefit increased to $40.00 per month from the Bureau of Pensions until her death in Rogers, Arkansas on November 22, 1941. She was eighty seven years old.

The End